Amid the Ashes and the Dust

Amid the *Ashes* and the *Dust*

Clay Mitchell

iUniverse LLC
Bloomington

Amid the Ashes and the Dust

Copyright © 2013, 2014 by Clay Mitchell

All rights reserved. No part of this book may be used or reproduced by any means, graphic, electronic, or mechanical, including photocopying, recording, taping or by any information storage retrieval system without the written permission of the publisher except in the case of brief quotations embodied in critical articles and reviews.

This is a work of fiction. All of the characters, names, incidents, organizations, and dialogue in this novel are either the products of the author's imagination or are used fictitiously.

iUniverse books may be ordered through booksellers or by contacting:

iUniverse LLC
1663 Liberty Drive
Bloomington, IN 47403
www.iuniverse.com
1-800-Authors (1-800-288-4677)

Because of the dynamic nature of the Internet, any web addresses or links contained in this book may have changed since publication and may no longer be valid. The views expressed in this work are solely those of the author and do not necessarily reflect the views of the publisher, and the publisher hereby disclaims any responsibility for them.

Any people depicted in stock imagery provided by Thinkstock are models, and such images are being used for illustrative purposes only.

Certain stock imagery © Thinkstock.

ISBN: 978-1-4759-8807-9 (sc)
ISBN: 978-1-4759-8808-6 (hc)
ISBN: 978-1-4759-8809-3 (e)

Library of Congress Control Number: 2013907648

Printed in the United States of America

iUniverse rev. date: 01/14/2014

For my precious PJ,
whose love and support helped me to
believe, to achieve, to draw closer to
God, and to be a better man.

And, for my beloved friend Jan Edwards who
always hounded me to finish, but never got
the chance to read the end of the story.

ACKNOWLEDGEMENTS

Thanks to my editors at Watercress Press, Alice Geron and Julia Hayden for their diligent editing of the manuscript. I am forever thankful for the thoughtful help and guidance received from my two sisters, Kathy Mitchell-Brown and Kari Mitchell, both talented writers and editors in their own right, who suffered through early versions of the script.

Inspiration is what makes a writer, and I must take a moment to say thank you to those who most inspired me to write this book. I'll start with my dear mother, Dee Mitchell, who always knew where my heart was and never failed to encourage me when she saw something that would make a good story. Thanks to my father who instilled in me the character to work until the job is finished. Thank you Shanky for your friendship, and for motivating me during my darkest hours. Most importantly, I want to thank my grandmother, Nina Mitchell, and the blessed men of God who dedicated their lives to bring His word to me. Among these giants, those who most touched my heart are Dr. Charles Stanley, Dr. Adrian Rogers, and my own beloved teacher, Pastor John Hagee. Finally, I look up and say a special thanks to my grandparents who live on my heart and inspire my characters.

AUTHOR'S NOTE

This book contains a fictional story with fictional characters. Although some of the events are true, and some of the locations are real, the story is entirely fictional.

This story was written not only to entertain you, but to help you understand that your life is not that different from anyone else's. We all go through valleys in our lives, from small daily challenges, to deep, dark valleys that can consume a lifetime. The depth and length of your valley is not determined by God, but by you.

The valleys occur because we live in Satan's kingdom. We have free will, and free will can lead to good things or to bad things. Life is all about learning to navigate the valleys. Just as we can't avoid sin, we can't avoid the valleys which are the terrain of a sinful world. Nor can we avoid pain, for God made pain the path to purification when he sacrificed his son for our salvation.

We do however, have a choice in how we deal with the valleys. We can fight this world, fight with God, and lead selfish, independent lives, or we can surrender our will to God, and ask Him to lead us out of the valley on the path He has chosen for us.

If you take nothing else away from reading this book, please let it lead you to read Galatians 5:16-26. The ways of the flesh are the path of least resistance. We immediately feel pity or anger when life doesn't go our way. If we allow these feelings to control us, they will take over our lives, leaving us vain and bitter. If, however, we can consciously try to avoid living in the flesh, and recognize our valleys as teaching moments that allow us to grow, first through humility, then through the resurrection of the spirit, we can begin to celebrate our lives as a journey full of opportunities to grow closer to God.

As you read about the main character, and notice the similarities to your own life, ask yourself if it is God who abandons us or us who abandon God. Enjoy the story. Peace be with you!

"So here's to the last cast,
timed perfectly to memorialize the day; you
know it probably won't yield anything, but
you can't leave without giving it your all.
It's all about proper endings; about
maintaining harmony.
Perfection is found in the doing,
not in the results.
And, so it goes, a clean shot just below the
hanging willow and up next to the log, a
glance across the lake, then to the horizon
just before the sun blinks goodbye; amber
sparkles on steel-blue water, Chad jumping,
and thoughts of her in the back of your
mind. She's always there. Thank God for her.
Thank God for everything."

~ 1 ~

A warm southern wind danced around the lake causing tiny blooms of ripples here and there on an otherwise glassy surface. Tyler Morgan cast an eye toward the horizon where a lone dark cloud had parked perfectly in front of the late January sun. The upper rim of the cloud glowed white-hot, and the sky below was ablaze in gold at the center, blending into amber to the left and right. Rays, like the fingers of God, shot out from the upper right corner, and all of it mirrored upon the steel-blue water of Sam Rayburn Reservoir.

It was his last day to fish with his father for a long time, and what better way to end a blessed day than with a divinely crafted painting in the western heavens.

Tyler Morgan laid his rod in his lap and sighed. He lifted his cap and ran his hands through his long, curly brown hair that immediately sprang back into a wild tangle.

"Looks like they're about done for the day," he said as he stretched. He looked back at his father, Charlie, who was still busy working a large willow tree by the water's edge. Tyler studied his father, admiring the master as he applied the techniques he had taught his sons at an early age. He still held the resemblance to Robert Redford that folks always went on about, only his frame had thinned considerably, and his brown hair was now heavily frosted.

"There ain't nothing there, Dad. I already threw in there."

"Yeah, well sometimes it's the second cast that gets 'em. Besides, I ain't done 'till the sun goes down, then it's one more cast for good measure. Let's work this point on around toward the house. What do you say?"

"You got it." Tyler smiled and looked down at his son who was bent over the side of the boat playing in the water; his own fishing pole carelessly thrown in the floor of the boat.

"Jake, how many times have I told you not to throw your rod in the floor, Son? Somebody will step on it and break it, or get a hook in their foot."

Without looking up, a sweet childish voice answered from the water's edge, "Yes, sir."

Tyler's muscles rippled as he ran his hands across his chest and arms, inspecting his tan. He leaned forward and grabbed his T-shirt off the back of his chair, slipped it on, then hit the trolling motor a couple times to keep the boat parallel with the shore. He spotted a shad running between a couple of stumps near the shore and cast his spinner-bait just beyond, hitting his mark as usual. A hard tug jerked his line taut.

"Hey Jake-o! Come here, Son, and hold Daddy's pole for a minute while I put up my tackle."

"Yes, sir."

Tyler winked at his father while the boy flicked the water off his hands and came to grab the pole.

"Hey. I got one!" Jake screamed.

"Well, pull him here, son."

The little boy struggled and stumbled about, trying to keep his grip on the rod. "Dad, I can't, it's too heavy."

"Yes, you can, Son. You're doing good. Fight him; keep reeling; don't give him any slack."

Tyler bent down and helped him reel, then reached over the side and pulled up a healthy, black bass. He laughed as his son jumped up and down with excitement, dropped the rod, and went to hug Charlie.

"Did you see, Grandpa? I caught a biggun'."

Charlie gave his grandson a big hug and pulled him up onto his lap. "I sure did. You caught the biggest one. Uncle Vince will fry him up for you tomorrow."

Jake put his arm around his grandpa's neck and watched as his father removed the hook. "I want to give it to Mr. Parker for his birthday."

Tyler exchanged grins with his father. "That's very thoughtful of you, Son. I'm sure he'll love it. How many does that give us for the party tomorrow, Dad?"

Charlie lifted the lid on the live well. "I'd say that's about fourteen."

"Oh, really? Well, that ought to be plenty. Let's go ahead and take it to the house so I can get them all cleaned before dark."

TYLER SLIPPED A NUMB ARM out from under his sleeping son, kissed his wife, Rachel, on the cheek, and threw on some jeans. The house was quiet, bathed in the red-orange glow of morning sunlight, and steeped with the pleasant breath of fresh air that wafted in through the curtains over the sink. It was the smell of East Texas in the raw; of lake water, pine trees, wood smoke, and fresh-turned earth. It was home and he was going to miss it.

He poured his coffee and headed toward the front porch where he knew his mother would be rocking in her chair, Bible in her lap, her gaze fixed on the sunrise over the lake, and humming her favorite hymn as she twirled her hair around her index finger. Mornings had always been their quiet time together, the time for heart-to-heart talks and soul searching – a time for mother and son to connect.

Tyler's heart lurched when he reached the screen door and saw her there. This would be the last morning he would share with her for a long time. He was glad they had slept over last night instead of going back home to finish packing. What if he never got the chance to sit with her again for their morning ritual? What if the cancer came back while he was living at the coast? He took a deep breath and set a course to make this morning a crowning memory of the precious moments spent with his mother.

"Good morning, Momma!"

"Good morning, Son," she said in a melancholic voice.

He gave her a kiss on the cheek and sat down in the rocker next to her. "Beautiful morning isn't it?"

She briefly looked his way with a smile, and he noticed her eyes were a little red and watery. Katherine Morgan was a strong woman, even stronger than his father. An avid horse person since she was old enough to walk, she was a lot tougher that her five-foot-three frame suggested. She was a single child and a bit of a tomboy growing up, whipping boys and barrel racing before she opted for a baton in high school. She made up for the passive attitude of his father; kicking him in the butt when he needed to stiffen his backbone a little. That iron constitution had been her saving grace when she was diagnosed with breast cancer, and it was her voice Tyler had always heard when he needed to find that something extra in his football days.

"Where's Dad? Is he out in the garden already?"

"Oh, you know your father. He was out there at first light, but he's gone after Vince now."

"Oh, good!"

Tyler took a sip of coffee and scanned the lake. He closed his eyes and was taking a deep breath when he felt his mother's hand on his arm. "I'm going to tell you something, Son, and I don't want you to think I'm being a nosey mother. Maybe I am, but I'm going to say it anyway."

He smiled and squeezed her hand. "Come on, Mom. You know you can tell me anything." He tried to make eye contact, but she continued looking away.

"Son, I know you have put everything on the line for this dream of yours. I want you to know that I'm proud of you, and I believe in you. I've seen you do things on that football field that were nothing short of a miracle, but business is business and if you can't afford it, you don't need it. You can't worry about impressing everybody right now. You have to start with what you got and it's gonna take guts and hard work to get where you want to be, but if you do it right, you'll never have to worry about someone else owning you. You have to start out like you want to finish."

He paused, staring off into the woods while trying to distill the true meaning behind her words. Perhaps she was just lecturing, saying something she felt needed to be said, or perhaps she wanted a discussion. Either way, he wanted to be sure that she knew her opinion mattered. "Do you think I'm doing something wrong, Mom?"

She began rocking and took a sip of her coffee. "It's your business, Son, and it's your family. I've heard all of this talk about a big fancy boat and a two-story condo on the water. I realize Rachel's from a wealthy family and I know you want her to be happy, but you can't put the cart before the horse. I know that's how everybody does it these days, but most of them are up to their ears in debt and will never see daylight."

Tyler studied his mother's profile for a moment while he sipped his coffee. "Mom, you know I always value your advice, but I'm not sure I understand what you are concerned about. Are you worried about Rachel or the business?"

"I guess I'm just worried about you, to be honest. Don't get me wrong, Son, we love her to death, but we just want you to be happy, and this whole thing just doesn't feel right. She's from old San Diego money and she's not used to roughing it. Port Aransas is not much more than a fishing village. You have a family counting on you now, and you have to be sure that you manage everyone's expectations."

"I think it will all be just fine, Mom. It's not like I just came up with this idea on a whim. I've put in two stints in the Navy and earned my business degree. With my diving and fishing experience, I think I'm pretty well set. Rachel's accounting degree will help with the books, and she's going to sit for her CPA as soon as things settle down. Don't forget, my old diving buddy from the Navy, Ray, is going to be my partner. He's from Port Aransas, and he knows all the right people.

His mother set her coffee down and turned to look him in the eye. "I hear what you're saying, Son, but that boat is going to cost an arm and a leg, and I know the diving equipment and all the store supplies are going to be astronomical. Where are you going to get that kind of money?"

"It's all been figured out, Mom. Ray's oldest friend, Brownie, is going to be our main investor for the startup costs. His family started a bank down there. He's seen our business plan and he's walking it through the bank to secure our business loan which he will personally guarantee. He'll be an owner for a while, but once the business is self-sufficient, we will slowly buy him out. As a matter of fact, I should hear something today from Ray about the loan."

Katherine folded her arms and sighed as she stared out at the lake. "I'll be praying for you, Son. I hope your dream comes true this time."

He looked into his coffee cup and twirled it around a couple of times. "Listen, Mom, I understand you don't like the idea of us being so far away. I realize this isn't the dream you had for me. I know you always wanted me to marry Jeanie and become a pro football player. So did I. I don't know why, but that dream was taken away from me. This is all I've got now."

Katherine remained quiet. He put his hand on hers and gave her a gentle squeeze, but she gave no response. She continued rocking slowly, her gaze still fixed over the lake. He saw a tear in the corner of her eye. Sadly, he realized this wasn't going to be the memorable morning he'd hoped for. He got up, kissed her, and walked back into the house.

AFTER BREAKFAST, TYLER HELPED RACHEL in the kitchen and was putting away the dishes when his father walked in with his brother, Vince. It was the first time Tyler had seen Vince in over four years, and that visit had been brief as he was shuffling from the Navy to college. For the last couple of weeks, Vince had been away with a new doctor who was helping him find a better way to cope with his surroundings.

His brother's appearance was still a bit of a shock to Ty after so much time apart. The part in his hair was much wider than normal due to the large scar where his skull had been wired together, and his left shoulder slumped where they had to rebuild his collarbone. His huge size and ghastly appearance were reminiscent of a horror movie monster, and had earned him the name "Frankenvince," courtesy of the local children. Tyler swallowed hard past the lump in his throat.

Poor Vince; he'd just signed his NFL contract and returned home for a couple of weeks before reporting to camp. Tyler had been helping his father clear the land for the new boat barn, but there were a couple of large stumps in the way that were taking a long time to dig out, and he couldn't get them to budge. Vince insisted on taking over. He was so proud of himself when he hooked a big chain up to the tractor to jerk them out.

The first one came easy, but the tractor struggled with the second stump, so he figured he needed to get a running start on it. No sooner had the slack gone out of the chain, than the tractor flipped over backwards on him. His head was split open and he broke almost every bone in his body. He'd actually died for a few minutes on the table at Lufkin Memorial Hospital.

His accident changed everyone – the whole damn town. High school football takes second place only to religion in the hearts of small-town folk. Even the preacher seemed to lose a little faith. Daddy stopped living and began existing. Mother seemed to lose her youthful step and cheerful glow overnight. She used to say, "You ain't supposed to outlive your kids. What he's got left ain't life at all."

Vince gave Tyler a big hug, then stepped back and lifted a Polaroid land camera from around his neck and took a picture of him. Tyler smiled. "Hey, I wasn't ready!"

Vince paid him no attention and went to hug Rachel. Tyler interjected, "Rachel, you remember my brother Vince from the wedding."

"Yes, of course!"

Tyler glanced at his father who began to offer some explanation.

"The new doctor gave Vince this camera to help him relate to things around him. He says it will help him to physically process things. He seems to like it."

Vince took a picture of Rachel, then Charlie ushered everyone out of the kitchen so that he and Vince could start preparing lunch.

Tyler was watching out the back door as Rachel took Jake for a walk around the garden when he heard his mother announce Mr. Parker's arrival. Katherine was busy setting up so Tyler answered the door.

"There he is, the man of the hour, Mr. Volney Parker. Happy birthday, Mr. Parker!" Tyler held the door as the family's oldest friend worked his cane over the threshold. Volney had been his grandfather's best friend and had treated the Morgan boys like grandsons after their grandfather died. His birthday had become an annual tradition around the Morgan household.

Tyler looked out at the old Ford Bronco in the drive. "By God, did you drive yourself?"

"Sure as hell did."

"Man, I hope I'm still driving at your age. Come on in. We saved the best seat in the house for you right over here in front of the TV where everyone can swing by and say hi to you."

Volney stopped just inside the door and looked up.

"Hot damn, it smells like the old camp house kitchen in here."

Charlie stepped around the corner of the pantry wearing an apron. "That's old Vince in there frying up your favorite fish! Happy birthday, Mr. Parker!"

Volney grumbled playfully, "Look what the cat dragged in. You becoming a cross-dresser? How the hell are you, Charlie?"

Charlie laughed and swatted him with a dish towel. "You old turd. You ain't changed a bit."

In the short time he'd been home, Tyler had been busy working on his business plan and traveling to and from Port Aransas to get everything set up. He hadn't spent much time with family and friends. He knew there would be some teary eyes as they came by the party to say hello and goodbye at the same time. As he stood next to his brother in the kitchen, he felt his heart sinking.

"Say, Vince, why don't I take that camera for you while you're frying fish so you don't mess it up?"

Vince paused and grunted, looking down at the camera around his neck. He took one last picture of the battered fish and handed it over to Ty.

"So do you think you're going to like taking pictures?"

"Yeah."

"I'm glad you finally found a doctor that can help you," He said as he squeezed his brother's shoulder.

"Yep."

As he set the camera aside, Tyler heard a commotion in the front room. He poked his head around the corner just in time to see Lester Radcliffe shaking hands with old man Parker.

Lester was just as he had remembered him, always overdressed as if he had to maintain his image as the richest man in the county. He wore a shiny, graphite-grey suit, complete to a shirt with French cuffs and a collar bar supporting an imported silk tie. Everything about him was perfect, except for the scarred and deformed finger on his right hand. Tyler reluctantly stepped forward to say hello.

"Mr. Radcliffe, how are you sir?"

"Tyler! I didn't know you were still here. I thought you were moving to the coast to start a new business."

"Yes, sir. We leave tomorrow."

"A deep-sea diving and fishing business, isn't it?"

"That's right."

"Well, let me know if you need any advice. Running a business is a lot trickier than it looks." Lester turned to Charlie who was standing dutifully by. "Charlie, let's take a walk. I want to talk to you about something. How long have you worked for me now?"

As they headed out the front door, Tyler looked over to see his mother standing off in the corner with a concerned expression on her face as she talked to Rachel.

"Tyler?" His brother Vince called him back into the kitchen.

"What's up, Bro?" He watched as Vince tossed a huge bowl of salad.

"We need more tomatoes."

"Okay. I'll run out to the garden and get some." He stopped at the kitchen window and looked out at his father and Lester down by the shore. Lester was gesturing with his hands as if describing the layout of something. After studying them for a minute, Tyler decided to take a little detour on the way out to the garden.

As he walked through the pantry he passed Rachel coming in from the front room. She raised her eyebrows and rolled her eyes. "Your mom hates that guy."

He laughed. "Oh yeah, you have no idea."

"Why? He seems nice enough?"

"He's a fake. He'll smile at you and cut off your ring finger as he shakes your hand."

"What?" She smiled uncertainly.

"It's a long story, Babe. He's part of the old Pine Island Country Club crowd. He's the reason that 146 acres behind us doesn't belong to our family anymore."

He gave her a quick kiss. "It's a long story. I got to grab some more tomatoes for Vince."

On the front porch, Tyler stopped to fill a cup with beer from the keg. He walked down to the shoreline and held the cup out in front of him as he approached Lester and his father.

"Mr. Radcliffe, can I offer you a beer?"

Lester stopped mid-sentence and threw a cold stare at Tyler. "Not now, son. We're kinda in the middle of something."

"Oh yeah, what are y'all talking about?" Tyler played dumb as he took a sip of the beer and set it on the ground to load a pinch of tobacco.

Lester turned his gaze towards Charlie as if to ask him to run Tyler off.

"Oh it's just business, Son." Charlie added obediently.

Tyler shifted to one leg and looked down as he stuffed his hands into his back pockets. "You know, I may be just out of college, but I have been out in the real world for a few years and I think I know a business proposition when I see one." He threw Lester a cocky smile. "I was just curious what you are planning here, Mr. Radcliffe."

Lester glared for a second, then jutted his chin into the air and turned toward the lake, scanning the horizon. The more he thought about it, the more sense it made to pitch Tyler at the same time he was pitching Charlie. He figured Tyler would find out anyway. At least now, he could paint a good story for both of them and he wouldn't have to worry about Tyler spoiling the deal.

He turned back to them and began nodding. "Okay, Tyler, fair enough. Your daddy happens to be in a very lucrative position right now. We have just started clearing land for the Radcliffe Resort which will be situated on the acreage behind us that used to belong to your grandfather. I'm going to start a corporation which will allow your daddy to own part of that land again, as well as participate in the profits from the resort which will eventually pass to you. Additionally, I'm offering to buy this place for our marina."

Tyler lifted his head which he had kept down the entire time Lester was speaking. He squinted one eye at Lester. "So just where are they supposed to go after being here all of their lives?"

Lester felt his internal salesman amping up. He looked at Charlie and slapped his shoulder. "That's a good boy you got here, Charlie. He's watching out for you." He turned his attention back to Tyler.

"That's the beauty of it, Son. As people get older, it gets tough trying to take care of a place this size. They start thinking about downsizing and looking for a place with easy access to doctors and hospitals. I know it seems sad to think about your folks that way, but it's a fact of life. Now, without my resort he might have a difficult time selling this place for a price that would amount to anything, but lucky for him he's in the right place at the right time." Lester put his arm around Charlie and gave him a squeeze to make him feel proud.

Tyler straightened his posture to address his father.

"Daddy, were you guys thinking about leaving here in the near future?"

Charlie shuffled about, but Lester made sure he kept his hand on his shoulder. "I don't know, Son. I guess if the right opportunity presents itself, we'll have to give it fair consideration."

Lester saw the opening and jumped in. "Your father has been my most loyal employee, Tyler. I wanted to give him first shot before we considered any alternate locations. This kind of opportunity doesn't come along very often, and it won't stay around too long neither." Lester tried to read Tyler as he watched the young man kick at the ground and look down the shoreline.

After an awkward silence, Charlie chimed in. "Ain't no harm in it, Son. It might just be an offer we can't refuse."

Lester felt his smile melting as Tyler froze and made eye contact with him. He spit without breaking eye contact.

"That's what I'm worried about." He worked his jaw and nodded at both of them before walking back up to the house.

Lester sighed and crossed his arms as he watched Tyler walking away. Charlie looked down, acting a little embarrassed. Lester put his hand on Charlie's shoulder again. "Don't worry about it Charlie, he'll come around when he's had time to think it through."

Charlie smiled and offered his hand to Lester. "Well, I better get back up there to the party. I appreciate you thinking of us, and let us know when you get something put together."

As Charlie stepped away, Lester turned back toward the lake to think. He picked up a rock and pitched it out into the water. "That's where my marina is going to be whether you like it or not, Tyler Morgan. Come hell or high water, Lester Radcliffe gets what he wants, whatever it takes."

Lester glanced back toward the house. He knew Tyler was going to be trouble. He had some time before he would need to move forward on acquiring the property. He figured he would let it lie long enough for Tyler to get settled down south and buried in his own business.

Tyler stepped cautiously through the rows picking tomatoes, thinking about last times, about fishing with his dad, rocking with his mom, and working the garden. His basket was almost full when he heard a familiar whistle.

He looked up to see his old friend and quarterback, Karl Dupree, standing at the edge of the garden. Karl had been a deputy now for a few years, and his football swagger had easily morphed into the gun-toting swagger of a cocky law man. He stood leaning to one side with his hat cocked, a toothpick in his mouth, and his arm resting on his gun.

Tyler threw him a big smile. "What do you say, Deputy Dog?"

A grin grew beneath the rotating toothpick, and his friendly blue eyes gleamed. Karl was a tall, good-looking man with wavy blonde hair and a slim, athletic build. He had always been a heartthrob with the local ladies and still spent many nights answering false burglar calls to the homes of lonely widows and divorcees. Tyler switched arms with his basket as he exited the garden and offered his hand to Karl.

"Did you come to pay your respects to old man Parker?"

"Yep, and to say goodbye to my best friend. Y'all still leaving in the morning?"

"Yeah, were heading out early."

"Wish we would've had more time together, Ty. Seems like you just got here yesterday and you're already leaving."

"I know. A man's gotta follow his dreams!"

They stopped at the outside sink and Tyler began rinsing the tomatoes as Karl scanned the garden. He chuckled.

"Funny how time flies. It don't seem that long ago we were getting yelled at for playing in the garden."

"Right? It's been hard seeing old friends and having to say goodbye."

"I see you got to say hi to Jeanie."

"What's that?" Ty looked up in surprise.

"Well, I figured you did anyway. I passed her and Terry walking from back here. They didn't look too happy."

"I'll be damned. I never saw them." Ty stood from his washing and stared at the corner of the house in a daze. "That's weird."

"Well, it doesn't surprise me. Terry is so jealous he never lets her out of his sight. She probably heard you were back here and came to say hi. I guess he wrangled her back in as soon as he noticed. I think he was in a hurry anyway to get to Lester's for the big unveiling."

Tyler turned off the water and stood again, rubbing his hands on his jeans. "Unveiling?"

"Yeah, for the new resort Lester wants to build on your grandpa's old land."

Tyler scowled. "I just heard. Guess I'm the last one to know anything around here." He put his hands on his hips and squared his jaw.

"Sorry, Bud." Karl frowned and pushed his hat back. "By the way, I saw a truck sitting out by the turn to Lester's with our local thugs stuffed in it."

"No kidding?"

"Yeah, the same three jerks we always fought in high school – Bobby Buell, Cooter Faulk, and Doyle Kitchens. Joe-Glenn Hill was with them too. You may not remember Bobby, he left before his junior year, but who could forget that scrawny Cooter? He followed Doyle everywhere. You remember, he's that white trash that pulled Lisa Peterson into his car in the Pizza Hut parking lot and tried to have his way with her."

Tyler chuckled as he folded his arms. "Oh yeah, we whipped him and Doyle both that night, didn't we?"

"Yeah, didn't take much." Karl grinned widely.

Tyler cocked his head and squinted. "Isn't Cooter the one they tried for murdering his parents or something?"

"That's right; they just up and disappeared one day." Karl peered over the top of the bag as he loaded a chew. "They never proved anything though. Guess who paid his legal fees and ended up owning the family farm when Cooter couldn't pay him back?"

"Let me guess; Lester?"

"Yep, he rents it back to him now."

"Well, what the hell is the richest man south of Dallas doing running with those dirt bags?"

"Oh, I don't think they were with Lester. I think they were waiting on Terry to come back up from here. I heard he is going to hire them to work at his new John Deere dealership. He probably invited them to the unveiling and I'm sure Lester won't be too thrilled about it."

Tyler picked up the tomatoes and started for the back porch. "This place just gets weirder by the minute."

Karl stopped outside the porch. "Listen, Bud; the sheriff wants me to stay available, so I can't hang out. There's supposed to be a seriously dangerous storm headed this way."

"How is Coach these days? I still can't believe he's our sheriff!"

"Kinda weird huh?" Karl spit and grinned.

"Yeah, almost as weird as letting Lester fund his campaign. Stranger things have happened, I guess."

Tyler adjusted the basket to shake hands again. "Well, take care of yourself, buddy. If you get some time off, get your butt down to Port Aransas and I'll take you fishing."

"You take care too, my friend. I'll look forward to it." Karl shook hands then slapped Tyler's shoulder as he turned to leave. "You guys keep an eye on that storm."

"Sure. No big deal." Tyler sighed and watched his best friend disappear around the corner of the house.

~ 2 ~

After lunch, Tyler walked around the room where he'd grown up, taking inventory of his life as he revisited all the trophies and newspaper clippings. He stopped in front of an old photograph and plucked it from the mirror frame.

"It's going to be hard for you to leave here isn't it?" Rachel leaned against the door frame with her arms crossed.

"Hey, Babe. I didn't see you there. So Vince finally let you out of his sight, huh?"

"Moose took him home a little while ago. He was getting upset because he ran out of film. He's a wonderful man, Ty. I think we bonded. You're lucky to still have him in your life."

She nodded at the photograph he was holding as she walked into the room. "You know, Vince says that photographs can show us secrets; things the world has hidden from our eyes to keep our hearts from knowing the truth."

"Really? Vince said that? That's kinda profound for him. It must have been his therapy talking."

"That's her isn't?"

"Who, you mean Jeanie?" He shrugged. "Yeah, that was a long time ago."

"Evidently not long enough." She unfolded her arms and walked up to him as he was placing the picture back where he'd found it.

"Babe, don't start on that again. You know better than that. Besides, we're out of here tomorrow to start our new life at the coast."

She put her arm around him, leaned into him, and sighed. "I just know how she looked at you when she came by to say happy birthday to Mr. Parker. She just stood there watching you for the longest time. I think she really just came to get one last look at you."

He pushed her back gently to look at her. "You watched out the window or what? I didn't even know she was here until Karl told me."

Rachel shrugged. "She's a real beauty with that gorgeous blonde hair and those heavenly, sky-blue eyes. She's so joyful and naturally attractive that she even makes me want to hug her. Your mom sure seems to think the world of her."

Tyler took his wife by the shoulders. "Rachel, you are my wife and I love you with all my heart. I love our beautiful son, and I am blessed to have both of you. I can't control how someone looks at me, and you should know beyond any doubt that you and Jake are my whole life."

She smiled, took a deep breath, and gave him a warm, lingering hug. "They said to tell you they're ready to cut the birthday cake."

"All right. I guess we should head that way." He began to follow her out, but stopped short of the doorway. "Oops, I forgot my beer. I'll be right there, Honey."

He walked back into the room and grabbed his cup of beer from the dresser. The Bible his mother had given him after his knee surgery was sitting nearby. He lifted the Bible and smelled the leather. "Thank you, Lord, for my beautiful family and for giving me another chance at life." As he set the Bible down, he looked at himself in the mirror. *Jeanie is beautiful, and she still touches my heart, but she is a married woman and I am a married man whom God has blessed with a new direction. You can do this Tyler. With God's help, you can do anything.*

NEAR THE END OF HIS life, Volney Parker grunted with a deep sigh of relief as Tyler helped him sit down in a homemade Adirondack chair overlooking the ever-changing shoreline of Lake Sam Rayburn. Today was the anniversary of his ninety-first year on this earth. As he patted Volney on the shoulder, Tyler realized that the anxiety of being in small places with more than a handful of people was becoming unbearable for his old friend. Nevertheless, the old man was a bit of a hero to him, having outlived all of his family and friends despite his partiality to hand-rolled smokes and what he called his *Joy Juice.*

He smiled proudly as Volney wiped his forehead with a napkin and looked around the porch.

"Forty-eight years."

"What's that, Mr. Parker?"

Volney coughed and ran his hand across the arm rest, admiring the quality of the wood. "Your grandpa Angus, crazy Joe Gentry and I built this porch together with our bare hands forty-eight years ago."

Tyler felt sorry for him. "You miss them, don't you?"

"Those were days rich with the dreams of young, able-bodied men of sharp mind, strong work ethic, and simple, Godly ways."

"Too bad things have to change so much."

"Oh hell, I've seen a lot changes in my long life, many of which I never understood. I'm here to tell you, I've come to the notion that it's not all about the here and now."

"Is that so?" Tyler folded his arms, slightly amused, but no less impressed as always by his wise old friend. "What's it all about then?"

"I think there's an eternal war between Good and Evil taking place on a higher plain. This world where we live is like a breeding ground for souls. The old Devil wants you to live in the flesh so he can win your soul, and the Good Lord wants you to have faith and live according to His word so you can have life eternal. I believe a man's life is a fight for his soul, and represents only a small incursion within one of many battles that take place over many lifetimes."

Surprised at the deep thoughts of his old friend, Tyler posted his hands on his hips and grinned. "So are you saying that we live more than once?"

"I don't know too much about that, but I do believe that events from long ago can become part of the template for a man's life. Things you would never dream could touch your life will suddenly play an important role, and things yet to come that you have no idea about now, will strangely become part of your story. We judge everything by the spectrum of our own lifetime, so we can never understand nor appreciate the full wonder of God's plan, the intertwining of it all, and the eternal wisdom of God."

Tyler smiled and slipped his hands into his pockets. "I'd be willing to bet most people never put much thought into that."

"That's why most people don't have much faith; they just ain't lookin' at the bigger picture. I've learned that if we can't see the reason for something that happens, it's a sign of the Master Plan at work."

Tyler nodded, considering the events of his life as he watched Volney close his eyes and lift his head. Without opening his eyes he added, "I used to have an old Indian friend who said the most important events were marked by the winds of change. He said the faithful ones could always sense it."

"It makes sense, I guess." Tyler was deep in thought when a familiar fragrance stirred his senses. He recognized the smell of rain blowing in from across the lake. Curiously, a gust of wind lifted the hair from Volney's shoulders, and he seemed to be nodding a pleasant greeting to all things inevitable as he studied the worn handle of his cane.

With a deep breath and a long sigh, Tyler patted the old man on the shoulder. "I guess I better run back in and see if I can help clean up. Are you going to be okay out here?"

Volney grinned and blinked. "I'm good."

WITH THE DISHES DONE, TYLER stepped away from the family and back out onto the deck where the keg sat, iced down in a large gray trash can. He poured a beer and took a drink as he headed over to talk to Volney. He tried to squat next to the old man's chair but felt a twinge in his knee. Volney looked at him and shook his head.

"That old football injury is still bothering you, huh?"

Tyler frowned as he stretched and rubbed out his knee. Feeling the breeze again, he turned and looked to the south.

"Boy, it's black as pitch over there. There was a severe weather warning on TV earlier. They said something about thunderstorms with possible tornados, and a flash flood warning for Nacogdoches and Angelina Counties."

"Yeah, I reckon it's fixin' to come a frog-strangler."

"You think so? What exactly is a frog-strangler anyway?"

"Damn if I know, but it's gonna rain like hell. I can feel it in my bones. Can you smell it?"

"That's probably that shirt you've been wearing for the past three months."

"Hell if it is, you little smart-ass. I wash this damn shirt every week."

"Well, if you'd ever open your dang birthday gifts, you'd see I bought you a new one. I picked out a pretty red one. I figured you needed all the help you could get."

The old man grinned as Tyler pumped the keg. "Widow Cox still thinks I'm purty."

"Ah hell, she's just after your money."

"Oh, I 'spect that's a fair trade. Say, it sure was good to see old Vince again. I ain't seen him in quite a spell."

"Well, he moved out to the river house near Boggy Slough. He likes it better there; no one to stare at him and whisper remarks back and forth like he can't hear 'em."

"Damn shame what happened to your brother; you too, for that matter. I always figured I'd be watching both of you in Cowboy blue one day."

"Yeah, me too, Mr. Parker; me too. You know, I was mad about it for a long time, but I finally realized that it just wasn't part of God's plan for us. I mean, if you think about it, I never would have gone into the Navy, I wouldn't have become a diver, and I wouldn't have met Rachel and had a beautiful son. I've been blessed."

The old man grunted and looked down at his feet. "Oh yeah, you're blessed, but you're still a young man. You gotta lot of life ahead you, boy. Just remember that a man's faith gets tested many times. It's easy to feel blessed when things are going your way. The real test is when you're in the valley, when things are the darkest. Will you surrender to His will or turn away from Him and become angry at Him for letting you suffer?"

"Hell, I've been tested enough for one life, I think. It's finally time for things to start going my way. I've got everything ready for our new life at the coast. You need to come down with Mom and Dad when they come and let me take you fishing."

The old man coughed and wiped his mouth. Tyler walked to the front of the porch and looked out over the lake. He was a little touched by what Mr. Parker had said about his football career. Truth was, he'd dreamed of being a Dallas Cowboy ever since he could hold a football, but the championship game of his senior year ended that. It had been some time since he'd thought of it; of Terry Radcliffe missing all those blocks, of Terry going on to college with Jeanie Stinson and him staying behind.

Jeanie, his Jeanie, or so he had always thought. They had been inseparable since he was seven. The year after high school had not only marked the end of a lifelong friendship with Terry Radcliffe, but it had also marked the end of his dream to marry Jeanie, his childhood sweetheart. He found it somewhat poignant to be thinking of it now as he prepared to start life over on the coast with Rachel and their little boy.

Jeanie was probably a couple of hills over at the Radcliffe place now, attending the grand unveiling with Terry. To think she had been standing only a few yards away from him and he had never known she was there. A light pain in his heart forced him to take a deep breath. As he slowly exhaled, he wondered if Rachel was right; that Jeanie still had feelings for him. Their parting had been so sudden and so mysterious. They never had any closure. *Why, Jeanie, why*? As he shoved his hands into pockets and threw his chin up to the sky, he knew he would forever be haunted by that question.

His love for Rachel wasn't the same kind of love, but it was a good love, a love consummated by the beautiful son they shared together. He sighed, feeling proud that he'd overcome many obstacles, and confident that he was finally pointing his life in the right direction.

The sliding door eased open and Tyler smiled at Rachel as she let Jake out to come see him. He knelt down and gave his son a hug.

"Hey there, Jake-o boy. Are you coming to see daddy?"

"Uh-huh." His son buried his face into his chest as he hugged him, but he quickly pushed away and held a Hot Wheels car up to his father's face.

"Look at my race car."

"Yeah, Boy, that's a cool one. I bet it's real fast."

Jake's face went blank. Tyler watched as his son became entranced, looking over his shoulder at the sky behind him. He tried to get Jake's attention, but the little boy just stared ahead, wobbling slightly as a worried look began to grow on his sweet little face. Before Tyler could figure out what was going on, his son hugged him, gave him a kiss on the cheek, and ran back to the door. Tyler watched curiously as Rachel let the child back inside.

"Well, that was weird."

He stood, walked back to the edge of the porch, and looked out across the lake to the approaching storm.

"Do you think little kids can sense the danger of a storm?"

Old man Parker coughed and spit. As Tyler looked back, he noticed the colorfully stained napkin his old friend had stuffed into the front of his shirt.

"You want to change out that napkin before I bring you some cake?"

"Naw, hell naw, it's just gonna get dirtier. I ain't got room for cake yet. Say, why don't you grab me one them beers? I need to belch and that's about all that damn stuff's good for."

"You got it."

He handed Mr. Parker his beer and watched him take a long drink. Then he looked nervously back over his shoulder again. "I'm getting a little worried about that sky over there. It's looking serious, don't you think?"

"You dern tootin'. It's been a rumblin' and a tumblin' to beat hell. I 'spect we'll be feeling the winds here right directly. Now listen, I'm going to tell you sumpin'." Mr. Parker took another drink and burped loudly. "That there ain't no ordinary storm and that boy of yours knows it."

Tyler was tickled with the old fellow and wanted to laugh, but suddenly he felt the hair on the back of his neck stand up. He spun around to look at the lake again.

"Wow! Here come the winds. So you reckon there's something special about this one, huh?"

"I've seen it before, like in sixty-five when they was filling the lake, the storm that took old man Moore." He pointed with a crooked finger. "That there's a life-changer. There's death in them clouds. Ever once't in a while the Good Lord sends a reminder."

"I hope it ain't *our* death." Tyler squatted next him, ignoring the pain in his knee. "I've heard Daddy tell the story about old man Moore. He used to own the Moore farm before the lake swallowed it."

"Yep, that's right. It was a beautiful farm."

"I fished it many times with Dad growing up. They used to say old man Moore would come into town ever so often with a wad of cash to buy stuff, but no one could ever figure where he got the money. Is that really true?"

"Sure 'nough. Moore was a gambling man; not much else for him to do. He inherited that farm, but not much money. I figure he got mixed up with the wrong crowd, just like your Grandpa Angus."

The sliding door flew open and several people rushed to the edge of the porch, looking across the lake. Tyler jumped up as they rushed by him.

"What's going on?"

"Tornado sighted over by Hanks Creek," someone shouted.

"I doubt you can see it from here. Hanks would be a couple of points past that last point to the left," Tyler added.

Rachel stepped up next to Tyler and grabbed his arm. "Oh my God, it's completely dark over there!"

Old man Parker cleared his throat nervously. "You got a transistor radio?"

"Good point," Charlie answered. "We may not have power here in a minute. I got one out in the boat."

Tyler nodded at his father and patted old man Parker on the shoulder. "Good thinking. Dad, why don't you get everybody back inside? I'll run and get it."

Tyler helped old man Parker up from his chair. With everyone inside, he stopped for a moment to study the storm, wondering if he could see the tornado. It looked as if night was coming across the lake. Like an apocalyptic prophecy, it seemed to slowly swallow all signs of life as it moved forward. For the first time he could remember since he was a child, fear gripped him. Hail began to fall and he knew what that meant.

The winds increased to a howl as he set off for the boat barn that stood about thirty yards closer to the lake. The waves thundered against the shore, and he could hear a faint sound in the distance like a chugging train coming from the other side of the lake. Pine needles stung his face as he reached the boat barn. The wind caught the huge tin door as he tried to ease it open, but he managed to get a foothold and pull it closed behind him. He turned on the light, but by the time he got into the boat, everything went dark.

~ 3 ~

Outside, the wind roared, and the hailstones were getting larger, slamming into the tin barn in a deafening barrage that sounded like fireworks exploding. Tyler knelt in the floor of the boat and reached through the darkness, feeling his way up under the bow and over the anchor. His hand fumbled past the life vests until he finally came across a familiar tubular shape. He withdrew the flashlight and clicked it on. A slow cracking sound came from outside, followed by a loud thud. It sounded like a huge limb must have landed right next to the barn. Immediately, he thought of his dad talking about how weak pine trees were and how dangerous it was leaving them so close to the house.

The lock on the rod box wasn't clasped, thank goodness. He didn't have the boat keys. Inside, he found the old weather radio and tucked it under his arm. He cast the light down to find the trailer fender and stepped out. As he peeled the door open, the wind was even stronger and the hail had given way to torrential rain. It took all of his strength to keep the door from smashing to pieces against the hickory tree behind it. By the time he got it closed and latched, he was soaked to the bone.

Tyler was horrified by the sight of the lake as he ran for the house. The shoreline roared like the North Sea, and behind it nothing but white fading into black. Somewhere in the blackness, not far from shore, the deep, chugging engine noise was drawing closer, and he began to hear a hideous gurgling, as if a tub drain the size of a swimming pool was losing the last of its water.

By the time he reached the porch, the gurgling which had become high-pitched, mushroomed into a hideous and horrifying eruption which sounded like a herd of elephants crashing through the woods. He dove inside the dark house, shouting for everyone to take cover, then switched on the radio and searched for a signal. Rachel and Jake huddled up next to him, in the corner behind the bar. There was a loud tone on the radio followed by a prerecorded message:

> This is not a test. National Weather Service meteorologists are tracking a large and extremely dangerous tornado in the Sam Rayburn Reservoir area of Nacogdoches and Angelina counties. The tornado was spotted over Hanks Creek Marina and is moving in a north-northeasterly direction at approximately sixty miles per hour. Winds from this storm can reach in excess of two hundred miles per hour. Residents along the lakeshore near Shirley Creek Marina and in towns north and northeast of the lake should seek shelter immediately. Again, this is an extremely dangerous and serious life-threatening situation. This storm is capable of producing extremely high winds, flash flooding, and strong to violent tornadoes. If you're in the path of this tornado, take cover immediately!

Soon there was another loud crack and an earthshaking boom. The winds screeched like a whirl of demons and the windows shook fiercely. The house creaked and moaned wildly. Tyler wondered if it would all rip away at once or just slowly peel away in a flurry of swirling debris, sucking people up into the mix and tossing them far away. He pulled Rachel closer to him, and together, they held Jake as tight as they could.

Nine people hunched against the back wall saying prayers and listening to the gargoyle-wind, clawing and tearing to get in, ripping the shingles from the roof. Jake began crying and tried to crawl deeper into his father's lap. Like a handful of war refugees sitting against the wall of a bomb shelter, they listened helplessly as the death train howled above them.

When hell's fury had passed, they sat motionless in the dark with only an occasional flash of lightning to let them know they weren't alone. Soon Tyler could hear his son sniffling and others catching their breath and counting their blessings. Eventually, the roaring thunder of the wind diminished, but the rain droned hard and steady, drowning out all other signs of life. Finally, the sky lightened a little, but inside it was still too dark to get around easily.

Katherine Morgan broke the silence. "Everybody okay? Y'all just stay put. I'll run and get some candles."

After a few moments of rummaging in the kitchen, Katherine appeared with a lit candle and a handful of others. They gathered in the front room comparing notes, as Tyler and his father stepped outside to survey the damage.

Huge limbs were scattered everywhere; the ground was covered with fresh pinecones and straw, as a soft rain fell. The next thing Tyler saw was the top to the boat barn lying down by the lake. A few more minutes and he might have been lying down there with it. Two of the large pines by the lake were uprooted and lying across the yard, and the old oak between them had the top torn out of it.

Charlie's old metal john boat, which had been leaning against the trees a few feet from shore, was now lying on the Morgan's front deck, and there was a huge gash in the corner of the house where it had crash landed. The keg of beer was sitting upright thirty yards out in the woods as if it had been purposely placed there. Tyler walked over to inspect it; all the ice was gone.

He caught up with Charlie, now making his way around the house, checking the roof. To their relief, not many shingles had been lifted, but around back, one of the large pine trees had fallen and missed the back steps by mere inches. A smaller pine leaned on the wires strung from the service pole — which was now bent about thirty degrees to the North.

"We got damned lucky." Charlie mumbled quietly.

"Yes, we did, Dad, but we got a hell of mess to clean up."

Tyler's cellphone rang. It was Karl Dupree.

"You guys all okay? I hear that thing went right through there."

"Yep. It got close enough to rip the roof off the boat barn and curl my hair, but everyone is okay and the house didn't get much damage."

"Thank God. When I was leaving there I saw that black sky way off in the distance, and by the time I got home I was getting calls of hail and high winds over at Hanks Creek. You ought to see the marina. It's all twisted and tore up; parts of it up in the trees and boats are all over the damn place."

"Anybody hurt?"

"Nothing too serious, thank goodness."

"Thank God for that."

"Amen, brother. Well, I just wanted to check on you. I gotta lot of ground to cover before dark so I better get off. You guys still leaving in the morning?"

"I think so. I need to check with Dad to see if he needs any help, but otherwise we're headed south."

"Well, good luck to you, Buddy, and congratulations again. I'll be waiting for that invite to go catch my first sailfish."

"You got it. Take care, Karl. I'll be in touch when we get settled."

THE SUN PEEKED OUT FOR just a moment, but quickly vanished as the day waned on toward its second nightfall. Tyler heard his cousin Mike and his wife Sarah saying they would rather stay the night than try to brave the debris-strewn roads and heavy rain that continued to fall. As for old man Parker, there was no way he could go anywhere. He lived on the other side of the bridge and down the road a piece near a small community called Marion's Ferry, and he couldn't see to drive through heavy rain anymore. Tyler wanted to stay, but there was no room and he still had a little light packing to do at the rental house.

As they loaded into the car, his mom and dad worried over them. Charlie lifted Jake and slid him into the back seat while Katherine walked over to kiss Tyler.

"Son, there are plenty of sheets. I could make a bed of the two couches downstairs for y'all. I hate to see you leave now. You don't know what to expect out there."

Tyler gave his mom a kiss and a big hug. "We'll be all right, Mom. I'll call you when we get to the house."

Mike and Sarah came up to say goodbye as Charlie took another stroll over to investigate the leaning service pole. Mike stood directly in front of Ty looking worried.

"Ty, you can't possibly be thinking of hauling your family off through a storm like this. You've had a few beers. Stay here. We can play dominoes and you can drink all you want."

Ty smiled and slapped his cousin on the shoulders.

"Don't be such a worrywart, Mikey. The worst is over. We're only a few minutes away and I ain't drunk."

Charlie walked back to them with his hands on his hips, gazing up at the sky.

"I hate to see you guys go, but you better hurry, looks like there's another band coming and it looks nasty."

Tyler looked around. "You sure you don't want me to stay for a few more days and help you clean this up, Dad?"

"Nah, that's what insurance is for. Besides. I can get Vince to come help me. You need to get your business set up, Son."

Tyler hugged his father, who waited patiently as he climbed into the car, then leaned down and spoke through the window.

"Be sure you slow down over the hill before Joshua Creek. It used to get bad enough in the old days, but since Radcliffe has been clearing land, we haven't had a hard enough rain to know what it's gonna do. Hell, it could be a damned river by now."

"Don't worry, Dad, I'll be careful. I grew up crossing that creek. We'll be fine."

"Yeah, well, just don't take any chances. If it's running, don't try to cross it. It's deeper than it looks. You remember how deep that gully is. I ain't telling you nothing new."

"I got it, Dad. Love you guys."

As they pulled away and headed past the back pasture, the heavy rain intensified.

"Man, I don't think I've ever seen rain this hard."

"Tyler, are you sure this is a good idea?" asked Rachel.

"It's just rain, Honey. The tornado is long gone, but if it'll make you feel better, I'll stop here and wait for it to slow down."

"Yeah, I think that would be better."

Tyler put the car in park and turned to look at his little boy. "What do you think about all this rain, Jake-o?"

His son turned a worried face to him for a moment, then returned to his window as he stared wide-eyed at the sky and pumped his legs back and forth.

"I hate not having him in his car seat, Ty. I can't believe I let you talk me into running over here without it."

"Relax, Babe, *I* never had a dang car seat. Besides, we didn't have time to switch it out. For goodness sake, we're only a couple of miles from the house."

He put his arm around her and gave her a long kiss. "Just think, Baby, a couple of days from now we'll be sitting on our deck on the channel drinking Bahama Mammas and watching the sailboats float by!"

She sighed and leaned her head against his shoulder. "I'm so proud of you, Tyler. We're so blessed. This is a dream come true."

"It certainly is, Honey. We are blessed. Ninety-eight is going to be a year to remember." He chuckled. "For a minute there, I thought that tornado just might be the end of us, but the Good Lord protected us." He gave her a sweet kiss, then reached back and squeezed his son's leg. "I bet Jake-o's going to be a surfer boy and drive all the girls crazy!"

~ 4 ~

Katherine Morgan turned from the TV and stood looking out the window at Lufkin Memorial Hospital as the news coverage of the tornado continued.

"We go live now to Garrison Ward who's standing where Hank's Creek Marina used to be."

"Thanks, Gina. Folks, if you look just behind me here you will see several pieces of twisted metal wrapped in and out of these trees. That metal used to be out here in front of me as part of the marina. There were over a hundred boat slips, a store, a café, and some gas pumps out on the end which are now completely gone.

"Now I want to show you something else if I can get the camera to pan down here at my feet. This small piece of concrete where I am standing used to be the beginning of the ramp which led out to the floating marina, and as you can see, there's absolutely nothing left.

"Up on the hill behind me were rows of trailer homes that were rental units for the visiting fishermen, but as the camera pans across the area, you will see that almost every home has been demolished as if a bomb hit here. Incredibly, there are parts of these homes and this marina that have been reported as far as three miles away. The miracle of it all, Gina, is that only a few people were injured, and no fatalities here. Unfortunately, that can't be said for other areas hit by this vicious tornado. Back to you, Gina."

"That's right, Garrison. It is a tragedy for some of our viewers today as the death toll from the storm has now reached nineteen. We were just informed that two more were lost on the north side of the lake in Nacogdoches County. Their car was found mangled a few hundred feet from a private creek crossing. It is assumed that they attempted to cross the flooded creek. There was one survivor, believed to be the driver, who is now hospitalized and in stable condition. Two are reported to have been lost; their bodies as yet have not been recovered, and the names are not yet being released."

Tyler woke, clawing wildly and gasping for air. "Jake! Where's Jake? Rachel?" His mother turned quickly from the window and ran to his side.

"Tyler, I'm here. Relax. It's okay, son. You're all right."

"Where's my boy? Where's Rachel?" He shouted frantically as he tried to comprehend the alien surroundings of the hospital room.

Though still delirious, he could tell his mother was trying hard to keep her composure, but he could see through her weakly constructed facade. He knew she had bad news for him, and he could feel her pain filling the room. She wrapped her arms around him and put her head on his chest to hide her face.

"Momma?"

His mother slowly lifted her face and looked into his eyes. He stared back at her for a moment, his brow furrowed and his eyes grew large, then suddenly his face turned to stone. She reached out and touched his cheek, but her affection didn't register with him. He felt her hands cupping his face as she began shaking her head.

"I'm so sorry, son. They're still looking for them. Karl's been out there for two days. He'll find them, Ty, he'll find them. You just gotta have faith, son."

His face remained unchanged except for the tears that gushed down his cheeks. The bleakness of the hospital room confirmed his reality.

As his mind raced back to his conversation on the porch with Volney Parker, his heart emptied into his gut.

"Have faith, Son, just have faith. We are blessed that you have been saved."

He gritted his teeth and turned his face to the wall. "No one is blessed." He felt his mother's face pressing down against his, and her tears dripping down his cheeks. In shocked disbelief, the words spilled from his mouth in a guttural utterance.

"My family is dead. I should be too. How can you talk about blessings? What God would do this?"

TYLER LAY MOTIONLESS, BIOLOGICALLY ALIVE, but nothing more. His mother lay across him on the bed as the nurse came in, followed closely by the doctor. He felt her rise stiffly, as if she had exhausted the last of her energy. After a moment, the doctor stepped back into the hall. As if coming from a world outside his own, Ty could hear the conversation through the wall.

"He's okay to talk to, Sheriff, but keep it under five minutes, please."

Sheriff Warren McKinney walked into the room. He gave Katherine a hug and mumbled something as she collapsed helplessly into a chair in the corner. Tyler stared straight ahead, still stone-faced as the sheriff greeted him.

"That was a serious bump you took on the head, Bubba. How are you feeling?"

Ty lowered his eyes but didn't say anything. The sheriff let out a long sigh and pulled out his pad and pencil.

"I know this ain't the best time for this, son, but I gotta do my job. I guess you know by now, they're still searching for Jake and Rachel. Your daddy has been riding with Karl, but so far all they've found is the car. Both windows in the front seat were open, and the back door behind the driver's seat was open. I know this is hard, Tyler, but anything you might be able to remember could help us find them."

Tyler's face broke up as he stared down at his clinched fists. Outside he could hear Rachel's father, Henry Fuller, arguing with the doctor, who was trying to keep him out. It was all like a bad dream as Henry and the doctor crashed through the door.

"What the hell were you thinking, taking my daughter and grandson out in that storm when you'd been drinking? Mister Tough Guy, huh? You sorry-assed drunk. You killed your family with your drinking; trying to be a tough guy and cross a flooded creek. How tough do you feel now, you sorry bastard?"

"That's enough! Get the hell outa here!" Sheriff McKinney grabbed him and escorted him out of the room, as he carried on shouting, "I hope you never get over this. I hope you suffer the rest of your godforsaken days. I'll see you in court, Killer!"

The sheriff pushed him into the hall, then stuck his head out the door and roared at someone unseen, "It's about time you got here. Nobody else comes in here. Got it?"

Tyler felt his mother's weight upon him once again. His heart had completely burst inside and he was numb all over as she squeezed him and moaned in great agony.

SHERIFF MCKINNEY SIGHED AND TURNED toward the window, struggling with his emotions. His reflection in the window showed a large man of six-four with burly arms and a square jaw. He could take just about anything physical that his job demanded, but he had never been as tough on the inside.

He thrust his chin up to take the knot out of his throat, then lifted his Stetson and wiped the sweat from his balding head. Not many years ago he was the coach of their championship football team, and Tyler was the hottest prospect to ever come out of Texas high school football. No one was more heartbroken than Coach McKinney when he saw Tyler go down with his leg twisted sideways as if it didn't even belong to him. Here he was again, standing on the sidelines, watching Tyler's life being torn apart. After a few deep breaths, he regained his composure and helped Katherine back to her chair.

"Please, Kat, I just have a few quick questions and I will be out of here." Tyler rolled his head to the side and stared out the window. "Okay, Tyler, what do you remember about the accident?"

Tyler blinked a couple of times, then mumbled, "There's no way I tired to cross the creek."

"Well, that ain't how it looks, son. Maybe you just can't remember too well. The toxicology report showed you still had some alcohol in your system, but that test was taken quite some time after the accident."

"I wasn't drunk."

"Your cousin Mike is saying that he'd asked you not to drive. If you didn't try to cross the creek, how did the car get in the water?"

"I don't know."

"How many beers did you have that afternoon?"

Tyler's chest heaved, and tears began to swell in his eyes.

"You understand that we are going to have to ask your family these questions. What do you think caused the car to get into the creek, Tyler, if you didn't drive it there? Did you leave it in gear?"

Tyler's jaw tightened and his lip began to quiver. "No. I don't know. I don't remember what happened. I remember being in the car and seeing the flooded creek, but then everything goes black."

"Why were you even there? Why didn't you just go back?"

His jaw dropped in agony as the pain forced its way out. "I was going to. I don't know; I don't remember. Oh my God! My sweet boy; my dear wife!" He let out a loud moan and started bawling uncontrollably.

Katherine jumped up from the corner.

"That's enough, Sheriff. He doesn't remember anything. Can't you see he's in pain? For God's sake, that's enough."

~ 5 ~

Another sunrise on an empty heart. Anxious and perturbed, a still-athletic and dark-tanned Tyler Morgan, sporting his usual tank-top, shorts, and sandals, paced the length of his 28-foot Glacier Bay. The cat-hulled, center console, offshore fishing boat had become the center of his universe.

The sun had yet to rise over the Port Aransas Marina, but he was already an hour late getting on the water. He sat impatiently in the bow seat, sipping his coffee, glancing repeatedly at the growing light in the East.

2002 had turned out to be a tough year, and the last couple of months hadn't brought enough business, draining the bank account and putting him dangerously behind. He had promised himself he'd work harder this year, get caught up on the boat payment and maybe buy some new electronics, but most of January was already lost, and things weren't looking too good.

His clients were late again, giving him extra time to think, something he usually tried to avoid at any cost. Keeping busy was the only way to cope, but he'd done all he could do. The boat was ready; he had bait in the box, gas in the tanks, and the charts were programmed for the day's fishing trip.

Dammit, come on, he thought. He stood and stretched, twirling the last sips of coffee around in the bottom of his cup. Disgusted, he pitched the contents overboard, tossed the cup on top of the console, rubbed his bad knee, and cursed as he ran his fingers through his long, curly brown hair.

Two cups of coffee and three cigarettes worth of waiting and he was starting to simmer inside. It wasn't the waiting that angered him. He was a patient man, the mark of a good fisherman, but left alone today, he knew he would soon be consumed by the inescapable horror of his own memories. For God's sake, today of all days, he had to stay busy.

He stood and cast his hazel-brown eyes across the Port Aransas Marina again, past the quietly docked sailboats, out between the jetties to check the wave heights, and then back again to his watch. The sun was starting to crest through a long strip of clouds on the horizon, a familiar sight that took him back to his childhood on Lake Sam Rayburn.

Quiet, beautiful, and unseen by most eyes on this planet. Such were the quiet dawns of his youth, fishing the shoreline near the house with his father and brother, saying a silent prayer to welcome the glorious day, and hoping for an early bass while waiting for the light to show them the way across the lake to their favorite fishing holes.

"Dad?"

"Yeah, son?"

A young Tyler cast his line toward the bank, his Houston Oiler cap pulled down to the point of forcing his ears to bend outward. His big brother, Vince, yelled, "Dang it, Ty. You thowed over my line again."

"I can't help it, the boat keeps movin'."

Charlie Morgan turned to face his sons. "All right, boys, don't start. I don't want to hear any of that today. Brothers are supposed to help each other. Besides, you both oughta be in church this morning with your momma."

"Dad?"

"What is it, Tyler?"

"Do you think Grandpa gets to go fishin' in Heaven?"

Vince glanced at his father, then back to Tyler and laughed. "There ain't no lakes in Heaven, stupid. People just sit around on clouds and listen to Jesus talk and sing songs and stuff."

Charlie smiled as he cast. "Now hang on, Vince. I don't think that's exactly right." He laid his rod down and turned toward his sons again.

"Let me tell you boys something that you should never forget. Maybe this will make up for you not being in church this morning. First, that was a good question, Tyler. The most important thing, guys, is that we should never quit thinking about what Heaven is like because God wants us to focus our lives on Him. You should never stop praying and never stop asking God what He wants you to do. No matter how bad things get for you, you should start every morning thanking Him for all of His blessings and offering your life to Him to use according to His will. That's called having faith. We'll never know all the answers, but if you live your life that way, you'll be rewarded and end up in Heaven and get to see for yourself." As Charlie turned back and picked up his pole, his line went taut. "I'll be darned, looky here! Looks like old Dad drew first blood today!"

The boys stared wild-eyed as their father reeled in a large bass. Tyler looked up to the sky as his brother quickly cast in the same spot where his father had caught the fish.

TYLER CLENCHED HIS JAW AND sighed as he watched the virgin sun starting to climb the mast of a large catamaran across the Port Aransas channel. There would be no silent prayer for him this morning; instead, he would wage the same war he waged every morning since he woke up in that hospital room five years ago and watched his mother shake her head, her face crushed and wet with tears, as her unforgettable words, "They're still looking for them," echoed between his head and heart.

His cellphone rang. It was too early for the bank to be calling. He answered without checking the number. "This is Tyler. Yeah, we're all ready, just waiting on you guys. Oh, really. Ah, okay. Nope, that's cool. I'll be here."

He slapped his phone closed and shoved it into his pocket, took a long breath, and stood for a minute with his hands on his hips while he tried to temper his instinctive reaction. The insurance executives were postponing for a couple of hours. *Grown men, corporate leaders, and they act like school boys when they get away from their wives.* He tried to think good thoughts. At least he would still get paid today, but he didn't like having his schedule changed. He'd spent a week painstakingly planning the trip, checking weather and wave heights, and they had managed to screw it all up in one night.

There was too much time to fill now. He checked in the stow under the captain's seat for his bottle, a little shot in his coffee would take the edge off, but no such luck. He'd have to run back up to the house. On second thought, it was going to be a long day out on the water; maybe he should just stick to beer. He dug through the ice in the cooler, but all he could find was sodas. *Shit!* How could he have forgotten the beer? Frustrated, he slammed the lid and ripped out a few more cuss words.

He went to the back of the boat and sat with his arms crossed, deliberating over whether he really needed to make a special trip for booze. The thought of using this spare time to pick up a few groceries for tomorrow was all the convincing he needed. He grabbed his wallet and keys out of the locker above the console, jumped out of the boat, and headed back up the pier.

TYLER POINTED HIS TRUCK TOWARD the rising sun and put his visor down as he squinted for the road. A news alert on the radio about a tornado caught his attention so he reached over and turned up the volume. His cellphone rang again, but he couldn't see the road, much less answer his phone. A quick glance showed that it was his dad calling from East Texas. He decided he would call him after he returned to the boat.

The report on the radio said that a violent storm had ravaged Oklahoma last night, and an F-3 tornado had claimed two lives. It was an all too familiar story, a different place and time from the one that destroyed his life five years before, but uncannily familiar, right down to the day. That drink couldn't come fast enough.

Tyler sat in the parking lot of the grocery store, arms crossed over his chest, squeezing as hard as he could to fight off the pain. As the report of the tornado and flooding ended, he reached out and shut off the radio. He shook his head to clear his watery eyes and tried taking a deep breath to push away the memory, but to no avail.

He punched the dash and stepped out of his truck, slamming the door as hard as he could. He didn't know whether to be mad at himself or at God; whether to feel sorry for himself or for the family he lost. A rush of emotions swam through his soul, uncontrollable and chaotic, like debris coursing through a flooded river. The only thing he felt sure of was that he wasn't supposed to be here. There was no way he was supposed to be here. He'd been cheated out of life and death at the same time.

Fumbling down the aisles, he struggled to stay focused, but he soon felt himself slipping away.

"Pardon me." A man bumped into Tyler while reaching past him for a twelve-pack. Tyler's head hurt as his eyes tried to focus on the beer cooler in front of him. "When I can't make up my mind, I just grab whatever's on sale." The man smiled and moved on down the aisle.

Tyler unfolded his arms and rubbed his face. He had no idea how long he'd been standing there. He grabbed some beer and headed to the front.

"Mister, your change."

"Huh? Oh yeah."

"Have a nice day sir."

Tyler nodded and walked out of the Port Aransas Grocery Store. He squinted, checked his watch, and slid his sunglasses down over his sore eyes. He still had a few minutes to get back to the boat before his hung-over clients showed up. He stopped at the curb, fumbled through the bag, and pulled out the Tylenol Extra Strength. He lined the arrow on the cap, bit off the top, jammed his finger through the foil seal, and gulped down three or four pills, not really caring how many. He cradled one of the twelve-packs, ripped a hole through the top, and jerked out a semi-cold beer. He popped the top and slammed it as he started walking.

"Get back by the car!"

He heard a mother's voice yelling frantically in the parking lot. An old muscle car was skidding around the corner and coming down the row toward her children who had exited the car on the opposite side from her.

Tyler sprang into a full run directly at the oncoming car. With a crow-hop, he fired the half-empty beer can squarely into the windshield where it exploded as the car slid to a halt. He dropped his sack on the hood and tried to rip open the driver's door. Finding it locked, he slammed his fists onto the roof and snarled through the glass at the driver.

"You stupid punk, slow this piece of junk down. You're gonna kill somebody."

The kid inside looked like he'd seen a ghost. He threw the old GTO into reverse and started cussing. Ty's groceries rolled off the hood and spilled onto the ground. When he got far enough away, the driver rolled his glass down and shot the finger at Ty. "Crazy old bastard!"

"Get back here, coward! I'll rip that arm off and beat some sense into you with it!" Tyler snarled and glared after the car until it skidded out of sight. Behind him, the lady was holding her smallest in her arms while the older child clutched her leg. They stood there frozen in fear, like three Hoot Owls staring at him.

"It's okay, Mister. We're fine. Thank you."

He stood there in a daze, staring past them as his heart pounded in his temples.

"Mister?"

The sound of the truck horn startled him back to reality.

"Hey, dude, are you gonna stand there all day?"

Ty looked around to see he was still standing in the middle of the parking lot. The lady with the kids was heading into the store with her arms around both of them. She paused, appearing grateful but cautious. She shouted, "Thank you," and disappeared into the store.

Ty put a shaky hand up toward the driver of the truck as a muffled voice barked from inside.

"Come on, move it, dope head."

He clenched his jaw, glared for a second, then stepped out of the way and salvaged his groceries.

THE PARKING LOT OF MIRACLE Reef Aquarium was mostly empty as he cut through to skip the light. It always gave him a quiet sense of pleasure to know they never had much business. He slowed and thought back to when the sign above the building read *Go Deep Dive Shop and Guided Fishing*. He remembered how proud he was the weekend he came down to check on all the final details, and how he couldn't wait to surprise Rachel and Jake. They never got a chance to see it, and after he missed a couple of payments, the owner promptly took it back and started the aquarium for his daughter.

He parked in his usual place above the docks next to Woody's Bait Shop and reached into the sack for another beer. He paused, getting the urge for something a little stronger. He slid his hand under the seat, feeling for the soft, crumpled twist of brown paper.

His face grew warm and his eyes burned. *God, I miss them.* He pulled out the whiskey and took a long pull. A couple more and he could take that deep breath and wipe the excess from his lips. George Dickel had become his best friend and counselor, and a brief session every morning was critical to his stability, especially today.

His cellphone rang. The display showed Cartwright. Craig was a perpetually cheery guy who was great at selling treasure dives to retirees, but he'd never found anything. He always had exciting stories about old ship's logs and deep sea coordinates of wrecks that had never been dived on, where a fortune in Spanish gold awaited him and his hopeful partners. No doubt Craig wanted him to dive with him again, but he didn't feel like being cheered up right at the moment.

He walked up the stairs of his dockside home clutching the torn bag with TV dinners poking out of the bottom corner. After putting away the groceries, he headed back out to the truck, grabbed the three twelve-packs, and started down the pier.

Some neighbors in the slip next to his who were washing down their boat after a long night of fishing caught his eye, but not his attention. He just wasn't in the mood for idle talk.

"Mornin', Ty."

He waved without looking and kept walking.

"Hey, Ty."

Tyler found it odd that People seem to forget how the water makes sound carry. He listened to their conversation, shaking his head as he climbed into his boat.

"Leave him be, man."

"Why, what the hell's his problem?"

"It was today, five years ago. Today's the anniversary, so just let him go."

"Oh yeah. Well, it looks like he's already been drinking."

"Probably, and he has a charter today. I'll swear that guy's going to kill himself one of these days."

"Hell, if I had caused my wife and son to die, I probably would've cashed in my chips a long time ago."

"Oh, believe me, he might not be the type to take himself out deliberately, but after some of the stuff I've seen him do out there, it's a wonder he's still alive."

"So I've heard. I happen to know he ain't no Eagle Scout around town neither. You heard about him tearing up those two rig hands down at the Sand Bar this summer, didn't you?"

"Yeah, that was actually kind of funny."

"Right! Who takes on two rowdy guys by himself and walks away with the other guys ending up in the hospital, one giving birth to a pool cue and another trying to swallow a nine ball?" They laughed.

"In a weird way, having nothing to live for can set you free."

The two men grinned and shook their heads as they went about drying off the hand rails.

YOU WANT TO TALK ABOUT *setting you free, buddy? I'm not even supposed to be alive.* Tyler stood from the ice chest he'd been sitting on, took a deep breath and stared at the water for a second. Fighting the urge to drift away in self-pity, he dutifully stuffed the contents of two twelve-packs inside the ice chest and shoved the other one into the locker.

It was a necessity to always carry an extra twelve-pack of beer just in case they came across a shrimper. Shrimp boat crews were usually Mexicans who spoke little English, and the beer was worth its weight in gold after a few days at sea, or in this case, a five-gallon bucket of shrimp.

He parked himself on the bow seat where he could look out across the marina and put his feet up on the gunwale as he popped the top on another beer. Checking his watch, he reckoned he had another thirty minutes to wait before his clients arrived. He sighed as he pushed past the pain, waiting for the beer to do its trick.

Soon he'd be out on the water again. Each time it was less fun, and each time just as painful. Not once had he pointed his boat between the jetties without thinking of the family he'd lost and the life that never was. Usually, he managed to push it out of his conscious thoughts, but it was still there; a quiet whisper somewhere back in the warehouse of his mind, jingling through a chime of memories each time he cleared the jetties.

What had once been a lifelong dream to live each day exploring above and beneath the rolling sea was now a sea of monotony. He seemed to be constantly surrounded by city pukes who pretended to be brave seamen; weekend warriors all, and none of them knew jack about being out there. All they seemed to know how to do was screw up gear, blow through beer, and puke all over his boat.

He was a man trapped in a world where minuscule joys kept him going because his heart wouldn't allow him anything more. There was another cold beer after this one, then some jerky, then he could break to take a dip of Copenhagen. After that, more cold beer and perhaps some fried fish later. The minute joys kept him rolling through the day the way the sea rolled through the bow of his boat, and they were all he had now. The big joys, the golden dreams had all let him down.

~ 6 ~

The seas were at one to three feet and beginning to lie out. It appeared to be a perfect day for fishing, but Tyler knew better. There was a nasty storm about 200 miles out that looked to be headed their way. If his best friend and diving buddy from the Navy, Ray Minton, found out about it, he would insist they head back to port. Tyler needed the money, so he decided to roll the dice.

They were tied off at the Baker North Rig some 45 miles out, and Ray was busy cutting ballyhoo for drop-fishing. Ray had the look of a castaway, wiry and leather-skinned with sandy hair. He was a hell of a diver though, and extremely knowledgeable about anything to do with the sea.

Tyler propped his feet up and looked down at his customers. One fool was already badly burned on his shoulders and the other was leaning over the side selling Buicks. The one thing he had told them at the bar the night before was no tequila.

He cranked up the Stevie Ray Vaughan and let the Texas Flood carry him away. The chorus of haunts started again like they had every day for the last five years, quieted only slightly by the click-crack of the beer tab and subsequent slurp of foam.

The rolling seas lulled him into a stupor. He wondered if he'd made a mistake passing up Cartwright's phone call. An invitation to dive another wreck for lost gold was sounding pretty good about now. With his luck, the one time that sucker would finally locate a treasure, he wouldn't be there. The thought of finding gold took him back many years to his first infatuation with treasures, back to his childhood when he'd first learned in class about Fletcher's gold.

"Tyler Morgan, where are you going with that sharpshooter and bucket?"

Tyler heard his mother hollering out the kitchen window just as he was rounding the corner of the front porch and ready to make a break for the garden.

"Me, Terry, Karl, and Jeanie are going to hunt for Fletcher's gold."

"Come back in here for a minute, son."

He dropped his head and released his tools to the earth.

"Yes, Ma'am."

Once inside, he leaned against the counter and fidgeted with the leftover dough from the morning's biscuits.

"Don't mess with that. I'm going to make dumplings out of it later. Now, what are you going on about with this gold?"

He perked up and dusted his hands against his britches.

"Fletcher's gold is buried around here somewheres. We learned of it in class yesterday. I figured on going a hunting for it."

"Who's Fletcher and why would his gold be buried around here?"

"Miz Willard says he was a robber and they attacked some American filibusters who sacked San Antonio after capturing it when it was still Spanish Texas. The filibusters was gonna take a bunch of mule-loads of gold and silver to Louisiana, but some other robbers attacked them and took their loot."

"You mean filibusterers?"

"Yes'um. Anyway, this Fletcher feller was part of the other gang, but one of the fili-bus-ter-er's leaders got away and got Jackson's cavalry to attack the gang and they was all killed sept'n for Fletcher and some other guy. He got put in jail, then they said he could go free if he would fight in the battle of New Orleans."

She shook her head and rolled her eyes. "Well, that's one heck of a story. So what happened?"

"They both fought, but one of them, the other guy, was killed, and, well, Fletcher fessed-up that they had tooken the treasure off the El Camino Real and up a creek. They stuck it under a small cliff that made like a cave by the creek. Miz Willard said it was somewheres around here and that men had looked for it in the Twenties, but no one ever found it. But Mom, there's a place down the draw a bit on Joshua Creek that I think could be it. So, me and Terry, and Jeanie and Karl is going to go hunt it up."

When he saw his mother's stern face melt into a warm smile, he knew she was about to grant him his adventure.

"You go ahead then, son, but watch out for snakes and be sure you're back here by dinner."

"Yes, Ma'am."

"And don't you lose that shovel or your daddy will take a switch to you."

"EARTH TO CAPTAIN TY."

Tyler snapped and looked down at Ray, who was holding up a fat red snapper.

"We finally drew first blood, Captain."

A call came over the radio. It was the captain of the *Sea Legs*.

"Fish on, that's number two."

Tyler reached over and turned it up as he listened to the ensuing conversation between *Sea Legs* and the large Hatteras called *Reel Accomplishment*.

Below him, his clients were taking notice of the conversation as well.

"Hey, Captain, shouldn't we be heading for the billfish by now? That's the second one they've hooked into this morning."

Ty looked down at the big-bellied executive with burnt shoulders who stood glaring up at him with his hands on his hips.

"I just wanted to give you guys a little taste of everything."

"Yeah, well, I'm about ready to taste the fight of a big marlin while the bite is on."

Tyler nodded. "Double or nothing on your fee that you have the biggest bill on the dock tonight."

"You're baited and ready to drop," Ray said to the client as he looked up at Ty and smiled.

The two clients looked at each other and laughed. "You got a deal, champ."

Tyler smiled again at Ray, who had just climbed to the helm. "Works every time. They just spotted a rip current out close to our favorite rig."

"The Falcon!" Ray said with a wide grin.

"Yep, soon as they lose their bait or catch another fish, pull them in and I'll head out just beyond it to the shelf."

Ray laughed. "You crazy bastard. One of these days that's going to catch up with you."

"Grab yourself a beer, man."

Ray shook his head. "Nope, I don't pop the top until all the fish are cleaned and I am on the couch at home. Otherwise, I get tired and slow."

Ty burped and spoke at the same time. "Sounds like a good plan."

Ray squinted and punched him lightly. "Remember, we were gonna dive the rig for some grouper and jacks so don't overdo it today."

"Do I ever?"

"More like have you never?"

"You're worse than an old woman, Ray."

Ray stepped down as he heard one of the fishermen shouting that he had a fish on. "Yeah, well, you're enough to make an old woman out of any man."

THE SUN WAS JUST PAST its peak and getting hotter. There were several beer cans at Tyler's feet. The Stevie Ray Vaughan CD was cycling back to the first song, so he popped it out and searched for another CD. He flipped through the ragged CD holder, half-listening to some news on the radio.

An announcement about Space Shuttle Columbia came on. They were discussing possible damage to the craft resulting from a suitcase-size piece of thermal insulation that had broken off from the external tank, striking the Columbia's left wing.

He shook his head at the thought that there was a shuttle in space and he hadn't even known about it. There was a time when the whole world stopped, even class, to watch a launch into space. He found a Van Morrison CD and slid it in. 'Stranded' was the first song to play. *Pretty damned accurate,* he thought as listen to the words, 'stranded between the Devil and the deep blue sea.'

AFTER A LENGTHY BATTLE WITH what ended up being a shark instead of the tuna they had hoped for, Tyler fired up and headed toward the seventy-mile mark for some bill fishing. The trip took a couple of hours, and the fishermen were crashed on their bean bags as Ty slowed the boat a quarter-mile from the huge oil rig. He lit a cigarette and turned to shout at Ray.

"Here's Falcon; where's that rip?"

"Keep going on past, I ain't seen nothing yet."

He pushed the boat on farther as the two fishermen were sitting up. About a mile past the rig he heard Ray whistle. He looked down to see him pointing at a long line of sea weed.

"There's your rip."

"Got it. What do you think?"

Ray stuck his leathery chin toward the horizon. "Those other guys are way south. I can just make out their boat over yonder. I say we put out the spread and run the rip for a spell, and if that don't bring something up, we head out past the shelf and bring 'em back across on a big arc."

"We're on the same page. Let's do it."

After a little more than three hours, the crew of the *Dive Play Right* was all but worn out from fighting big game fish, and Tyler was ready to move on.

"All in?"

Tyler waited for the go-ahead from Ray as they brought in all the lines. He stared into the rolling blue swells that seemed to go on forever. Of all the things in his life that had exploded or imploded or just gone to Hell, fishing was the one thing that had managed to stay within his grasp.

Today had been no different. He belonged on the water. He had known since the day he talked to Volney Parker on the porch that his life was pointed in the right direction, and he'd worked hard to get there. Why would God take his family and force him to go on alone? Why did he even wonder about God anymore? He cursed, crushed the beer can he was holding, then slammed it to the floor.

"Ho, relax, Captain, we're good," Ray shouted.

Tyler nodded and pointed to the large reels that were posted on the gunwales. "Move those damn Penns up to the top rack. We won't be needing them anymore."

He pulled in his spreaders and threw the twin Mercury outboards into gear. With an impressive 480-pound blue marlin, one average white marlin, and a large wahoo caught and photographed, he headed straight for Falcon to dive the rig for grouper, ling, and amberjack.

Ty inched the boat forward as Ray balanced himself on the bow and lassoed a large upright pipe below the rig. Once he had the boat tied off, Ray stepped down and grabbed his dive bag. He stopped as he was putting on his wetsuit and looked over at Ty with a grimace. "Are you sure you should dive? You've had a lot a beer today and you know that's a dangerous combination."

Ty busied himself with his regulator. "Ah hell, I'm fine. I'll just be a little more sore than usual tomorrow."

He smiled at the two sunburnt and weary clients as they sat up from their bean bags as they, in a quiet sort of awe, stared bug-eyed at the two seasoned divers working into their gear.

Ray grabbed his spear gun and took one last look at Ty before going in. "You about ready?"

"Yep."

"Listen, no death-wish stunts today. I just want to have a peaceful, easy dive, so don't do anything crazy. Okay?"

Ty laughed. "I never start out to do anything crazy."

THE TWO CLIENTS HAD DECIDED not to fool with trying to tackle the electric reel that Tyler had set up for grouper fishing. Instead, they sat bobbing in the shade of the huge rig, drinking beer and listening to the alien sounds of deep sea oil production.

Suddenly they heard a loud, sharp whistle like steam escaping from a high pressure valve. They both jumped up and looked up at the massive rig fully expecting something to explode. After a second, the noise pierced their ears again and they realized it was coming from the water.

They looked overboard and saw Ray with a diver's whistle in his mouth. He was clutching a wire stringer with two huge amberjack hooked through the eyes. The big executive reached over and, after a couple of failed attempts, managed to drag the fish up over the side and into the boat.

Ray jumped on board, hurriedly throwing off his gear as he ran to the bow to look into the water. The two clients were already in shock at the sight of the large fish, but Ray's hasty movements had them visibly shaken.

"What's going on? Was something chasing you?"

"Crazy-assed Ty; as I was coming up, I looked back and saw him spear a ling that was way too big for him to handle. It was taking him down, and knowing him, he won't let go. He's already lost two guns that way. I just hope he's watching his air."

A few long minutes went by and no Ty. Cussing and praying, Ray switched tanks and dove back in. He made his way down to the first cross-member of the rig and held on to fight the current while he studied the water below. His heart was pounding as he feared that this might be the day he'd always worried about; the day Tyler's reckless attitude met face-to-face with his latent death wish. Too many times he'd sat up most of the night with him, listening to him talk about the way he wanted to go.

Ray started to panic. He let go and swam down another thirty feet. He began to see sharks coming in and his fears worsened. He was about to assume the worse when suddenly he saw some color below him. He made his way toward it when he realized it was coming up quickly.

Within a few seconds Ty was almost upon him. When he swam up to him, Ray saw his eyes were huge and at that moment, Ty jerked his regulator away and started sucking his air. Ray motioned to give it back as he wasn't ready for the switch. Once he had the regulator back, Ray looked behind Ty and saw the big ling hanging below him. They buddied back to the surface dragging the big fish behind them.

Ty LAID ON THE BOAT exhausted as Ray was reading him the riot act. "You dumb-ass, you'd be dead if I hadn't changed tanks before I went back down. Hell, I'd be dead! That was way too damn close, Ty. Do you realize you shouldn't even be alive right now? Don't you freakin' get it? You're totally out of control man. I'm done with your crazy shit."

Three huge fish and one diver laid motionless in the bobbing boat, only one of them breathing. The two guests sat frozen in shock like two children watching their parents quarrel as Ty moaned and rolled up slowly.

"Maybe you should have just let me go."

Ray stared a hole through him. "If you hadn't saved my life in the Persian Gulf, I...we're even now, Morgan."

"Okay, I'm sorry. Thanks man. I knew I could count on you. I nailed that sucker right in the head. I can't believe he fought so dang hard and long."

"Bullshit! You know better than that man. Hell, it ain't no different from jumping a wild hog with a buck knife. With a ling that size, you know you're going for a ride."

Ty looked up at Ray and smiled. "Well, the ride is half the fun."

"You're a real jerk, you know that? You really don't care, do you? If you want to kill yourself, please leave me out of it. You could have killed us both, jackass. I hope you choke to death eating that damn fish."

Ray left his wet suit hanging half-on and went to the front of the boat to cool his fury as the two clients shrank back into their bean bags.

AFTER A LITTLE WHILE, Ty was fully recovered and Ray had regained his composure. He came back to the ice chest, still sporting a stern face, and dug for a Coke. Ty knew deep down that he was right, but he also knew he couldn't help himself. He glanced at Ray, making brief eye contact, and mumbled an apology to him.

After staring out over the water a few minutes, Ray frowned and offered his hand to Ty, and they sat going over the story again as Ty made a bourbon and Coke for himself and the two guests.

"We gonna eat good tonight, boys!"

Ray grinned and shook his head as he went about stowing gear for the trip home.

ONCE THEY HAD CLEANED THE boat and collected their double pay, Ty and Ray dropped off some snapper to be cooked at the Island Café.

While waiting, they stopped by the liquor store and picked up a fresh bottle of Crown Black and more Cokes.

THE LUSCIOUS SMELL OF FRESH fried fish filled the truck as they drove over to Brownie Farrell's channel-side condo to share their food and stories. Brownie's surname was Scott, but he was the only child from a family of four kids to have darker skin and black hair, thus the nickname.

Brownie's family started Farrell Coastal Bank before he was born, and although he played the role of vice president at the bank where Tyler had met him five years prior, he made his living investing in real estate, oil and gas, and whatever thrilling ventures he could find. The investment he made to back the loan for Tyler's business, part of which had already defaulted, was more of fun distraction than a true investment.

Brownie had gone to school in Corpus Christi with Ray Minton and Craig Cartwright, and they had all grown up fishing and sailing out of Port Aransas together.

TYLER AND RAY HEARD THE screams and laughter from the waterside deck as they cut through the garage.

Ray looked at Tyler and rolled his eyes. "Here we go."

When they arrived, they saw that Brownie had his customary accompaniment of local ladies which usually meant divorcees and gold-diggers. This time it was one of each. Brownie parted the women when he saw his friends approaching with two large sacks in tow. He knew exactly what the sacks represented, and he was all smiles.

"Hey, looky here, girls. Looks like we don't have to make a grub run after all. Get over here, you two fish-catching sons-a-bitches. Charlotte, Marianne, this is my oldest and dearest friend, Ray, and my new best friend, Tyler. If I'm right, they've brought us plenty of jack, grouper, and snapper fresh from the bowels of Falcon!"

Ray grimaced. "That just didn't sound right."

Fast women were never Tyler's style, and he found himself slipping away a little as the night wore on. Brownie was working hard on the younger Charlotte, who made no effort to hide her gold-digger status.

Twice, Tyler had avoided the advances of Marianne, who had quickly become attracted to him. She was an attractive lady, sexy and sultry, but her desperation showed through like the bra strap under her thin blouse. As he watched her settling for Ray, he stepped away from the festivities to catch some air out on the pier.

He lit a cigarette and sat with his legs dangling over the water. It wasn't that he didn't want to have fun; there was a time when he was the life of the party, but his life-sized problems overshadowed everything. Not even the booze could make them go away.

The sea water trapped by the docks had a nasty, pungent smell. No wonder he was at home here; it smelled like hell on earth. As he thumped his cigarette butt into the water, he heard someone closing in on him from behind. Brownie grunted and plopped down beside him.

"What the hell's wrong with you, buddy? Is that Charlotte hot or what? Marianne is a sexy damn thing, too. She's got an ass on her like a race horse, built for speed. Good thing you guys showed up or I would've had to make some hard decisions tonight, if you know what I mean."

Tyler shook his head and smiled. "I can always count on you to bring me back down to the bowels of reality, bud."

"Well, what's up? Celina got you p-whipped already?"

"Nah, that ain't it. I just got a lot on my mind today, man."

"Well, listen, I think I know what's bothering you, and I want you to know I already put the word in to get collections to back off for a spell, but regulations are regulations, and they can't hold off too much longer."

Tyler looked at his cockeyed friend who sat swaying gently next to him. He knew Brownie had good intentions, but he somehow lacked the sincerity of a true friend. He could attribute Brownie's shallowness to having grown up with no real sense of the character-building hardships that face most people.

"Guess you don't want to own another boat, huh? Listen, Brownie, I appreciate it, but you know how slow it's been these last couple of years. If they shut me down, they shut me down. Maybe it's for the best anyway."

Brownie put his arm around Tyler's shoulder and rocked him couple of times.

"Bullshit. I've known you for a few years now, Ty. You gotta good thing going. Everybody knows you can find the fish, but you just ain't all there. I know why cuz' we've talked about it plenty times before. Damn, man, what's it been; four or five years now? Ain't that enough suffering? Look at them beautiful girls having fun up there. Look where you live, man, and at what you get to do for a living. You just gotta accept what happened and move on. It's history, bud. You got your whole life ahead of you."

Tyler loaded up a dip of Copenhagen and spit.

"It's hard to accept something when you can't even remember exactly what happened or why it happened, and everyone says it was your fault."

Brownie took a deep breath and shook his head, appearing to gather all the sobriety he could muster and leaned in to Tyler. The whiskey on his breath reached Tyler before his words.

"You can't change the past, brother."

"I'm not trying to, but what nobody understands is that the shit that happened to me destroyed everything I believed in. I don't know who I am anymore, and I can't even seem to find a good reason why I should care."

A shrill voice called out for Brownie. They turned to see Charlotte carefully navigating the steps from the deck to the pier.

Tyler looked at Brownie and forced a grin. "She's looking for you, Casanova."

"Ah, I'll get to her in a second. What are you going to do; just let it all go and start pushing a shopping cart up and down the street? Three weeks and they take away your keys, brother. The condo and the boat are both three months behind. This ain't no time to get philosophical about your life. I'd help you, man, but my crap is all tied up right now."

"Brownie." Charlotte teetered down the pier toward them. Brownie slapped him on the back and rose to meet her. "I hear that when you find a woman you care about, or some purpose that you feel is bigger than you, then you'll care. If that happens, count yourself lucky because I never found it."

Tyler watched as he worked his way back up the pier toward Charlotte. "Come on, sugar-butt, let's get you back up here away from the water. I ain't in no mood to go swimming tonight."

Tyler spit and looked up at the crescent moon. A woman and a purpose, he thought. That was exactly what had been taken away from him five years ago, and that was the second time.

He heard laughter again from the deck behind him. Marianne started calling for him, and the others joined in. Might as well get drunk.

~ 7 ~

Tyler awoke to the smell of bacon frying. Celina Andres was an artist; a woman who saw beauty in the prickly pear cactus and harsh landscape of southwest Texas. It was no wonder that she was quietly in love with him, a rough man who required careful handling to say the least. They had enjoyed their intimate moments, but she was a loving friend more than anything else. He had made it no secret that the door to the bottom of his heart was indefinitely closed.

He had finally given her a key to his place last year so she could pop by and check on him, which she tended to do quite often. She had shown great patience with him, and proven that she was content to go at his pace until the raging storm in his heart grew still. If nothing else, she was a pacifier; someone to keep the loneliness from consuming him.

In a way, she was a mirror to his soul, a constant reminder that there was a good man somewhere beneath all the pain. The thought had crossed his mind on many quiet nights out on the dock, nights when he said little, but allowed her to see something in his eyes that suggested there was a different man deep inside his heart. Those moments were probably the only reason she hung around.

He rose and sat on the side of the bed. As he rubbed his head, he thought of what she had told him a few nights before. She had talked about God and how he uses us to help others if we allow Him to. She said that she'd always known that perhaps it wouldn't be her whom he would end up with, but at least she could be there for him now and hopefully help the man inside find his way back to the surface. It was the first time he'd heard her say anything that would cause him to think of her needs, and today, as the smell of bacon wafted up into his room, it carried with it an air of guilt.

Tyler found Celina standing at the stove forcing a pleasant smile as he hobbled in feeling crusty and brassy.

"Good morning, Tyler."

"Hey."

"I'm making bacon and eggs with hash browns; would you like some?"

"Maybe later."

"Okay. The coffee's still hot."

"Thanks."

Tyler opened the cupboard and started pulling out vitamin bottles.

"How's your head?"

"Fine. I've never had a headache in my life."

"That still amazes me. You drink until the wee hours of the morning, smoke, dip snuff, and you've never had a headache."

"Never."

Out of the corner of his eye, he saw her biting her lip, studying him cautiously for a few minutes while he sipped his coffee and shook the vitamins to keep them from sticking to his palm.

"I hear you tried to kill yourself again yesterday."

"Ray blows things out of proportion."

She stared at him for a long moment. "I waited for you last night to go have dinner."

He dropped his head and stared into his coffee cup. "Crap, Celina, I'm sorry."

"It's okay, Tyler. You can spend that day doing whatever you feel you need to do, and you don't owe me any explanation." She smiled timidly at him, then took a deep breath. "You had a couple of calls this morning. First the bank, then your father called."

"Yeah, he called yesterday, but I couldn't answer at the time. I meant to call him back."

She hesitated, dropped her head, then walked over to him quickly and put her hands on his shoulders as she spoke. "Tyler."

He frowned and shook his head. "No, I don't want you to offer me any money. I made a little extra yesterday that I can put toward everything, and Brownie's helping to hold off the vultures a little longer. I'll be fine."

She looked deeply into his eyes. "Tyler, it's about your father's call." She looked away for a second and held her breath. "Tyler, it's back."

He froze, looking down at the pills in his hand. He immediately recognized the statement as something he'd never wanted to hear. It took a second to sink in and take full affect. He took the pills in slow motion. She embraced him and put her head against his chest. His jaw was tightly clenched. She held him for a long minute, but he could feel his body turning to stone. Anger had always been his way of handling pain, and for the last five years, it was just his way. Tyler suppressed the anger at first, but it began creeping up slowly, then it emerged with a vengeance for having been suppressed. He shook as he spoke with a crackle in his voice. "Where is it?"

She looked up and her face was wet with tears. "Her lymph nodes; I'm sorry, Tyler, I'm so sorry. You need to go right away. They don't know how much time she has left."

As if she sensed the volcano of emotion about to erupt from within him, she stepped back and clasped her hands in front of her chest. "I know you're feeling angry and cheated right now, Tyler, but you have to gather your faith. Now is the time for prayer. Pray for her. Ask God to help her."

He pulled at his shirt and looked around for something to punch. "God? What God? Are you freaking kidding me?" He leaned toward her, yelling in frustration as he poked himself in the chest. "Look at my life, Celina. I'm living proof that if there is a God, He doesn't give a shit about us. I lost my career and the love of my life, then I watched my brother get turned into a monster, then I watched my wife and son mysteriously vanish before my own eyes. Now my mother is dying? The most Christian woman I've ever known? For Christ's sake, Celina, she already beat it once and now it's back again? How does that happen? Why? What kind of God would take so much from people who never did anything to hurt anybody?"

"The God you used to know and love, Tyler; the one who still knows and loves you. He is waiting for you."

"Bullshit!"

"God doesn't take from us, Tyler. He gave us the blood of His only son for our salvation. We live in a world of free will. He doesn't interfere with our lives, He only answers prayers from those who work to become knowledgeable in His word and seek to build a strong relationship with Him."

"More bullshit!" Tyler threw his coffee at the sink, clenched his fists, and let out a loud growl that sounded like a lion's roar. In the same motion, he slammed his fist into the refrigerator, leaving knuckle prints in the stainless steel and sending the contents within crashing. He pushed the back door open violently and stormed off down the pier to his small flat-bottom fishing boat, untied, fired up, and took off down the channel.

He drove numb for almost a half-hour with the wind in his hair and the sun burning his face and chest. All that he had adjusted to was changing again. It wasn't fair. She had just defeated breast cancer less than two years before. She'd been through so much already, why couldn't she just be left alone to live peacefully for her remaining years? She never hurt anybody. She was a churchgoing lady, a godly saint who helped with meals for the elderly. She was a good mother and a loving wife.

"Why weren't her prayers answered? What's the freakin' point?" He cried out as he looked up to the sky.

Several times, he just wanted to gun the motor and run the boat straight over the small bar islands just to see if he could make it fly. The

Red Fish Bar was coming up on his right. He needed a drink. He looked at his watch and it was just past twelve.

Tyler pulled in and tied up. There were only a couple of regulars inside watching a ball game, and the bartender was busy prepping.

"I'll take a six pack of Corona Light, a bag of ice, and a cup."

"You got it."

Back on the boat, he laid the beers in the small ice chest and poured the ice over the top, saving enough for his cup which he filled with beer. As he cruised down the channel, the beer began to bring his systems back on line. The wind and the salt mixed with his tears and made him feel like he was returning from a tribal war by the time he slowed for the marina and turned toward his slip.

Moving almost robotically, his emotions spent, he pitched the ice chest onto the deck next to the table, plopped into a chair, and lit a cigarette. Three beers were left. He sat staring at the boats gently lifting up and down, smoking and waiting for the fuse inside of him to burn out.

Celina stepped out with a plate of food, placing it delicately onto the table before him.

"I'm so sorry." Tenderly, she brushed back his hair from his forehead. When he closed his eyes, she slid into his lap and wrapped her arms around his neck. "You should eat something. Your bags are all packed but your dive gear is still in the truck where Ray put it this morning to get ready for the tournament. It was too heavy for me to lift."

He put an arm around her and squeezed lightly to say thank you. With as little effort as he could produce, he spoke back to her. "Just leave it. I'm going to wash up and get on the road. Tell Ray I'm sorry about Port Isabel. They can use the boat if they want."

She kissed his cheek and nodded, then rose and pushed the plate toward him. "Please eat a bite or two before you go."

THE STEAM FROM THE SHOWER had clouded the mirror, so he ran a towel over it until he could see himself. He was too young for his mother to be dying. His long, curly, light brown hair still had no threat of gray, and thanks to the barbell set Vince had bought for him when he signed his NFL contract, he still had the body of a college athlete. His beer-drinking had done a number on his eight-pack; now he could only count four ripples in his abs, and he had to flex for that. He combed his hair back with his hands, threw on some shorts and a tank top, slipped into his sandals, and grabbed his bag.

Celina was waiting on the upper deck outside the bedroom. He lifted his sunglasses from where they had been hung on a lamp shade next to the bed and slid them around his neck. He saw her looking in at him and he stopped, holding the bag, as she came through the door and up to him.

"I know you don't want to hear it right now, but I want to tell you something that you need to think about on your way home." She took him by the hands. "Ty, we all go through valleys that test our faith and remind us when we're living only for ourselves and not seeking the purpose that God has for us."

Tyler looked down and shook his head. "Why would God create us, and then cause us to live in darkness and suffering?"

"We created our own suffering by our disobedience."

"Oh, come on. Satan is the one who caused our disobedience. How are we supposed to stand up to a dark angel and his demons? If God is all-powerful, how did He not see that one coming? Why wouldn't He just go ahead and defeat the devil and let us have a wonderful, peaceful existence here on Earth?"

"Because, Tyler, if you love something, you have to set it free. If you find love coming back to you, then you know it's real and true."

"He didn't set me free; He abandoned me. You can save the clichés for the kids in your art class."

"But it's the truth. If He took control of everything, then His purpose would not be fulfilled. He created us to perpetuate his love and goodness; if He were to exercise His power over our world, He would be like a child playing with his toys; it would be pointless because He would never feel our love for Him that way."

Tyler stiffened and looked away in disgust. "My son wasn't even four years old yet. His death was completely senseless. Do you think God is feeling my love now?" He threw his bag over his shoulder and started to walk away when she grabbed his arm. He turned back quickly and looked her in the eye. "And don't tell me the wages of sin are death. He wasn't even four; he had no sins."

She struggled to hold back her tears, but maintained her grip on his arm. "Tyler I know I can't relate to your pain, and I don't have all the answers, but if you can just find the strength to stop rebelling and make an effort to renew your relationship with Him, He will guide you out of the valley. If you never turn to Him, your valley will only become longer and darker." She grabbed both of his hands and looked him in the eye.

"Five years ago you lost your family, and you turned away from Him. Now your mother is in God's hands. Don't you get it? It's not all about what happens to your mother, it's equally about how you grow from the major events affecting your life. What will you do this time? He is waiting for you to come to Him with thanks and praise; to show that your faith in Him is unrelenting no matter how much you suffer."

"Yeah, well I think He asks a little too much based on what He's done for me. If He wants my attention, tell Him to save my mother's life."

She released his arm and dropped her head. "Why don't you tell Him? Better yet, Why don't you ask Him?"

He pulled his hands away and sighed, trying to hold back his tears. She dropped her head to hide her own tears.

"I'll pray for your mother, Tyler, and I hope that you will soon find the end to this long valley that has consumed your life."

She looked up quickly and gave him a long hug. "You've got to find your faith again. When you do, He'll show you your purpose, then you'll understand. Please be careful."

He nodded.

"Can I kiss you goodbye?" She asked.

He blinked to give his approval, and she put her hands around his face and kissed him softly on the lips. Her touch was like a thousand flower petals and her love poured out over him, but there was no point of entry. It would be left on the surface to decompose and blow away with the wind through the window of his truck.

HEADING OVER THE CAUSEWAY, THE warm stench of sea kelp filled the cab like the smell of rotting flesh, as if somehow preparing him to witness the passing of life. He remembered the first time he smelled it. Death was on his mind then, too.

~ 8 ~

Tyler drove mostly numb for the first few hours of the drive. At a station outside of Victoria, where he stopped to take a leak, he watched a young teenage boy arguing and smarting off to his mother. *One day that kid will be making his last trip home to see his momma; that's when he'll be going down his list of regrets.*

COMING OUT OF HOUSTON, HE stopped for a six-pack, a large cup of ice too big for his cup holder, and a can of Copenhagen Long Cut. Celina's last words to him had been bouncing around in the back of his head the entire trip. Each time, they brought up the same questions. *Why would God allow somebody like me to suffer so harshly? All I've ever done growing up was show respect, go to church, pray before meals and at night. What have I ever done to deserve the test of Job? It must be a curse on the family, or maybe the scientists and the secular humanists have it right: We're all just randomly evolved monkeys, with some of us still clinging to the fireside sensationalism of primitive cultures, passing it down from generation to generation.*

When he hit the tall pines and red dirt around Cleveland, the memories started flowing into the cab like bees returning to the hive. They landed heavily on his mind, some stinging, some crawling slowly down his back and burrowing into his heart.

The last time he saw his momma, she hadn't long been without the blue handkerchief she wore to hide her hair loss. Her color had finally come back and her eyes had regained their warm glow. He'd only been able to enjoy her for a few days as he was busy with his business plans. How long could he bear to stay this time? Would he stay three days; maybe four? He couldn't take anymore than that, not there, not where every step he took and every thing he laid his eyes on reminded him of his wife and son and the horrible mistake he'd made.

He passed the place where the roadside widened a bit, and a row of huge virgin pines separated the highway from the railroad tracks. It was a place where the ground was worn into fine red sand from a million fruit stands that had come and gone. It was there, a lifetime ago, where he'd stopped on the side of the road to eat sandwiches with his grandmother in her 1960 Chevy Impala. He was probably four then, and she was taking care of him while his mother rehabilitated after losing his baby sister within hours of birth. He'd known everyone was sad, and even though they hadn't told him, he somehow sensed what had happened and was afraid to ask. Julia was the daughter his mother had so badly wanted, but would never have.

As he drove on, strange and out-of-place memories began to emerge about his mother; her slipping a velour shirt over his head for the afternoon session of kindergarten; her taking him and Terry to football practice and by the A&W afterward. He could see her footprints in the flour on the kitchen floor and smell the fried chicken as she banged a fork through the mashed potatoes. The old family movies played over in his mind. He could see her sitting on a blanket by the lake in her colorful culottes, smiling, making faces, and trying to hide from the camera.

Why couldn't he think of times more meaningful? She could be all the way across the house and still bust him for stealing cookies, even when he was deathly quiet about it. She once lectured him when he was eleven, after his neighbor and partner in childhood crimes, Jack Dickson, had somehow been accused of teaching eight-year-old Johnny Edwards how to masturbate. That talk was in the kitchen, too, accompanied by the sounds and smells of Mrs. Paul's fried shrimp and French-fries. He had been horrified.

Twenty-three miles south of Lufkin, his automatic pilot came on, warning him about the local police who used to set speed traps on both sides of the small town of Corrigan and hand out tickets for even slightly exceeding the speed limit. They had nailed him twice during his college years.

He slowed and caught the only light at the center of town. A couple of blocks past the light, he looked, by habit, for the old two-story house that once hosted Essie's Café, a quaint little kitchen for home cooking that the family frequented on trips to Houston while he was growing up. He would never forget being laughed at by the locals for wanting Miracle Whip to put on his meatloaf and purple hull peas. He had to look twice to be sure, but the entire building was gone. Only a cracked and buckling slab of concrete that used to be the driveway remained.

Time consumes all things without regard. Life goes on whether we like it or not, and before you know it, the things that you thought you could count on for precious memories are suddenly erased, and you realize the fragility of your memory, and the delicate finiteness of your existence.

Eleven miles north he approached the city limits of Diboll, the headquarters of Temple Eastex, whose mills had slowly chewed up all the virgin pines across most of East Texas and replaced them with weak, yellow pine saplings that grew in twelve-year patches of thicket so dense a man couldn't walk through, much less hunt. Just another sign of the times; times when man has become so smart that he can replace the wonders of this world with more economical substitutes.

He remembered pictures he saw when he was younger of dreamy forests full of loblolly and white pine so tall that the underbrush was choked out. Back then, a deer could clearly be seen almost 100 yards away in the dim light of the forest. In one picture, the trees were so big around they dwarfed the men who stood at each end of a six-foot, two-man saw. People back then had no idea how lucky they were to be able to see the world as it was originally created, uncorrupted by man.

Curving off to the right from the middle of town was an old two-lane highway that used to take the family down to Brookshire's place on a slough lake off the Neches River, appropriately called Cypress Lake. For a kid, it was an alien world where ghostly cypress trees wore veils of moss that hung wearily over the small brown lake and cypress knees rose from the grave in fifty-foot circles around the tree trunks.

The small, two-room clapboard house they usually stayed in was built the year his father was born and hosted an original potbellied stove. Fifty yards away, down the bank was a newer cabin built in the late Forties or early Fifties that wasn't much bigger. There, they slept on bunks in a screened-in great room serenaded by crickets and bullfrogs and other creatures of the dark swamp night so loud they made his ears ring.

Cypress Lake was a world apart from the rolling pastures and wooded hills he ran as a kid, a world full of deadly snakes, alligators, swamps, thickets, and a sometimes angry river that flooded the lowlands. He wondered if the place still remained untouched by civilization.

Halfway between Diboll and Lufkin he passed the old drive-in theater. The screen still stood at one end of the pine clearing, faded and falling to rot, and the grounds were packed high in old cars and junk metal. Memories of the gang in the back of Terry Radcliffe's pickup, watching movies in woven plastic lawn chairs and holding the girls' hair back when they got sick on cheap wine, echoed through his mind.

With Lufkin less than five miles away, his heart began to race and the haunting reminders of a life he'd tried to drown in sour mash began to whisper and moan. All those memories for the last hour and a half had just been distractions; a noble attempt by some part of his psyche to drown out the traumatic stress slowly descending upon him with each mile north he drove.

Tyler took Loop 287 north and skirted downtown Lufkin. He rolled down the window for some fresh air and immediately recognized something was different. The familiar smell of creosote was no longer in the air. While he should be pleased that he could take a deep breath without having to filter the pungent, oily odor from his lungs, he was strangely disappointed, as if he'd somehow lost another attachment to his childhood. The smell had been in the air for as long as he could remember, and it always took him back to the days and nights he spent at Grandma Bonner's house on Humason.

While sleeping in the front room, in the very bed his mother had grown up with, he would be lulled to sleep by the sweet smell of creosote drifting through the open window, and by the ghostly struggles of the semi trucks working their gears as they groaned through the lights on Timberline Avenue a few blocks away, before fading off north through the piney-wood Neverland.

Tyler's thoughts quickly refocused on the disheartening nature of his journey as he looked over just in time to see the Catfish King, his mother's favorite Saturday night eatery. Flaky white catfish filets cut into strips and fried to a golden brown were served with hot water cornbread sticks, pinto beans, coleslaw, and green tomato chili; he could taste it like it was yesterday.

Life seemed complicated then, but looking back, it was sweet and simple, and full of wholesome moments like Grandma Morgan's Sunday dinner after church where his dad always fell asleep watching Richard Petty in his number 43 Dodge. He wished it was yesterday. He knew exactly what he would do differently.

The light posts of Panther Stadium glowed in late afternoon sun against a bank of dark clouds and sent a shiver up his spine. Something about the way the amber light poured across the concrete wall of the stadium made his stomach tickle. He took the familiar turn off the loop and stopped at the far corner of the parking lot closest to the field. He stepped out, loaded a dip of snuff, and walked to the fence to look down on the old battlefield.

He could still hear the pre-game announcements coming over the small radio he'd kept on top of his locker. One game in particular would always be on a perpetual loop in the back of his mind, waiting for a quiet moment to take over his thoughts. In his current state, and staring down at the field where his life had changed forever, he clutched the fence and let it play in all of its infamous glory:

> "It's an uncharacteristically hot Friday night here in late November as the folks pile into Panther Stadium to watch what may very well be a historic night of record-breaking Texas high school football. The Panthers, who finished the season undefeated, are already in the record books for the most points and most yardage ever achieved in a single season by a Texas high school team. Tonight, they take on the Judson Hornets for the State Championship, and what could be a better name for a team that has literally buzzed their opponents with the best air show in state history, posting a record busting 27 touchdown passes in a single season."
>
> "Chip, the Hornets will definitely command the air tonight, but I think the real story is this dynamite backfield of the Panthers appropriately nicknamed TNT. Everybody who follows Panther Football knows that those initials stand for Tyler and Terry; that's running back Tyler Morgan and fullback Terry Radcliffe, who have been playing football in the same backfield together since they were seven years old."
>
> "That's right, Jim, it's an amazing story, almost like a fairy tale; this dynamic duo has literally blown away their opponents by scoring an average of over four touchdowns per game between them, and they booked more than 5700 yards rushing this season alone."
>
> "Truly amazing, probably a record that will stand for a long time, Chip. I'd like to see their lifetime yardage

accumulated. Do you think they'll end up going to the same college?"

"It's been talked about. I know that Tyler Morgan, or Scoop, as he is affectionately known around campus because of his incredible glove at shortstop, is the one of the hottest running backs ever to come out of Texas high school football. Most of those touchdowns are his. He has incredible speed, surprising strength, and the most sensational moves anyone has ever seen, but the question is, can he do it without the incredible blocking of Terry Radcliffe?"

"You make a good point. This Radcliffe guy is as big as a lineman and as fast as any fullback ever to play the position. He literally explodes the line with or without the ball, and it's like stopping a freight train when he gets rolling. I've heard rumors that they're both being courted by the University of Texas, and what a sensational team that would be, Chip, because their nemesis tonight, Kelly Howe, the quarterback for the Hornets, has reportedly already given the Longhorns the nod."

"Oh that would just be unfair to the rest of NCAA football, but what a joy it would be to watch."

"You know it would be a lot like watching the undefeated Miami Dolphin team with the talents of Griese, Csonka, and Kick again."

"Yes, it would, Jim. Butch and Sundance all over again, but perhaps even stronger and faster. Wow!"

Tyler opened his eyes as the pain from his past revisited his haunted soul. The sun moved behind the dark clouds and set their edges afire. As he marveled at the majestic glow, the sun found a weak spot in the clouds and a bright beam shot down from heaven, spilling down into the stadium, across the field between the five and ten yard lines, and right up to him. He rode the imaginary golden carpet back down to the six yard line, and back to the day when his special gift was taken away. His father had videoed the game, while his transistor radio provided the play-by-play.

> "What a game this has been. We've seen records shattered like cheap china. Both teams are doing what they do best. I don't know what's been more fun to watch, the explosive TNT backfield or the air extravaganza put on by Kelly Howe and his number one receiver, Michael Ray. Each team has posted four touchdowns, they're tied on penetrations and, with one play left, it all comes down to this, folks. The Panthers are six yards away from glory in what's turned out to be one of the most awesome football games ever played in Texas high school football history. The story tonight for the Panthers has been Tyler Morgan. Terry Radcliffe has been uncharacteristically ineffective, missing blocks and bumping into Morgan on several carries, but the intelligent and elusive Morgan seems to always find a way to turn adversity into a success story."
>
> "He does indeed, Chip, and it's just a shame that Radcliffe has been off his game tonight because I think this game wouldn't have been as close if he'd been there tonight like he was all season for Morgan."
>
> "I don't know what the deal is, but I sense some animosity between the two long-term friends tonight. There were times it almost appeared they were arguing on the sidelines and even on the field a couple of times."
>
> "Here comes Dupree back from the sidelines with the play from Coach McKinney, and here we go, folks. The Panthers are huddling back up after that long time-out."

"You know, it almost appeared Morgan and Radcliffe were jawing at each other again as they went back into the huddle."

"Indeed it did, but there's significant pressure on these young men out there tonight. Nevertheless, this will be the last play of the game. All glory for both sides rests on this last snap of the ball. For the Panthers it means the State Championship, and for the Hornets it means they save the fort and live to fight in overtime."

"Okay, guys, here we go. This is for all the glory. Coach is calling for power sweep option right. Terry, you gotta make the block this one time, man, and clear the way."

"Screw that. Why does Morgan always have to be the hero? He steals my girl and now he gets all the glory, too? You called his number the last two times we were down here. They're all going to be keying on him. They'll never expect the first man through to have the ball. You gotta call my number, Karl. Come on, man, I need this."

"Cut the crap, Terry, Coach calls the shots, not me, so do your damn job. Now this is for all the marbles, so let's go get it guys; on two."

"Piss on this." Terry lagged behind.

"The Panthers are lining up. Radcliffe is just standing there staring at the defense with his hands on his hips as the rest of the team is getting set. Quarterback Karl Dupree is looking back at him and pointing at the clock. Now Radcliffe is slowly getting set. The crowd is singing *TNT, they're dynamite*. They have five seconds to snap the ball, no chance for an audible. They have to go with the play they set in the huddle and hope for the best. There's the snap. The backfield is rolling right; Dupree fakes a short pass and pitches out to Morgan, who has Radcliffe leading him around the right side. Radcliffe throws a block, and he's knocked back into Morgan.

Morgan bounces off, gets hit hard by Williams, but shakes his grip and grinds toward the goal line. He's got two more closing as he reaches the goal. He jukes, both defenders collide as they hit him."

"Oh!" Tyler could still hear the crowd moan.

"Oh my God his leg, he twists; he's still going; he's in! Tyler Morgan is in for the score! The game is over, and the Panthers are the State Champs!"

"He's done it, and what a way to end it. Tyler Morgan has won the game despite another poor block from Radcliffe. He somehow got past three defenders who had him dead in their sights at the three-yard line and still managed to punch it into the end zone."

"Oh boy, what a play; and Jim, it's not looking good down there on the field right now. They're motioning for the team doctor to come over. Morgan is down and he appears to be in great pain."

"Boy, you hate to see that. It looks like it was a knee. I don't like the way that leg was flopping around. The doc is going have trouble getting to him because the field is just being mobbed right now by the purple and gold."

"Yeah, it's gotta be that right knee, Chip. Washington's helmet went squarely into the knee. He tried to make it go limp, but his cleat got caught in the grass and the knee looked like it bent backward about five inches."

"Boy, there's a lot of people at UT holding their breath right now."

"Well, we can only hope that it wasn't as bad as it looked. There could be multiple torn ligaments and that could be a career-ender. Let's just hope for the best."

"You know, I wish we could show you the replay. How he was able to twist and thrust on one leg into the end zone is simply amazing. He wanted that score so bad he wasn't going to let anything stop him, not even his own physical limitations, it seemed."

"What I can't understand is how Williams, who goes about 160 pounds soaking wet, took Radcliffe, who's easily on the up side of 215, right off his feet. One has to wonder if it's somehow related to the strange events we witnessed just before the snap."

Tyler opened his eyes again, as the late sun peeked from behind the clouds and stroked his face. He reached down and rubbed his knee. Always the same question; why was he given so much just so it could be taken away so early? High school heroes who never make it in the world beyond become living ghosts in the minds of their followers. A person moves on through life, but the hero is forever stuck in the past, a haunting memory of what could have been. His memories of glory had transformed into reminders of a curse. He spit and wiped a tear from his eye. It was time to go see his mother.

~ 9 ~

On the right, just before the 103 exit, was the old mobile home dealership where he worked shortly after graduating from high school. He was happy then; as happy as he could be at least; learning a new trade, making real money, and dreaming of a life with his girl Jeanie, whom he'd loved since he was a boy.

The lot was barely noticeable now through the saint augustine grass that had reclaimed the drive. The small timber fence that lined the front was rotted and falling. In the back of the lot, he could just make out the remnants of an old single wide, disintegrated almost beyond recognition and half covered in grapevine and honeysuckle.

East on 103, less than a mile past the loop, he prepared himself for the rotten-egg smell of the paper mill, but the stench never arrived. As the mill came into sight, he saw that it had been shut down.

The huge brick stacks stood like monuments to the city's past. The mill had become a rusting village of twisted pipe, and sheet metal buildings with ladders leading into every nook and cranny, set alongside by several sets of railroad tracks no longer in use.

Seeing the ladders, he was reminded of his father's story of when he delivered Cokes during his college years. Frequently, when they passed the mill, he would tell the boys of how he used to balance his way up the ninety-degree ladders with a wooden case of 6.5-ounce Cokes in each hand. He once marveled at how someone could be so strong as he studied his father's forearms draped over the steering wheel. The thought always occurred to him; one fall and he might have never been born.

Farther east, the tall pines began to close in on him as the highway narrowed from four lanes down to two, with the occasional climbing lane on the steeper hills. Every few miles on both sides of the highway, he would pass the ghostly relics of the many bait and tackle convenience stores that had come and gone during his childhood. Some had been converted to antique stores when the lake first started its economic decline, and some were transformed with little effort into someone's home, while others were simply boarded up and left to rot.

When he first started fishing with his dad at the age of four, the bait and tackle houses with their bubbling tubs of minnows and goldfish were far more interesting than the hot days he spent fishing on the lake. The first thing he'd do was grab a Yahoo chocolate drink and head for the live bait, minnow bucket in tow, while Daddy filled the boat with gas and fetched the ice chest for drinks and snacks.

Everything was gone. Not one bait store left on the 26-mile run from the loop to the lake. When he saw the bridge, a couple of miles in the distance, he remembered there was one last place on the right before the bridge.

Ewing Park used to sell gas, rent cabins, and had a dandy live bait shack next to the small grocery store. It was nestled sweetly beneath tall virgin pines that ran right up to the bank of the lake. Behind the store was a line of boat barns for rent. His daddy used it for some time until he built his own next to the house. He could still smell the creosote poles and hear the sound of the corrugated tin door swinging open, rattling the lock and chain when it hit against the knotty pine root that kept it from opening too far.

He slowed and dropped over the shoulder into the parking lot, passing near a forgotten old sign that read *Ew..g P..k* with gaping holes in the rotted yellow plastic. The signpost was rusted beyond recognition of its original color. The pumps were gone from in front of the store, but it looked like the store might still be in business. The windows were filthy and crowded with bug-ridden cobwebs and faded advertisements that read like a chronological history of East Texas commerce.

He was sure the sign that promised hunting and fishing licenses was an original, as was the bleached-out Beechnut Chewing Tobacco sign still in the same corner of the window by the door. The screened-in porch that once hosted the bubbling live bait wells was piled high in rotting lake-related sundries and old outboard engine parts. Beyond that and toward the back, were old cars with doors slung open and missing hoods, a pile of tires, a homemade minibike with no seat, and a half-starved dog of no particular breed. This was not his East Texas. The East Texas of his youth was a rich and thriving place, where fishing was at the center of the universe.

The row of boat stalls was collapsed in the middle, with the culprit, a large virgin pine tree, still lying through the center. The end of it had been cut off and the limbs piled out to the right. Apparently the work had become too taxing as they had obviously remained there untouched for several years. All the little one-room cabins had become permanent homes, and now the once-beautiful piece of prime real estate with boat ramps on the lake looked like a hobo town from the Great Depression.

He pulled back out onto the road and started across the bridge. Most of the trees in the lake had died off by the time he was in high school. They had run a course of disintegration over the years. The last time he saw the lake, not many trees stood more than a few feet above the surface at normal water level. He fully expected to see mostly water with an occasional stickup here and there where there had once been forest, but to his amazement, there were tree trunks everywhere and strips of land jutting out where he'd never seen land before.

The concrete ramp for launching boats, which he'd always wished he could see the end of, was now fifteen feet above the water line. It wasn't nearly as remarkable as he'd fantasized as a kid. The lake was low, very, very low. Had it died? Can lakes die? It had a dam that controlled the water level, and it was the main source of water for that part of East Texas. Maybe the old lake was trying to support too many people now.

Lake Sam Rayburn was supposed to be the largest man-made reservoir in Texas. As Tyler passed, west to east, over its northern end, it looked like swampland. The once well-submerged river bed of the Angelina River was now discernible as a forty-foot wide strip of darker water flowing from the open water of the cut and meandering through the stickups, disappearing to places he'd known as a child from the back of his father's boat; places like Stanley Creek, the Moore farm, Odell Creek, and Hog Wallow; places where the fish were abundant and beyond his ability to appreciate back then.

Like most kids, cold fried chicken, cheese crackers, orange pop, Vienna sausages, and Oreos were the highlights of his day. The only thing that topped that was when they were catching white perch on live minnows. Sometimes they would haul in as many as a hundred fish. It was the subject of many a show-and-tell day for him at school.

The old Angelina looked worn-out, burdened by years of rationing its waters to the lake. Tyler never heard her real name, but the Spanish missionaries who first came to this territory called her Angelina, the little Angel. It was all in a book handed down from his grandmother, *Land of the Little Angel*, compiled by the Angelina County Historical Survey Committee. It was one of those yellowing, dusty books that he would pull from the shelf at grandma's house and fall asleep reading to the hum of the attic fan.

As he crossed the river bridge, there was still more lake bridge to cross, but he was already in Nacogdoches County. The little frame house that sat on the point overlooking the lake hadn't changed a bit. Probably on its thirtieth coat of paint, it sat like it was in a painting, untouched by the modern world that passed by a few hundred feet away at sixty miles an hour.

Just beyond the little house, he pulled off the road and sat staring at what used to be the Nacolina Motor Lodge. What had once seemed the shining symbol of modern civilization in a vast wilderness yet untamed by grizzly hunters and gangly fishermen was now a ghost town, rotting and forgotten.

The asphalt of the parking lot was slowly being swallowed by the perennial red dirt, and the red brick walls of the buildings were overgrown with weeds. Trees were growing next to the buildings. The roof sagged in several places, and doors were rotted and busted, with sheets of laminate peeling off and curling down.

A pain shot through his heart as he realized that he was staring directly into his past. He could trace all the footsteps he'd taken as a young boy, and recall all the dreams that had once filled his heart, dreams that had never come true. Somehow his life had gone the way of the lodge. There it stood; a storehouse of memories, yet a rotting corpse, barely recognizable from its former glory.

The windows of the old restaurant were dingy and cracked in several places, but he could remember the place as it was in its heyday, bustling with anglers of all sorts, eager to get their breakfast and beat the others to their honey hole. He could smell the bacon and sausage and taste the short stack with ribbon cane syrup. The orange vinyl booths were long gone where he would watch his dad devour his biscuits and gravy to the tunes of Charlie Rich, Kenny Rogers, Conway Twitty, George Jones, and the rest.

Dad knew all the fishing guides personally, and never a morning went by that at least one of them didn't stop by the table to say hello and drop a hint about where the fish were and what kind of bait they were hitting.

Fowler Burris, who ran the tackle shop and gas station next door, always laughed about the expensive baits he could sell to the city slickers who pulled up with their big, shiny bass boats. The old shop was boarded up, the gas pumps long gone, and old Fowler long buried. Last he'd heard, Mr. Lowery had bought the lodge and tackle shop and was going to fix things up, but that was some ten years ago, before his heart attack.

What a shame. Somehow he thought the place would last forever. After all, how would the biggest lake in Texas ever run out of fish? He always figured he would fill his thermos with coffee there, too, just like his dad. It was supposed to be where he would introduce his son to his first short stack with sausage and chocolate milk; where he could get a kick out watching his boy staring glassy-eyed at all the huge bass mounted on the walls, and the nine-inch pies turning in the glass pie case above the counter.

He thought of all the people who had come and gone, and of all the lives the place had touched, lives that had carried on along that vain course of invincibility the way we do, and that were now the dust of red country roads; legends of the piney island called East Texas.

~ 10 ~

Tyler turned off 103, over the cattle guard his grandfather installed almost a century ago, and onto the asphalt blacktop that had been a dirt road until he was in high school. His chest tightened and his eyes grew moist as he twisted through the stand of pines that hid his childhood paradise from the rest of the world. He passed the old sweet gum where his brother Vince fell and broke his arm and looked briefly to see if there were any remnants of the old tree stand.

Through the next draw and over the rise he saw the tops of the mighty white oaks that marked the boundary of Joshua Creek.

He slowed, taking in the last whispers of the red sun over the long, sloping pasture where they used to plant oats for the deer, not knowing how he would feel or how he should feel, when the crossing that claimed his family came into full view. His eyes were flowing now, and the pain was pressing hard into his chest. He stopped the truck and looked down the creek line where his whole life had been carried away in the angry torrents of the ninety-eight flood.

He could see the sweet but worried smile of his wife and the innocent look on his boy's face as he played with his Hot Wheel car. It was the last he saw of them, and the last thing he remembered that had made any sense in his life.

This was the place he knew he could never face on a daily basis, the reason for leaving and never wanting to return. The creek was brushy and dry now. Not even a trickle of water flowed. There were no grim reminders and no sign of regret. Nature can be so heartless in that way. There were fresh flowers at the monument on the high bank, but he didn't want to go there yet. Today, it was all about his mother, and he didn't want her to see the same pain in his eyes that she saw the last time he was there.

He sat and stared up the road, waiting to get control of his emotions before driving on. The brown paper bag was out from under the seat and he was untwisting the cap before he even realized he had it in his hand.

By the time he reached the top of the next rise, the sun had gone, but the sandy road and all things of lighter color still glowed in the fading bluish light of dusk. Under a sky of burning coals, he started into the long turn through the small stand of blackjack oaks and hickory that bordered the open pasture next to the house. As he was coming out of the turn, he was almost run off the road by a dark vehicle with its bright lights on. He stopped and looked back, but the car kept going.

When he reached the house, there was no sign of anyone there. The porch was dark, but he could see light through the three offset vertical windows in the front door. His father's old truck sat off to the side of the house, next to a leaf-covered rise surrounded by bricks that used to be the lily garden. Behind it he could see linens hanging out on the line to air, faintly glowing in the growing darkness, eerie and solemn in the mimic of apparitions.

He stepped onto the porch and gave a quiet knock. No answer. He tried the knob and found it open. Once through, he closed the screen door quietly behind him the way he'd been taught.

"Mom, Dad?"

All he could hear was the sound of the TV. The front room was dimly lit by the lamp next to his father's chair. It still smelled like home; like garden dirt, laundry, antique furniture, and a million home-cooked meals. He heard some shuffling in the Kitchen. As he walked through, the floorboards creaked in the pantry area, a sound he hadn't heard in a long time, but more a part of his life on this earth than any other sound he'd ever heard.

"What did you forget?"

"Hey, Dad, it's me, Tyler."

"Son?"

When their faces met, his father couldn't hold his up. Charlie Morgan began crying immediately. His entire body slumped.

"Dad?"

Tyler grabbed his father and wrapped his arms around him. "Dad what's wrong? Where's Momma?" His father's shoulders began to pump. "Daddy? Where's Momma, Dad? Is she here?"

His father lifted his head and looked him in the eye as best he could. "She went so damn fast. I didn't have time to get the news out, I couldn't tell everybody. Some of her best friends don't even know."

"What? What are you saying, Dad?"

"You didn't know?"

"No, Dad. Know what?"

"Your Momma's gone home, son."

Tyler lost all composure as his father fell into him. He felt the weight of his father leaning on him for the first time in his life. He held him tight and cried hard. After a few minutes, Charlie pulled away and grabbed a cup towel to wipe his face.

"I was trying to figure out what to say to you, what words to use, the words that you'd remember for the rest of your life. I just couldn't bring myself to the task. I'm sorry, son."

"It's okay, Daddy."

"What are we gonna do now?"

"Don't try to think right now, Dad. It's going to be okay. I'm here with you now."

After a short while, his dad pulled away and sat at the table. Tyler sat next to him; he had so many questions.

His dad pointed at an apron hanging over the chair next to him. "She was just wearing that yesterday. She was feeling horrible, but she fixed me some biscuits and sausage and coffee before we went to the monument. Afterward, I carried her to the doctor. When we got there, they took her blood right away. It weren't ten minutes and they were rushing her off to the hospital. She was there for almost three hours when they asked her where she wanted to be when the time came."

He stopped for a moment to regain his composure. "They said by the looks of things, she should've already been pickin' out her harp a long time ago. Do you know she said she wanted to be at home? So I took her home. She wanted to sit on the porch and look at the lake. She told me all the things she ever wanted to say, told me some things to tell you, too. Near the end she said they was all there around her, just smiling and waiting. She seen her momma first, then her sister and her daddy.

"After a little while, all she said was 'Isn't it beautiful? Praise the Lord, isn't it just the most beautiful thing?' Then her eyes closed. She was smiling and reaching out when she slumped over. I carried her to bed and pulled the sheet over her. The coroner left about a couple of hours ago. They took her down to Gibson's to fix her up." He examined the backs of his hands, then looked blankly at Tyler. "What am I gonna do without her?"

Tyler couldn't stop the tears, but he did his best to stay strong for his father. He reached out and squeezed his hand. "We'll get it all figured out soon enough, Dad. I'm here with you now. Just don't worry, okay?"

Tyler pulled back and wiped his face. He watched as his father picked at a burnt spot on the vinyl place mat in front of him. He noticed the large freckles on his forehead and the fine wisps of white hair that floated above them. His platinum-rimmed glasses seemed much bigger than they used to. In a waterfall moment, he suddenly realized that his father was just a simple man who loved and lived for his wife.

For most of his adult life, Tyler had harbored a certain amount of impatience with his father's excessively contented disposition. On many occasions, his father had appeared completely disengaged from the aggressive actions of others, avoiding conflict at all costs. He was obsessed with security, and he shied away from anything involving risk. Observing this, Tyler had promised himself at a young age to never lose his zest for adventure or allow his curiosity to grow idle. Looking back, he realized that life changes us in ways we can never be prepared for.

In contrast, his grandfather had been a maverick among men; an adventurer, an entrepreneur, and a fighter. With only an eighth-grade education, he mastered most anything he attempted, and became legendary at some. He was still the source of many fireside stories to this day, but his inability to be content with even the good life found him wrestling with the bottle and losing his hard-earned estate at the late night gambling tables of the infamous Pine Island Country Club.

It was a generational pendulum that Tyler hoped would end with him. The way things had turned out, it appeared that was a certainty.

"Why don't you go lie down, Dad? You've been through a lot today."

"Yeah. I'm feeling kinda tired."

"Come on, I'll help you in there. I still gotta get my bags anyway."

He helped his dad into bed and walked out onto the porch. He stopped and stared at his mother's rocker, then looked out across the lake at the last thing in this world that she ever saw. The moon was rising, large and yellow; it looked close enough to touch. He wondered if she knew he was coming to say goodbye, if it would have made a difference; if she would have held on. If only he'd known she was so close. He would have at least called ahead.

He sighed and put in a dip of snuff. The sheet on the line lifted and hovered about in ghostly fashion. He turned and put a hand on the old rocker and gave it a push. "I love you, Momma. I wish I could have told you one more time. I wish I could have held you and said goodbye to my momma."

His tears weighed him down, and he fell to his knees clutching the post and watching his pain drip onto the grass below him.

BACK INSIDE, HE CHECKED ON his dad and saw that he was already sleeping. By the looks of the bottle of tranquilizers by the bed, it must have been Dr. Tinkle who had almost run him over coming up the drive. He must be in his late eighties by now.

He eased back across the pantry and went to his old room where he pitched his bag at the foot of the bed and looked around at the life he once knew. He poured himself a shot of whiskey and walked over to his desk where he picked up a picture of him standing next to his Mom holding a blue ribbon watermelon. He took it back to the bed and lay down with it, staring at every detail until his eyes grew heavy. He remembered the first time he saw it. He'd been playing with his football and waiting for his friends to come around for a game when she called him into the garden.

"Hey Ty."

"Ma'am?"

"Get over here and look at this."

Tyler pitched his football up toward the porch and ran out into the garden. When he reached his mother, he gasped. She held back the vines so he could see it.

"Is that the biggest one you've ever seen?"

"It's gigantic. How are we gonna lift it?"

"It's not ready yet. It still has some growing to do."

"Still? It's gonna get bigger?"

"Oh, yeah; you oughta run into the house and find your daddy's camera just in case the critters or ants get to it before then. In fact, bring that Sevin dust off the back porch, too."

"Yes, ma'am."

"Looks like that special fertilizer you and your daddy made is doing the trick."

"It sure does. I think we got us a prize winner."

"Might have. Now run and get the camera and see if your daddy wants to see it."

Tyler ran out of the garden hollering, "Dad!" He ran into the house and the screen door slammed behind him. "Dad!"

"What did I tell you about that screen door?"

"Sorry. Dad we got a biggun'! You gotta see it; it's bigger than Miz Wilson's pig, and it's our special fertilizer that done it."

"What is it, a watermelon?"

"Yep. Them Georgia Sweets we planted. Mr. Parker was right about that fertilizer. You could feed a whole Southern Baptist revival with just one melon; this one anyway." Charlie smiled at his boy and squeezed his shoulder. "So, Dad, Mom said get the camera and the Sevin dust and tell you."

"Okay, son. The camera is in there in my chest. I'm gonna grab some coffee." He pointed Tyler into his bedroom and turned to tap the coffeepot to see whether it was still warm. He paused and smiled, looking out the window toward the garden where his wife was pulling weeds.

"I don't see it."

"It's in there. Keep looking."

"Where?"

"Look under the papers."

"I did."

"Look again."

Tyler shuffled through the newspapers, pulling some out and laying them on the floor next to where he dropped his football. He finally located the camera, which he set aside while he retrieved the newspapers. As he started to put them back, the headlines caught his eye and sparked his curiosity.

> Man Disappears as Last Night's Flood Puts Property 6 Feet Under!
>
> As the storm grew in intensity last night, authorities began to speculate that Sterman Moore might not have made it out. His property, the Moore farm, was straddled between a year-round creek and the Angelina River, and had been slated for complete submersion by the swelling waters of the new Sam Rayburn Reservoir,

but that submersion was not supposed to take place for another four to five weeks, according to Texas Corps of Engineers officials.

"Last night's storm was far beyond what anyone had expected, but the other two residents in the same proximity as Mr. Moore were reported to have made it out to relatives around 9:00 PM, about an hour after we posted the warning on local radio," officials reported. Friends of Moore said he was a hardheaded and elderly man prone to drink too much in the evenings and that he rarely listened to the radio. Search teams are still working through the newly flooded woodlands in attempts to locate Mr. Moore.

"Dad, why do you keep all these old newspapers?"

Tyler sat on the floor next to his father's bed where the wooden chest his grandfather had brought back from the war stood open. Charles Morgan came in from the kitchen and sat on the bed next to his son, sipping his coffee.

"Those are full of interesting stories. They're all the stories that caught my dad's attention over the years. I've added a few myself. Most of them I consider to have unfinished business. Let's see that." Ty handed him one of the newspapers and jumped up onto the bed next to him. "Watch out, boy, you'll spill my coffee." He positioned the paper to where he could read the article with one hand. "Oh, yeah, the Moore story. You know who this is, don't ya?"

"No sir."

"Don't you remember me telling you about the Moore farm that's under the lake now? I took you fishing there a few times, and I told you about the old truck that's still down there under the water. Just a piece down from that is the old school bus that stalled out at the bus stop, and they just left it there. One time the lake got low enough to where you could kinda make out the roof."

"Oh yeah!"

"Your grandfather sold that truck to old man Moore just before the lake got filled. I actually sat in it at the dealership."

"Wow! It's still there?"

"Yep, what's left of it anyway, after eight years under water."

Tyler looked at the article in a trance. "So did they ever find Mr. Moore?"

His dad folded the paper and stood. "No, they never did. That's why I say there's unfinished business." He pitched the paper back into the trunk and tousled his son's hair.

"Tyler?" A holler came from the yard.

"Oops, there's your momma. You better get out there with that camera. Why don't you help your mom pick us a mess of peas for lunch?"

"Yes, sir."

"Tell her to bring in some spring onions and a few peppers, too."

Tyler stopped before leaving the room. "Dad?"

"Yes, Son?"

"Was Grandpa's death unfinished business, too?" Charlie stared at the boy for a moment, then looked down at the stack of papers on the floor just past the trunk. "I don't know, son. Now run along. Don't forget the Sevin."

Tyler ran out the front door and was well past the porch when he heard the screen door slamming behind him. "Sorry, Dad!"

AFTER FINISHING HIS WORK IN the garden with his mom, Tyler slipped back into the house to put away the camera and grab his football. Heading back out the door, he stopped, peering through the hallway at his father in the kitchen. He watched as he refilled his coffee and turned to look out the window toward the lake. A strange sadness came over him as his father set his coffee down and placed both hands on the counter, lowering his head with a deep sigh.

Ty heard his mom knocking her shoes off on the porch and hid in the dining room to avoid being captured and put to work. He peered through the crack in the door as she eased into the kitchen in her gentle way, carrying a basket of fresh picked vegetables.

"We got some nice corn for dinner, babe. I picked some tomatoes and okra, too. I figured we could have peas, cream corn, fried okra and some of that meat loaf from the other day."

Tyler said a quiet cheer as Charlie turned and nodded. "Thanks, Hun; that sounds great."

"Why are you wearing your dress pants? It's Saturday. I thought we were going to can some chow-chow today?" His mother's voice seemed agitated.

Tyler saw his father frown. He could hear the disappointment in his voice. "Radcliffe wants to finish inventory today so he can get the dealership back to normal by Monday."

"Can't the shop guys finish counting parts themselves?"

"I'm the controller, Baby. It's my job to oversee it."

She slapped the towel in her hands and threw it over her shoulder as she turned to the cupboard.

"Kat? What's the matter with you?"

"It just makes me sick, that's all. Every time we set out to do something, Lester Radcliffe has to snap his fingers and you go running."

"He's my boss."

"You ought to be his boss. That was your daddy's dealership and everything around here was your daddy's land before he screwed him out of both."

"Kat, not this again. It was years ago. What was I supposed to do? My daddy took to him, he was a good salesman and a drinker and gambler just like my dad. I can't change the past. I went to college, my father died, and Lester took over."

"You had to pay for your last two years on your own because of him. Just look at all the things that man has put your family through. Besides, Angus didn't like him one bit after he disappeared and came back. How can you work for him?"

"Where else is an accountant going to make the kind of money I make there? Besides, when Lester took over, Dad negotiated for me to have a job there and earn stock options so that I could eventually have some ownership."

"So how did he take over to begin with? He's a cheater and probably a whole lot more."

"Oh, Kat, we've been through all of this. Nothing was ever proven. At this point, what's done is done."

"Don't you think it's funny that his family never had anything? He disappeared for two years after old man Moore died, and then he shows up rich. Where did he get the money to gamble with?"

"I don't know, and I don't care. Like I said, I can't change the past." He walked up to her and put his arms around her. "Do I not provide enough for you and Tyler? Are you unhappy with me?"

"I just hate him. I don't trust him. I wish he'd never come back so that you could have inherited what was rightfully yours. He's nothin' but a liar, and a crook. I'd take my daddy's pistol and shoot him right between the eyes if it wasn't against the law." He hugged her for a short while until she appeared to calm down, then tempered her mood with a soft kiss on the cheek. "Where's Tyler? I wanted him to start on the yard when he got done helping you in the garden"

Katherine broke from his embrace and began filling a large pot with water. "Terry and Steve were coming by, and they were going to Karl's to play football with the other boys."

"Football again? That boy's got football on the brain."

"There's worse things. It's served his brother well. He's got letters from five different colleges and he's not even a junior yet. Its only natural Tyler would follow behind him. They both got loads of talent."

"I guess. Can you believe that Steve? He's getting to be as big as a bull moose."

"Of course, you knew he would be just by looking at his momma and daddy. That Terry is handful too. A slick talker that one; seems downright impulsive the way he's into everything."

Charlie took a drink of coffee and smiled. "He's a good kid. He's got lot's of charm. He'll make a good salesman one day."

"Maybe so, but I think Lester does him no good by not spending much time with him. Going unchecked, that could amount to trouble as he gets older. Anyhow, they'll probably go swimming in Retha's pond after playing ball so I imagine we won't see Ty till supper."

"Guess we'll jump on that yard in the morning after church. I better head out now, honey."

"It's good Tyler has a passion, Charlie; it keeps him out of trouble."

He smiled and nodded, then gave his wife another kiss on the cheek.

Ty slipped out quietly and eased the screen door closed.

~ 11 ~

Tyler woke up and saw that he was still dressed and he'd left the lights on. The picture fell off his chest and floated to the ground as he sat up. He placed it back in the corner of the mirror frame and went into the bathroom. Some things never change. Other things change too much. Same old bathroom, same old toilet where he used to have urine sword fights with his big brother Vince.

As he walked back into the room, Tyler noticed the old war chest sitting at the foot of his bed. He wondered if the old newspaper clippings were still there. He lifted the lid and rummaged through the old memories, mostly stuff from his football days. Under the top shelf he found the old newspaper clippings. He glanced through them, taking in the headlines again as he poured a couple of shots of whiskey into a small juice glass he had taken from the kitchen.

Land Prices to Skyrocket When Lake Reaches Pool

Officials said Friday that the new lake which has now been commissioned as the Sam Rayburn Reservoir, is projected to reach pool level by mid-1966.

"When we reach pool, many landowners will find themselves with lakefront property. Some may have as much as thirty acres of lakefront, while others may end up with only an acre above pool, which means their land may stand between large land owners and the new shoreline," offered Retha Johnson of Retha's Realty. "Their property values will likely skyrocket as they wait for the highest bidder to come along."

Tyler slid the paper back into the stack and withdrew a few more, leaving a couple on the ground where they fell out.

Angus Morgan Ruined

Yesterday, Angus Morgan signed over 146 acres of prime lake view ranch and farmland that had been in the Morgan family for over a hundred years to settle gambling debts. Just five years after Studebaker announced they would be closing their doors, the former local Studebaker dealer met before Judge Townsend to settle a string of debts he had mounted while playing cards at the Pine Island Country Club, a private hunting club in Angelina County.

Lester Radcliffe, the new owner of the Morgan place, except for the five acres on the lakefront where the old Morgan home place sits, said he has no immediate plans for the place and would like nothing more than for Mr. Morgan to be able to buy it back from him when he got back on his feet. Lester was made a minority partner in A. W. Morgan Motors as a settlement for the remaining gambling debts.

He threw the paper back into the trunk and reached for the two on the ground. The first headline found him staring, wondering what his grandfather must have been like.

Angus Winston Morgan dead at 64

In the early hours just after dawn on Wednesday, Angus Morgan was found dead in his bathroom from what the coroner has ruled as heart failure. Morgan's blood toxicity was reported to be the cause of the heart failure. The alcohol levels were near fatal on their own, but the coroner found traces of diazepam, the key ingredient of Valium, which led to respiratory failure and subsequent heart failure.

Morgan had lost most of his property a few months ago in a poker game where his best friend, Joe Gentry, reported that a group of his so-called friends got him liquored-up and took advantage of him at the card table, equating to stealing his land and other valuable possessions. Gentry went on record as saying that Lester Radcliffe and others who were regulars at the club knew Morgan, who was prone to becoming heavily intoxicated, was a man of his word and that he would not welch on his bets. When asked to comment, Radcliffe and others offered their condolences and cited that their old friend would be truly missed.

Joe Gentry Dies in Bizarre Accident

Whiskey and valium were apparently linked to another death in Angelina County this week. Authorities say that Joe Gentry died late Thursday afternoon after apparently falling into a burn pile behind his home on the Old Moffitt Road. An empty bottle of Old Crow and a prescription of Valium were found on his kitchen table which led authorities to the conclusion that he must have had too much to drink and taken a Valium before setting a pile of rubbish afire behind his house. It is suspected that in his state of inebriation, he must have fallen or passed out while trying to manage the fire. A large sheet of plywood that was found still burning on top of him was believed to be standing nearby when he fell. His body was discovered within two hours of his death by Sam Miller of 309 Humason. Sam, a lifelong friend of Gentry, was coming by to take him along to run the dogs when he discovered the body. Mr. Miller is not a suspect at this time.

Tyler pitched the papers back into the chest and laid down in the dark, listening to the crickets. The same melodious chirps seemed to chime in from all the same places as they had in the past. The old house was a place where time stood still, but lives changed and people came and went like the seasons.

What would his daddy do now? How much more could he die without physically dying?

Gibson's Funeral Home was moderately packed as Tyler looked out across the sea of faces; some he knew and some he didn't recognize anymore, or perhaps he never knew. Some were glancing at him with cautious eyes and whispering with covered mouths, no doubt still sensationalizing over the thought that here among them was the very monster who got drunk and killed his family. He watched an old man navigate his walker up to one of the front rows while people waited patiently behind him.

Here and there children fidgeted or spoke too loudly. His father looked older, but good as he greeted old friends with their sympathies extended. The music played "A Closer Walk with Thee" as Mrs. Washburn whispered to him.

"Okay, Tyler, we're fixin' to get started. When this song ends you'll want to start your eulogy."

He nodded and turned his attention to a nearby conversation. Lonnie Hicks and his wife Christina were sitting on the front row with their little boy Walt. Lonnie was Vince's best friend in high school and one hell of a receiver, but he didn't have the money or grades for college. He'd done well for himself and his family, though, as a master electrician. Little Walt was bouncing around, crawling in and out of their laps and asking questions nonstop.

"Daddy, why do people care so much when someone dies?"

"Because it hurts their feelings."

"But we didn't come here when all them people died in that big wreck the other day."

"We didn't know none of them son."

"How come Miz Morgan died?"

"She had a disease that kilt her. Now hush with all your questions."

"Miz Tubby said it just ain't fair that God took her. How come God didn't love her no more?"

"He did. She was a good woman so he took her to be with Him."

Walt crossed his arms and sat back with a scowl. Lonnie and Christina sported puzzled looks. She put her hand on her son's head and leaned down to him. "Why, what's gotten into you, Mr. Walt?"

"Now I know why everyone's sad. Life ain't fair. You gotta be good to get Christmas presents, but if you're good, God will kill you so he can have you."

She gave him a big hug and laughed. "That's not exactly how it works, son. We'll talk on it some more later."

Tyler turned his attention back to the song that was ending. Miz Washburn was making faces at him. He smiled at her and nodded, blinking as a thank you. He'd thought about this moment many times before and reckoned that most people did, but now the time was upon him; it was for real.

He'd grown up with most of the people there. They had all aged just as he'd imagined. Their smiles were the same except a little rounder and more wrinkled. Their clothes still represented the simple, traditional side of life, and their eyes still glazed as if they lived in a time warp or in the fixed destiny of a novel, intent on and content with simply dying one day themselves, never knowing the intricacies and wonders of an advancing world just a few hours down the interstate.

Pathetic, really; what the hell are they living for? What do they have to look forward to that makes them get out of bed every morning? They were all stuck in a place with nothing going on other than birth and death, with endless hard work and sad stories in between.

He stepped up to the podium and laid his notes before him as the song faded into history. Just before he spoke, a large, dark figure lumbered in the door and slid into the back row. There was something about that figure, something vaguely familiar, but he was too busy to think about it.

"Katherine Louise Morgan was born Katherine Louise Bonner on May 22, 1938. She was the daughter of Elizabeth Sue Bonner and Franklin Howard Bonner, both natives of Angelina County. Katherine met the love of her life, my father, Charlie Boy Morgan, at a barn dance on the Morgan Ranch in the late summer of 1953. She graduated summa cum laude from Stephen F. Austin State University with a degree in Elementary Education and became a school teacher at Coston Elementary where she taught math and science until she had her first son, Vincent Michael Morgan."

When he finished telling the brief and mostly insignificant history of his mother's life to the mostly insignificant and half-interested crowd, he looked up from his notes and was compelled to say something poignant, something that would make this day of death a little different and perhaps remembered out of all the thousands of days of death that these poor people would witness.

"So what's it all about, folks? We live these crazy lives full of heartbreak and disappointments only to be taken out by disease, tragic accidents, or some lunatic down at the cafeteria with an automatic assault rifle. I've heard all the canned responses. I know the wages of sin are death, but there's gotta be more to it than this. I mean, isn't it all kind of senseless? What are we missing? Why don't we fight to find answers to the hard questions? Why do we just sit around living and dying and going through the motions?

"Everyone here knows that my Momma was a good, God-fearing woman. At some time in her life, she helped every one of you in some way. As I look back on her life, I see a whole lot of giving, endless sacrifice, and more than her share of tragedy; yet, here she lies, called home early.

"Some would say that she was taken from us because God needed her more than we did. Well, I don't believe that. Dad and I both needed her. He needed his lifelong companion to enjoy their well-earned golden years together, and I needed the chance to show her that I was here for her and thank her for all the many years she was there for me. Unfortunately, I got here too late. I missed her by a few hours. How does that make any sense? How does it make any sense that we only have these few short years on this planet, and just when she has a chance to rest and enjoy it, she gets attacked by cancer again?

"Maybe I'm feeling a little selfish, but my mother was the only person who ever understood me. As most of you know, I kinda lost hope a few years ago, and I haven't been around much. I always knew somewhere down inside that if I could just come back and spend some quality time with her, she could help me find hope again. Instead, all I can do now is look up and say thanks for another hard blow. I know my mother is with God, but I wish I had her back. Our business here was unfinished, and frankly, His business I just don't understand."

Tyler paused and looked out at the empty faces; some of them teary, some of them just empty. The door to the back of the chapel opened and the large shadowy figure floated out.

"Frannie Logan wants to say a few words now."

TYLER STOOD NEXT TO HIS father by the graveside as the crowd nudged closer to hear Preacher Bill. He put his arm around his father and gave him a light squeeze when he noticed the Preacher and some of the crowd staring at something behind him. He looked back to see the large figure from the chapel making his way through the crowd.

When he drew closer, Tyler recognized the man as his brother. Vince was dressed in jeans with a black shirt buttoned to the top and a black coat. Hanging from a lanyard around his neck was the familiar Polaroid land camera. Every few feet he would stop and take a picture of the crowd. Before moving on, he would peel the back off the picture, wave it back and forth to dry it, and then stick it in his coat pocket. He stepped up to Ty and nodded as if they had seen each other every day for last few years. Tyler put his arm around him.

All through the ceremony, Vince moved in and out of the crowd as he continued to take pictures. When the ceremony had ended, Ty spent the next few minutes shaking hands and accepting hugs and special little speeches of the kind that people think they need to impart to the survivors. When he finally came up for air, he looked for his brother, but he was nowhere to be found.

BACK AT THE CHURCH RECEPTION hall, people came by and offered their condolences, ate, told stories about Katherine, laughed and cried, and yelled at their kids. As Tyler sat in the reception hall staring at what was left of Doni Simmons' famous moist-end brisket, Pearl's butter-fried chicken, and various assorted casseroles, he wrestled with the uneasy thought that his mother's death had played out just like all the others he'd experienced. No matter how much he'd always wanted it to be special, he'd failed to make it so. The traditions of their East Texas world had taken over and finished her off in the same casually ritualistic fashion that all others had passed with; nice and sweet, efficient and safe.

"When are you headed back, son?"

Tyler shook off his daze and fought to sit upright in the slick, steel chair. "I don't know, tomorrow I guess."

Charlie looked out the window as he spoke. The glare from the beautiful, cloudless day and the gentle movements of the large pecan tree just outside the window reflected on his glasses. "Thought we might go fishing."

"It's supposed to rain tomorrow, Dad."

"Yeah, but not much; it'll clear by early afternoon. That damn Henderson boy is always wrong anyway. His daddy couldn't ever read an almanac either. Maybe we could go then or wait until the next morning so that the water can settle a little more. You don't have anything you have to rush back to, do you?"

"I'd love to, Dad, but you know I can't stay around here too much longer."

His father sat with his hands folded in his lap, looking down at the toes of his dress shoes as he tapped them together.

"Have you been to the monument since you got here?"

"I passed by it, of course."

"You want me to go with you, Son?"

He shrugged. "I don't know. I'll probably stop by as I'm leaving."

"Okay."

Charlie looked down into his lap as he meticulously folded his hands together.

"What's wrong, Dad?"

"Ah, nothing. It's just that, well, I guess I was hoping maybe you could indulge your old daddy and stay one extra day. We may not get too many other chances to fish together."

"Don't say that, Daddy."

Ty nodded to Peggy Wilcox, who was waving back at them as she turned a little sideways and nudged through the door with an extra plate that she always said was for her decrepit old neighbor Ellie Dublin.

"Well, I'm just getting older is all. Fact of the matter is, it won't be long 'till I can't manage climbing in and out of that damned boat."

He looked over at his father who was sitting with his legs straightened, rubbing both of his knees. Despite his determination not to let anything stand in his way of putting East Texas in his rearview mirror right away, Tyler could see that the conversation would play over and over on his conscience for a long time to come. *What's one more day?* "Do you think we can still find them out there somewhere?"

His father perked up. "Why, hell yes. With the water so low, there ain't so damn many places for them to hide."

Tyler sighed and smiled at his father's enthusiasm. "Okay, Dad. I'll stay one more day. We'll go fishing Saturday, but then I really have to get back."

~ 12 ~

Tyler woke on Friday morning having slept much later than he had in a long time. Out the kitchen window he saw that the sky was overcast, which explained why he hadn't risen sooner; that, and the empty bottle of Dickel that he pitched in the kitchen trash as he walked in.

The coffee was burnt and had been turned off long enough for the pot to cool. He strolled through the house, and with no sign of his father, stepped through the washroom on the back porch and headed out the screen door.

The air smelled like rain and he heard the distant rumble of thunder. His daddy was in the garden tending to his winter greens. He watched him for a moment. He looked peaceful and well occupied, so Ty figured he'd leave him a note and slip off to town to grab some late breakfast.

> Dad,
> I ran into town for breakfast and then I'm going to go
> by and see Vince. I'll be back later.
> Love,
> Tyler

He knew where he was going before he got into the truck. The Sun-n-Pines Restaurant had been the hotspot cafe of East Texas since his grandfather was a teen. He couldn't count the number of times he'd sat at the old knotty pine counter listening to almost unbelievable stories as his father pointed out the actors sitting around the cafe.

When he got there, most of the crowd was gone. A fresh coat of paint was about all that was new about the place. The parking lot hosted a cop car, a Cadillac, a Harley that was probably the cook's, and a couple of typical East Texas pickups with lift kits and rims worth more than the trucks.

Inside, he took a booth by the window and grabbed a menu without looking up. The waitress strolled up and set a glass of water in front of him. "Coffee?"

"Yeah. How's the biscuits and gravy?"

"Same as always. I'll be back in a minute."

He watched with a slight snarl as she walked back over to the counter and began whispering to another waitress. The other waitress looked his way, but quickly turned back to her silverware when she saw him looking. Her frown had said it all. He could imagine what had been said; he'd heard it all before; *That's Tyler Morgan, the guy who got drunk and killed his family.* Five years later, and nothing had changed. He couldn't wait to be back on the road and as far away from here as possible.

He returned to his menu, but within seconds, the menu was snatched from his hands and he found himself staring into the unmistakable big country smile of Karl Dupree.

"Well, I'll be damned, Deputy Dupree. What did I do, double park?"

Karl smiled as he shook Ty's hand across the table. "Hell, I saw you way back past Denman Avenue, but I couldn't catch up to you. How the hell are you, Ty? It's good to see you again, old buddy."

"Same here, Karl, have a seat."

He waited for Karl to get seated, grinning a little as he watched him delicately place his Stetson upside-down on the table. "Listen, thanks for coming to the funeral yesterday, Karl. I saw you there close to the back."

"Sure. I wanted to come say hello after and pay my respects directly, but there was a wreck on 94 that I had to work. A woman pulled right out in front of an oncoming car and it T-boned her. She was killed instantly."

"Yeah, I heard about that. No one we knew, I guess."

"Nope. She was out of Tenaha. Anyway, I'm sorry about your momma, Ty. She was a wonderful woman and an inspiration to me."

"Thank you, Karl."

"Have you seen any of the old gang yet; Moose or Terry or Jeanie?"

"No, not yet. How is everybody?"

"Moose is still the same; a little fatter, but still strong as an ox." He laughed. "Just the other morning he got tangled up with old man Rogers while they were having coffee here."

"No kidding." Tyler was amused.

"Sure enough. The old fart is still as strong as buzzard's breath and was on top of Moose like a mountain lion in no time flat. Folks broke it up before Moose could get real mad about it. I think in a way he was proud of the old guy for still having the mustard."

"What the hell got into him?"

"Ah, he was feeling his oats and crackling on with something about the younger generations not having to work as hard as he did. You know these old farmers and ranchers around here; they're so full of piss and vinegar they get a little feisty sometimes. Anyway, Moose got a little tired of it and said something back to him that he didn't like."

Tyler chuckled. "Same old Moose. So is he still running his body shop?"

"Yeah, and he's doing good for himself, staying real busy. Terry has changed though, Ty."

"Has he?"

"Oh yeah. I'd say he ain't the same person at all no more. He used to always swing by Crossroads for a beer and hang out with us, but for the past few months he's been hanging out across the river at Slim's and he ain't got two words for me when we cross paths."

"What's with that?"

"Not sure yet, but I have my suspicions."

They paused for a moment as the waitress set Ty's coffee down. She shifted to one leg and pulled a pencil from her ear.

"Say, ain't you Tyler Morgan?" She spoke with a precocious grin that would hide any connections to a bet previously placed in the kitchen.

"Yeah, that's me."

She smiled real big and bounced her weight from one leg to the other. "Oh, I thought that was you. I bet you don't remember me. I'm Darla Hotchkiss. Well, it's Turner now. I used to be in your momma's Girl Scout troop."

He nodded and gave her a polite smile. "Oh yeah, I remember you. I'll be darned."

"Yep. So did you decide yet?"

"Uh, I'll have eggs with sausage, biscuits, and gravy."

"How you want your eggs?"

"Scrambled."

She looked over at Karl.

"Karl, you want anything?"

"No thanks."

They watched her walk away and Karl laughed. "Still the same old Ty, I see."

Tyler nodded. "Hey, this is where the tradition started, and I never had better biscuits and gravy outside of Momma's kitchen than right here. So, tell me about this stuff with Slim's. Is it still as rough as it used to be?"

Karl shook his head. "What, you mean with the weekly stabbings and monthly gunfights? Nah, it's quieter than it used to be, but they still raise a little hell every once in a while, and it's still a watering hole for junkyard dogs, that's for sure."

Ty paused for a minute and took a sip of his coffee, not wanting to appear too eager with his next question. "And Jeanie?"

"She's okay, but . . ." Karl's head dropped and cocked to one side.

"But what?"

"Oh nothin', she's fine."

The conversation lapsed momentarily as they both looked around the café. Tyler gazed into his coffee cup as he spoke. "I kinda wondered why she didn't come to the funeral."

"Well, they were out of town. They left Wednesday to go to Vegas; some convention or something. They came back last night. I pulled him over for speeding; pissed him off real good."

"I wonder if she even knows."

"Oh, yeah, she does. According to Joanne Denman, she wanted to stay here and go to the funeral, but Terry wouldn't let her."

"That's strange. Why would he do that?"

"Strange has become his middle name lately. I don't think they're very happy, Ty. In the last few months she seems to have lost that bubbly disposition that she always had. You remember, it didn't matter what kind of mood you were in, whenever you ran into her she'd make you smile. It seems like since Terry's business started having trouble, they've been having troubles, too."

"Like what kind of troubles?"

"Well, I hate to say anything because it's not confirmed."

"Not confirmed? What does that mean? Is she okay, Karl?"

"Well, I didn't tell you this, and you darn sure better keep it under your hat for now, but the word is Terry has been hitting her."

Tyler's jaw clenched. He fell back into his seat and grabbed the bill of his cap and worked it back and forth. He looked back up at Karl with fire in his eyes. "If I find that's true, you better get him before I do."

"Now hang on there, killer. That's why I didn't want to say anything. Don't you worry; I'm on top of it. Besides, he's been throwing a little extra money around here lately and I think it has to do with why he's hanging out down at Slim's."

"Why's that?"

Karl frowned and flipped his keys back and forth around his finger. "I kinda think he's running dope."

"You gotta be kidding me. Terry?"

"People change, Ty, and they do strange things when they're desperate for money."

"What makes him desperate? He owns a damn John Deere dealership, don't he? Besides, his daddy's got more money than anybody in East Texas."

"Yeah, well, I think he got a little crossways with Lester when he bought the old Winston place and remodeled the house. The word is he went in deep on it. He was trying to impress Jeanie because their relationship was getting rocky. Lester told him not to do it, but he did it anyway. Now he can't go to his dad for help; his pride won't let him."

"Hell, it ought to be rocky if he's gone to beating on her."

"Yeah, but I don't think that started until after he got upside-down in debt. He's been sitting on expensive flooring with the dealership, and the economy around here hasn't been the same since the drought. He kinda got hit from all sides at once."

"What do you think she's going to do? Do you think she still loves him? She never seemed like the type to put up with that crap."

"The truth of the matter is, I don't think she ever really loved him; not the way she loved you anyway. She used to always be bubbly and happy with you, but she's never seemed much more than just content with him. I think as time went on she began to regret marrying him. They've just never had that zing that you guys had."

The waitress came by and brought Ty's breakfast. She took another run at Karl. "You still don't want nothing?"

He shook his head and smiled.

Their conversation fell silent for a moment, and Tyler felt Karl's eyes upon him as he ate. He could guess what his old friend was thinking. He felt it too. It was strange to be sitting there talking with one the best friends he'd ever had as if no time had passed between them. It had been several years since they'd seen each other, and in a way, that friendship had been filed away as a memory. They were like two strangers with the same past.

Karl thumped the table. "I want to let you eat, old buddy, but I just had one last thing I want to ask you."

"Sure. Shoot."

"Do you think there's any way you can talk to Terry before he gets too far gone?"

Tyler kept his eyes down as he reached for his coffee and took a sip. "I don't think that's such a good idea."

"No? Well, I tried talking to him, but all he sees is this badge. I can't get through to him as a friend anymore. We were never much friends to begin with. Are you sure you can't pay him a visit just for old time's sake and see what comes up?"

Tyler put his fork down and sighed. "Maybe you don't remember, but Terry and I ain't exactly friends anymore, Karl. Besides, now that I know he's hitting Jeanie, I don't think I could so much as look at him without wanting to knock his head off."

"That's a shame, Ty. You guys were practically joined at the hip from kindergarten through high school. I know some things came between you, like the block he missed in the championship that ruined your career, and . . . well, the fact that he ended up with Jeanie. I know those things are hard to swallow, but I guess I figured there still might be some brotherly love there."

"Yeah, well, you figured wrong. I got my own problems to worry about. I don't much give two shits about anybody else's problems right now. Why don't you just bust his sorry ass and put him in jail?"

Karl shrugged and squirmed a little. "Well, I just might have to do that. You know, Ty, as your other best friend, I can tell you that it doesn't make sense to be carrying around a grudge for so long. It's sad, man. You guys were everybody's heroes. I just think life is short and old friends are rare. Besides, it only hurts you when you shoulder animosity like that. It's like carrying around your own little bag of plutonium."

Ty went back to work on his biscuits. "Deputy Dupree, you're right about one thing; old friends are rare, even more rare than you might think. When you stop living in the past, you find these things out."

"You know I'm still your friend, Ty. If it'll help at all, you can bend my ear with it. At least then you'll be able to get it off your chest. I bet you ain't never shared it with anyone."

Tyler slammed his fork down. "What do you do, sit around watching Dr. Phil all day? What difference does it make, Karl? Let him make his own decisions. I don't owe him anything. I swear, you people are amazing! I ain't seen you for five years and you pick right up with me like I just went away for the weekend or something."

"You people? It's not all about you, Ty, and it's not even about him. If he don't straighten up, he could really hurt Jeanie. Now maybe you can't make a difference, but how can you know that and not try?"

Tyler shoved his plate away and took a long drink of water. He set the glass down and looked around the empty restaurant for a moment. He pushed his hat back on his head and leaned on the table looking at Karl. "That son-of-a-bitch may or may not be the reason I lost my career; that I can't prove for sure, but he took away the love of my life after I had sat and told him how much I loved her."

"Come on, Ty, you went away to the Navy."

"Okay, Dr. Karl, let me drop a little information on you for a minute, old buddy. You want know what really happened? I'll tell you. Terry had been sending love letters to Jeanie behind my back during our senior year. She didn't want to tell me because she didn't want to ruin my and Terry's friendship."

"Oh wow! You're kidding me!"

"I shit you not. She liked both of us, but she was secretly in love with me. We made a love pact when we were in seventh grade, but I just figured it was what all kids do. I knew I had strong feelings for her, but it was awkward since we'd been friends for so long. I had no idea she felt the same way until she cornered me at Pizza Hut after we beat Nacogdoches the first year. Even then, we knew we were still too young to do much about it. We wanted to save ourselves for marriage so we always did everything as a group. You know what I'm talking about. You were part of the group."

"Oh yeah, and we had some good times."

"Well, sometime after I started dating her seriously, Terry and I went to the lake one night and ran some trotlines. We drank too much beer and I poured my heart out to him about Jeanie. After that, he pretended to step back out of the way, but he was secretly sending her letters and going to her house to try to compete for her."

"My gosh. When did you find out?"

"Just before the championship. He'd gone to her house to ask her to wish him luck. They were standing out by his car and, when she went to give him a quick hug, he tried to kiss her. She pushed him away and told him she was in love with me. Ellen Trout was riding by on her bike at the same time, and Jeanie knew it would be all over the school, so she called me over after he left and showed me the letters."

"Oh shit. So that's why he was so pissed at you during the championship game."

"Yep."

"Well, all's fair in love and war, Ty. Hell, the guy was smitten with her and he had to act true to his heart. You'd have done the same."

"You don't get it, Karl. He wasn't smitten with her. He was screwing every girl he could. He just wanted to conquer her, primarily because he knew I wanted her. He's a rotten, jealous asshole. He always wanted to one-up me and he figured out a way to do it."

"Okay maybe you're right about that, but friends screw up, especially teenagers."

"Yep, and if that was all there was to it, I probably could have looked the other way, but what he did to me in that final game I can't forgive. I believe he was trying to make me look bad in front of her and the scouts. He never missed a block for me all season, and he missed four in that game. The last one ended my career. I lost my scholarship. I lost everything, including Jeanie."

"I gotta admit that was strange. I couldn't believe what I was seeing. He said he was sick, didn't he?"

"Yeah, right; that's what he told the team, but he and I both knew better."

"So what happened between you and Jeanie?"

Tyler sighed. "I don't want to talk about it, man. That was a long time ago."

"It's just strange, that's all. You guys were inseparable."

With another long sigh, Tyler retreated to the window. He sat quietly for a long moment, watching the sunlight bounce off the cars as they drove by. He frowned and rubbed his face with both hands before looking back at Karl. "You remember we had all agreed at the beginning of our sophomore year that we'd go to UT?"

Karl nodded.

"I was a shoo-in until I lost my football scholarship. Terry, of course, had no problem getting in. He had a partial football scholarship and plenty of money to boot, but Jeanie didn't have the money."

"Yeah, neither did I," Karl added.

"Well, I'm sure you remember that at the last minute, the Radcliffe Scholarship went to her. The inside scoop was that Jamie Reynolds was supposed to get it, but I think Terry told his dad to give it to Jeanie. Then Lester Radcliffe bought a duplex for Terry to live in while he was at school, and guess who got to live in the other house for free?"

"Oh my God, Ty, I never knew any of this."

"It gets worse. We were calling each other steadily for a little while, and then her calls stopped and I couldn't get her to answer mine. I tried writing several letters, but she never answered any of them. I was joining the Navy and wondering why I had lost her. As a last-ditch effort, I left a message for her to come see me off, but she never showed."

"Unbelievable! Man, I'm sorry, Ty. So, you really never knew what happened to make her leave you. Now I'm seeing Terry in a whole new light. Looks like he's been a freak for a long time. I don't blame you for not wanting to see him." After a quiet pause, Karl nodded. "Fair enough. I guess Jeanie is on her own until I can nail him."

He rose and shook Ty's hand. "By the way, Della has some great ribbon cane syrup back there, but she keeps it a secret."

Ty smiled. "Good to know, but I think I hit the wall with those big-assed biscuits."

"Don't be a stranger, old friend."

"Yeah, I'm leaving Saturday afternoon, so if I don't see you again between now and then, take care, Karl."

Karl tipped his hat. As he watched him walk away, Tyler's gut began to turn. "Hey, Karl, wait a minute." He leaned back in his seat and frowned as Karl walked back over to him. "Look, maybe you're right. I guess I could stay for a couple more days, but I'm only doing it for Jeanie. I'll try to talk to him but I can't promise you how it'll turn out. It may end up in a blood bath. I ain't much of a bullshitter."

Karl smiled and shook his hand. "Just don't kill him."

"No promises." Ty watched as the deputy sheriff sauntered out the door. A friend since childhood, Karl Dupree was the high school quarterback, King of the Court, Valedictorian, and voted most likely to succeed. He probably would have gone a long way, but he lost both of his parents the summer of his junior year.

They were all skiing up on Rayburn out of Sandy Creek. It was his mom's turn to ski and his dad insisted on trying to take the skiers straight up into the Attoyac River so they could get some different scenery rather than skiing in circles all day. The river was wide and he knew it well, but there was a hard left turn getting into the mouth of it from the open lake. Karl's dad made the turn fine, but there was one of those high-dollar bass boats barreling way too fast down the river. Mr. Dupree jerked back on the throttle and his mom was dropping into the water when the boat hit her. The impact nearly tore her head completely off, and the prop mangled what was left of her.

Karl blamed his father, saying that if he hadn't shut it down, she could've swerved to miss the boat. He wouldn't talk to him for over a month, then it was too late. They found his father's boat running around in circles in the big opening in front of Sandy Creek, but he wasn't in it. They never found his body.

~ 13 ~

Ty paid his check and drove slowly through town. As he looked around at all the aging and abandoned store fronts, his throat choked and his heart seemed to sink to his gut for the days gone by. Apart from making him feel old, it saddened him that all the friendly, family owned businesses had been replaced by large corporate warehouses.

He passed the old department store where he'd spent many a Saturday morning. He slowed and looked through the dirty windows at the empty building, conjuring up memories of his grandmother buying him car models and plastic trucks with a bag of marbles tossed in the back, Hot Wheels, and pearl-handled toy Colts in a real leather holster. What was ever wrong with Perry Bros. Department Store anyway? It had plenty of different stuff just like Walmart, but it had things Walmart didn't have, like a quaint little lunch counter and malt shop that made the whole store smell good. He couldn't count the days he'd spent running his Hot Wheels across that speckled Formica counter, while he was eating the best grilled cheese in the world with a Dr Pepper milkshake and waiting for Momma to pick out fabrics.

Tyler turned the corner and slowed as he passed the bus stop where he'd waited for Jeanie all those years ago. The old wooden bench was long gone and had been replaced by shiny aluminum benches bolted to the concrete. The talk with Karl had stirred up thoughts and emotions that he hadn't dealt with in a long time.

He pulled over for a moment and stared at the new benches. It was hard to believe all the years that had gone by since he sat there as a younger man, facing a new life, trying to fill the hole in his heart.

The day he was set to leave for the Navy, Tyler was eager to test his skills at diving, but sad to leave everything and everyone he knew behind. He barely passed the physical because of his knee, but his incredible muscular condition made up for it. He sat on the edge of his bed with his bags at his feet, taking final inventory of his room and rubbing his right knee.

He turned and looked at the Jacques Cousteau picture above his bed, then glanced at the deep-sea posters above his desk. He closed up his backpack, then got up and strolled around his room looking at pictures of Jeanie and him together, pictures of friends at the lake, and pictures from his football days.

He picked up the old Shakespeare reel that had belonged to his grandfather and spun the handle. He set it down and stepped over to take one last look at his glory wall, carefully examining his trophies and newspaper articles.

His father tapped on the door and walked in to help with his bags. "Got 'em all ready, son?"

Tyler looked back and nodded quietly, glancing down at the bags. Charlie walked up and put his arm around him, looking at the wall with him. "You made me the proudest father on earth, son."

Tyler put a hand on his dad's shoulder. "Thanks, Pop."

"Are you sure about this? My offer still stands. You'd make a great salesman."

Tyler pulled away and grabbed his backpack off the bed. "I appreciate it, but I can't see myself as a car salesman the rest of my life, and no offense Dad, but I'll be damned if I'll do anything that puts money in the pocket of a Radcliffe."

His father sighed and lowered his head as he shoved his hands into his pockets. "This will always be your home, son."

Tyler paused from picking up his suitcase. "You always said to follow my heart. You know how much I've always wanted to be a diver."

"I know you'll be the best damned diver they've ever seen, too. I love you, Son."

"Love you, too, Dad."

"Did you say goodbye to your brother?"

"Yeah, listen Dad; you got to get him out of that old barn and back into the house."

Charlie lifted his hat and scratched his head as he glanced back at the barn. "We'll see. He's happier there son."

"Still, it ain't right."

Together, they rounded up the bags and started out of the room. "You be sure you write your momma often, you hear?"

"Yes, sir."

THE SEPTEMBER MORNING HAD BROKEN quietly without a formal introduction of the sun. Tyler stepped from the porch under a cotton-white sky and tossed his bags into the back of the truck. A cool breeze lifted the first leaves of fall that speckled the green lawn. He heard the screen door creak and close softly behind him. His dad stopped, sported a sympathetic smile, and leaned on the truck bed. He turned to see his mother standing on the porch, wiping her hands on her apron. He walked back up to her and hugged her gently, kissing her on the cheek.

She held firm for a moment, then released her tears and squeezed him with all of her might. "You do yourself proud, son. Don't let your momma go too long without seeing her baby again."

"I won't, Momma. I love you."

"I love you, too, son. Be sure to call now."

"I will, Momma."

He watched her wave as they turned down the long dirt drive. By habit, his dad slowed and looked across the pasture for deer. After sharing a quiet moment with his son, he sped up and passed through the small stand of sweet gum and hickory. "Nice cool breeze this morning. Guess it's time to start the winter garden, don't you think."

Tyler briefly smiled at his father but his thoughts were elsewhere. He was retracing his footsteps across the East Texas foothills of his childhood, revisiting the thoughts of a rambling boy in his cutoff jeans, running like the wind, barefoot down the shoreline on amber summer evenings that seemed to last forever; a boy whose world still held the promise of mystery and adventure. He wondered how he'd let so much time pass and so many dreams fade away. At least he'd held onto one. It wasn't how he'd envisioned it happening, but he was finally on his way to being a diver.

A YOUNG TYLER MORGAN, EAGER to take on the rest of the world the way he'd taken on half of East Texas on the football field, sat on the bench in front of the bus station with bags piled on the ground next to him. His bus was called and he stood and said goodbye to his father.

As he watched his father pull away, his thoughts quickly turned back to Jeanie – where they had been all morning. He had asked her to come see him off, but she never showed. Such must be the life of college girls he thought. Why had she stopped calling? Why wouldn't she answer the phone? His heart ached, and inside he was falling to pieces, but he couldn't let anyone see him crying, so he toughened up and pitched his gear to the driver.

He looked back a couple of times as the bus crawled out of the station and headed down Denman Avenue toward Timberland Drive. With a heavy heart, he said goodbye to the only life he'd ever known as the bus wound its way through town before straightening south onto Highway 59.

LEAVING THE BUS STATION AND the painful memories behind, Tyler stopped at the Circle K on Denman Avenue and picked up a six-pack and a cup of ice before heading out to Vince's place near Boggy Slough.

Down Highway 94 about six miles, he passed through Hudson where his father had gone to elementary school. Except for a new convenience store where the Hudson General Store and Feed used to be, nothing had changed. Farther down the highway, He pulled off at the entrance to a dirt road. Finding the gate unlocked, he continued down the road that ran between two beautiful pastures studded with grand oaks.

Just beyond the pasture, the road turned to white sand, and the world turned dark from the tall pines. He crossed an old wooden bridge and came to a turnoff with another steel gate. He sat there for a moment, clutching his brown paper sack, trying to wash away the memories staining his conscience, and preparing his heart for a visit with his broken-down hero. He pushed the bottle back under his seat and fumbled through his keys for the one his dad had given him.

His chest tightened as he wound through the forest toward his brother's home. A sense of hopelessness flooded his being as he turned through a busted-up barbed wire fence and into a dirt yard. The old house was nothing more than a shack. The outer walls were covered with small animal skins and deer horns. A couple of old rockers stood on the porch, and off to the left was a large oak with the top burned out of it, probably from a lightning strike. Nailed to the trunk was a huge meat hook with a fish head stuck on it where someone had recently cleaned a catfish. Below the hook, the trunk was stained black in old blood.

Tyler put both arms over the steering wheel and rested his chin on his hands. His heart sank, and all that he could think was, *'What a place for a number one draft pick to end up.'*

As he stepped from the truck and headed for the door, he realized that he hadn't had too many personal conversations with his brother since the accident that had almost killed him.

He snorted and took a big breath, then stepped onto the porch and practiced a big smile. He knocked on the door and listened for footsteps. All that he heard was a wispy breeze rustling the dried leaves of a small red oak on the side of the house and some birds chirping. He hollered for his brother.

"Hey, Vince, it's me, Tyler." Nothing. He tried the door and found it open, so he pushed it in slowly. "Vince, are you in here?"

The smell of fish grease almost knocked him over. He stepped inside and was immediately besieged by what he saw. Every wall inside was covered with pictures held up by thumbtacks. There must have been thousands. The house only had three rooms and a screened back porch. He found the kitchen empty, but the stove was still warm and the large iron skillet on top was still full of grease and browned cornmeal. He shoved the last five beers of the six-pack into the refrigerator next to an open pot of beans and set a new bottle of George Dickel on the counter.

Across the den was the door to the bedroom. An old bed with a deep hollow in the center and a chest of drawers with the laminate cracking off were the only furnishings. The door to the back porch was standing open, so he made his way out and down the old wooden steps that had seen better days.

Out in the leaf-covered backyard there was a water spigot dripping into a large washtub and an old lawn chair beside it with a busted strap hanging from beneath. Walking toward it, he began to notice blood everywhere, some of it congealed with bits and pieces of innards scattered throughout. To his relief, in the tub were several filets of catfish submerged in bloodstained water.

With a deep sigh, he put his hands on his hips and looked out through the woods where he saw a trail leading away from the house. He stood there for a moment wondering if he should just leave. He was about ready to go when he heard a faint sound coming through the woods that sounded like water falling onto water.

He reached into his pocket and loaded a dip of snuff, spit, then started toward the sound that led him down the footpath and into the woods. He'd only walked for a couple of minutes when the trail opened up to a small slough lake, and there on the bank was his brother with another washtub. Fish heads and guts floated on the surface where they were being attacked from below by a hungry swarm. He watched his brother cleaning the tub and figured he would announce his presence after he'd finished. He battled with the mix of pride and pity that plagued him as he looked on.

Vince suddenly raised his head, and then swung around violently with a growl. In his hand was a huge knife readied for attack. Tyler was caught completely off guard and slipped as he tried to step back.

"Vince no, it's me, Tyler." Tyler watched as a faint smirk came across his brother's face. He put the knife away and chuckled as he came to help him up. "You asshole, you knew I was there all along, didn't you?"

"Uh-huh." His brother's reply was like the grunting of a grizzly bear, and the big, playful hug he gave him was no different. He squeezed Tyler hard, making him feel like a rag doll.

They walked together back through the woods to the house where he helped Vince bag the catfish filets he'd left soaking in the tub.

The drawer next to the refrigerator was packed with a huge roll of wax paper and freezer bags of all sizes. Ty opened the freezer to put some filets in and was surprised when Vince grabbed it from his hands. He watched his brother wrap the filets in a single band of masking tape, and with a black marker, he wrote the date on the fish. Ty looked up into the freezer that was packed with all sorts of game, every one dated and marked by type, and all placed according to age from front to back. Vince drew a fish symbol with whiskers and smiled as he handed it to him and nodded for him to put it away.

With the fish all put up, Ty washed up and grabbed a beer for each of them. "You still like beer, don't ya, bubba?"

"Oh yeah." Vince patted his little brother on the shoulder and pointed him into the den.

With only a small couch and a chair to choose from, Ty chose the couch as it looked far less worn. "So how have you been, Vince? Are you doing good?"

"Uh-huh."

"Are you still happy here?"

"Uh-huh."

"Does Dad come out and see you a lot?"

"Uh-huh."

Ty was beginning to worry that his brother's vocabulary had gotten worse after being out in the woods alone for the past five years. He looked around at all the pictures on the walls, trying to find something to talk about that would give his brother a chance to have a real conversation. "So when did you start taking all these pictures Vince?"

"Mostly when I got here."

He stood, went to the coffee table, and picked up his camera, and put it around his neck. He took a picture of Ty, then sat back down, waving the photo back and forth to dry it. After a moment he looked at it and smiled, then threw it to Tyler. Ty looked at it and laughed, partly because he found his brother's actions to be somewhat humorous, and partly because he found it so traumatic he needed a release.

"That's me, ain't it?"

"Uh-huh." Vince smiled.

"Do you ever run out of film?"

"No." He reached down by his chair and opened the top drawer of an old filing cabinet that doubled as an end table. He motioned for Ty to take a look. The drawer was full of film and batteries. "Dad brings more every week."

"Oh, that's good."

"Yeah, he gets all my stuff."

"So you never leave here, Vince?"

"No."

"Would you like to go somewhere? I could take you somewhere; get you out of here and get you some new scenery for a change."

"It's not time."

"What do you mean, it's not time?"

"The lady said no. I have to rest and take my pictures. She'll tell me when it's time."

"Oh really? What lady?"

"In the forest. She said to take pictures of everything. She said to take lots of pictures of the bad men."

"You're saying there's a lady who lives out here, too?"

Vince seemed a little confused. He looked down and started fidgeting with his camera.

"You said the bad men? Vince, who are the bad men?"

"The men in the swamp," he said without looking up.

"Oh, okay." Ty's heart sank a little more. He remembered the doctors saying that Vince would say some confusing things and not to be alarmed. They'd hoped that it would only be temporary.

Vince swallowed the rest of his beer and burped loudly. They both grinned at each other. Ty burped back at him, and they had a good laugh. He jumped up and grabbed two more beers, squeezing his brother's shoulder as he handed him his beer.

"Well, when you think it's time, I'd like to drive around the old country roads with you again, bubba. Just for something to do, you know?"

"She said it's almost time."

Ty sat and lifted his beer toward Vince. "Good. I can't wait."

"It'll be good. We'll be happy."

"Yes, we will, brother."

~ 14 ~

As he was leaving, Ty looked back at his brother sitting on the front porch and struggled to hold back his tears. He drove the rest of the day down asphalt-covered back roads and one-lane dirt roads that led through the third world of deep East Texas.

Most of the old wooden bridges he'd loved while growing up, painted in the contrast of oak shade and sunlight, were long gone, taking with them the reminders of those who had built them. He drove past rolling pastures laced with hand-cut posts and rusted wire, and snaked through pine thicket in the rationed sunlight of early winter, looking for precious memories, finding some just where he'd left them, while others had either turned to a loosely connected web of remnants or had completely washed away with time, leaving only the ghostly reflection of emotions, connected to something he wished he'd never forgotten.

He tossed the empty bottle out the window and into a pine-straw covered ditch before reaching the highway. He was totally numb now, just where he liked to be. He crossed the bridge over the lake, pulled off at Etoile Park and drove down by the boat ramp to watch the sunset. The lake was still and empty, its glimmer steadily fading, much like his heart.

Tears came to his eyes as he thought of all the lives that had gone by, touching his along the way, and all the dreams that had died with them, most of them before they did. He'd enjoyed beautiful evenings much like this as a young man, his heart full of zest for a world glowing with mystery and promise.

He used to wonder what his purpose would be, and what he would end up doing that would make his life worth living. He used to look around, feeling full of piss and vinegar as his father used to say, and wonder why so many others seemed to give up or simply fail. Sitting here now, in the late afternoon of his life, he wondered if the whole thing about finding purpose was just a good story to keep people from knowing they were failures. After all, he'd never done anything to hurt anybody on purpose, but God had taken everything from him and left him hopeless. How could a man with no hope have a purpose?

THE MORNING WAS WELL LIT, but the color of the sun had yet to make its debut over the tall pines on the eastern bank. Tyler stopped on the porch to stretch and test the temperature. The air was dry and cool, but not cold. He threw his coat back inside, sauntered down to the boat stall and hooked the boat up to the tractor.

He checked the plug and the rod box, tested the battery on the trolling motor, and backed the boat down to the lake. Ever since he was fourteen, he had been in charge of backing the boat into the water. By then, Vince had grown tired of fishing and could think of nothing but football and girls as he headed off for his first year of college where he would continue to set records.

With the boat in the water, he sat back and watched his dad coming down the hill like he'd done a thousand times before. He always took the same path to the left of the fish cleaning table and made the same mini-hop over the roots that grew on the small ridge that marked the high water line. Everything looked the same, but everything had changed; everything from the way his father's clothes hung on him to this distraction called life that surrounded their fishing trips.

"Where do you want to go this morning, Dad?"

His father sat with a grunt and slid his thermos under the console. "It don't matter to me, Son. Too bad the lake is so damn low. You know, we used to find a warm, sunlit bank and work it with spinner-baits, but the damn lake is so low I wouldn't know where to go."

Tyler smiled. He had enjoyed many wonderful mornings studying the sandy banks for swirls and watching his bait slide into the clear water and bounce across the sticks and roots on the clay bottom; steam rising to the promise of a warm day, and the dew on the willows, glistening in new sunlight. His heart tingled with anticipation.

He looked closely at his father's face as he rose, at the orange glow painted on his whiskered skin from the rising sun and the fog escaping from his breath, and quietly swore to make this day as beautiful and cherished a memory as any fishing day they ever had together. "I can't wait to get on 'em, Dad."

Charlie seemed a little embarrassed by the sudden intimacy.

"Stanley Creek is always good, but it'll be full of boats this morning. We might ought to go over to Odell Creek and see if there's enough water. If not, we can fish the old pond at the Moore farm or slide out and hit some of the bends in the river. The ramps are all closed on that side of the lake, so there may not be anybody around."

"Sounds good to me; looks like it's going to be a clear day when these morning clouds blow off."

Tyler backed the boat out and started across the huge lake he'd come to know so well as a child. It wasn't just a body of water surrounded by piney points and wispy willows; it was a part of East Texas history where water covered old farms, rivers, creeks, road beds, and even towns. Every part of the lake was identified by these old landmarks, and in that way they lived on beyond their drowning and gained new fame by the fish caught above their watery graves.

The old boat seemed to be running good as they cleared the stumpy area and sped into the north-south cut. When the lake was first made they had cleared wide cuts like fire lanes through the forest so that the boats would have a way to navigate the lake. Over time, the wind and waves consumed most of the trees, slowly eating away their trunks at the average water line. Growing up, it was common to sit by the water's edge to catch the sunset and hear a tree falling somewhere across the lake. Now, as each day dies, the grand old lake dies a little more.

Today, since the lake was so low, the cuts could be seen again, marked by stumps that had risen from the grave. Some of the stumps hosted v-cuts through their centers, left there by weekend warriors in their super-duper bass rigs who learned about busted transoms and stainless steel props before they ever learned to catch fish.

As Tyler slowed and turned into the opening where the Angelina River curved through ancient cypress stumps, he could see that the cove he wanted to fish had no water in it. Odell Creek dropped into the lake at the back of the cove and wound through at least 300 yards of dry land where the lake used to be.

He shut it down and turned to talk to his dad. "Boy, it's low, isn't it?"

Charlie appeared a little awestruck as he canvassed the area. "Lower than I've ever seen it."

"What do you think? Is there any use in trying to get back there to the creek and fish in it?"

"I ain't too sure you can get back there to it. The river makes a big bend about 100 yards up there and you'll have to find where the creek meets up with it. Otherwise, it's too shallow to try to cut straight across to it."

Charlie craned, trying to get a good view of the creek back in the cove. "It looks awful inviting back there, though. You can see where the creek cuts through dry land back yonder and it looks deep and clean."

"Well, do you think there's fish back in there? I'd be willing to bet nobody's been in there for quite some time."

"Yeah, I would imagine there is, as long as the creek is deep enough and it looks to be. We can try it, Son. It'll be fun trying and if we can't make it, we'll turn back out and head straight to the Moore farm to fish the old pond."

"That sounds like a plan."

They followed the Angelina until it started bending back toward the cut and looked for what might be the creek channel. The water was only two feet deep when they got out of the river bed. Ty raised the big motor and used his depth finder to locate where the creek bed might be. After several minutes of meandering back and forth with his trolling motor, he found a spot where the depth dropped to seven feet.

"This must be it. I'll just use the trolling motor to get us back there."

"There you go. You can kinda see where the creek is. It ain't very wide, so you'll need to stay between them larger stumps that mark the edge of the old creek."

Tyler looked back at his father and nodded. It had been a long time since he'd heard the sage-like quality of his father's advice. There was something primitive about a father and son being out on the water; something that required a father to always take the position of experience, give advice, and tell stories involving lessons that could never be forgotten.

Soon they reached dry land halfway back in the cove where they could easily follow the creek. Tyler stopped trolling and turned to grab his rod. His father was already tying on a worm.

He watched him work as a slight breeze lifted his line. His movements were slower now, his eyes squinted, and he somehow lacked the eager anticipation of the first cast that used to define his love for fishing. Tyler knew he was trying hard to move on, but his broken heart and his fears of a life of perpetual loneliness had obviously taken their toll. At least he was still going through the motions and hadn't given up.

"I had a long visit with Vince yesterday, Dad."

"Oh, that's good." Charlie bit his line and pitched the worm into the water.

"I couldn't believe his house was completely covered with pictures."

"Oh, yeah, he takes pictures of everything, and I don't think he's ever thrown a picture away."

"Well, I knew the new doctor had him start doing that last time I was here, but I had no idea he would still be so infatuated with it."

"No, me neither. He was heavy into it at first, but then he slacked off a bit. Then, for some reason, shortly after your accident, he became obsessed. At first, he was keeping them in albums, but he got tired of having to look so hard to find his favorite ones so he just started tacking them on his wall. He started in his closet; then moved through the house. I asked him one time why he suddenly picked it up again, but what he said didn't make any sense so I just left it alone. It seems to give him some purpose."

"Do you remember what he said?"

"Something about a lady in the swamp and some bad guys." Charlie frowned and shook his head as he cast.

"Yeah, he told me the same thing. He said he was supposed to take pictures of the bad guys. Did he ever show them to you?"

Charlie shook his head. "Nah, I never asked."

Ty got hung and trolled over to work his bait free. When he finally got it loose, he pulled his flask out of his pocket and took a couple of swigs. He saw his father look over and frown, but he didn't say anything.

After a few more casts, he watched his father reel in and lay his rod across his lap. "What's wrong, Dad, are you tired?"

"There's something I promised your mom I'd tell you, Son, and I guess now is as good a time as any."

Tyler took a deep breath to absorb the shock and tried to reply, but could only look at his father and nod.

"She sure missed you these last few years, Son, as did I, but she was always better with her words when it came to this sort of stuff, and she had plenty of time to think. I don't remember it word for word, but I'll try to do it justice."

Tyler set his rod in the boat. "Okay, Dad, I'm listening."

"She said to tell you first how deeply sorry she was for you that you lost your family, and that no one could tell you how it felt because there are no words to describe such pain. She also said that if living your life the way you have these past few years is the only way you can manage, then you just go right on ahead and do it.

"There was only one small thing she wanted to ask of you. She wanted you to take one hour out of the rest of your life, walk into the church, sit down alone, and ask God to forgive your sins, to cleanse your soul, and to accept your life to be used for His purpose. She said if you could just do that to honor her dying wish, she would promise to join you there and to whisper into your thoughts the words that would heal your wounds and allow you to live again. She always wanted more than anything to have the chance to do that one last thing for her son."

Charlie wiped his eyes on his handkerchief and cast without saying another word. Tyler stared into the water through teary eyes for a moment, then got up and went to the back of the boat to hug his daddy.

Without another word between them, he made his way back to the front and was soon fishing again. Silently, they worked up the creek with plastic worms, throwing under fallen logs and contemplating events too late to change.

They made the first bend and were well into dry land when Ty set the hook and was bringing up a good fighter.

"Keep your line tight. Don't give him no slack; he'll jump and spit out the hook."

Tyler laughed as he worked the fish. "I wish I had a nickel for every time you told me that."

Charlie smiled and started to say something else when he suddenly froze, then slammed his back against the boat seat, jerking his rod high into the air. "I'll be damn, I got one, too." He set the hook with a big grunt that rocked the boat. "How long has it been since we were catching fish at the same time?"

"Years. I bet mine's bigger."

"Bet it ain't. Oh lord, get the net."

Tyler laughed. "I'm a little busy over here."

"Well, hurry up. This is the lake record."

With both fish finally in the boat, Tyler released his and paused for a nip of bourbon while he watched his father working to free the hook. "Need some pliers, Dad?"

"I think so. He damned near swallowed the hook."

Ty pitched him the pliers. He finally freed the hook and held up a large mouth black bass that was somewhere just north of five pounds.

"Nice fish, Daddy."

"Well, where's yours?"

"I let it go. It was too damned heavy to lift anyway. I just kicked it over the side before you saw it 'cuz I didn't want to hurt your feelings."

"Horse shit, I saw that fish you caught. It wouldn't have made a pecker on my fish."

"Yeah, well, your fish ain't a pecker on the lake record either."

Charlie laughed and smiled widely, holding the fish up to examine it. "I guess not. It sure felt good, though."

They laughed and winked at each other before releasing the fish to fight another day. As Tyler was taking another shot of whiskey, he saw his father spit on his worm and cast again.

"You've been hitting that stuff hard since you got back, Son. Is it just being back here that's making you do that or do you always drink like that?"

"Some days are better than others. Being here don't help, but I don't want to talk about it, Dad."

"I watched your grandpa wreck his fortune and eventually kill himself with that stuff, Son."

"I'll be fine, Dad."

"Yep, well, I heard you say that before, then I watched them pull your half-dead body off a tree limb. It won't bring them back, Son. They're gone to a better place and we have to move on. It's what they'd want for us."

"I wish it were that easy."

"It don't ever get easy, but you'll learn to live with it a lot better when you get your head and your heart right. I hope you'll think about what your Momma said."

Ty nodded and cast his line.

"Come on, Dad. Let's just fish."

~ 15 ~

Tyler cast out his line and waited for it to drop. As he worked his worm across the bottom, he noticed his father was taking a break, just sitting quietly and watching him.

"It ain't them you're a hurtin' for, you know. It wasn't you who died that day, but you seem to want to make it so. Your momma and I loved them, too. For the past five years we've been forced to feel like we lost you, too, that day. Now she's gone and you're all I have left. I know I'm talking too much, but I'm scared, and I hate for you to see more of that damned bottle than you see of me, Son."

A couple of deer stepped out of the woods and grazed toward the creek, breaking the tension and interrupting their conversation, but what his father had said was sinking home inside Tyler's heart.

He knew his dad hadn't wanted to say it straight out, and though it seemed to come from somewhere outside of himself, he had gotten his point across. His mother had missed him, and in a way, he'd cheated her out of her last years with him. Now he was doing the same to his father. He'd never stopped to think about anybody loving him and wanting to spend quality time with him. All he'd ever thought about was the time he'd lost with his wife and son, and the fact that if he'd listened to his father that day, his life would be quite different now. He laid his pole down and lifted his hat to rub his head.

Charlie cleared his throat. "Do you remember the first time you wanted to be a diver, Ty?"

Swallowing past the lump in his throat, Tyler put his hat on and lifted his rod to cast again. "Not really, do you?"

"Yep. We were sitting right over there at the Moore farm. I had just told you the story of how that truck ended up on the bottom. When I finished telling it, your eyes lit up at the prospect of exploring it. I told you the only way you could do that is to learn how to dive, then you could explore a whole world under the water that most people never get to see. That's when you started watching Jacques Cousteau and became infatuated with diving."

Tyler smiled. His father's anecdote had worked.

"I saw the newspaper clippings about him the other night. Tell me that story again, Dad. It's been too long since I've heard it."

He watched his father working a tap on his line, but it was gone before he could react to it. He popped the worm a couple more times, then let it lie as he grabbed a bottle of water from the cooler and drank a few sips.

"Well, let's see, it was back in sixty-five when old man Moore strolled into your Grandpa's Studebaker dealership and paid cash for a fancy black and white Transtar Deluxe Studebaker truck. Everyone wondered where he got his money, but your grandpa didn't pay it any mind. I was sitting in that truck writing all the numbers down last time I saw it.

"They had just finished building the dam and most of Moore's property was slated to be underwater before the end of the year, but the flood of sixty-five brought water over his land three weeks before he was supposed to leave. It was a horrible flood that took several lives and left his property under six feet of water. The house and barn were partially collapsed when they got here, and they could just see the top of the truck a couple feet under water.

"They figured Moore would wash up somewhere between here and Hanks Creek if he didn't make it out, but he was never found. Some say he was a bit canny and would have got a kick out of making folks think he was dead. He always talked about going to Montana, and he didn't have any kinfolks left anyway. My suspicion is he never made it out, because I know he wouldn't have left that truck behind."

"Why didn't they dive around here to see what they could find?"

"There's plenty of controversy surrounding that question. See, your grandpa, Joe Gentry, Judge Jack Reynolds, Sterman Moore, a young Lester Radcliffe, and Coach McKinney were all poker buddies and members of the Pine Island Country Club. I think it was the coach and Joe who came forward and said that Lester was hotter than hell mad at old man Moore the night before he disappeared. He said Moore accused Lester of cheating, which he probably was, so he refused to pay him the money he owed him."

"Wow, I don't think you ever told me this part."

"No, I suspect I didn't. Now, as the story has it, Lester figured he could take old man Moore, so he told him he wouldn't let him leave until he paid up, but the old man was stronger than skunk piss, and he knocked Lester's cocky ass out cold. When he came to, Moore had already gone home, and before Lester stormed out, he said the old man would pay for what he done."

"So why wasn't there an investigation?"

"I think Judge Reynolds intentionally blocked it long enough for the lake to reach pool because Lester got into his pocket pretty good that night as well. Anyway, there were a lot of changes going on around here then, and by the time they were able to go back out, the water was thirty feet deep in this area. Since there was no family to push for an investigation, they never had one.

"Lester wasn't seen again after that night for over a year. The word was he'd left town saying he had a sick relative to tend to, and since there was a storm to blame where other people had died, it just kinda all fell by the wayside."

"So why would the Judge block the investigation? If he could've busted Lester, he wouldn't have had to pay him back."

"Ah, hell, the Judge and many others didn't want people poking around in their poker business. My daddy told me before he died that he remembered that Lester owed the Judge over five hundred dollars, but he never mentioned it again after Lester disappeared. There's more than one way to skin a cat, I guess. A little tit for tat if you know what I mean. Another thing my daddy told me was that old man Moore and the Judge were old enemies, and they were always fighting over something as they were growing up, including a young Russian girl whom Moore later married. It kinda makes you wonder."

"I'll say it does. On the other hand, maybe the truck got stuck and Mr. Moore got caught by the rising river while trying to make his way out on foot."

"No telling, really. One thing I know for sure though, when Lester Radcliffe came back to town he was a wealthy man. He said his relative had died and left him a tidy sum. He joined right back up with the Judge and the others despite your grandpa's objections."

"But I thought Grandpa liked him."

"Angus Morgan thought Lester was the cat's meow when he first hired him as a salesman, but after he came back he never liked him. He was cocky, throwing his money around, and bought his way back into the circle of friends. I think your grandpa just put up with him after that because all the others were his friends and they all hunted together.

"One night, when you were just a young boy, my daddy just about cleaned Lester out at the poker table. Then, six weeks later he lost everything he had right back to Lester. He'd never lost more than a few bucks before that. They got him drunk, ganged up on him, and took him to the cleaners by cheating him. That's how Lester ended up with part-ownership in the dealership and most of our land. Daddy never would admit that he'd been taken; he was too honorable not to pay his debts and too proud to admit his friends had stolen from him. Two weeks later, I found him dead on the bathroom floor full of whiskey and Valium."

Ty started to cast and laid his rod back in his lap, remembering the article that he found in the chest. "Valium! Why would Grandpa take Valium?"

"No one knows son. My daddy never took pills. You could hardly even get him to take aspirin."

"Well, didn't anybody ask questions?"

"Of course, Grandma and I both went to see the Judge, and he acted like he'd look into it. Joe Gentry, who was there at the poker game, came around saying he'd gotten drunk the night your grandpa died, but he thought he'd remembered Daddy winning big; deeds and such. He said he thought Daddy had won back everything he'd lost plus some. Then old Joe up and died eight days later. They found him burnt up in his fire pit behind the house."

"I saw that article, too, but I had no idea the story behind it all. I can't believe that everyone couldn't see through that."

"Well, after a short investigation, they claimed he'd gotten drunk and stumbled into the pit. They were downright determined about it. Momma got scared and didn't want no part of it anymore. She said we couldn't bring back the dead nohow. The Judge never really turned up anything about your Grandpa's or Joe's death except that they found a prescription of Valium in Joe's house."

Tyler sat with his rod across his lap staring out across the lake. Except for an occasional breeze that kissed the surface, causing slight ripples here and there, everything had gone still. He looked back at his father who was working his worm diligently across the bottom. "That all sounds so crazy to me, Dad. Smells like there was some kind of conspiracy."

"You never know. One thing's for sure, you can't fight big connections in a small town." Charlie laid down his rod and stood to pee as they inched around another of the many bends in the creek. There was a large tree lying across the creek a few feet ahead of the boat, so Ty set his rod aside and leaned back to stretch. "Well, that was worth it, wouldn't you say?"

"I'd say so. How many did we catch, four or five?"

As Tyler began to answer, a deafening boom echoed around the lake. Tyler jumped in his seat, and his father almost fell into the lake. A small concussion wave followed. They looked to the sky to see smoke trails and debris falling. Suddenly, there was a tremendous rushing sound and a big splash somewhere out in the lake.

"What the hell was that?" Tyler exclaimed to his father.

"Something blew up. I hope it wasn't them damn terrorists again." Charlie zipped up and turned to look out across the lake.

"I heard what sounded like something falling from the sky and hitting the water just over there by the Moore farm. Look, it looks like there's a big wake over there. Do you think a plane crashed?"

"I don't know, son. That's kinda what it sounded like. That was a big splash, whatever it was. It's a little far to tell, but I don't see anything floating on the surface, do you?"

"No, but maybe we ought to get a closer look."

Tyler and his father sat in shock, looking up into the sky and out across the lake for a minute. "I think it was right in the middle of the Moore farm. Close your tackle box, Dad, and I'll head that way."

As they made their way out of the creek and into the river, Tyler fired up the big motor and they cruised around a few hundred yards to where the old farm used to be. He shut it down quickly and called to Charlie, pointing to a break in the stumps along the river side and a straight run of open water about ten feet wide, with tree stumps along each side trailing off away from the river.

"I can see where the old road was that led to the house. This must have been where his river bridge was."

"Darned if it don't look like it."

Tyler began to notice a haze in the sky and could almost feel something falling in the air, but he couldn't define it. He putted along between the stickups that would have been trees lining the drive long ago. When they reached the opening that would have been the old home place of the Moore farm, they slowed to an idle and looked around. "Look how the water has changed. Whatever it is, it hit bottom pretty hard and stirred up a lot of mud."

He shut down the engine and they floated around and speculated for a bit as they looked for evidence of what might have happened. Both men stood with their hands on their hips watching the mud bubbling up to the surface.

Charlie scratched his head. "Hell, maybe it was a damned UFO."

Tyler grinned, but he wasn't ready to rule out the possibility.

"You reckon it could have been a meteor? Look how the water looks like it's boiling over there."

"I doubt it, Dad. That looks more like air bubbles. A meteor would have been traveling a lot faster. It would have made a much bigger splash and displaced a massive amount of water. I don't think we'd be sitting here if that was the case. My guess is something fell out of the sky; maybe a satellite part or something. You hear of that stuff falling out of orbit sometimes."

Tyler plopped down and swiveled in his chair looking back at his father with an embarrassed frown. "Speaking of orbit, wasn't the shuttle supposed to be returning today?" He looked back at the muddy water. "Oh dear God!"

Charlie grunted and sat down. "It wouldn't be the first time. I guess we'll know soon enough. One thing's for sure, if there were any fish here, they're long gone now."

"Good lord, Dad, how could you think of fishing right now? Say, do you reckon whatever it was would show up on the depth recorder?"

"I don't see why it wouldn't. Let's check it out."

He put down the trolling motor and turned on his depth recorder. After a moment, he saw a sharp rise on the display.

"There's something right down there. It looks like it's about six feet high and not very wide."

His father blew his nose and refolded his handkerchief. "That sounds like the truck. I believe this is about where it was."

Tyler cut hard to the left and headed toward the old tree line through what seemed to be the center point of the muddy water. He watched the line on his display shoot up, bounce up and down a bit, then finally crawl back down.

"Wow. That was weird. I think whatever it was is right below us now. I've never seen an image like that before."

Charlie perked up. "Did it look like it had wings?"

"No, not that I could tell. It was about the same height as the truck, but a lot longer and wider, and jagged across the top."

Charlie looked up into the air. He put his hands out wide with his palms up and snorted. "What the heck is in the air? It's almost like a real fine ash or something? I wonder if some volcano exploded somewhere."

"I don't think so, Dad. Too bad I don't have one of those GPS deals so I can mark the spot."

"Hell, you know where we're at. There won't be no problem getting back here."

"Yeah, I guess not. I'm thinking we might oughta head back and report it. After that we can grab a cheeseburger at the marina and catch the news."

"That sounds hunky-dory. I'm getting pretty hungry. Come to think of it, one of them cheeseburgers with lots of onions is starting to sound awful inviting. Besides, I'm dying to know what the hell is going on around here."

~ 16 ~

The sound of sirens began to grow in the distance, and along with them, way down inside, a small part of Tyler Morgan that had been dead for several years was slowly waking. There was new energy in the air. It was a familiar feeling, and for once it hadn't come as the result of a personal tragedy. For the first time in a long while, he was part of something outside of his own personal misery.

"I guess someone knows about it. Here they come."

Tyler smiled at his father and fired up the big motor.

When they finally reached the café at the marina, the TV was blaring with special announcements and the whole place was buzzing with conversation. Tyler quickly discerned from the newscast that Space Shuttle Columbia had blown apart on reentry and all members of the crew were lost.

> NASA officials have confirmed that Space Shuttle Columbia, Flight STS 107, has broken up during its landing approach to the Kennedy Space Center in Florida. It appears that all members of the crew have been lost. The cause of the disaster has yet to be determined.

As they drove down the farm road from the marina, they were passed by black Suburbans with lights flashing in their grills. Out on the highway next to the bridge a county vehicle was sitting on the side of the road. In front of it, something was roped off. As they passed by slowly, Tyler could see something lying on the ground that was obviously metal and badly burned around the edges. It looked to be a small piece of the fuselage or one of the shuttle's wings.

THEY SPENT THE BETTER PART of the afternoon in front of the TV, watching all the new reports coming in from all over East Texas. The largest accumulation of debris had fallen at the Nacogdoches airport. A plane had been taking off when a piece of one of the shuttle's engines slammed down onto the runway in front of them. Fortunately, it was far enough ahead for the pilot to be able to avoid it.

As they showed the pictures of the astronauts who were lost, Tyler thought about how their families must feel as the nation looked in on their personal tragedy with differing amounts of shock and sorrow. Only friends and family could really feel the pain, but countless heroes of sensationalism chimed in for their moment in history. He remembered the ashen mist that fell on him and his father while fishing out on the lake, and thought of how fitting the graveside eulogy *Ashes to Ashes and Dust to Dust*. There he was with all of his problems, ashes falling, dust rising; life was truly a battle amid the ashes and the dust.

It was good, he thought, that the announcers were talking of a nation in mourning, but was it real? Did the nation really care for those who were lost, or were they mostly excited that they had something sensational to focus their meaningless lives on?

He watched the faces of the people who had found pieces of the tragedy on their property. They seemed excited to be a part of history, eager to be on television for their fifteen minutes of fame. There was a boy of about fourteen describing in detail with his heavy East Texas accent how he and his friend found a partially burned leg in his pasture.

His eyes grew larger as he explained that the boot was still on the foot. City by city, across several counties they reported in, proudly boasting of their finds. Some were caught trying to hide the pieces in their homes, and one man already had a piece for sale on eBay.

Ty couldn't decide which was the bigger tragedy, the accident or the way people reacted to it. The entire third world of deep East Texas had come alive with the falling ashes of the modern world raining down upon them. They watched the President's speech confirming the breakup of the orbiter.

The reports were starting to repeat, and Ty was growing tired of hearing the words "Breaking News." He stepped outside to join his father who had left earlier grumbling "What a shame" under his breath. He walked out, patted his dad on the shoulder as he walked by him, and leaned against the post looking out across the lake.

Tyler could hear his dad shifting about and rubbing his hands together as he looked across the lake to the beautiful, blood-red gloom above the distant shoreline.

"It's getting cold." Charlie muttered.

Tyler didn't respond to his father's remark. He had something else on his mind. "They'll never find all the bodies. They may find most of them, or at least the biggest parts, but never all of them. Someday a boy will be squirrel hunting with his grandpa and he'll come across something completely foreign to him, lying half buried in the pine straw, or one day they'll cut down one of these tall virgin pines and they'll find a rotted, barely recognizable piece of history mangled in the canopy."

"Tragic events happen in threes."

"I don't think Mom's death would be considered a national tragedy, Dad."

"Mark my words. There'll be a damned tornado or a bus wreck before the end of the week."

Tyler snorted and frowned as a cool breeze slipped under his collar. His father was a smart man, not of the type given to superstition, but he'd been known to hang on to some of his backwoods anecdotes, probably because he was just a little sentimental about the simple ways of his upbringing.

Ty buttoned his shirt another button and crossed his arms. "Dang, it definitely is getting cold."

He turned to see if his dad had heard him. He was gone. He shoved his hands deep into his pockets and spit. The deep red hues had faded over the lake. Only a sliver of violet remained as evidence that it was ever there. He heard the six o'clock news signing off and took one last look at the black monoliths protruding from the purple water. He listened to the screech of a crane and the slap of a monster bass echoing from somewhere near the small island in front of Hog Wallow, and went inside.

"You hungry, Son?"

"I could eat."

Charlie browsed the dishes on the counter; mourning food left by friends and loved ones. He went down the line, turning back foil and lifting glass lids as Tyler sat at the table thumbing through the paper. "We got Miz Hill's dumplin's; there's chicken spaghetti from I don't know who, and this lasagna looks inviting."

"Who's it from?"

"Says Nelvis-Jean. I'll be damned, I didn't know her to ever cook much."

"Give it to the dog."

"Son, that ain't very nice.

"Yeah well, it ain't very good neither."

"Don't look so bad."

"Go on and eat it then."

Charlie looked it over for a minute. "You say it ain't no good, huh? Smells good."

"Gave me the shits the last and only time I ever ate it."

"Hum, guess that's why she never cooked much."

"Guess so. What else is there?"

"Chicken casserole; meatloaf; uh, mystery dish; baked beans, and some sliced honey ham."

"Baked beans?"

"Yep, and here's the topper, Miz Traugott's banana puddin'."

"Guess I'll eat sure enough. Man's gotta have something to put that puddin' on top of."

Tyler went into the bathroom to wash up.

"Hey, Dad, are you saving this piss in here for anything?"

"No, go ahead and flush it. I'll make more here directly."

"LORD, WE THANK YOU FOR the many kind blessings bestowed upon us and for the good friends you provided us. We ask that you make a special welcome for Momma, and watch over her until I get there. We thank you for this food you've put before us and ask that you bless it to the nourishment of our bodies. In Christ's name, Amen."

"Amen."

"Them dumplin's would have been the first thing your momma would've eaten, had it been me to take the first walk."

Tyler got a lump in his throat. He watched his dad shoveling food into his mouth, head down, one foot up in the chair, arm draped over his knee to support the shoulder that went bad thirty years ago. He'd seen him cry for only the second time in his entire life a few days ago. It was different when his grandmother died. Everything and everybody was different. She was 94, and everything seemed part of a natural order then.

At his mother's funeral, his father had been strong until they were standing by the graveside. It had almost brought him to his knees when he looked up and saw Barbara Ann there, standing off away from the family, her beauty faded, but not forgotten, her gray hair curled beneath a black silk hat with a short, black lace veil. Tyler could see his father's insides exploding at the sight of her.

Barbara was Katherine's best friend from high school, and they had somehow drifted apart some fifteen years ago. Yet there she was, doing her duty, crying; probably counting the missing years and wondering the reasons for missing them. A quick kiss and a hug, and she disappeared as quietly as she had come, but Tyler remembered the warm feeling her presence had imparted upon all of them. It was like there was an unwritten code that friends who had been so close would always be there until the end, no matter what had come between them.

Tyler watched his father's methodical movements as he reached for dessert. Apart from a profound lack of aggression, Charlie Morgan was a hard man, raised by one of the last of the great generation, and he held his own, at least until he lay next to that empty pillow at night. Fifty-six years is a long time to go without sleeping alone. Somehow, stumbling from his recliner at three in the morning and falling into bed without ever fully waking made it tolerable.

"Your momma always said she'd get the recipe for this puddin' but she never did. Every time she asked for it, Miz Traugott would just bring over a fresh puddin'. I don't think she wanted to share the fame much."

Charlie rationed a spoonful into Tyler's bowl. "That ain't gonna cut it."

"Keep your britches on, I ain't done yet. You know, I'll never forget the first time I tried this stuff. She brought a fresh batch by that day after you scored the winning touchdown in the championship and ruined your knee."

"Yep, I remember that. She knew I loved it. Every time I mowed her yard she would have a bowl of puddin' and a cold Dr Pepper waiting on me."

Charlie took a large bite and sat staring at the faded floral wallpaper. "I never knew that," he said, smacking. He slurped some milk. The glass seemed to fall hard on the table. Without looking up at his son, he continued. "They say memories can either be a blessing or a curse."

Tyler studied the marks on the old table. As if reading his mind, Charlie spoke into his bowl as he positioned another bite.

"My God, where did all the years go?"

Tyler woke to the sound of a cardinal singing outside his window. In the brief few seconds before he opened his eyes, he was a child again. Conditioned thoughts trafficked in quiet reminders being whispered from his mind to his heart. Sunday mornings were always thick with the smell of pancake batter being browned, fresh sausage from Renfro's split and sizzling in shallow water, and the enveloping warm smell of roast coffee. It was a symphony of delicious fragrance accompanied by the rhythmic turn of his father's newspaper and backed-up by melodious sounds of country gospel on the radio. He could still hear the shuffle of his mother's house shoes from the refrigerator to the stove and her sweet voice humming "Amazing Grace."

Tyler opened his eyes to the thought that his mother didn't make the coffee this morning. He could smell coffee, but no pancakes and sausage; a stern reminder that something had changed and someone was missing.

The cardinal sounded even closer now. He rolled over and looked out the window to locate the bird. His eyes drifted out across his father's half-acre garden. The winter garden was never as bountiful as the spring garden since only half of it was being worked. How would he ever do it all on his own now? Would he even try anymore?

He watched a squirrel playing in the red oak and saw old Speck sitting patiently below, ears cocked, tail wagging occasionally. A flutter caught his attention. There on the bird bath was the cardinal. It turned in circles and chirped, as if complaining that the bath hadn't been refilled. Even the birds missed her.

He rose, stopped for a cup of coffee, and went through the quiet kitchen toward the sound of the morning news. The floor of the pantry squeaked and the old Frigidaire hummed as he stepped through to the living room. His dad spoke without taking his eyes off the TV.

"Did you get some coffee?"

He raised his cup and nodded as he flopped into the large recliner that still had the sewing kit on the floor next to it. "Have they found anymore pieces?"

"Helicopter crashed; killed one of the search teams. That's number three." Charlie got up and shuffled past him without looking, his coffee cup leading the way. "I need another cup of Joe."

Tyler watched a little longer, then walked out onto the porch to sit for a spell. He watched the gentle lap of waves on the shoreline and took a deep breath of the East Texas morning air.

The old shoreline held many fond memories of long, carefree summer days where he would run up and down in his cutoff blue-jean shorts, barefooted and shirtless, his skin toasting golden brown in the unforgiving sun, catching his own crickets and selecting the best cane pole from the bunch that lay drying on the floor joists under the house.

He thought of Karl's comment about how Jeanie used to look so in love with him. It had been in the back of his mind since he'd heard it. Along the shoreline in front of him, several years ago in the spring of his life, he'd walked hand in hand with Jeanie Stinson with his heart pounding. They had walked over to the point and sat in the tall green grass watching the evening sky heal from a midsummer storm. The colors were still vivid in his mind, as was the comfort of the cool breeze and the promise he shared with his first love that day.

She had told him that she loved him, and she promised she would wait for him and never marry another. He had found an old beer tab and placed it on her finger, and he quietly stayed in love all the way through high school despite the jealous intrusions of Terry Radcliffe who had always wanted her for himself. Now Terry had her.

A twist of fate had taken his future and placed her in the arms of his once best friend. He grew angry thinking about it, and about how it seemed he'd been cheated out of everything he ever wanted. He walked out to the truck, poured a shot of bourbon in his coffee, and stirred it with his finger.

Charlie walked out onto the porch and sat in the love seat next to the wall. "So I 'spect you'll be headed south today."

Tyler turned his rocker sideways so he could see his father, who was sitting like he always had with his legs crossed and his hand with the coffee cup draped across the top knee. "I'm not much in the mood to travel today. I'll probably just head out first thing in the morning."

His father's top leg began to bounce slowly, and his eyes seemed to light up a little as he lifted his cup to his mouth. "Maybe you could help me fix that toilet in my bathroom. The damned thing runs constantly. I think it needs new guts."

"Yeah, sure, I can run to town in a bit and grab a kit. Do you think Medford Hardware is open today?"

"They'll open after lunch. His wife runs the store on Sundays so he can fish. She always meets her girlfriends at the Diner for lunch. Your momma and I used to go there on Sundays too. We always watched them sitting together on the long table by the salad bar, cackling like a roost of hens. Your old girlfriend Jeanie was always there. Your momma used to say the same thing every Sunday. "Things might have been different if Ty would have married her.""

Tyler stopped rocking and sipped his coffee. "Dad, was Momma disappointed that I married Rachel?"

"Oh, no, Son, she loved her to death; we both did. I think she just always took to Jeanie like the daughter she never had; seeing her grow up and all."

Tyler stood and turned toward the shoreline. "I sure do miss Momma. Trying to stay busy and keep your mind off it just don't work. It's like something or someone catches you the minute your thoughts get idle and whispers to you that she's gone."

When he realized what he said might have hurt his dad, Ty turned to show his sympathy. Charlie buried his emotion in his coffee cup. "I've got sausage from Renfro's in there. I was thinkin' of whipping up a batch of drop biscuits and having you grab a fresh jar of Momma's pear syrup from the back closet."

Tyler dropped his head and nodded. "Sounds good."

AFTER EATING, THEY WASHED THE dishes and moved to the den to relax for a spell. Charlie looked at the clock. "Oh heck!" He grabbed the remote and started flipping channels rapidly until he found what he was looking for.

"That's Dr. Stanley, isn't it?"

"Yep. Old Liver-lips, as your Momma used to call him. She sure liked his preaching; said it was well prepared and easy to follow. Him being Baptist didn't hurt none either, I 'spect."

"Yeah, I 'spect not. Do you remember when we used to watch the Jubilee every Sunday morning, Dad?"

"Sure do. I wish it was still on. That was some sure enough good music."

They turned their attention to the preaching. The strong and reassuring voice of Dr. Stanley saying, "Now listen," was like the comforting drone of a car engine to a restless baby.

TYLER HADN'T REALIZED HE WAS dozing, and he was startled when his father stood to walk out onto the back porch.

"Well, I think I'm gonna put my boots on and head out to do a little work in the garden. I need to check on my sweet potatoes."

Tyler stretched for a moment and looked around at the empty house, then followed his father out onto the back porch. "I'll go with you and give you a hand."

~ 17 ~

Many years had passed since he'd thrown on the boots to help his dad in the garden. Back then, his mind worked on his future as fast as his hands worked the soil. Today, his mind was empty, vacant like his soul, and it was all he could do to keep pace with the sound of his heartbeat.

He moved about pulling weeds and cleaning up around the sweet potatoes while his father moved over to work on the turnip greens. "Do you think you'll keep the garden going, Dad?"

"Oh, I 'spect so. It won't need to be as big as it was anymore." He bit a turnip, shook his head and spit. "Seems like yesterday I was worried about making it bigger. I always pictured you and Vince having a gang of rug rats that I'd have to holler at to stay between the rows."

Ty looked up and smiled but his father was bent over inspecting his greens. They worked on silently, listening to the cardinals and the mockingbirds, and to the tearing sound of weeds separating from the ground; both of them moving in rhythm with the earth, both, no doubt, contemplating what the future held for Charlie Morgan and his garden.

A sharp pain in his knee pulled him out of his blissful trance. As he stood to stretch and check his progress, he realized he'd been hearing the dog barking for some time. He looked over to see his father sitting with his arms wrapped around his knees, listening, smiling, and looking up into the tree tops with the sky reflecting off his glasses.

"Sounds like Speck's got that old fox squirrel treed again. It's the funniest thing to watch that squirrel a-teasing him. He'll run down the tree just a-shakin' his tail and barking to beat hell. He gets as close as he can just so he can drive that dog crazy."

Charlie held one finger up and wiggled it back and forth. Ty laughed and went to give his father a hand up. They walked together out of the garden, welcoming the cool breeze off the lake. The sun came and went through lazy, late morning clouds. Shadows flashed across the yard as if snapping photographs to be retrieved some time later in life when Tyler Morgan would walk the garden alone.

Speck joined them from his hunting trip as they washed up in the outdoor sink that Charlie had fashioned with a garden hose. When he'd finished, Tyler rolled his sleeves back down and patted his dad on the back. "Well, I guess I'll head to town for that toilet repair kit."

"All-righty. If you take a notion, you oughta stop and grab some of Maggie's meatloaf while you're there. She still makes fresh fried okra, cream corn fresh off the cob, and fresh purple hull peas with cornbread to go with it. I'm sure you haven't eaten like that in quite a spell. It'll do you good."

Tyler smiled at his father. "Okay, maybe I'll do that. Sure you won't come with me?"

"Naw, I got some mail to go through, then I think I'll warm up something while I throw some fresh greens on for dinner."

"Good enough, I'll be back in a bit." Tyler starting walking off, then turned back to his father who was gazing out at the garden with his hands on his hips. "I love you, Dad."

AFTER PASSING BY THE HARDWARE store and finding it still closed, Tyler headed for some lunch. He reached Maggie's Diner a little past noon and found a booth with a window to the street. He ordered a Coke and inquired after the meatloaf and fixin's that his father spoke of, and sure enough, it promised to be just as he'd described.

The place was mostly full and noisy with the after church crowd, but it wasn't long before a laugh echoed across the room that tickled along the shoreline of his memory. He was looking out the window at Alman's Home Furnishings where he'd worked during the summer before his senior year. The job had been fun except for the backbreaking chore of delivering sleeper sofas. He could never figure out why Alman insisted on keeping the sleepers on the second floor. When he heard the laugh again, he turned to find where it had come from.

He looked toward the salad bar and tried to study the diners at each side of the long table of women without being too obvious, but to no avail. There were just too many people coming and going. The waitress came by with his Coke and directed him to the salad bar for his salad and bread. He nodded and waited for a moment, then slid his flask out of his pocket and dropped a little bourbon into his Coke to take the edge off. As he sipped his Coke, he wondered what he would say if he saw her.

He looked at his reflection in the window. He was still a good-looking man, but he could have aged better if he'd really cared. Finally, he decided that it probably wasn't even her and that he was being foolish.

He threw his napkin onto the table and headed straight to the salad bar. Without looking around, he grabbed a plate and started loading up. He dared not look up, but his ears were sharply tuned to the voices at the table. Steam rose in a thick cloud from the hot rolls as he lifted the lid. He dug down a little and picked one out that looked extra buttery. He was having no luck deciphering voices from the nearby table and was beginning to feel silly again, so he headed back to his table.

Thoughts of laughing down old dirt roads with Elroy Lumpkin in the furniture delivery van mixed together with the wonderful flavors of fresh spring onion and deviled eggs as he worked on the last few bites of his salad. He'd all but forgotten about the familiar laugh when he heard the shuffling and scooting of chairs that announced the large table being emptied. He glanced up but was quickly blocked by the waitress wearing a large grin and asking him to move his salad plate so she could spread out his lunch.

By the time the waitress quit asking questions and stepped away, he saw that the table had been cleared out. So much for auld lang syne. The knot in his chest released, and with a deep sigh he bowed his head to bless his food.

~ 18 ~

Jeanie Stinson-Radcliffe washed her hands and dolled herself extensively in the mirror before stepping out of the bathroom of Maggie's Diner. She'd seen a man at the salad bar whose frame and disposition had sent an instant tingle through her body, but she hadn't been able to study him long. There was something about the way he stood, always leaning on one leg or the other, that created an aura of exceptional agility and athleticism; and there was something about the manner in which he used his hands, precise like a surgeon, that feathered along her spine and entered her chest like the first cool breeze of autumn.

The bright glare from the street and the rising steam from the hot rolls had made a cloudy silhouette of him, and by the time she'd broken away from Annie Boyd's long dissertation on why teachers should still be able to paddle, he had disappeared.

She opened the bathroom door and walked slowly through the diner, casually glancing from table to table, feeling her heart sink a little lower with every step until she decided it was all a foolish whim. She figured she had no business getting excited about seeing him anyway. Sadly, she was a married woman with enough problems already, and probably no jewel in the eyes of man who lived around tanned, hard bodies at the coast. She let out a resolute breath and quickened her step toward the door.

As she neared the door, she took one last casual glance down the window line, and there he was again, the lithe figure from the salad bar, sitting in a booth next to the window. Could it really be him?

All the years rushed by in a whirlwind. Her soul was soon flooded with memories; the long walks by the lake, the promise made in the midsummer of her life under a late afternoon, kaleidoscope sky; the beer tab ring which she still had in her keepsake box stashed away in some forgotten corner of her closet; chasing each other through the woods on their motorcycles in the early evenings of summer with a newfound sense of freedom, while contemplating possibilities of love as they flew through the explosion of fireflies at dusk like a spaceship at warp speed careening through the universe.

She stopped, fidgeted for a moment, and then pushed on the door. As she started to move out onto the sidewalk, her heart budded open, sending waves of anxiety through her body. Her arms weakened against the growing weight of the door, and she found herself back inside. Unsure of where her spirit was taking her, she stepped cautiously toward the man with curly hair tumbling out from beneath his cap. As if watching herself from afar, she saw her hand falling upon his shoulder.

"Tyler?"

"Jeanie!"

He almost lifted the table off the ground trying to stand up and give her a hug. She laughed and all of her anxiety drifted away. She spoke into his ear as he hugged her. "I'm so sorry about your mother."

"Thank you, Jeanie."

"I'm sorry I didn't get to come to the funeral, Ty. Terry had a convention in Las Vegas and wanted me to go this time."

"It's okay, I understand. I know how much she meant to you. Please, sit down."

She glanced around the restaurant briefly, then sat across from him. A sudden awkwardness flushed over her. "It's awful about the shuttle."

"It's terribly sad. I can't believe we lost another one. Dad and I were fishing when it happened. We heard something big fall into the lake close to us."

"I was in town shopping. Can you believe all the pieces that fell around here? Especially at the airport; it's a wonder that no one got hit by anything."

"Some people seem to think it was another terrorist attack; something about a bright flash like a rocket just before it broke up. You know one of the astronauts was Israeli."

She paused, looking into his eyes for a moment, as if reveling in the freshness of his face, and trying on old feelings to see if they still fit. She wanted to find a way to break the small talk and reconnect, but maybe it was too soon, or maybe she was afraid of what she might start feeling again.

"Oh my Lord, do you think that's possible?" she offered.

"Who knows? I doubt we'll ever know the full truth anyway."

She watched as he mixed Miracle Whip into his meatloaf. A smile came across her face and she relaxed further.

"You know, you're still the only person I've ever known to mix mayonnaise with their meatloaf."

"Best way to eat it. It has to be Miracle Whip, however; mayonnaise just doesn't do the trick." He looked up and grinned.

"How are you, Tyler?"

"Like my momma used to say, I got up this morning; a lot of people didn't."

"I know it must be hard, Ty. I couldn't imagine losing my momma right now."

"Thanks. I just wish I could've made it here in time. Not getting to say goodbye is the hardest part."

As he went to take a bite, she noticed a shimmery glow to his eyes. Her heart clutched, seeing he was trying hard to swallow past the lump in his throat.

A tear formed in the corner of her eye and she tried to wipe it away quickly before he saw her. She noticed everything about Tyler Morgan; it had been that way as long as she could remember. She loved to watch ideas form on his face, and she was mesmerized by the strong, yet graceful way his body moved when he skipped rocks across the lake;

his bronzed skin glowing in the amber light of sunset; that old straw hat and the cutoff jeans; and always, always chewing on something; a straw, a blade of long grass, or his nails, as he conjured up visions of what the future would hold.

"How's your daddy, Tyler?"

"As well as can be expected I guess, but he's taking it hard."

"I need to go out and see him."

"He'd like that. He poured another shot of whiskey from his flask into his Coke and she cringed a little.

"Ty, I think good friends are an important part of the healing process. I think they're even more important than family in a way. You expect family to be there by your side because they're going through the same thing you are, but when a friend takes the time to show you their love and support it's something more of a gift, and the gift is healing."

Tyler smiled. "That was beautiful. Come out and see him, Jeanie. I'd like it, too."

Her tears came harder and she dove into her purse for some tissue. "I should have been there for you, Tyler, and I should have been there five years ago, too."

He stopped eating. "Hey, it's okay."

"No, it's not. I wanted to come to you, but he wouldn't let me. I should've come anyway. Anyone can see you are still tormented. You didn't get to heal."

Tyler's face flushed as he held a deep breath. She could feel his pain mixing with a desire to reach across the table and hold her, and it only made her want to cry more. He sighed and shook his head. "It's hard to heal when you don't know all the answers."

She wiped her face and reached her hands across the table to him. "Tyler, I just want you to know that I, well, I think it's just awful, the things that people were saying, and I never believed it for a minute. People can be so cruel. I mean, it's hard enough without all that. It's not fair what some of us have to learn to accept."

"I appreciate that, but you never learn to accept it. You just deal with it, and live in eternal confusion trying to figure out why things happen the way they do. Some days are better than others, but no day is as good as it could've been."

"Does it ever come back to you? Do you ever remember anything more?"

"Nah, it's always the same. It starts out clear, then ends abruptly; nothing but a blank screen."

"Ty, I know you would have never been careless with them. If it's any consolation, I know it wasn't your fault. You just gotta have faith. The good Lord will clear it all up when it's time."

He released her hands and sat back with a long sigh. "It's been five years, Jeanie. I can't for the life of me figure what He's waiting on."

"Maybe He's waiting for you." She could see her words sinking in as he paused and stared out the window. She stared at his profile for a moment, at the muscle flexing at the corner of his jaw, and the sweet spot just below it where she used to place little kisses.

"Enough about me." He turned abruptly before she could dim her admiration. "Karl tells me that you and Terry have been having some troubles."

She began breathing again as she pulled her hands off the table and stiffened her posture. "Nothing we can't handle. I'll have to talk to Karl about spreading rumors."

"Rumors? What rumors?"

She started feeling nervous, fidgeting with her tissue, and looking around.

"You know that thing you said before about friends? It goes both ways, Jeanie."

"We've been going through some rough times, but I'm sure it'll get better soon."

"You know, a good friend once told me it ain't fair what some of us have to learn to accept."

"I didn't say ain't." She forced a smile.

"Is it true? Is he hitting you?"

She looked away from him, threw the Kleenex into her purse and started trying to zip it up but the zipper was stuck. Tears were beginning to pour from her eyes again.

"Jeanie."

"I have to go, Ty."

"Jeanie, wait. It's been so long."

"Please, you're going to make a scene."

"Meet me later then."

"I can't. I'm sorry, I have to go."

He stood and grabbed her arm, and she looked back over her shoulder. "Jeanie, you can't let it go on. You've got to do something about it. I'm here to help you."

She waved her hand in front her face to blow away the liquor from his breath. "There's nothing I can do, and it's not like you can help me, so just let me go before you cause a scene."

~ 19 ~

Tyler released Jeanie's arm and stood watching as she walked out the door, bumping into Karl as he was walking in. A familiar pain echoed deep within his heart. Karl strolled up to the table with his thumbs hooked under his gun belt and a big smile on his face. "Well, now, what was that all about?"

Ty sighed and raised his eyebrows. "I'm not sure, but I think I screwed up."

"Did you try talking to her about Terry?"

"Yeah. She clammed on me."

Karl slumped. "Well, heck, what did you expect? I asked you to talk to him, not her. I guess she'll be giving me a piece of her mind here directly."

"Yeah, I guess she will."

Ty took a drink of his Coke and looked out the window for her. Karl smiled and shook his head. "If I'm not mistaken, I think I see something brewing in your eyes, and I think I like it."

Tyler felt a bit frustrated as he went back to eating his lunch. "So what brings you in here, Karl?"

Karl defrosted his gaze and shook off his thoughts to address what he'd come to talk about. He slid into the booth where Jeanie had been sitting. "I was looking for you. I guess you heard about the helicopter crash."

"Yep." Ty slipped his flask out of his pocket and dropped a little more hooch in his Coke where the waitress had refilled it.

Karl pulled off his cowboy hat, squinted, and scratched his head. "Damn, Ty. It's not even one o'clock on a Sunday."

"Yeah, well, I had to take a break and get some sleep; otherwise I wouldn't have stopped last night."

"Very funny. Anyway, what I came to tell you is that one of the divers who was assigned to do the searches on the north end of the lake was killed. He was in that helicopter when it crashed. They want to get someone on it right away so I told them about you; Navy certified and all. They want you to show up at Ewing Park tomorrow at eight. The pay is damn good."

"Forget it."

"What?" Karl looked confused. "Why?" He sat up in the booth and rested his elbows on the table. "Do you know what kind of money you're passing up?"

"Karl, I appreciate you putting in the word for me, but I've got to get out of here, man. This pitiful town is killing me."

Karl narrowed his eyes and snapped, "I beg to differ with you, my friend. I think the only thing killing you is you. What the hell is so bad about the town you grew up in?"

"Look, don't take it personal, Karl, but it makes me sick. Every time I look up, some busybody is whispering about me, 'There's the murdering drunk.' Nothing changes; no one has any intestinal fortitude, and everyone is on a Radcliffe payroll someway or another."

Karl grimaced. "Oh come on."

"No; it's disgusting, Karl. Jeanie is letting Terry beat the crap out of her, everyone knows and nobody does a damn thing about it. It's the same as when my grandfather was killed. Like my daddy said, you can't fight big connections in a small town. It is especially true when nobody in that town has the guts to stand up for what's right."

Karl pulled off his hat and examined it. "What happened to you, Ty? I know you've suffered a great deal, probably much more than most, but healthy people bounce back from that kind of stuff. I know your momma taught you better than that. She certainly helped me. Besides, you used to always be a little crazy and take on challenging things just to make life more interesting."

"You live in the past, Karl. I was a different person then. We were kids; grow up! This whole damn town needs to grow up."

Karl frowned with disappointment as he slid his elbows back off the table and sat back. After a moment he laughed.

"What's so funny?"

"Do you remember the time you concocted that scheme to keep us from having to go to school? We dug that hole at the bus stop and covered it in pine straw, and when the bus came around, it fell in." He laughed more and Ty finally looked up. His stern glare slowly melted into a grin. "Seemed ingenious at the time, but I didn't think about the fact that everyone would know it was me who done it since the bus was stuck in front of my drive."

"Your daddy whooped both us, then we had to fill the hole with tablespoons."

Tyler smiled as he took a drink. "I had blisters bigger than Dallas for a week."

Karl continued. "What about that time you were feeling adventurous and got me to go out with you in that little plastic boat you got for your birthday? We paddled that damn thing all the way to Hog Wallow 'cuz you said you knew where the fish were."

"Hey, we caught fish, didn't we?"

"Yep, we sure did. We almost turned over three or four times, too, then that thunderstorm popped up on us and the waves almost swamped us. We had to tote that damn boat over our heads for two miles down the shoreline in the pouring rain. You said it was our Navy Seal training." He laughed.

Tyler grinned and looked into his old friend's eyes. "I remember stopping about halfway and sitting under the boat listening to it rain. After the wind blew through, the lake had laid out flat and the rain was coming straight down as big as marbles. We worried about whether we would end up going to Vietnam, and what it would be like to kill somebody."

"I'm glad we never found out."

"Me too." Tyler took a deep breath. "Thanks for the memories, but all of that doesn't change anything. Like I said, I was a different person then. I had dreams, and I had no idea that everything I cared about would be taken away from me for no reason. The sad thing is, even if I wanted to try to make it all change, being back here has only reminded me that some places don't accept change. People would rather talk about what's wrong than work to change anything. You don't think I see them pointing fingers at me still, after five years? Yet, what do they do when someone truly evil, like Terry Radcliffe, attacks one of them directly? They scatter and hide like little rats and whimper to each other. So you can have your ratty-assed little Radcliffe-ville, I've got clients to take fishing and an independent life to get back to where I never have to kiss a Radcliffe's backside."

"Now, old buddy, I'm kinda taking your words a little personal here."

"Take it however you want, Karl, but you have to ask yourself if you really make any difference. You work for a man who gets his campaign money from Lester Radcliffe. Do you honestly think you can do anything around here that Radcliffe doesn't approve of?"

Karl sighed and looked at his hands as he rubbed his thumbs together. "So you think you're doing a lot better by drowning yourself in whiskey while you're here, then running away as soon as you can? Maybe folks around here can't figure out how to fight back, but at least they haven't run away."

"Screw you, Karl. If I was the law, I'd be nailing Terry for his drug-running and put him under the jail for hitting Jeanie. As for Lester, somebody needs to knock him off his damn high horse.

"Look, as far as I know, Lester hasn't broken any laws, but I understand why you have a hard-on for him. Listen, Ty, sometimes being the law makes it harder for you to do what you know is right. You, on the other hand, have a little more wiggle room to try to make a difference, but you don't have the balls to hang around here and stand up for your own father, for Jeanie, or for yourself."

"It's got nothing to do with balls, Karl."

"Call it whatever you want, buddy, but when the cards turned for you, you couldn't stay here and face your demons and try to make a difference. You're the one who hasn't changed. After all you've seen since you've been back, you still just want to self-medicate with your booze, make your sideline judgments, then run away back to your carefree life of no responsibility where you can feel sorry for yourself the rest of your Godforsaken life."

Tyler exploded across the table and grabbed Karl by the collar. "It is Godforsaken, and you got no idea what it's like. I shouldn't even be alive." He squeezed harder and gritted his teeth. "Who the hell do you think you're talking to?"

Karl turned his head to avoid the cloud of liquor as he lifted his hands in the air. He gave Ty a second to settle, then looked him in the eye. "That's what I'm trying to figure out."

They stared eye to eye for a long moment before Ty released him and sat back. He turned and waved for the waitress to bring his ticket as Karl stood. "I've lost family too, Ty, and I lost my best friend when you left and you've never looked back. Do you think that feels good?"

Tyler took a long drink and looked out the window as Karl sighed and turned his hat in his hands. "You know Ty, Sometimes we get so caught up in our own pity that we forget the people who love us and need us. I know where all of this is coming from. I know this is not about you and me. You're just letting off a little steam and I don't blame you. For God's sake, your momma just passed away and you didn't even get to say goodbye. Terry stole the greatest love of your life, and now he's abusing her. Your dad got screwed out of his job and all of his retirement funds by Lester, and don't think I don't know how it feels for you to cross Joshua Creek and think about the most horrific day of your life. After all, I was the one who pulled you off that limb thinking you were dead."

Ty looked around as he was speaking as if to say he wasn't listening until he heard something about his dad's retirement funds. "What did you say? What do you mean, my dad got screwed out of his retirement funds?"

Karl sighed and flopped his hat on the table again as he sat. "I thought you knew."

"No, hell no. What's this about?"

"The letters went out last week. The development has been shut down."

Tyler pounded the table in frustration and leaned back with a sigh. "I saw a letter on Dad's desk. He said it was a statement on his retirement investment, but he didn't say he'd lost it." He pulled out his flask and poured more bourbon.

"Maybe he hasn't had a chance to look at the last one yet. Ty, the RRC project is bankrupt."

"Bankrupt! Hell, they haven't even started building anything."

"The letters say the money is all gone."

"But how? I can't believe my dad would even invest with Lester."

"Well, plenty of people did. I expect your dad did because it was the only way he could regain some ownership in your family's land and have something to pass on to you. Before he was asked to retire, Lester convinced him and all the employees to funnel their retirement into the project for part ownership in the resort."

"So what happened to the money?"

"I'm not sure, but I suspect it has a lot to do with the fact that he hired his friends to do all the development work. As you know, they cleared all the land, built curbed roads, ran electrical lines, and the whole bit."

"My God, Karl, they started clearing land five years ago before I left."

"Yep, he started clearing land on his own before he formed the corporation, but I hear what you're saying. It should've taken a few short months to get it ready, and nowhere near what it cost, but they kept making changes. Then someone discovered that the site work wouldn't support the architect's drawings for the hotel and marina without a substantial investment in additional foundation work and drainage control. When that work was done, there were no more funds. They had planned to get financing from CNB for the main construction, but

CNB pulled out, so Radcliffe bankrupted the corporation." Karl leaned in to speak lower. "Besides that, we both know he's always wanted your daddy's land to build the marina. The location is perfect, being right next to the cove."

"Yeah, I remember. That sorry sonofabitch; I can imagine the kickbacks he got from his buddies. So now what happens to the 146 acres?"

"Radcliffe sold it to the new corporation for twice what it was worth. The terms were 50% down and the rest of the payments due in monthly installments after the place opened for business. He had a clause in the contract that said if the corporation failed to make the payments, he would reassume ownership of the property, but since the business went bankrupt, it accelerates the clause."

"How convenient; that sorry crook. Are the owners going to sue?"

"I doubt it. No one can afford representation, and most of them work for him so they'd be jobless if they tried. If they did happen to find someone to take on Radcliffe and his slew of lawyers, it would have to be on contingency, and by the time they paid all the expenses and gave the lawyers their cut, there wouldn't be enough left over to make it worthwhile for them."

"So that's it. That bastard gets his land back with all the improvements and now he can finance the construction with his buddy Marion at the State Bank and own the damn thing straight out."

"I'm sorry; I thought you knew, Ty." The waitress brought his ticket and he counted out some bills while deep in thought. Karl straightened his collar and put on his hat. "Look, I'm sorry I said those things, Ty. I hope you know I'm your oldest friend and I . . ."

"Forget about it, Karl. I guess I deserved it. No need to say anything more."

Karl stood to leave. "She still loves you, you know. Anyone could see it. Think about that diving job. The Moore farm is on the list of dives thanks to the report you gave us. I would think you'd find that dive especially interesting. You can let me know in the morning. If I don't hear from you, take care of yourself and stay in touch, old friend."

Tyler was steaming by the time he got in his truck to head home. He slammed his fists into the steering wheel and cursed. He pulled out his flask and finished it off, threw the truck into reverse, and skidded out.

He pushed back his anger long enough to let Mrs. Medford sympathize with him about his mother's passing while he bought the toilet repair kit, but he was seeing red again when he stepped out the door. With dark blue clouds looming on the horizon behind him, he put the pedal to the floor and pointed the truck into the sun.

By the time he reached the house, Tyler was cooling down, but he'd already come up with at least five ways to brutally murder Lester and Terry both. He stopped on the porch to take a deep breath and prepare himself for a talk with his dad.

The smell of greens boiling with ham hock filled the house as he stepped inside. He raised the bag into the air to say he'd gotten the repair kit when he saw that his father was slumped over in his chair asleep. When he walked closer, he could tell he had been crying. He was clutching something made of fabric that appeared to be homemade. He started past the chair to take the toilet parts into the bathroom and accidentally kicked a bag on the floor. He looked down to see that it was his mother's sewing kit.

On the table in front of his father was an opened letter. Tyler looked at it and saw that it was from the RRC. He scanned it and stopped at the words "Filed for Bankruptcy."

The anger returned. He put the repair kit on the counter in the bathroom and headed back to his room. He pushed open the door so hard that it bounced off the wall and came back and hit him, which only made him madder. He grabbed the bottle of Dickel off the dresser with a wild sweep of his hand. One of his trophies fell over and his Bible crashed to the floor, releasing a folded piece of paper that flew out and danced across the room. He kicked at the Bible in disgust and stepped over to the window.

As he stared out his window, he filled a juice glass with bourbon and emptied it once for Lester, once for Terry, and once for himself. The Morgan curse was alive and well. His mother was taken by it, his brother was mangled by it, it claimed the lives of his wife and son, his father was still being punished by it, and now Jeanie was slowly being beaten by it every day just because she had loved him. He turned and threw the glass, smashing it against the wall heater. With the bottle in his hand, he slipped out the back porch and wandered past the garden and across the field behind it, all the way out to the white oaks of Joshua Creek, tracing his own footsteps down the path he'd run many times as child, and drowning himself in sour mash.

~ 20 ~

Tears began pouring down Tyler's cheeks as he stepped down into the creek, trampling small bushes and vines underfoot. The trail he'd walked a million times as a child was grown over and almost unrecognizable, but he didn't care. He made his way along the creek for a few yards stomping and cursing until his foot got caught in a blackberry vine, sending him tumbling down into the dry creek bed. His knee caught a tree root on the way down and he rolled around in the creek bottom in agony.

He squeezed his bad knee and gritted his teeth, then let out a gut-wrenching yell. He cursed everything and everybody as his whiskey emptied into the dried leaves. His mind filled with the long series of disappointments his life had been as he looked up to the sky with rage.

"So, you're waiting on me, huh? Well, here I am! You destroy my brother, take my future away from me, and if that ain't enough, you give my first and only true love to a beast who beats her." He sat up with his fists raised to the sky and screamed as loud as he could. "What do want from me?"

He lowered his head and dropped his arms into his lap, breathing heavily. "I don't understand. I finally find love again, make a beautiful son, and you take my family from me. How could you? Why did you take my mother after making her suffer for so long? My poor dad, pushed around all his life by that evil bastard Lester, yet he has everything and we have nothing. Why, God? Why would you let such bullshit happen?"

He looked around for his bottle and found it empty. Growling like a mad man, he smashed it against a tree, cutting the back of his hand.

He rolled around in agony, crying, yelling angrily, and pounding his fists against the ground. "What's the freaking point? You've made everything I've learned about you seem wrong. Where's the reward that was promised?" In anger, he tried to run up the creek bank shouting at the sky. "Why don't you just take me? All you've ever done is punish me. Well, I'm through. What the hell do you want from me? Bring it on."

He stepped onto the soft lip at the top of the bank that was covered in leaves and rolled back down into the bottom. He laid there for a short while with his face in the dirt, his knee aching wildly, waiting to see if anything else was going to start hurting. He rolled over and looked up at the sky. He was weary inside and out, and feeling broken down to nothing.

"I need something, God. I need something to give me a reason to go on. If you're really up there, now's the time to either help out or take me. Just strike me down and end it all because all of this just ain't worth it." He struggled to his feet, dragged himself up the creek bank, and sat on an old hickory stump where he used to sit as a child, .22 rifle in hand, waiting for a fox squirrel to challenge him.

He thought about how life seemed like a magical place back then, full of mystery and golden promises. He thought of all the wonderful dreams that had slowly died, one by one. Like finding Fletcher's gold, they had all just been the foolish dreams of a naïve child. His life had become a nightmare instead. He took some leaves and wiped the cut on his hand, it was just a scratch.

Tyler put his head down on his arms and cried while visions of those he'd lost replayed in his mind. What hurt more than anything else was the feeling that he hadn't been good enough or strong enough, or smart enough to prevent the horrible things from happening that destroyed his life. He couldn't do anything to save his knee, he couldn't stop Jeanie from leaving him, he couldn't protect his wife and son, he couldn't save his mother, and he couldn't prevent his father's financial demise.

THE SOUND OF THUNDER ROLLED out of his dreams and into reality as he lifted his aching head to see the dark clouds above him. He didn't know how long he'd been asleep, and he had no idea what time it was. A strong breeze entered the woods, howling and rustling toward him like an invading army. He rolled his head back and closed his eyes, waiting for its stiff, cold breath to lift his hair and put its hands around his neck.

The wind began to swirl in gusts, over-stretching the open arms of the white oaks that creaked and moaned under the stress. He could smell rain and the rotting corpse of the earth where it had been wetted upwind of him. The naked limbs above him rattled and crashed together like a herd of stags doing battle. Through the rolling canopy he could see the sky to the north was badly bruised.

As he stood to get a better look, he heard a gushing, gurgling sound and watched as a small wave of muddy water pushed across the dry leaves and sticks, making its way down the creek. He'd always wanted to see the first push of flood waters as they announced the coming surge, and now he watched as the boiling water carefully surrounded the whiskey bottle he had smashed, slowly pushing it along and washing it away.

He made his way up out of the woods and followed the wood line down to the road as the rain began to fall. He thought of his cursing to God and wondered if this was his answer; more rain. The sound of rushing water was growing with intensity as he limped toward the bridge. By the time he stepped out onto it, the rain was coming hard and heavy. The creek was flowing fast and he could clearly see it rising, swelling above the midpoint on the bank.

He was beginning to shiver a little as he walked up the small rise overlooking the creek where the monument had been placed. He stood before it, reading the words for the first time. It had been his mother's idea, placed there on the anniversary of the accident almost eight months after he'd left for the coast without looking back.

Rachel Marie Morgan   Jake Henry Morgan
1969 - 1998   1994 - 1998

"In loving memory of our beloved wife and mother Rachel and our beloved son Jake whom the Lord took home all too early.

We carry you with us wherever we go.
We were blessed to share your love. May God delight in you as we have."

He fell to his knees and stared past the monument to the last place he'd seen his family. How odd that he'd been gone so long only to return at the precise time that another flash-flood was threatening. Mesmerized by the torrential current building below him, he slipped down the bank by the bridge and sat near the water's edge, staring into the churning water as his mind drifted back to the day he lost his family.

TYLER'S FEET WERE GETTING WET. As he came out of his deep trance, he realized the water was rising extremely fast. More water poured into him as he tried to climb the bank. He lost his grip on the grapevine he was trying to use as a handle and slid backward into the water. The current begin to take him. Before he knew it, he couldn't breathe and he was under water, tumbling and disoriented.

His body bounced off something large and solid and it sent him busting up through the surface. As his head poked through the murky boil, he saw the approaching arm of a huge white oak limb, and with all of his might he lunged for it, smacking into it with such force that it knocked the wind out of him.

He struggled to find a grip as the current seemed to tug harder and harder at his body. His mind began to race. He couldn't breathe. How stupid could he have been to be where he was. His arms began to tire and he couldn't seem to lift his legs from the water. He felt a presence as if he was beginning to watch himself, and he knew the battle was almost lost.

He closed his eyes, praying for strength as he focused on clinging to the powerful limb of the large tree that was his lifeline. A thought entered his mind. *This is it. So this is how I go, hanging on to the same limb that miraculously saved my life five years ago. Maybe I was supposed to go then, maybe that's why I have been in Hell. Well, you know what? Fine by me God! I ain't got nothing left. It's all up to you, You want me, you got me.*

He began to feel a great sadness as he closed his eyes and remembered his mother's words, recounted to him by his father.

"Lord, take my life, for it is yours. Do with me as you wish. If this is how I should go, then take me now, but what a shame because I never got to do anything for you. If you have other plans, then know that I'll let you lead me to do your work." He heard a soft whisper like someone blowing in his ear, and he remembered hearing his mother's prayers as he lay in the hospital room. Suddenly, there was a loud crack and a splash. He strained to see back up the creek and saw a good-sized tree headed toward him.

Could he have been wanting for it to end this way all along? He always felt he shouldn't be alive. Did he somehow bring himself to this predicament by some sort of subconscious premeditation?

He clenched his body and rabbit-breathed in anticipation of the pain. He could see in his mind's eye his body being ripped apart by the rapidly approaching tree and churned under the rushing current. He only hoped he'd be knocked out before he had to experience such a horrific death.

In a flash, all of his battles on the football field came back to him in a medley of memories, all tied together in a common emotion. A swelling came from deep within that he quickly recognized as his survival instinct. As the tree hit him, it slid under him and lifted him from the water, giving him the extra boost he needed to sling a leg over the limb. With all the strength he had left, he curled himself over the top.

He rested for a moment, listening to the victory that was his breath panting inches from death. Once his body began to feel real again, he inch-wormed his way back to the trunk and dropped down onto solid ground. He lay there still in shock with the words repeating over and over across his lips, "Thank you, Lord, you must want me alive for some reason. You lifted me up. Thank you, Lord."

In a short while, he had regained some of his strength. He rose and walked back up to the monument, fell to his knees, and cried. His tears came harder than the rain. For a long time he cried, letting five years of pain and denial flow from his heart.

When the tears and the rain had all but smothered the fire inside him, he grabbed the granite rock and slowly pulled himself up, kissing the stone as he stood. "I love you, Rachel. I love you Jake-o, my sweet son. I pray that I may know you again. Please forgive me for causing your lives to end. I'm so sorry."

Tyler started down the stone steps feeling weak and hopeless, his legs still wobbly from holding on so long against the current. *Well, God, you finally got my attention. You got me talking to you again. Don't waste it this time. You might not get another chance.* He missed a step, causing his legs to split apart. A menacing pain shot through his groin as he slid down the small rise. He rolled a couple of times and came to rest in a muddy ditch where something sharp stabbed his hand. He jerked his hand up, but there was no blood. Curious, he dug into the mud and withdrew a shard of hard plastic. As it washed clean in the rain, he could see it was a piece of taillight. He studied it for a moment, then rose and shoved it into his pocket as he started back home.

Mud caked on his boots, making them heavy as he trudged across the field and headed back toward the house. He had been handily defeated, but at the same time, he knew he was a survivor, and not just physically. Each step brought a new resoluteness about his existence.

For the first time in as long as he could remember he felt like he was supposed to be alive. The adrenaline rush had brought with it reminders of his innate ability to overcome adversity, and of the sheer joy he derived from victory. In his heart was a certain clarity that he was a vastly different man from the one who stomped to the creek in a drunken rage.

There was a distantly familiar calmness about him, a quiet confidence he hadn't known in a long while. Hope returned to his heart as the heavy rain cleansed and humbled his weary soul.

He was battle-hardened and scarred, like he had been through Hell and back, like he used to feel after a long, hard-fought game in the cold, wet autumn of his youth when the quest for glory was all about football and the battle was all about pride. Win or lose, he'd always been proud that he'd given it his all, and he always had the cuts and bruises to prove it. What did he have now? What should he feel? He hadn't been giving it his all; he'd been running like a coward, hiding behind the booze, and feeling down on himself like some kind of bench warmer with no pride nor confidence, just waiting for the game to end.

By the time he reached the garden, the rain had stopped and the sky was beginning to open up. The world was bathed in a yellow-green light as he stopped and rested against the garden fence post. He fell to his knees and placed his hands on his thighs to stretch his back. Tired and humbled, he studied the finely set rows of greens and sweet potatoes delicately placed by his father's hand and freshly watered by the hand of God. Words began to pour into his mind as if they were spoken by another.

"The pain that was trapped inside has come to the surface where it's been transformed to physical pain; and now that pain can heal and you can live according to your purpose. That's what you have now, clarity, singularity of purpose. You have been purified. Take care of your father and rescue your love. Go fight the good fight and know you've given it your best shot. Feel the glory of battle once more."

THE FOOTPRINTS BETWEEN THE ROWS, left by him and his father, were almost washed away, just like the whiskey bottle he carried to the creek. He looked up to see a rainbow arching over the house, and he laughed. "Okay, that's a little melodramatic, don't you think?" He shouted to the sky.

The cardinal returned, landing on the garden fence a few posts down from him. He watched as it fluttered around to find a comfortable spot, then shrilled out a crisp, clear whistle that broke the silence of the dripping earth. Old Speck walked out to the garden's edge, shook himself, and sat looking at Tyler, blinking with a pleasant pant as if to say, "Hey, dummy, don't you know to get out of the rain?"

As he took a deep breath and stretched his groin, a rush of serenity come over him. He suddenly realized that for the first time in five years, he was feeling calm, reposed, and tranquil. The urge to grab a bottle to numb the pain seemed completely foreign to him, almost sickening. He was disgusted just thinking about it. With Speck following closely, he walked to the edge of the house and looked down at the lake. A curtain of tears, kissed golden by the late angle of the sun, fell from the pines between him and the shore; and behind them, the water was relaxing after its stormy surge, lapping against a fresh, new shoreline of leaves and straw. The world smelled clean, purified.

He walked through the back porch and kicked off his shoes. He could smell something warm and delicious coming from the kitchen as he stuck his head in the door.

"Hey, son, where have you been? I looked all over for you."

"I went for a walk."

"In this storm? Are you nuts?"

"Not anymore. I went down to the crossing, Dad."

His father tightened his jaw and nodded as he looked him up and down.

Tyler frowned and shook his head. "I didn't know it was coming and I got caught out in it. I'm going to wash up and put on some dry clothes."

WHEN HE RETURNED TO THE front room, his father was eating from a large bowl of fried okra and watching a movie. He poured some off into a smaller bowl and offered it to Tyler.

"Hey, Ty, come get you a bowl of this okra. This is *Tombstone*; you ever seen it? Val Kilmer makes the best Doc Holliday I ever seen."

Tyler smiled and took the okra. "It's my favorite movie, Dad. He saw the brown canvass his father had been clutching earlier lying across the table. "What is that anyway, Dad?"

"Your momma made that for me. It's a rod holder. She never told me she was making it. I found it in her sewing kit as I was going to put it away."

Ty picked it up and inspected it. "Wow, that's pretty handy."

"Ain't it nice? You know I was always complaining about how my rods were all cluttered up and always in the way. I guess she got tired of my whining."

"I guess so." Tyler noticed that the RRC letter had been put away. He searched for a way to start the conversation. In a way, it was none of his business. He didn't know what to say, so he let it ride and enjoyed the movie with his dad.

After a short while, he went back to his room to throw on a warmer shirt. The shard of tail light was sitting on the desk. He picked it up and studied it again, and decided to keep it with him as a reminder that he was putting the problems of the past behind him. From now on he wouldn't run from his troubles and drown his sorrows in whiskey. From now on he'd fight the good fight and accept both defeat and success with dignity and grace.

He saw the Bible on the floor and picked it up. As he did so, he caught his reflection in the mirror. An old thought recurred to him. *You can do this Tyler, with God's help you can do anything.* He searched for the paper that had flown out, and found it under the corner of the bed. He started to put it back inside the Bible when he realized he didn't know what the paper was. He sat on the bed and laid the Bible next to him as he unfolded the paper and started reading. It was in his mother's handwriting, and he couldn't remember ever seeing it before.

> To Tyler from Mother,
> Son, if you are reading this I have probably gone home. I know this stuff will come back one day and

I don't think I will have the strength to beat it again. As God is my witness, I will give it my best shot, but just in case He has other plans for me, I wanted to say some things to you that no one would know except you.

You see, Tyler, I asked God to reveal this letter to you when he knew the time was right; when it would do the most good. So, when you read this, take note of what is happening in your life. I will bet God is already preparing you.

Do you remember what I told you when you hurt your knee? When things look the bleakest, when you feel hopeless and think you can't possibly go on, that's when you know He is with you, that's when it is time to pull yourself up by His robe and start fighting. When you do, all the angels in heaven will fight by your side.

Your daddy needs you now more than ever, Ty. Vince, God bless his sweet soul, lives in his own world, and your daddy has no one left but you. He has sat by and watched as Lester Radcliffe slowly stomped his family into nonexistence. If I'm right, they will still be vying for whatever he has left. You are all that he's got. He's not a fighter, but you are. I know you still have it in you. They think you don't have any heart left, and they are counting on you to run like you did before. Don't let them take what's left of the Morgan family down without a fight. Remember, you can turn and walk away from an ant pile, but not from a mad dog. Sometimes you have to take a stand and fight the good fight. Good, bad, or indifferent, sometimes you have to see it through until the end. God is waiting for you, son. Always remember my favorite verse and you'll do just fine.

> "Trust in the Lord with all your heart, And lean not unto your own understanding; In all your ways acknowledge Him, And he shall direct your paths."
> God Bless You. I Love You. I'll see you in heaven!
> Momma

Tyler held nothing back as the pain poured out of his heart and onto the letter. He crumbled to ground by the bed and wept.

When he finally rose his stomach was in knots, but he felt renewed again, as if he'd been through an even deeper level of cleansing. He laid the Bible back on the desk and put the note in his pocket. Just before he stepped away, he noticed for the first time since he'd come back home that a picture he'd put away many years before was back on the corner of the chest of drawers. It was a picture his mother had taken of him with Jeanie, standing on a floating sun deck they had made.

A trail of pure gold stretched out across the water from behind them and angled up to the sun above the pines on the far bank. His hair was wind-dried and curly and hers was long and stood out from her side as it tossed in the wind. They both had a look of strength and confidence, of everlasting youth and beauty; naive champions, untested in the battle amid the ashes and the dust.

Tyler opened the window to let in the cool breeze and the smell of rejuvenated earth. He needed a few minutes to just be alone and let things soak in. He took a deep breath, then turned to the bed. He laid back and closed his eyes. Today he'd heard the message he'd needed to hear for several years.

"Thank you, Momma. Thank you, Lord."

~ 21 ~

Tyler rose, returned to the window, and looked out at the garden where his father had been sitting earlier, listening to the dog. Mom was right. Dad was totally lost now. He needed his help. He knew he had to find a way to talk to him about the investment. He needed to find a way to fight back.

In his closet he found an old flannel shirt that whispered stories of hunting trips and Thanksgiving holidays gone by. A stabbing pain in his chest reminded him there would be no more Thanksgiving dinners made by Momma. Such spontaneous and uninvited reminders, laced with lingering sadness, were sure to revisit him for the next few months, as day in and day out, he would likely run across little things in his life that held fond memories of her.

He threw the shirt on over his T-shirt and noticed that the sleeves were too short to button, but that didn't matter. He rolled them a couple of times, buried his nose in the sleeve, and took a deep breath as he headed back to the den to watch the rest of the movie.

His father was stretched out in his recliner with his head supported by one elbow on the arm rest, but he sat up when Tyler entered the room. "They're about to have the gunfight."

Tyler sat down and smiled at his dad. The poor guy couldn't hide it. He had a hole bigger than Dallas in him, and he was trying hard to fill it with the son he'd lost five years ago.

"I got some ice cream in there and some chocolate syrup if you want something sweet."

"That sounds good. I might go get me some here in a minute."

Tyler watched the commercials in silence, going back and forth between the TV and his father's profile. He decided to throw out a comment before the movie came back on. "Say, Dad, I ran into to Karl earlier and he told me that the Radcliffe Resorts Corporation had gone bankrupt. I noticed you had some letters from them around here. Did you have a lot invested in it?"

His father frowned and dropped his head. "I didn't know how to tell you, Son, but I lost everything I had."

The weight of the world seemed to crash upon Tyler's shoulders, and he fought to maintain composure. "Dad, Karl said Lester talked all of his employees into letting him funnel the profit-sharing plan into it, and that he pilfered the money out through a host of contractors who were friends of his."

"Yep, I think that's about the gist of it. Before they let me go, there was a meeting and considerable hype about how much money we all stood to make. We all agreed to let them sell the stocks and invest in the resort." He sighed and rubbed his bad shoulder. "Ain't nothing much we can do now, son. The money is gone."

"Wrong, Dad. I'll tell you what you can do now. You can all get together and sue his ass off."

"It won't do no good. His lawyers are too powerful. Besides, most of the investors were employees whose jobs are even more critical to them now. Like I said before, you can't fight big connections in a small town."

"Dad, for once in your life you have to stand up for yourself; you have to fight just for the principle of the thing. He's been running all over you all of your life. Whether you win or lose, that man deserves to be stood up against."

"We ain't ever been much at fighting, son. Besides, you'll be running back off to the coast soon, and I just don't have anything left to fight for."

"Bullshit, Dad. You've got everything left to fight for because everything is what he's trying to take from you. Lester is a bad man, and he'll continue to do bad things until someone decides they're going to take a stand against him. It doesn't matter if you think you can win; what does matter is that you take action and fight the good fight."

"You can't beat him, son. He's just too big."

"Dad, you're not listening to me. Do you remember when I used to get down before a game when I thought the other team was too big, too fast, and too strong to beat? You used to tell me that it ain't the size of the dog in the fight, but the size of the fight in the dog. Without a fight, he wins for sure, but if we fight, we may just cause things to happen that will bring an end to him."

"I just think it may cause a lot more trouble. People might start dying around here again."

Tyler paused and looked into this father's tired eyes. "Look, Dad, I'm not going back for a few days. I've decided to stay here and help you get through this mess. I was offered a job diving to find pieces of the shuttle, and I'm going to take it." Tyler sat on the table in front of his father and grabbed him by the shoulders. "Dad, all my life I've watched you turn the other cheek and go with the flow. Look at where that's gotten you. I know I ain't been much count these last few years for you and Momma, but that stops today. This man is wrongfully taking what belongs to our family, and there's no better reason to stand and fight. If you don't fight, you'll be left with nothing. We have everything to gain and nothing to lose."

Charlie stared blankly at his son. Tyler could tell that his words had struck a cord, and his father was trying to compute the idea of fighting. "I hear you, son, but I don't know what to do. I've always found it better to put my energy in other directions rather than spend it fighting a lost cause. Aren't we supposed to turn the other cheek?"

"Dad, earlier I found a letter mother wrote me before she died. She had stuffed it into my Bible. What she wrote was eerily well timed, as if she chose this day to reach down from heaven and show it to me. Everything is coming clear to me today.

"You see, most things here on earth require the will of man to happen. That's what changed when Christ shed his blood on the cross for us. God doesn't orchestrate our lives anymore; He waits for us to have the faith to orchestrate it properly for ourselves, and through that faith is where his strength and guidance comes to our aid. It's what the old cliché really means, *Evil flourishes while good men do nothing.* Without us taking action, there's no way to pit good against the evil of Lester's actions, and he will prevail as he always has.

"Dad, except for Vince and each other, we've both lost everything that ever mattered to us. I've spent the last few years punishing myself because I didn't have anyone else to fight. I believe if we don't act, it'll show a lack of faith, and even though I've been a bad example of it, I truly believe that all good things come through faith. I don't know about you, but I'd rather go down as a warrior fighting the good fight than as a victim with no faith."

His father leaned into him and hugged him. Tyler held his father tight, and for the first time since he was a running back, he had the strength and motivation to make a difference.

AFTER THE MOVIE ENDED, TYLER stood and stretched. He checked the time. "Don't they have a service at 6:30?"

"Yeah, I believe they do."

"Do you want to go to church, Dad?"

"No, son, I'm sure I'm overdue, but I just don't feel up to it. You go ahead."

TYLER SAT IN THE BACK, and when the service ended, he waited for the church to clear so he could go up and pray on his own. He sat looking through his Bible for the note his mother had written him when he remembered he'd put it in his front pocket. As he closed the bible, his senses peaked, and the wonderful smell of perfume filled the air. He looked up into the sweet smile of Jeanie Stinson Radcliffe. "Hello, Ty."

"Hey there."

"It's good to see you in church. I think the last time I was able to get Terry to go to church was when I married him."

"That's too bad, but I can't judge him too harshly. That was probably the last time for me as well."

Pleasure exuded from her smile as she sat next to him. She giggled lightly and nudged him with her shoulder.

"I usually go to morning worship, but I was lazy today. You're the last person I expected to see. Are you okay?"

Tyler posted a halfhearted grin and looked down at his Bible. "I had one of those life altering events today, Jeanie. I challenged God and He answered me. He showed me how to forgive myself and take the fight to someone else."

He felt her staring at his profile for a long moment. He could tell her soul had been caressed by the sorrowful winds that blew from his words. His heart was heavy, but the mere presence of this woman who brought the first tingle of love into his life so many years ago was quietly uplifting. "I think your mother would be proud of you. I know I am."

As he looked up, a couple was walking by and stopped to say hi to Jeanie. "Hey, Miz Jeanie, I haven't seen you come by the shop lately. You haven't been letting Rhonda Carlisle do your hair, have you?"

"Oh no, Trisha, I wouldn't dream of it. Are you kidding me? Just look at this mess." She noticed them both looking at Ty as he was flipping through his Bible. "Oh, you guys know Tyler, don't you?"

Tyler stood and gave a nod to Trisha. "Trisha, how have you been?"

"My God, Tyler Morgan, I would never have recognized you with all that long hair. I need to get you into the shop." She laughed at herself as Tyler smiled and offered his hand to Bobby. "Hey, Tyler Morgan. I remember you from the first couple of years in high school, but you disappeared after that."

Bobby stared at him without returning the handshake, and then looked at Jeanie with disgust. "Yeah, I know who you are. Let's go, Trisha. I want to catch the basketball game."

Tyler sat back down and watched as they left.

"Don't mind him. He's one of Terry's hunting buddies. I'm sure I'll get to hear it from Terry now."

"Why do you say that?"

"Don't tell me you've forgotten about the small town rumor mill. We do have a past you know."

"Oh, hell."

"Tyler Morgan! We're in church."

"Sorry."

"You know what, Ty? I don't care anymore. People just need to get over themselves. We aren't doing anything wrong. We're old friends and we're in a church, for goodness sake."

He smiled at her.

"What are you smiling at?"

"Nothing. You just sounded like the old Jeanie there for a minute."

She grinned and looked down at her hands. "Yeah, I did, didn't I? You want to go grab a cup of coffee or something? Terry stays at the club all day on Sundays betting on golf games, and playing poker. He won't be home until after eleven."

"Sure, but I'd like to sit quietly here for a few minutes first if you don't mind."

"Oh, I'm sorry. Here I am going off at the mouth."

"Don't worry about it. Can you wait for me?"

"Of course. I'll be on the bench out front. Take your time."

"Okay."

Tyler watched her leave, then rose and walked to the front of the empty church. He took a seat in the front row and read his mother's letter again. He thought about what his father had said about her final wish, and he knelt and closed his eyes.

Jeanie bounced up from the bench as he walked out the front door of the church.

"Well, did you put in a good word for me?"

"I sure did, believe it or not."

They walked north on First Street toward Nolan's coffee shop, taking in the cool night air and talking about what stores used to be where in the old days. They found a booth near the back at Nolan's, one they used to sit in after games all those years ago.

Tyler Morgan was a man full of fresh new feelings. He could feel his burdens lifting as he looked into her eyes and followed her every word. He felt good about this new turn in his life, about fulfilling his mother's last wish, and about offering his life to God.

After a few good laughs, they paused and sipped coffee. He noticed that she seemed to be trying to work up the courage to tell him something. He smiled to let her know he was listening.

"Tyler, there's something I need to tell you, a lot of things actually, but I don't know exactly how to start."

"I think you just did."

She cocked her head and smiled. "Seriously, Tyler, I owe you an apology for the other day at the diner. I shouldn't have just walked out on you like that."

He put his hand on hers and squeezed it lightly. "It's okay. I had no right to just come straight out and ask you something so personal."

"Yes, you did; you had every right. You just caught me off guard and ill-prepared to talk about it. I didn't know what to do, so I panicked and ran." She paused and looked down.

"The truth is, Ty, he has hit me, and on more than one occasion. At first I thought it was my fault because he was drunk and I pushed him past his limit by getting in his face and asking him too many questions. He was lying to me and I knew it. I badgered him because I was so hurt, and he lost it and pushed me so hard that I hit my head against the bed post. He apologized and bought me flowers, and I thought it was over, but the next time was worse.

"He was drunk and high on cocaine, and he tried to deny he'd been using drugs. I was furious with him, and I was trying to dig in his pockets to find it when he struck me in the face with the back of his hand. That was a month ago and I haven't forgiven him."

"My God, Jeanie, I'm so sorry. Are you still in the house?"

"I sleep in our spare room now. Last week he came home really late again as usual, and he wanted to come into my room. When he found the door locked, he banged on it, and I refused to open it, so he bashed it in. I tried to fight him off, but he kept saying I belonged to him, and he tried to have his way with me. In the scuffle, his elbow caught me in the eye and I had a black eye the next day."

"This sounds so crazy, Jeanie. What's happened to him?"

"He's just lost it. We hit some hard times and the true Terry finally came out. A few months ago we invested a great deal of money into the dealership thinking spring would bring us a boost in business, but this drought really hurt us. His father told him not to go into debt, but he did it anyway, so he was too proud to ask his dad for money when we needed it. We were already over our heads because he had to buy a farm and build the biggest house in Nacogdoches County.

"He tried the bank, but they said he was already too far in debt to qualify for a loan. He was looking for a temporary investor when he ran across Rob Davis, the guy who owns Slim's across the river. Rob lent him enough cash to catch up on his payments, then showed him how he could make a lot more."

"Let me guess; trafficking drugs."

"Yep. Then he started using and he became a monster. He won't admit that he has a problem. I tried to help him, but he's like a completely different man now. Sometimes he acts almost normal, but most of the time he treats me with complete indifference and gives me stupid excuses for staying out late that a complete idiot wouldn't believe. I'm convinced he has a girlfriend."

"Maybe it's time you just got out."

She grabbed a few napkins from the dispenser to wipe her tears. "I've already called a lawyer. Excuse me." He watched as she slid out of the booth and went back to the restroom. After a few minutes, she returned, looking a little more composed.

"You okay?"

"I'm fine. Thanks for listening, Tyler."

"Listen, I want you to know that this crap is going to stop right now. I'm going to talk to Terry and make sure that he never hits you again."

"Tyler, no! You can't do that; he'll know we've been talking. He'll go nuts and do something crazy."

"If he does it again, I'll do something crazy."

"Please, you can't. I'm already planning to talk to a lawyer about getting out. Just let me do it my way."

"That's going to take a long time, Jeanie. Have you at least filed a report?"

"No, but I'll be okay."

"We'll see."

The waitress came by and refilled their coffee. She pointed to the pie case and informed them that the last piece of Dutch apple wouldn't make it through the night and offered to warm it up for them, on the house. Tyler accepted and offered to pay for a scoop of vanilla ice cream to go with it.

"I haven't had Dutch apple since the day before I left for the Navy."

"It's really good here, and the ice cream was a great idea."

The pie arrived and they both dug in. "Speaking of going into the Navy, what ever happened to you that day, Jeanie? Did you not get my message or did you just change your mind? I waited for you as long as I could."

Jeanie set her fork down slowly and looked up into his face. She took so long to answer that his words repeated slowly in his mind until he was beginning to feel bad for asking. Without any attempt at creating drama, he feared he had surreptitiously reached into her soul and opened her secret hurt locker.

Her eyes watered. "I'm so sorry, Ty. I wanted to come, but Terry took off without me and I didn't have a ride."

"But, why didn't you call?"

"I did; I called the house, but no one answered. Then I found the note Terry had left for me. It said that you had asked him not to bring me and that he didn't know how to tell me so he just left."

"Oh my God! Jeanie that was a lie. I was dying to see you."

She pumped her shoulders. "Well, it pretty much broke my heart in two anyway when I found out about you and Stacy Conners. I figured that you had gotten lonely and settled for her."

Tyler's mouth dropped open. He was so stunned he didn't know what to say. "Jeanie what on earth are you talking about? What does Stacy Conners have to do with anything? I was never with her."

"She called me to apologize, Tyler."

He threw his arms upon the table and dropped his head. "So that's how he did it."

Jeanie looked at him as if she had been stabbed in the chest. "You mean it wasn't true? They tricked me?"

She started crying, and leaned sideways onto his shoulder. "Oh my God. All this time it was a lie. My heart has never stopped hurting. I always knew we were supposed to be together, and I just couldn't believe that my heart would lie to me. I'm so sorry, Ty, but I knew then that I had to get over you, and the only way I could do it was to never talk to you again."

He grabbed her hands. "Jeanie, Sweetheart, it was a lie. The thing about Stacy was a lie, and the note was a lie."

She slid away from him in the booth and fumbled with the napkin in her lap. "So why didn't you keep trying? Why did you give up on me?"

"I tried a couple of times, but you never answered the phone. I wrote you three letters and you never answered them either so I finally gave up."

She looked up at him confused and teary-eyed. "You wrote me letters? I never got any letters." Her face contorted violently and she turned away from him. "God help me, Tyler."

He placed a hand on her back. "God help us."

She leaned into him and he wrapped his arm around her. Years of quiet desperation began to unwind inside of him. He wanted to worry about who may be watching, but his heart was finally starting to crank again, peeling off years of protective paint that he had so feverishly applied to prevent his undoing. His heart tickled at the familiar sensation of her affection flowing into him, and somehow it seemed to find the same place that it had occupied all those years ago.

She sat up after a short while and wiped her face. "Do you think we ever know our purpose in life?"

"I used to think so. I used to think my purpose was to be a great football player and loving husband to the girl of my dreams."

She laughed and worked on her eyes some more. "I used to think my purpose was to be a good wife and mother. I married a jackass who hates children . . . so stupid."

~ 22 ~

Tyler woke Monday morning with a newfound sense of purpose. He rolled over and looked out the window across the garden. Everything was fresh and untouched in the lavender light of dawn. He said a quick prayer, slid out of bed and threw on his jeans. When he turned the corner to the kitchen he saw his father standing with his hands in his armpits, looking out the window at the lake. The coffeepot was spurting and gurgling on the counter next to him.

"Good morning, Dad."

"Hey, son, I hope I didn't wake you. This coffeepot is getting old and creaky like me. If it gets to sounding anymore like the damn toilet, I don't think I'll be able to drink the stuff."

Tyler chuckled and grunted a bit as he sat down and stared out the window past his father. He pulled the shard of taillight out of his pocket and rubbed on it as the coffeepot burped.

"It's struggling mighty loud, but I needed to get up anyway. I'm supposed to report for diving duty today, remember?"

"Oh, that's right. I forgot about that. Going to help search for shuttle pieces, are you?"

"Yes, sir."

"I think it's finally finished. What do you want in your coffee?"

"Just one sugar."

Charlie pulled two cups down from the cupboard and spooned sugar into them. "Where will you be diving? Do you know yet?"

"Nah, I don't know where they plan to start us, but I do know that Karl promised I'd get the assignment for the Moore farm since I was the one who knew where the piece landed." His father handed him his coffee and aimed himself into the chair at the table across from him with a throaty groan.

"That ought to be real interesting. Maybe you'll finally get a chance to see that truck you've wanted to see since you were a kid."

"Yeah, I hope so. I'm eager to dive it, but these guys are precise and technical about their recovery operations. I doubt they would allow it."

"You don't say. Well, I 'spect you might be right about that."

His dad looked over the top of his glasses. "What is that you got there?"

"Oh, it's a piece of a taillight, I think. I found it in the mud yesterday down by the crossing."

Charlie grew silent and turned around to grab his paper off the counter. "If I was you, I'd throw that as far out in the woods as I could. It won't do you no good holding on to it, son; just cause you pain."

Tyler sighed and stuffed it back into his pocket.

"You may be right, but it has kinda become a talisman for me. I gotta feeling I should hang on to it for a little longer."

Charlie cleared his throat. "You gonna eat 'fore you leave?"

"Is that biscuits I'm smelling?"

"Yep. I ate earlier, but I saved you a couple, and there's two pieces of sausage left. You want me to throw some eggs into the grease for you?"

Tyler looked at his watch. "No, Dad, that's okay. I'm not real hungry yet, and I gotta hit the shower and hightail it outa here. I'll just stab them biscuits with the sausage and take 'em on the road with me."

"Okay. I'll wrap 'em in napkins for you."

"That'd be great." Tyler grinned at Charlie and nodded. "It's going to be good to hang out with you again, Daddy."

Tyler could tell he caught his father a little off-guard as he watched him stick his chin out with pride and take a deep breath. "It's good to have you home, Son."

TYLER HEARD HIS PHONE RINGING as he was crossing the cattle guard. A doe had run out in front of him as he was headed up out of the ravine from Joshua Creek, and when he hit the brakes, his phone had slipped down from the seat.

He stopped just before the highway and reached down to the floorboard and up under his seat looking around for it. His hand came across the crumpled soft paper that contained his whiskey bottle. He slid it out, opened the top and took a good whiff. His phone rang again, so he put the top back on and threw the bottle in the seat next to him. When he finally located his phone and pulled it out, he noticed his hand was shaking.

"Good morning, Hoss."

"Hey, Karl, I'm just getting to the highway."

"Good. I'm glad I caught ya. Don't bother going to the office. Just head on down to Shirley Creek Marina and I'll meet you there. The ramps on the north end of the lake are all too shallow so they want to launch from the small ramp there at Shirley. Meet me up at the cafe. They want have a meeting to coordinate everybody."

"Okay, sounds good. See you shortly."

"Yep."

TYLER WALKED INTO THE CAFÉ where he'd spent many a Saturday morning as a child. All the tables that used to be occupied by local fishing guides and their hopeful, bug-eyed clients clutching a steaming cup of coffee, had been rearranged conference style. A small group of men were huddled around a large map of the lake that had been set up on a situation board in the corner. Red pins saturated the map in a wide trail across the northern end. Not wanting to interrupt, he shoved his hands into his pockets and leaned against the counter.

As he waited, Tyler looked around the old café and store and took inventory of all the changes. The comic book rack where he used to pore over Sgt. Rock and Sgt. Fury comics as a kid was long gone, as were the rows of tackle where he used to stand with his Texsun orange juice over crushed ice, dreaming of catching the big one while he waited for his pancakes to get ready.

Boston Blacky, as Uncle Joe used to call her due to her jet black hair that was dyed and stacked on top of her head, was no longer at the grill. Everything from the grill to the store area seemed much cleaner and less cluttered. There were no more life preservers or oars hanging on the walls, no fishing nets, ice chests, racks of fishing poles, or bait buckets. A view of the lake still filled every window, but it was like Christmas without trees or lights, the ghosts of fishings past had long disappeared, taking with them all the cozy surroundings of their utilitarian existence. Karl walked in behind Ty and slapped him on the shoulder.

"There he is."

"Hey, Karl."

"Come on, I'll introduce you to the agent in charge."

Tyler followed him over to the group as they were disbanding and finding their seats. Karl walked up to a tall, thin man with curly gray hair and glasses wearing khaki trousers and a white dress shirt under a gray cardigan. "Excuse me, Leonard."

"Oh, hi, Karl."

"Special Agent Leonard Wisilosky, this is Tyler Morgan, the diver I told you about."

"Good to meet you, Tyler, and thank you for coming aboard on such short notice. Our next diver in line was going to be more than a week out, and we just can't afford that kind of delay. Please call me Len."

"Hello, Len, my pleasure."

"We're going to start the briefing, then I'll get with you afterwards, if you don't mind. Please, take a seat."

"Sure, thank you."

Tyler listened carefully as Len explained in great detail the calculations involved in speculating where major pieces of the craft had fallen. They had found many pieces already on the ground, and by working back on their calculations using velocity, weight, wind speed, and currents combined with the estimated explosion pattern, they were able to locate probable areas within the lake for their search zones.

When the briefing had finished, Len came over and sat on top of Tyler's table.

"So, Karl tells me that you dove for the Navy."

"Yes, sir. I am also Combat Diver Certified."

"Wow, the best of the best. So I am sure you are familiar with the protocol here." He looked up and motioned for two other gentlemen to come over. "Tyler Morgan, this is Agent Frank Quintero. He'll be driving your boat and guarding your cargo, and this is Johnny Pargas from NASA, who'll identify, record, and process any pieces found. I understand you have all the necessary gear?"

"Yes, sir, I have my own gear."

"Well, I have to inform you that we can provide gear for you if you so desire, but we're not authorized to reimburse you for the use of your own gear."

"No, that's okay. I prefer to use my own."

"Understood. Well, if no one has any questions, when Mr. Morgan completes his paperwork, you guys are free to launch. Frank will show you to your boat."

Tyler spent almost an hour going through all the paperwork and was glad to feel the wind in his hair as they took off toward the north cut. Frank leaned over and spoke to Tyler over the noise of the wind and motor. "I understand you were raised on this lake." Tyler nodded. "Our first objective is the splashdown that you reported. I have coordinates, but I'm glad to have you aboard. Just point me where we need to go."

"You got it."

They turned north into the long cut that led past Stanley Creek where Tyler and his brother and father had spent many golden days wrestling bass from their favorite and most profitable fishing hole aptly named the Christmas Tree Hole.

He canvassed the area, looking as far back as he could to see if he could spot the old hole. In his mind, he traveled beyond the hole and around the point where the lake opened up into deep banks, stickups, and a labyrinth of willows that outlined the creek that gave the area its name.

It was there as a young boy in the back of his father's boat that Tyler had mastered the art of the trolling cast with a willow-bladed chartreuse spinner-bait. Hitting the perfect spot over a fallen log or next to a large stump had become an art form by the age of twelve. He'd even learned to cast left-handed, thumbing the open face of his bright red Garcia 5500 and starting his retrieve just as the bait was hitting the water. The technique was one his father had taught him to reduce the splash, simulating a spider leaping from one of the many lime-green willows that hung precariously above the pollen-laden water in early spring.

Before long, he recognized the outline of the Angelina River snaking back and forth through the stickups to the left of the cut. Somewhere, in one of those bends in the river, a thousand fishing trips ago, he had hooked into a giant catfish with a white-speckled spoon.

The fish was so large that he thought he'd hung on a submerged stump, and he'd laid down his rod to wait for his dad and brother to make a few more casts before untying to retrieve his lure. When he looked back at his line, he noticed the slack had gone out. As he started reeling in line, he found it so heavy and difficult that he thought he was pulling in a large limb, but when he finally got the fish to the boat and told doubting Vince to grab the net, the huge mouth of the 44 pound appaloosa catfish breaking the water scared Vince enough to make him fall backward into the boat.

Tyler spotted the opening of the river where it intersected with the cut before snaking out through the dead trees again. He tapped Frank on the shoulder. "See that opening there next to the tree with one limb?"

"Yeah."

"That's where we want to go in. You're going to want to slow it way down and take it easy through there."

Tyler talked him through the river a little ways and pointed out where the huge submerged stump was that he high-centered when he and Karl had come through too fast as teenagers. They both had to jump into the water that day to work the boat off the stump, and to his relief, the boat had sustained no damage.

They found the old road bed that led to the main pasture of the Moore farm with no problem and were soon at the spot where Tyler and his father had seen the water boiling a few days earlier.

Tyler motioned for Frank to pull over to a large stump and tie off the boat while he readied his gear.

When he had finished his dive prep, he sat on the edge of the boat and rolled off into the water. Diving freshwater was different; less predators for one thing, and the depths, at least here, posed no threat. The biggest difference that he noticed right away was visibility. The water of Rayburn was rarely clear, but even at its clearest, the visibility was less than ten feet.

With his depth at twelve and a half feet, he began to make out a large, bulky object in front of him. He threw his light on it and it lit up like a Christmas tree. There were two long tubes on each side twisting around a cluster of pumps and metal tubing. From the pictures they had shown him back at the marina, Tyler immediately recognized this was an engine. He took a couple of pictures and headed back to the surface.

As he broke water, Frank and Johnny were leaning over the side. He hollered up at them.

"It's an engine."

Johnny began writing furiously and grabbed his phone to call it in. Frank grabbed a marker buoy and tossed it over the side. Tyler slid the cable through his hands and found the clip at the end. He blew out his lines and went back down to tie the buoy onto the engine. When he reached the surface he checked the sign on the buoy:

KEEP AWAY!
Danger of Contamination!
Do Not Enter Water!
Do Not Tamper with Sign!
Property of the US Government
Violators will be prosecuted to the fullest extent of the law

Back at the marina that afternoon, the pictures posted on the discovery board confirmed his initial assessment. There, next to the picture he'd taken of the shiny mass in the murk, was a photo of the brand new engine taken after it was certified. A sadness came over him. Little did they know when they took that picture that it would end up on the bottom of an East Texas lake. His was the second engine that had been found. The first one had landed at the Nacogdoches airport, but the last one was still missing.

Len came up to Tyler from behind and slapped him on the back as he was looking at the pictures from his and other finds.

"Good job, Morgan. NASA is extremely grateful for all of your help so far."

Tyler shrugged. "Just doing my job."

"Listen, we need to talk before you get swarmed here in a minute."

"What do you mean?"

"KTRE Channel 9 is on their way out to interview you; local boy makes good, large shuttle piece found, etc., and I need to make sure you know what you can talk about and what you can't say."

"Oh, great."

"Hey, it comes with the new job, buddy."

AFTER THE INTERVIEW, TYLER MOSEYED around the marina a little to stretch his legs. He stood at the top of the boat ramp thinking back to the time when a boat belonging to friend of his father slid off the trailer as they were pulling it out of the water. Tyler had been standing on the trailer fender, holding on the boat rail as kids will do, taking a ride up the steep ramp. Charlie was driving the truck and his friend Joe was still sitting behind the wheel of the boat. They had only gotten halfway up the ramp when the boat slid off and skidded a few feet down the concrete ramp.

Tyler remembered bailing out as soon as he felt the boat sliding. When he rose from the ground, the first thing he saw was Joe sitting there casually with a silly look on his face. The cigarette he was about to light was broken and pointing upward where it had smashed against the steering wheel. Tyler was horrified thinking that he was about to hear all kinds of yelling, but instead, Joe just blinked his eyes and grinned.

LESTER RADCLIFFE PULLED UP BEHIND Tyler as he was standing above the boat ramp. He rolled down his window and hollered at Tyler. "Well, I'll be damned. Is that you, Tyler Morgan?" As Tyler turned, Lester watched his smile slowly melt into a glare.

Tyler walked up the car and pulled out his tobacco. "What can I do for you Mr. Radcliffe?"

Lester grinned like an opossum eating acorns. "Now that ain't no way to greet an old friend. I heard you were back in town. Sorry to hear about your momma, she was a good woman."

Tyler spit. "Much obliged."

"I hear you were diving over near the Moore farm today. Did you find anything?" Lester worked to maintain a friendly smile.

"In fact, I did. You'll hear about it on the news tonight."

"I was just curious if you got a chance to see the old truck down there. I've always wondered if it was still there."

Tyler frowned and shook his head, but didn't say anything more. Lester was growing weary of the weight of Tyler's surly expression. He looked away for a moment, then put his car in gear.

"Well, do me a favor and take some pictures of it if you get to see it. I'll pay you for them. That's something I've always wanted to see."

"Maybe I'll do that." Tyler spit again.

Lester started easing away. "Tell your daddy I said hello."

Tyler nodded. As he pulled away, Lester reached up and positioned his rear view mirror where he could see Tyler. "Dammit."

TYLER WAS WEARY WHEN HE got home. Dad was out in the garden, so he moseyed out that way and stood for a moment with his hands in his pockets watching his dad checking and cleaning up around his sweet potatoes. He wanted to help, but the ground was soft, and he didn't have any boots nearby. Speck came up to say hello and kept trying to jump up on him, so he climbed onto the Farmall Cub and grabbed a pinch of tobacco. The sun was almost gone, and as he sat there waiting for his dad to finish, he glanced about the place.

He listened to the echoes of times past as he watched the ghosts enjoying family, food, fellowship and life in general. There were countless good times had in that old yard; times when family and friends would come out to help in the garden and they would all sit around in the backyard shelling peas and listening to the stories of old in the long, sweet, lazy afternoons of early summer.

Daddy and Uncle Bill would fry catfish and bass, and drink beer until long after dark. They all seemed to get happier as the night went on, then someone usually got mad and raised cane about something. The kids would all play hide-and-seek in the nearby woods, and somebody always got in trouble for trying to hide in the garden amid the corn stalks.

Tyler noticed the remnants of the old ice cream maker behind the shed, dilapidated and half-covered in tall grass. He'd learned at an early age how to apply the rock salt so that it didn't get into the cream and ruin the taste. Momma had always wanted to put peaches in it, but none of the kids liked junk in their ice cream. He never remembered the cream ever being ready, just the churning, slow and constant churning that seemed to last forever.

He looked back and saw his dad making his way out of the garden, head down, always inspecting, old Speck walking patiently behind him. When he reached Tyler, he began speaking without ever looking at him.

"Well, how was your first day on the job?"

Tyler was surprised that he even knew he was there. It was as if old Speck had gone out there and told him.

"It was good. I found out what we heard hit the water over at the Moore farm."

"Oh, you don't say. What was it?"

"It was an engine from the shuttle."

"Well, I'll be damned. I'm glad it didn't land on us."

"Yeah, that might of ruined our day."

As he followed his dad into the house, Tyler's phone rang.

"Hello?"

"Hey, Scoop."

"Man, I haven't heard that in a coon's age."

"Ha, I figured you hadn't. I still ain't never seen anybody scoop up a ground ball the way you used to at shortstop. Listen, I wanted to call and see how you and your daddy were getting along, and I wanted to tell you to get your skinny butt over to the Holiday Inn tonight to watch some basketball with me and the boys. Bring your daddy, too."

"I didn't know you liked basketball."

"Hey it's a sport which requires drinking if you watch it. Give me a pitcher and a big screen and I'll watch freakin' lawn bowling."

"Well, thanks, Moose. I appreciate the offer." Tyler said, laughing."

"Hell, it ain't no offer, it's a damn command. You ain't got no excuse. Now, get your butt over there and have some beers with us and let's have a good time."

"Well, since you put it that way, I guess it would be good to see the old gang. I don't know if you can count on daddy, but I'll do my best to get him to come along."

"Kick-ass! We'll see you there, Ty."

"All right, man."

~ 23 ~

Tyler pulled into the parking lot at the Holiday Inn and found a parking place. As he'd expected, his father had bowed out and was going to rub some liniment on his bursitis and lie down early.

He locked the truck, checked that there was nothing in the back that could be stolen, and headed into the Relief Pitcher sports pub. As he approached the door, he heard an angry voice around the corner and a loud slam that sounded like fists being pounded on a hood. He stepped back and walked to the corner for a look.

There were four men standing by a small pickup. One man was leaning with his back against the hood facing the other three. He was rambling on about something while the other three were jeering and barking at him. They were just out of reach of the nearest light post so he couldn't make out who they were. The largest man slammed his fist down on the hood again and started yelling.

"Dammit, I made promises based on what you told me. People are starting to get pissed and I don't like being put out like this. I'm due in Houston Thursday after next. You got till one week from Wednesday or I'm gonna take it out of your hide." The guy leaning back against the hood started whining something, and he was quickly interrupted. "I don't give a shit how you do it, just get it done. I don't want to hear talk. I want to see action. Damn you asshole." The bigger guy punched him, and he fell back onto the hood as the others laughed and hooted. "Let that be a reminder. No talk, just action."

The three men started walking toward Ty, and he waited to see them go under the light. Once he got a good look at their clothes, he disappeared inside the hotel.

There was no trouble locating Moose once he was inside the club. Tyler heard his booming voice over the crowd as he was stepping into the bar. He stopped at the corner of the bar and looked down into the pit of tables situated to face the big screen. All he had to do was locate the biggest guy. Moose definitely lived up to his nickname. He wore an old soiled and wrinkled cowboy hat pushed back on his head with his curly black hair pouring out everywhere, and he wore a scraggly beard that had never really filled out. His arms looked like huge oak limbs jutting out from the sleeveless cowboy shirt that he wore untucked.

No sooner had he found Moose than he heard a voice shouting from below. "Scoop! Hey, there's Tyler Morgan."

He smiled and waved at Kip Reed, the short, but stocky second baseman who was seated with Moose and four others. Moose jumped up and raised his huge arms wide. "Scoop!"

The whole crowd took notice. "Get down here, hero!"

He walked down as some people in the crowd were applauding. He had no idea what was going on. After giving Moose a big hug he got the full story. "Hey, hero, we just watched you on the news. You're a national hero! Way to go, champ."

"Ah hell, that's getting a little carried away. How's it going, guys?"

Moose grabbed the pitcher, which looked like a beer mug in his huge hand, and poured Ty a beer. "Make room, boys!" He shoved a skinny fellow, whom he later introduced as Danny Pitts from the shop, out of his chair playfully and stuck it behind Tyler. He sat and gave them the story of how he found the shuttle engine, and they caught up on some old times as they watched the game.

At half-time Tyler went to the bathroom and was on his way back to the table when he bumped into one of the three men from the parking lot coming around the bar. His red flannel shirt was a dead giveaway. He looked up and they were all three standing there. "Watch where you're going, jerk-off."

Ty stopped and looked the guy in the eye. It was Bobby Buell, the punk from church. He got close enough for Bobby to feel his breath.

"Give it a break, pal."

Bobby cocked his head and grinned. "Hey, Terry, look who's here."

Ty looked up to see that the big guy was Terry Radcliffe. He checked Terry's knuckles and saw where one of them was a little busted. Standing next to him was Doyle Kitchens, the high school bad boy who got kicked off the team for smoking pot on the bus and was always smart-mouthing teachers and getting into scrapes with the law.

Terry squinted and clinched his jaw for a minute as he looked Tyler up and down. Slowly his face melted into a smile.

"Well, I'll be damned. Tyler Morgan, get your butt over here and let me buy you a drink, old friend."

Tyler forced a grin, shot his eyes at Bobby, and stepped up to the bar next to Terry. Terry put his arm around him and gave him a squeeze. "Just look at you. How long has it been now, man? Let's see, four or five years at least."

"Yeah, something like that."

"You still got your business down in Corpus? What was it, a dive shop or something?"

"Yeah, mostly guided fishing now."

"Hey, you hear that, guys? We need to get old Tyler here to take us deep sea fishing. How much does something like that cost?"

"Well, that depends on what you want to go after, but usually about five hundred a day."

"Damn. I'd like to get paid five hundred dollars a day to do nothing but fish." Bobby interjected his two cents, still working at trying to get Tyler peeved, but Tyler only sighed and shook his head. "So would I." He turned back to Terry. "So, how about you? What are you doing these days, Terry?"

"Well, you know, I have the John Deere dealership here, right?"

"Oh, that's right."

"Yeah, well, it's going okay."

"That's good. Boy, I guess this drought has really made an impact on a business like yours."

Terry finally got the bartender's attention and ordered a couple of drinks for them. He turned back to Ty, then looked at his friends and laughed. "You just got to know how to diversify your interests."

They all laughed except for Tyler, who knew exactly what he meant. He watched as the bartender poured two double shots of bourbon.

"Here we go." Terry grabbed the shots and stuck one in Tyler's face. He didn't want to take it, and he damn sure didn't care anything about sharing drinks with Terry, but he'd promised Karl he would talk to him, and he knew that it wouldn't go over well until he warmed up to him a bit. He took the shot and stared at it for a second while he told himself this was an exception.

Terry let out a boastful toast. "Here's to old times, to TNT."

Tyler lifted his glass and clinked it against Terry's. "To TNT. Down the hatch."

They took the shots and slammed their glasses on the bar. Terry motioned to the bartender for another round. "That's right, you're a Navy man. Well, congratulations on becoming a hometown hero. I saw you on the news today."

The longer he stood there, the easier the whiskey went down. Tyler looked over several times to Moose and the gang who were glancing back at him time and again. The game had started back and he really wanted to go hang out with real friends. Bobby and Doyle were steadily eying him, and Terry's friendly act was starting to wear on him. This wasn't the place to have a serious talk and he knew it.

He slapped Terry on the back. "Hey, listen man, thanks for the drinks. It was good seeing you again. Looks like the game is back on." He stuck his hand out to shake and Terry took it.

"Are you sure you won't have one more?"

"Maybe later, bubba."

"Well, maybe we can catch up some more after the game." He felt Terry's grip tighten a little as he spoke. "There's still a lot I want to talk to you about."

"Yeah, sure; same here." Ty returned the hard squeeze and winked. He nodded at Doyle and Bobby, who had started their own conversation while he'd been standing there. Bobby just stared back at him with as much loathing as he could muster. Tyler grinned and shook his head as he walked off. He heard Bobby saying something as he walked away. "Yeah, we'll talk again soon, hero."

When he sat back down next to Moose, he got the third degree from him. "What the hell you doin' hanging out with that asshole?"

He put his arm around Moose. "It's a long story, buddy, but believe me, it ain't for the good company he keeps. What's the deal with this punk Bobby?"

"Look, man, they're all scum in my book. Bobby Buell hooked up with Terry a couple of months ago. He used to go our school but he got kicked out for stealing parts from the auto shop. They met up again out at Slim's. I think he's the reason Terry got mixed up with the dark doings he's into."

"So you know about that too, huh?"

"Hell, everybody knows."

"Well, look, Moose, I had a long talk with Jeanie last night and she told me some things. I'm trying to figure out what I can do to help her."

"You mean about him hitting her? Everybody knows about that, too. Karl's done told her all she's gotta do is file a complaint, but she ain't done it."

"She just wants out, Moose."

Moose looked up at the bar where Terry and his gang were standing, then casually turned back around. "I know you're thinking on talking to him, but don't worry, I got a feelin' he's planning on talking to you first. The way those guys are staring down here, I get the notion they're already on to something about you."

"Bobby saw me talking to Jeanie last night in church. He probably followed us and saw us sitting at Nolan's."

"That'll do it. Terry is as jealous as they come, and those two losers he hangs out with would rather fight than eat. They love to keep him stirred up so they can get their jollies watching him go off. My guess is they got him stewing over you trying to weasel in and get Jeanie back."

"Well, that ain't true."

"Don't matter; it makes for a good reason to fight. You better watch your back there, Scoop."

Tyler was soon distracted by the game and the occasional stories that were tossed around about close games and wild parties by the lake. By the time the game ended, he was feeling pretty stung. He walked up to the bar to pay his tab and get a glass of water. The music was turned up after the game went off and he was signing his tab when he felt someone nudging up next to him. Terry put his hand on the back of his neck in a manner which made him wonder if it was friendly or threatening. His instinct was to employ his training, but when he saw it was Terry, he quickly relaxed.

"What's with the water? You ain't quitting already, are you, Squibby? Hell, I thought you were a champion booze hound."

Ty forced another smile. "I've had enough tonight, man. I'm already on the road to recovery."

"Well, shit, don't take off yet. We're gonna head out to Slim's. Why don't you go with us?"

Tyler shook his head and slapped Terry's shoulder. "Not tonight, old buddy."

"Well, hell, we haven't had time to talk. Why don't we step outside for a minute? This damn music is so loud I can't hear myself think."

"Sure, I'm not leaving just yet anyway."

He nodded and followed Terry through the club. He noticed that Doyle and Bobby were tagging along behind him, and when he passed within range of Moose, he threw a glance his way. Moose had a mug turned up, but he caught Ty out of the corner of his eye and winked.

They stepped out onto the sidewalk, and Terry stopped and shoved his hands in his jacket. He stumbled slightly and took rest against the wall. "Damn, it's cold out here."

Tyler's defense mechanisms came online when Doyle and Bobby circled and joined them, and he was glad he still had his snap.

He glanced at the two vultures, then looked at Terry. "It's been a long time, Terry."

Terry lit a cigarette. "Yes, it has, Ty. I began to wonder if we'd ever see your mug around here again."

"Well, I began to wonder if I'd ever come back, but you know what they say, home is where your family and friends are."

"Oh, yeah; your parents, your old buddies, and your old girlfriends. Right?"

Tyler dropped the smile and clenched his jaw. "So what did you want to talk about, man? We're both a little drunk and it's far too cold to sit out here and relive old times. Why don't we get together for lunch or something?"

Terry stood out from the wall and puffed on his cigarette while his honchos shuffled. "Life's been hard on you, Ty. When times are hard, it's easy to look for someone to blame. I know you must still harbor some resentment for me; not because I did anything directly to you, but I did go on to play ball at UT like we both dreamed, and I did end up with the girl of your dreams." He chuckled. "You remember that time we had just got back from water skiing and we sat in the boat till sunset after Jeanie left? You told me you was gonna marry her someday. You remember that?"

Tyler sported a half-smile and chuckled lightly. "I guess we don't always get what we dream for, do we?"

Terry rubbed his chin and pointed his cigarette at Ty. "No, we don't.

You see, that's just it. Sometimes we get to figuring that we'll never have what we wanted unless we just try to take it."

Tyler was beginning to lose his patience. "Are you trying to tell me something, Terry?"

Terry stepped in front of him and thumped his cigarette into the parking lot. "Okay. Here it is. You and I go back a long way, Ty, and I always looked up to you. Hell, I even wanted to be you at one time. No matter how hard I worked, or how well I played, you seemed to always get the glory. But now, Ty, Jeanie and I are happy, and by God, I want it to stay that way. Do I need to say anything else?"

Tyler glanced at Doyle and Bobby, who were stiffing up. He remembered the incident earlier in the parking lot and recognized the patterns. "What are you going to do, Terry? Punch me, too? Do you think people don't know what you're up to? You think they don't know you're hitting your wife? Look at yourself, man. Look where you are. Is this really where you want to be, and who you want to be? You used to be the best friend I had in this world, and now I barely recognize you. You took a wrong turn, pal. You don't need to worry about me. You need to worry about yourself. You need to get your shit together before you're in too deep. You've got too much to live for to be doing the shit you're doing. What the hell are you thinking?"

Terry stuck his chin out and clinched his fists. "I was trying to give you some slack, Morgan. I know what you're up to. The tables have turned. Now I'm the one with the glory, and all you got is your bottle and your fishing pole. You think you're gonna weasel in here and reclaim your glory by any means you can? Well, I'm gonna tell you one time and it's gonna be the last time. Bobby here seen you with my wife yesterday looking mighty friendly. You stay the hell away from her or I'll rearrange that pretty face of yours and send you back home in a body cast."

Ty sprang into Terry and slammed him against the wall with a thud that seemed to shake the building. He pressed him against the wall in a sleeper hold and spoke right into his ear. Behind him, Ty could hear a commotion, but he was focused on Terry. "If you ever hit Jeanie again,

I promise you're gonna get to take your best shot because I'm gonna come after you with everything I got, and buddy, all Hell is gonna rain down on your ass." He squeezed tighter. "Are you hearing me or do I need to leave a reminder on your face the way you did that poor bastard earlier?"

Terry squirmed and chirped, then finally nodded. Ty released him and immediately looked behind him as Terry slid down the wall. Moose was standing in a half-squat with Doyle's head under one arm and Bobby's under the other.

"Hey, Scoop, thought I'd just even up the odds a tad for you." He bumped their heads together just hard enough to stun them and they fell to the ground. Tyler smiled and shook his head as he walked over and shook hands with the big guy.

"Thanks, bud, I owe you one."

Terry climbed to his feet and his two goons scrambled to his side rubbing their heads. Ty stared at them as he loaded a dip of Copenhagen and spit. "You jackasses had enough or do you want to finish what you started?"

Bobby popped off as he took a couple of hesitant steps forward. "Oh, we'll finish it. You can bet on that, asshole."

Terry grabbed his collar and pulled him back. "You're gonna wish you had finished it tonight, Morgan, while I was good and drunk. Next time you won't be so lucky, and that time's coming."

Doyle lit a cigarette and put in his two cents as they started walking away. "You can bring your big ape with you next time, too, 'cuz I got something for his ass."

As they watched them moving away around the corner, Ty and Moose turned abruptly to the sound of a car pulling up behind them. The lights on the cruiser were flashing red and blue beams across the parking lot as it came to a halt next to them.

Karl got out with a crooked grin on his face and walked up to Ty with his hands on his hips. "What's going on here, guys?"

Moose grunted. "Oh, just taking out the trash."

Karl smiled at Moose and accepted his outstretched hand.

"Moose, thanks for looking out for him."

"I'm gonna' head back and finish my beer. See ya later, Scoop."

"Okay. Thanks again, Moose."

"Scoop? I ain't heard that in a long time. So is this what you call 'talking to Terry'?"

Ty frowned and slid his hands halfway into his front pockets. "Hey, man, he didn't even give me a chance."

Karl waved his hand in front of his face. "Damn, Ty, how much have you had to drink? You smell like a dad-gum distillery."

"What, are you gonna make me walk a straight-a line now, Karl?"

"Hell, I know better than that. You ain't never walked a straight line. So talk to me. Is that blood?" Karl walked over to the wall and examined a trail of blood smeared down the wall. "Ty, you're treading on thin ice. You gotta stop with the drinking. You got too bad a temper."

"I did stop."

"Well, it sure don't smell like it to me."

"I didn't want to drink with him, but I had to warm up to him."

"Well, it looks like that went over well."

"He called me out here to talk; said it was too loud inside and he wanted to catch up. I figured I could catch a dip for a minute, so I obliged. He started in right away trying to beat around the bush and hint about me seeing Jeanie. I told him he didn't need to worry about me, that he needed to get his shit together because he was blowing it. After that he came straight out and threatened me. I guess I lost my temper."

Karl sighed and pushed his hat back on his head. "Good thing Moose showed up. That Doyle's been known to be pretty good at swinging some steel around." He sighed. "Well, I guess this was a dumb idea to begin with. Maybe I need to start leaning on him myself. Listen, you drew blood. He's gonna use it against you, so be ready."

"Yeah, well, he can bring it all he wants. By the way, I found out what happened between Jeanie and I that ended everything."

Karl cocked his head. "You don't say."

"I had a talk with her after church the other night. It seems that Terry concocted a story that I had left her for Stacy Conners."

"You're kidding! I can't believe she would fall for that."

"He had Stacy call her to apologize."

"You're shitting me!"

"Nope."

Tyler sighed and shook his head. "Something else you should know, Karl. When I pulled up here, I heard a commotion around the corner. When I went to take a look, I saw those three ganging up on some guy in a small red pickup with a camper. Terry popped him pretty good. He was yelling at him about not coming through for him. He said he had till Wednesday week to come through or he was going to take it out of his hide."

Karl looked up and scratched his neck. "That'd be Joe-Glenn Hill. He used to be a top notch mechanic but he's been a heavy boozer for the last five years. I figure him for the runner. Boyd Hicks said he seen him twice lately, way up in Rusk. That's a long way from home for a swamp rat like him. They've been busting meth labs left and right up there."

"Looks like you got your hands full, old buddy. Say, did you have any luck getting that list of RRC investors?"

"I found out who can get it for you, but you're not gonna be too happy about it." He grinned. "I can't have nothing to do with it, so you're just gonna have to suck it up."

"That could only mean one thing. Stacy."

"Yep."

Karl broke out laughing. "I'm sorry. I know it ain't funny, but I couldn't help it."

"That's cool. I should've figured as much. I guess I'll go ask her for it tomorrow."

Karl got serious and stared at Tyler for a moment. "I hope you know what you're doing. This is nothing short of declaring all-out war on them and they got a mighty big army."

"It's gotta be done, Karl. A man's gotta stand for something."

Karl sighed and slapped him on the shoulder. "Just be careful."

Tyler smiled. "No problem."

"Be careful driving home, too." Karl hollered as he walked back to his car. He stopped next to his car and turned back to Tyler. "Wait, put your head back and your arms straight out to your sides."

Ty shot the finger at him and they both laughed.

"I got your back, brother." Karl touched his hat.

Tyler nodded and spit.

~ 24 ~

Tyler was standing at the end of the marina staring at Terry's yacht when he heard his phone ring. He saw that it was Karl and waved goodbye to Frank as he headed back up the hill.

"Hey, bud."

"Hey. They all just left to go out on Terry's boat. They're gonna have a poker game this evening. Now would be a good time for you to go see Stacy."

"Yeah, I was just standing right in front of his boat and there was a guy in there setting stuff up and getting it ready to go out. Thanks, I'll go and see her right now."

"Oh and listen to this, Ty; rumor has it that she and Terry pretend to go to breakfast once or twice a week, but they really go to the boat for a morning romp. Floyd Newman says they manage to get that big-assed boat rocking sometimes, and you can sit and drink coffee at the café and see ripples coming out of the marina when the water is dead still. That's just in case you need a little help persuading her to cooperate."

Tyler laughed as he crawled up into his truck and fired up the engine. "You gotta be kidding me; thanks, man."

"Don't you love small towns?"

"Home sweet home."

Tyler pulled into the Ford dealership and strolled across the showroom, slowing to look in as he passed by a red and white Mustang GT500. He could only see one salesman, and he was with a customer. He slipped up the stairs and walked up to Stacy's desk. She was turned toward the filing cabinet looking in the mirror she had hung there with double-stick tape and talking to one of her girlfriends on her cellphone.

"And listen to this, he said there's a convention in Nebraska next month and we's gonna pretend were going to it, but he's gonna take me to Tahoe instead." She squealed, and Tyler cleared his throat, making her jump like she'd seen a ghost, and sending her phone flying across the floor. Blushing, she hurried over to it and picked it up. "Sherry, I gotta let you go; there's someone here."

He watched the terror in her face melt away as her expression transformed into the sultry look of temptress. With a wink and a smile, she snaked up to him. "Why, Tyler Morgan, to what do I owe this honor? My, oh my, how long has it been?"

"Hi, Stacy. It's been too long, that's for sure. Get over here and give me a hug."

She responded gladly with a quick kiss on the cheek and a tight squeeze. She stepped back, straightened her skirt, and tossed her hair. "Just look at you, boy, you're still just as muscular and fit as you ever was."

"Oh, I got a few more pounds on me, but look at you, still built like a dirt dauber; big at both ends and little in the middle."

She giggled and squirmed, then sat back in her chair. "Lester ain't here. He went fishing with Terry."

"Yeah, well, I'm not here to see Lester. I came to see you." He grabbed her left hand and rubbed his thumb over her ring finger. "I can't believe you're still single. I figured somebody would have gobbled you up a long time ago."

"Nope. I'm hard to get. Oh, listen I'm sorry to hear about your momma. I always liked her since when she carried me to the hospital that time Bernie Wascum took a handsaw to my arm for telling on him.

You know I still got that scar?" She held her arm up to his face where he could smell her perfume.

"Yeah, you sure do, don't you? Listen Stacy, I came here to talk to you about something important that's bothered me for many years."

He leaned over her desk and cut down the space between them. Her eyes grew a little bigger as she relaxed a little and started to grin. "Tyler Morgan, what are you doing?"

"This is serious, Stacy. I know you haven't seen me for a long time, but I've been through a lot lately and it got me to thinking. You remember when you led on like you and I were fooling around together the year after high school?"

She bobbled her head a little, not knowing how to answer and looked down. "You still mad about that?"

He put his hand under her chin and lifted her head.

"You know what, Ty, I was young and stupid then, and . . ."

He put his finger in front of her lips and cut her off.

"Shshsh. I'm not here to settle a score. Granted, it screwed up my life, but I'm here to tell you that I forgive you and that I want to give you a chance to make it up to me."

She raised her eyebrows and grinned. "Really?"

"Really. You see, after all I've been through, I feel like life is too short to carry a grudge, and it's also too short not to live every moment with the one you truly love." She squirmed some more and melted a little closer to him. He ran his finger down her nose and rose up. "Here's the deal. I know how you feel about Terry. I heard you talking just now on the phone, and I heard Floyd Newman talking to some old guy over coffee this morning about slipping up to Terry's boat and listening to you two making love on those early mornings down at the marina."

She sat back as her eyes popped and her jaw dropped. "Stacy, I think you deserve each other. I saw him the other night at the Holiday Inn, and after he got a few drinks in him, he just couldn't shut up about you. Hell, I feel like I've seen you naked myself."

She gasped. "Tyler Morgan."

He winked and shrugged. "But don't worry." He leaned on her desk again. "I've still got the hots for Jeanie and he's got it bad for you, so if I can take her off his hands, you two can be together."

She pursed her lips and squinted. "So, what do you want me to do?"

"Well, I figured that I could get her real easy if I just told her that you two were screwing around, but then I started thinking that I should give you a chance to make up for what you done and not be vengeful." She started nodding.

"Listen Stacy, It just so happens that my daddy wants to put on a little shindig out at our place for all the RRC stockholders to help get their mind off their losses, and I knew that you could get me a copy of the list. I know it ain't much, but at least it's a token of forgiveness and that's enough for me."

She smiled and shrugged, looking a little disappointed. "Sure, if that's all, I got it right here."

Tyler saw where the RRC files were when she opened the file cabinet to retrieve the list. He started thinking he would really love to be able to go through the files and make copies of anything that might be evidence before Lester had a chance to shred them. He could send them to Pat Horton, a lawyer from Victoria whom he'd taken fishing many times. Pat loved to get after the bill fish and had offered his services many times if Tyler ever needed legal help.

When Stacy walked to the copier to make a copy of the list, he followed her and stepped up behind her.

"You know, Stacy, I've got to be honest with you. When I finally got over being mad at you about telling that lie about you and me, I started kinda wondering what it would've been like if it was true."

He slid his hands around her waist, and she leaned back into him as she hit the button to make the copy. He spoke softly into her ear.

"I never told anybody, but I always had a little crush on you in high school, so I began to wonder what it would be like to just get crazy with you one time."

He nibbled on her ear, and she spoke with a shiver in her voice. "Well, we got time now. Ricky is the last one here and he's probably about done with his customer."

"He won't come up here?"

"No. He's a freak. He always runs home to watch his pornography."

Ty paused for a moment, trying not to laugh. "How's about we fulfill a little fantasy for each other, sexy girl?"

"Oh, yeah." She squirmed.

He whispered in her ear as she gave him the copy. With a playful purr, she went into the conference room, and began taking off her clothes. He started closing the door behind her.

"I'm going to wait a few minutes until you are on the table so I can walk in and act surprised."

"Oh, how fun!" She gave him a devilish grin as she unbuttoned her shirt and he closed the door. He went to the file and pulled out all the files for RRC, put them into his jacket and rolled it up under his arm. He hurried downstairs and found Ricky tidying up his desk and sorting some paperwork.

"Hey, Ricky?"

"Hey, do I know you?"

"No, I was bringing something up here for Stacy. She asked me to tell you to meet her in the conference room right away."

Ricky looked at him, puzzled. He winked at him. "Believe me, judging by the toy she bought, you need to hurry."

He smiled and walked out.

Tyler pulled over across the street where he could see the conference room window. It took a couple of minutes before he saw the light come on. After he heard a muffled scream, he laughed and headed for home.

Almost a week had gone by, and Ty had contacted everybody on the list. The papers he'd faxed to Fitzgerald and Horton had been made into transparencies, and Jeanie had managed to get the meeting hall at the church. All he needed now was for Pat Horton to call with the good news that they would take the case. The meeting was set for tonight, and he hoped that everybody would overcome their fears and get fighting mad once they saw the evidence.

Ty put everything in his briefcase and walked back into the kitchen. "Whatcha' cooking, Dad? It sure smells good."

"Oh, I got a little deer shoulder slow-cooking in that electric skillet over there with spring onion chives, and I got a bit of mashed potatoes and some string beans with bacon and onion. Do you want some cornbread with it?"

"No, that's too much trouble. It sounds good enough as it is. I can't wait."

Ty sat in his customary place at the left side of the table near the door and watched as his father proudly shuffled back and forth tending to his masterpiece. His daddy was always proud of his cooking but was his own worst critic. Everybody at the table could be bragging on him and he would still say something like "Well, it ain't as good as I've had, but I reckon it'll make a turd." That was a sure sign he hadn't yet gotten all the compliments he wanted.

"So where did you dive today?"

"They moved us to the cut yesterday."

"You didn't get a chance to explore the old truck?"

"No. I tried, but I didn't get to spend any time on it. I asked to go back down, but they said it wasn't authorized. It's a shame being how it was so close to us, but it wasn't inside the radius of the authorized dive and they keep things super tight."

"Well, I guess they have to do it that way to know what they got."

"Are you coming to the meeting with me, Dad?"

Charlie put the lid back on the skillet and sat at the table crossing his long legs. "Oh, I guess I will. Aren't you worried about Lester or his boy showing up and causing a stink?"

"I thought about it, but I can't let that stop us."

"I still don't know what good it's gonna do. If I know that bunch, they'll find a way to scare the dickens out of these folks and that'll be the end of it, but like you said, I guess we have to try." He stood with a gentle moan and shuffled over to the refrigerator. "You gonna want sweet milk or buttermilk?"

"Sweet milk. You know I ain't never learned to drink buttermilk."

He watched with a look of disgust as his daddy filled a glass with ice and poured the thick, clumpy buttermilk over it. After he took a long drink, sporting a milk mustache, he poured Ty's milk and set them both on the table. Ty smiled.

"Got milk, Daddy?"

"Huh?"

Charlie laughed and wiped his mouth.

~ 25 ~

There were several cars in the parking lot as Ty and his dad pulled up to the church. They went inside and greeted all the investors. After the room had filled to capacity, Tyler got everyone's attention and called the meeting to order. Just as he was about to begin, the door creaked open and in walked Jeanie.

A murmur grew from the crowd when they saw her. She walked timidly around the back as if she were wearing a scarlet letter.

Ty motioned to her to come up front. "Jeanie, there's an empty chair up here."

She walked slowly to the front, dropping her head occasionally under the weight of all the eyes upon her. A voice from the crowd rang out. "What's she doing here? That's the crook's daughter-in-law." The heckler was joined by an affirming chorus.

"Now hang on a minute." Ty raised his voice to get everyone's attention.

"Jeanie is a stockholder, too, and she happens to be the one who arranged this meeting place for us."

She whispered to Ty, "That's okay, I can leave."

Another voice rang out, "How do we know she ain't a spy?"

Ty looked at her. "Do you want to tell them?"

She quietly pulled off her sweater and draped it over the back of the chair. With a deep sigh, she looked down at her hands as she turned the ring on her finger. With another deep breath, she turned and walked over next to Ty to address the crowd.

"I believe what's happened to you folks is wrong, and I don't want any part of it. I lost some money in this investment, too, but Lester paid us back and that wasn't right. Of course it wasn't the exact amount, and he called it a loan, but that's when I knew for sure it was wrong. If it's anyone's business, I plan to leave Terry. Margie there has already offered me the extra room in her house and I plan to take her up on it. I'm not stupid. Everyone in town knows he's messing around on me, and as most of you suspect, he's been abusive. Now that I've aired my dirty laundry, if you still want me to leave, I'll go." She glanced at Ty and slipped past him to grab her sweater off the chair.

"Hang on, Jeanie. How about a show of hands, folks? Who thinks it'd be okay if she stays?" Most of the crowd raised their hand. Margie stood and started clapping for her and the rest of the crowd obliged. Charlie came from the front row and put his arm around her, as Tyler began to address the crowd.

"Okay, now that we got that settled, I guess you all know why we're here. Five years ago Lester Radcliffe got the keen idea to build an all-inclusive lake resort on the property he won from my grandfather in a poker game back in the late sixties. The idea seemed good at the start because, as we all know, the local economy has suffered greatly as the lake has grown older. The Radcliffe Resort Corporation should have been a successful project, and it should have been completed two years ago, but it's been severely, and we think criminally, mismanaged."

The door busted open and Terry walked in steaming. He looked around at the crowd as if daring for someone to look at him wrong. "Well, well, well, what the hell we got going on in here?"

Doc Peavy unwound his six-foot-four frame and stood to face Terry. "Young man, we're having a peaceful assembly of the stockholders of the RRC, and the meeting is open to invitees only. Your presence is an unwanted disturbance, and we'd appreciate it if you'd kindly remove yourself."

"I second that motion," Ty interjected.

"Third," a voice rang out and others followed.

Terry looked around the room and snarled. "I don't give a shit about your stupid-assed meeting. You fools are all wasting your time anyway. My daddy ain't done nothing wrong. I'm just here to collect my wife. Come on, Jeanie."

"I don't want to go with you, Terry. I'm staying here."

"The hell you are. You're my wife and your place is with me." He started crossing the room toward her and Ty stepped in front of her.

"You heard her, Terry, and so did all these folks."

Terry stopped and glared at him, then he turned to the crowd. "This man assaulted me the other night. He got drunk at the Holiday Inn, called me out into the street saying he just wanted to catch up on old times, then he took me by surprise and attacked me. He caused me to have to get four stitches." He took off his cap and showed the crowd where his stitches were. The crowd mumbled. "You all know me. Most of you have done business with me and I treated you fair and square, but this here is the same man who got drunk and killed his family; you all know about that."

Ty grunted and moved toward him, but Jeanie put her hand on his chest and shook her head. Terry continued. "This is the same man who used to be in love with my wife, and the same man whose father just lost his money with RRC. He's come back into town to settle a score with whomever he can, and he'll soon be arrested right in front of your eyes for assault." He turned to Ty, who was boiling and ready to rip him apart. "Ty, I gave you a chance. I even fought with myself not to file charges since we go so far back, but there ain't no telling who you might end up hurting, so I had to go and report you."

Jeanie stepped forward. "Terry, stop. You're just making a fool of yourself. These people know what you've been up to; they've seen the way you've changed and they've seen the bruises on my face."

Ty stepped around Jeanie. "This show is over, Terry, and we have business to tend to, so it's time for you to move on."

"Oh, I'll move all right, and so will all these good folks, just as soon as they come to arrest you, but I ain't leaving without my wife. Our business is between us and no one else. If you aim to try to stop me, you're interfering in personal business and I'll have every right to whoop your ass. Moose ain't got your back this time, so you better watch your damn mouth."

Charlie stood and faced Terry. "No, but he's got me behind him."

Ty put his hand on his dad's shoulder. "Dad, it's okay. I got this."

"Like you said, son, it's time to stand for something."

Their attention was quickly averted as the door flew open again. Deputy Karl Dupree stopped momentarily inside the door and scanned the room.

"Hold on now, let's everybody settle down here. There ain't gonna be any fighting or you're all going to jail." He walked up between Terry and Ty, then turned back to Terry. "Terry, I need you to go on home and cool off."

"The man is cavorting with my wife, Karl. He assaulted me and I want him arrested."

"Let me put it this way, Terry. You got five seconds to make a bee-line for that door, get your butt in your truck, and get the hell out of here, or I'll arrest you first for public disturbance and inciting violence. Now move." Terry squared his jaw and gave Jeanie a stone cold stare before turning, knocking over a chair, and stomping out. Karl sighed and turned back to Ty.

"Okay, Ty, this isn't me talking, it's the deputy sheriff. Tyler Morgan, you've been accused of physical assault against Terry Radcliffe. Please turn around and put your hands behind your back."

"Oh come on, Karl, you know this is bullshit. You were there."

"I didn't see everything, Ty. I got there after the scuffle. For what it's worth, you know I believe you, but I have to do my job. Now please, bud, turn around and don't make this any harder than it already is."

Ty cursed and turned as ordered.

"You have the right to remain silent. Anything you say can and will be used against you in a court of law. You have the right to an attorney, and if you can't afford one, one will be appointed for you by the court. Do you understand your rights?"

Ty frowned and nodded. Charlie stepped up next to his son.

"Please, Karl, do you really have to do this?"

"Sorry, Mr. Morgan, but I have to follow procedures. You can do me a favor, though. Go by and ask Moose to come down and give a statement. He was there and he can probably help backup Ty's story."

"You got it." Charlie slapped his son on the back. "Don't worry, son, you'll be out in no time."

Karl escorted Ty out the door and over to his cruiser. He caught Terry out of the corner of his eye walking toward Jeanie as he helped Ty into the back seat.

"Oh shit."

"Don't let him take her, Karl, he'll hurt her."

Karl threw Ty's briefcase onto the front seat and turned to see Charlie and Margie protecting Jeanie as Terry was pleading his case to them. The sheriff came over the radio.

"Karl, did you pick up Tyler Morgan yet?"

"Yes, sir, Sheriff, he's in the car now."

"Lester and Stacy are claiming he stole some documents from their files here at the dealership. It appears he pulled a fast one on Stacy."

The sheriff started laughing. "You won't believe this. I'll have to tell you the whole story later, but Stacy wanted to file sexual assault charges against him because he got her to go in the conference room and take her clothes off, and then he sent Ricky Dawkins in to meet her." Karl listened as the sheriff cracked up again, then started laughing himself. "Anyway, Karl, just make sure you confiscate any documents he has on him. I'll let them know he's in our custody and tell them to come on in to make their statements. I'll see you in a few."

"You got it, Boss."

Karl looked up to see Terry had his finger pointing at Jeanie and was inching closer to her while Charlie and Margie stood firm.

"Oh crap." He looked back at Ty, who was watching out his window. "How have you managed to cause such a mess after being in town only a week?"

Ty just looked at him. "Go get him before he hurts somebody, Karl."

"Yeah, yeah."

Karl walked back over to Terry and stood with his hands on his hips. His stuck his chin up in the air and took a deep breath.

"Okay, you two, listen carefully. Terry, are you still trying to take Jeanie home with you?"

"Of course. She's my wife and she's not well."

"I'm in no position to judge her mental capacities, or yours either for that matter, so let's just leave that out for now."

"Jeanie, do you want to go home with Terry?"

"No. I'm going to stay with Margie. I don't feel safe at home."

"Why don't you feel safe at home?"

Jeanie dropped her head. "You know, Karl."

"No, Jeanie, just like everyone else in town, I suspect, but that's not enough for me to act upon. If you have a complaint against Terry, you need to come to the office and file it formally. Then I can do something about it."

"You butt out, Karl Dupree." Terry snarled. "This ain't none of your business. You're just creating trouble where there ain't none. The sheriff is gonna hear about this."

"Okay, Terry, at this time I'm going to start reading you your rights. You've disrupted a private gathering and you're creating a public disturbance. I already asked you once to leave. This is your last chance. Jeanie has made her choice and she doesn't want to go with you, so move out."

Karl pointed toward Terry's truck.

"This ain't the end of this."

"You better hope it is."

"You're on his side, Karl, I know you are, you sonofabitch." He walked away, jumped into his truck, and skidded out in a spray of gravel.

Karl grabbed Jeanie's arm and walked her over to his car to get away from the crowd that was slowly gathering around the steps of the church. "Jeanie, listen. I'm not trying to tell you what to do, but you need to know your rights. The best way to keep him from bothering you is to file a restraining order against him. To do that, it's best if we have a statement from you showing you have a reason to believe that he's potentially dangerous to you."

"Oh, Karl, do you think all that is necessary right now?"

"In situations like these, you never know how somebody will react. It's always better to take early precautions than to react after the fact. If we have a statement on file from you before anything else happens, it'll help build your case."

"Well, it all sounds so scary."

"I would think that he's scarier. Think about it, Jeanie, and don't take too long."

"All right, I will. Thank you, Karl."

Karl looked over at Charlie and nodded a thank you to him. Charlie nodded back.

KARL WALKED TY INTO THE office and told him to sit down. He threw Ty's briefcase on the desk and sat across from him with a big sigh. He looked up at Ty and shook his head, then he started laughing.

Ty looked confused, then started smiling. "What's so damn funny?"

Karl leaned on the desk and folded his hands. "Really, Ty? You got Stacy to go into the conference room and remove her clothes, then you sent Ricky in to meet her, or whatever?" They both laughed. After a moment, Karl threw his hands up. "This job just gets more interesting by the day. Good move. That serves her right for what she did to you and Jeanie, but what in the world possessed you to pull that one on her?"

"It didn't start out that way. I just wanted the list of investors, which she gave me after I convinced her that I knew she and Terry were having an affair, but when she opened the file drawer to get me the list of investors, I saw the RRC files."

"Wait. Stop right there. I don't want to know after all."

Karl scratched his head and winced. "Look, the sheriff is at the dealership right now listening to Lester and Stacy who are claiming you stole the list."

"Yeah, so I heard. My God, Karl. They're coming at me from all sides. First Terry, now this. That's not true, I didn't steal the list. She gave it to me, or a copy of it, that is."

"Well, that ain't the song they're singing. They're also claiming you made copies of other files. You're stirring things up, Ty. What did you expect?"

"There's no way they would know that."

Karl put his hands up in front of him. "I'm going to pretend I didn't hear that. My guess is they're just trying to make things as hard as they can for you. The more they can smear your name before a trial, the better their case is gonna look. So, as long as you don't have copies of anything but the list you are okay." He paused, then looked at Tyler sideways. "That's all you have right?" Karl nodded trying to help him along.

"Well, not exactly. All I have is those." He pointed to the briefcase.

Karl raised his eyebrows and perked up in his chair. "What? No, wait. I don't want to know what's in there. Look, Ty, Radcliffe ain't no dummy. He's worried you might know what's in those files, so he's already planning on how to get them thrown out as inadmissible evidence. Didn't your attorney tell you that they wouldn't be able to use them?"

Ty slid down in his chair and frowned.

Karl sighed. "Oh, boy. Well, they will. Look, I'm going to do you a favor. I've got no reason to look in this briefcase; that's the sheriff's job, but whatever you come in here with has to go in that locker. I'm going to step in there and find out where the sheriff is. When he comes back, he's gonna want to look in there, so for your sake I hope there's nothing incriminating in there." He stood to walk out and Ty tried to ask him something.

"But what am I . . ."

"Nope, not another word." Karl cut him off. "Man, it's hot in here.

This window just leads to an old alley, but the wind can sometimes make it through here."

He raised the window and looked down with a laugh. "Our dumpster is just below the window. It kinda makes it handy for a lazy guy like me who never liked taking out the trash. I'll be right back." He grinned and shut the door behind him. Ty jumped up, grabbed his file out of his briefcase, and went over to the window. He looked down and saw the dumpster and chuckled. He grabbed some rubber bands and wound a few around the file before letting it drop into the dumpster below. Quietly, he closed the window and went back to his seat.

Charlie was there early the next morning to pick up his son from jail. Ty jumped into the truck and stuffed his briefcase between the seats. His dad reached up on the dash, grabbed a cap, and pitched it to him. "Thought you might want your cap."

"Thanks, Dad."

"So I guess you got the day off, huh?"

Charlie pulled out and headed toward Timberline Drive.

"Yep. Karl said he talked to Len and told him I was being harassed, so he gave me the day off."

"I guess Moose came through for you?"

"Yeah, so far anyway. The judge should be setting a hearing in a couple of weeks."

"I figured you might want some good breakfast so we'll stop at the Sun-n-Pines if that's okay."

"Sounds good."

"I got a call from Lester this morning."

"Boy, he didn't waste any time, did he?"

"Said he wanted to apologize for his son's actions. He wants me to come by Friday for lunch; something about a peace offering."

"Horse shit."

"Yeah, well, I figured I'd hear what he had to say and see what he had to offer."

"What do you mean, offer?"

"He said he wanted to make an offer on the place that would include extra what it was worth to make up for my losses."

"Dad, five years ago, before I left for Port Aransas, he was going to make you an offer. What happened with that?"

"Your momma said no."

Tyler looked at his father as he drove. He could see the pacifist ideals in every wrinkle of his blue-jean shirt, and he knew that Lester's offer was appealing to him because it meant he didn't have to fight. Perhaps he should just let it all go and let his father get a tidy sum of money and find a nice little house somewhere to spend the rest of his days. Maybe he would even live longer if he didn't have to step over a thousand memories every day. Mom was his whole world. She was the rock and he was the moss. Without her, he could no longer grow.

"Just be careful, Dad. Don't agree to anything without it being on paper and letting me and Mr. Horton look at it first."

"Oh, don't worry, son. I know what he's up to. He's been trying to get it for years."

~ 26 ~

Tyler had looked all over the house and out in the garden, but his dad was nowhere to be found. He walked out onto the porch and stood looking down toward the lake when he saw his father standing next to the shore. He thought he was fishing at first, even though it wasn't quite five yet and still a little early for the evening feed, but then he saw him reach down, grab a rock and skip it across the water.

He knew then that his father was seriously thinking about selling out. He was already counting memories and trying to decide if he could take them all with him.

Ty's phone rang. "Hey, Ty, this is Pat Horton. We've been looking through these documents you sent us. You got the transparencies we sent you, right?"

"Yes, I did, Pat, thanks."

"Well, listen, there's definitely some funny business going on here. Almost every vendor and subcontractor has charged two to three times what they should have. It's cleverly disguised with amendments, but they don't make sense when you look at the whole picture."

"Well, that's great news. So we got him."

"Not so fast. There's something I have to ask you, and it's quite serious."

"Okay."

"These files are the whole case, Tyler, so I have to ask. How did you come by them?"

Tyler sighed. His whole world melted, and that familiar pain in his heart told him he'd screwed up again. "Honestly, Pat, I swiped them and made copies, then returned the originals."

"Ah, man. We can't use them, Ty. I'm sorry, but they can't be submitted as evidence or they'll be thrown out, then anything in them is off limits. Without these, you don't have a case unless you start from scratch. You'd have to file the suit, then we would have to gather depositions from all these people and hope we find a crack in their stories. We can do that, but it will be time-consuming and costly, and we wouldn't even be able to get started for probably three to four months due to our case loads."

Tyler glanced down at his dad's silhouette on the shoreline. "Yeah, we don't have time for that. So basically, Pat, what you're saying is that we're screwed."

"Ty, this guy is clever, but he's got a big head and he thinks he's smarter than everyone else. You just need to dig deeper and find something concrete. You may have to go way back, but I'm sure he has some skeletons in his closet. Just go deeper and find those skeletons."

Ty hung up and melted into his mother's rocker. The sun was listing lower, casting his father's shadow longer onto the bank. He thought of all the investors he'd let down by his impetuous mistake. Maybe his father had it right all along. Maybe it was better to let things happen without a fight. Maybe he should have never even tried to test the road that day and just taken his father's advice and stayed over. Where had fighting gotten him in his life? He fought for an extra yard and it ruined his career. He played the tough guy fighting the elements and lost his family, and now he'd tried to be slick and fight the big guy on the block and he destroyed everyone's chances.

Here he was rocking in his mother's chair; the chair she should be sitting in now, watching her husband down by the lake, greens cooking on the stove. Maybe his horrible accident which took him away from her these past few years somehow took away her strength to fight the disease that plagued her.

He thought about his family. His wife should be hugging up to him now as the day cooled, both of them gazing down toward the lake watching their son learning to skip rocks while tugging on his grandpa's arm. Friday would have been his birthday.

Tyler's chest tightened and a knot went from his stomach into his throat. Well, that was it. He'd failed and now his father had no choice but to take Lester's offer. Maybe it was time to pack up, grab a bottle, and head back to Port Aransas.

He watched his dad meandering back up the hill from the lake. He stopped and looked at Momma's rose garden that was in sad shape, then moseyed on up to the porch. He walked past Tyler silently and sat with a melancholy moan in his favorite spot.

"Well, son, I've been thinking long and hard on it, and I just can't seem to change my mind." Tyler held his breath and braced for the impact as he sat forward and turned to look back at his dad. They made eye contact for a long, quiet moment, the glare from the late sun on the lake reflecting on his father's glasses. Tyler frowned and started shaking his head. Charlie cleared his throat. "I've decided we're having squirrel and dumplings tonight."

Ty exhaled with a chuckle and leaned back in his chair. "You finally got that squirrel, huh?"

He looked back at his father and saw that he was grinning. Tyler grew serious again. "I know what you were really thinking about out there, Dad. I wanted to help you save this place, but I just got off the phone with Pat. They can't use the evidence I gave them. They said it wouldn't hold up; illegally obtained. Looks like I screwed everything up again."

Charlie frowned and looked at his nails. "Don't be hard on yourself, son. At least you were trying. No one else had the guts to."

Tyler sighed and bent forward with his elbows on his knees. "I really thought it was going to work."

"Don't worry about it, son. You're doing your part. The good Lord will do his. Now I don't know about you, but my stomach has been up three times to see if my throat's been cut."

Tyler smiled as his dad pulled himself up with a grunt.

"You want some help in there?"

"Come on, we'll find something for you to do that you can't mess up."

INVESTORS HAD BEEN CALLING ALL week, and Tyler was telling them one by one about the high cost of depositions, the time it would take to even get started, and how, without hard evidence, the case would rest on their ability to find inconsistencies in the testimony of the subcontractors. He failed to mention the fact that he had screwed everything up by stealing the files and giving Lester's attorneys a gateway for having them dismissed.

When he woke on Friday, he rolled over and stared out the window at the garden as he'd grown accustomed; a habit that had started long ago in childhood. He didn't feel like working today. Talking to upset investors all week had him run down. He had gone from hero to horse's ass in their eyes and his, too.

Today his father would probably take Lester's offer and it would all be done. Like he had said at dinner, he could put some money away for a retirement home, and he probably couldn't live long enough to spend the rest. It appeared that even he'd learned not to count on Tyler Morgan.

Tyler sighed deeply, wondering how long it would be before he came back to this part of the country for another funeral. He would pass by this place and see a new lock on the gate. Lester would finally own it all; a forty-year quest would be completed, and someday Tyler Morgan would drive by the place with no more right of passage than some traveling salesman who, like most passers by, probably wouldn't even notice the gate, much less contemplate the world beyond it where a hundred years of family history came and went. The world would never know that it was a place where loved ones married and died, and where a young boy grew to a man in a place he'd always called home, then watched his family get washed away forever in an instant. As for Tyler, he would never even see his family's graves again unless he groveled before Lester Radcliffe.

Tyler dressed and wandered into the kitchen where he found cream-of-rice on the stove. A few strips of bacon garnished some cinnamon toast in the oven. There was something homey and unmistakably country about food that smelled as good as it tasted. As he sat and ate, he looked through the window over the sink like he had a thousand times before, out past the willow tree, up to the sky, and back down to the shoreline. His father shuffled in with his coffee cup leading the way as usual.

"Good morning, son. Today's the big day."

"Morning, Daddy. Yes, it is. You know what else today is?"

His father poured his coffee and coughed. "What's that?"

"Today would have been Jake's eighth birthday."

Charlie stirred his coffee slowly. Tyler knew he was searching for the right thing to say while feeling a little guilty that he had been so focused on himself. He stepped over to the table and sat opposite Tyler, smiling sympathetically.

"Wonder what he would've wanted for his birthday?"

Tyler shrugged. "Probably a mini-bike or a new fishing rod if he was anything like me."

"Oh, I think he would have been just like you. Why don't you ask for the day off, son?"

"Nah, that's okay, Dad. I'm better off keeping busy."

"There was a boy his age on TV just a bit ago. Seems his dog drug up a partially burnt leg from the field out by their house. They didn't say which astronaut it belonged to. Poor kid didn't know how to react. He was a little excited, as a kid would be, but he was traumatized just the same. You could see it in his eyes."

"You know, it's funny, Dad. I heard a boy talking about death with his father at momma's funeral. His dad told him all the right things about why we die that you hear in church and all, but the kid just saw right through it. The truth is, we don't understand death, and we don't know how to handle it."

"Well, everybody's got to go sometime, son. We just all end up going different ways at different times."

"Yeah, but when you study it all, it just doesn't make any sense, Dad. People die all over the world every day in different ways from old age to sheer tragedy. We seem to be able to accept some without a second thought, while others we get hung up on and it stays with us the rest of our lives. Even if it's a stranger, sometimes we never forget it."

"I think it all has to do with whether you're confronted with it, and if so, whether you choose to deal with it or just put it out of your mind. I think if you deal with it, you can learn to accept it, but if you don't, it'll always haunt you."

"That's sounds about right. The thing is, Dad, I guess I just don't understand why God would create us just to watch us fail to be perfect, then die."

Charlie took a long drink of his coffee and followed Ty's stare out the window. They watched the fog rising from the lake and greeting the blue sky that promised a bright, clear day.

"I'll tell you what I heard your momma tell Mrs. Holcomb when her husband died. She was asking the same questions and your momma opened her Bible and showed her first this phrase, then that. Betty was feeling guilty because she went to play bridge the night he passed. He'd said he wasn't feeling right, but she was so looking forward to her bridge night that she just gave him some aspirin and sent him to bed. She found him there stiff as board when she got home. His heart had given out on him.

"Yeah, I remember the story."

"Anyway, your momma laid her Bible down and grabbed that woman by the shoulders and said, 'Betty, God put us here to learn from Him, not to question Him. If He thought you needed to know the great plan while you walked this earth, He would have put it in this book, but you can't teach rocket science to a first grader. Now I'm sorry everything can't happen according to your plan, but the fact is, it's His plan we have to go by and Thank God for that. You just need to remember two things; stuff happens and God loves you.'"

"That sounds like Momma. I just wish it didn't have to be so painful."

"Yeah, believe me, I know, Son. Dr. Stanley says that pain is purifying. He had a sermon just the other day about walking through the valleys of life. He was reading Psalm 23, you know it. He said something that struck a cord in me. He said that the answer to the question why does God let this happen is "The Purifying Work of Pain." He said that pain gets our attention, and it helps us focus on the things in life that really matter. Sometimes it's for us, and sometimes it's for others around us whose lives we affect. The dark valleys bring about change and shake loose the stuff that's clogging up our lives; helps us focus on what's important."

"It sounds like a mighty harsh way to get your point across."

"Yeah, but pain equals growth and change in God-fearing people, Son. The most important thing I learned from that sermon is that the valleys we go through serve a purpose to get us to the next mountaintop; a higher mountaintop of greater understanding and vision. In short, it's when we're given our greatest lessons, and we must respond correctly to them to ever get out of that valley. You see, Son, you gotta let God do His work, and even at the time when you are feeling the greatest pain and confusion, you have to stop fighting and start listening, then thank God for the purpose that He has for you so that you can reach that next mountaintop. If you fight with Him and question Him, you'll never reach higher ground and you will be left in darkness due to your lack of faith."

"Wow, Dad, I never heard you talk like that."

Charlie glowed with pride. "Yeah, I kinda surprised myself with that one."

"Maybe it wasn't just you talking."

"Well, I've been reading your momma's notes that she kept in her Bible. Maybe it's her talking through me. Just remember that it was Christ's pain that gave us our salvation."

"I guess that kinda answers why some people are so affected by death; if they choose to question things instead of accepting God's will, then I guess they never get past it because there are no answers here on earth for those kinds of questions."

"That's right. It's kinda like football practice. Salmon Kreske was a great running back in my time. He used to say first God created football practice, then he created Hell. But, look, if you stood around questioning why practice had to be so hard and so painful, you wouldn't get through it, you wouldn't learn from it, and you'd never get to play in the game."

Tyler grinned, "No pain, no gain."

"There you go."

~ 27 ~

Tyler worked mechanically, feeling melancholy, as he prepared for what would be his final dive. With an empty heart, he descended into the murk, casting his light to and fro, looking for anything that didn't belong on the bottom of the lake. Seemingly out of nowhere, he began to hear his inner voice echoing through the darkness of the deep.

"Therefore; just as through one man, sin entered the world, and death through sin, and thus death spread to all men, because all sinned." Romans 5:12.

"We all must die, and no one shall know the day of his passing, but all should praise His glory and His mercy, for He has gone to prepare a place for us, a place beyond the valley, a place called Paradise. There is a mountain of reward for those who kept their faith through the valley of death. Let us not think woefully on the passing of our loved ones, for if we are to have faith and we are to truly exercise that faith, then we are to celebrate and give praise for the release of our loved ones from the valley.

"Mourning cannot be for the one who has passed, for the dead cannot hear your cries. We mourn for ourselves, for our loss, and in this way, we place ourselves in a position of higher importance than the one whom we have lost. Let us focus on the life, the accomplishments, the love, and the

new life everlasting for our loved ones. Let us remember, above all else, that as long as one is remembered and loved, and as long as their teachings live on inside of us, they can never die, and in this way we can see and feel the earthly compliment of their life everlasting.

"Now if we died with Christ, we believe that we shall also live with Him." Romans 6:8

They were the words he should have said at his mother's funeral. The voices inside his head that seemed to have come from somewhere outside of himself subsided as Tyler broke the surface with a small piece of burnt metal in his hand. He pushed his mask up and swam over to hand it to Johnny, who was leaning over the side.

As they wound through the stumps and stickups headed to the cut, Ty leaned his head back and let the wind dry his hair. It was cold, but the pain was endurable and strangely welcoming. The whole time he'd been diving he was thinking about the darkness of the deep, and how everything was more confusing in that darkness. Life is that way, the long night of the living.

He had many memories come back to him today; images of his son and times they had shared together during his short life, and images of his wife and of the love and intimacy they enjoyed. He'd seen their faces there in the deep and felt their love. For the first time since he'd lost them, it wasn't haunting to him, but more like forgiving, like they were saying goodbye, like they were saying have a good life.

The boat turned up the cut and powered up over the small chop in the water. The winding hum of the engine and the repetitive bounce of the bow were hypnotizing. He focused on the broken layers of clouds backlit like burning embers of the dying sun. His inner voice was screaming to overcome the popping of the wind in his ears.

He asked himself how much he'd learned since he was last careening across the lake in the closing hour of the day with his skin glowing bronze, his hair tossed like an old mop, and his thumbs roughed up from handling bass. He'd known then that those precious days spent with his father and brother would become cherished memories; the beautiful sunsets, bookmarks for his recollection, but here he was thumbing through those recollections, and what had he really learned?

ON THE WAY UP TO the house, Tyler stopped on the rise above Joshua Creek and walked up to the monument. He placed a brand new fishing rod with a shiny red reel against the pink stone and stood back.

"Happy Birthday, Jake-o, my dear, sweet son. I hope you catch a big one, little buddy. In the flash of an eye, I'll be there to fish the great lakes of Heaven with you. Grandpa will come, too. He'll show us all of his favorite holes, and teach you how to skip rocks. I love you son, and I sure do miss you, hot shot. Daddy is so sorry for letting you and Mommy get . . ."

He fell to his knees and sobbed.

CHARLIE HAD FRIED CATFISH, FRENCH fries, and hush puppies ready for dinner when Ty walked into the kitchen. He was excited to see Ty and show off his dinner. Tyler saw his dad's enthusiasm and decided to pump himself up a little.

"Hey, Dad, where did you get the fish?"

Charlie spoke as he fished out fries and dropped them onto a plate covered with paper towels. "Man, we sure caught 'em today. David Holt came by and carried me a fishin' with him. He's been baiting a hole for a couple of weeks now over by the Deer Stand where the river swings by there, don't you know? He threw out some sour corn and we dropped some big shiners down and caught our limit."

"Smells great. I can't wait to eat."

"Well, go wash up and we'll dig in."

Tyler said the blessing and took a couple of bites. He waited for his dad to get situated and started on his meal, then asked him about the lunch meeting with Lester.

Charlie chewed on fish and hush puppies and raised his eyebrows to take a big swig of sweet tea. "He made a darned good offer; two, in fact."

"Two?"

Tyler rested his forearms on the table's edge and waited for his dad to finish washing down his food.

"Yep. He made an offer of $200,000 if we're out in 30 days, and an offer of $160,000 which is good for three months."

"I thought he was going to offer you what the place was worth plus extra to make up for your losses? Dad, the place is worth every bit of $300,000 as it sits. Plus, you lost over ninety grand with the RRC."

Charlie reached into his pocket, pulled out a check and slapped it on the table with pride. Tyler picked it up hesitantly and looked at it.

"What did you sign, Dad?"

"That there is a check for ten thousand dollars, son. It's a nonrefundable deposit for a six-month first right of refusal on the place." He smiled with pride. "I got him, son. I don't even have to sell and that money is all mine."

"But, Dad, it also locks you in at the price he's offered, which is way below what he promised you. Now you have to make a decision within a few days or you lose $40,000. If you take the offer by then, you still lose $100,000 off what the place is worth, plus the $90,000 he was supposed to offer on top of that."

"Well, like he said, son, people ain't lining up to buy this place, and I ain't gonna last long with all my resources depleted the way they are."

"Don't you think he knows that, Dad? This was his plan all along. He's still going to go through with the resort. He always needed this place for the waterfront. Without it, he didn't have a marina. If anything, he needs it worse than a normal buyer and should be paying a premium for the land alone, not to mention the payback for your losses. You could have come away with close to $500,000. Hell, he's spending money he stole from you and the other investors anyway."

Charlie picked at his fish. "I thought you'd be proud of me, son. I can still spend the check and I don't have to sell."

Tyler looked at the check again, then sat back in his chair. "No, it's okay, Dad. We'll just have to make it work for a few months until we can get him back to the table. It's okay, it'll all work out. You did good. This is probably the best way to deal with him anyway. He'll probably start raising the price when he sees you're not biting. Just promise me you'll take me with you next time."

Charlie nodded. "Eat your fish, it's getting cold."

Tyler lay in his bed staring up at the stain around the light on the ceiling that had been there as long as he could remember. He knew he couldn't last there for six months. He had bills to pay in Port Aransas and a business that was already in jeopardy. His job with the Feds would be winding down soon and he knew he'd have to go back. No matter how he looked at it, he couldn't make it work. Maybe he could talk Lester into raising the price a little more. His screw-up with the files loomed over his head again. Too bad they couldn't find something concrete to nail Lester on. He closed his eyes and apologized to his mother.

He reached over to the night stand, grabbed his Bible, and read Psalm 23, then unfolded his mother's note and read it again. Perhaps his recent failures were part of God's plan. Maybe He had a reason. He decided to leave it in His hands.

With the lights out, he listened to the crickets chirping their East Texas lullaby and thought of carefree days spent working the shoreline in cutoff jeans with a cane pole, and waiting for Jeanie to come sit beneath the great pine on the point to catch the sunset.

TYLER WOKE IN THE MIDDLE of the night and bounded up to the side of the bed. There was something repeating in his dreams that stirred him to consciousness. "You may have to go deep, but I'm sure he has some skeletons in his closet." It was what Pat Horton had said. Something in his mind had clicked at the time, but not loud enough for him to recognize what it was. It all made sense here in the middle of the night. Perhaps a touch of serendipity, or perhaps a whisper from God, the answer might have been right below him all along on the bottom of the lake at the Moore farm. He checked his clock; three-o-five. Sunrise would be in less than four hours, but he just might have enough time. He jumped out of bed and threw on his clothes.

TYLER STRAINED TO FIND THE entrance to the river through the darkness. There was intermittent cloud cover, and the half-moon was no help for seeing stumps near the waterline. He dug through the rod box and found a spotlight. He plugged it into the console and it lit up the water like day in front of him. Slowly, he wound through the river channel until he came to the old road to the Moore farm.

AS HE DESCENDED THE BLACK water, he thought about the consequences of getting caught making an unauthorized dive in a posted area without permission. He checked his watch; three-forty-six. Was he doing it again? Was he going to screw this up, too? He didn't even know what he was looking for; he was just moving on a hunch.

Before long, he caught a glimpse of the old truck in his light. As he neared, he got that familiar feeling that something was in the water with him; something big.

Tyler swam slower and cast his light around looking for the source of his uneasy feeling. He flashed the light to his right just in time to see a huge gator mouth staring at him. He flinched and reached for his knife. The animal turned and he saw it was an alligator gar. It was at least five feet long and big enough to take a mean chunk out of him if it wanted to, but he'd never heard of a gar attacking anyone as long as he'd been around this lake. As he pushed forward to the truck, he only hoped his encounter wouldn't be that one exception which boggled the minds of aquatic biologists and made front page headlines.

His light panned the length of the truck. Silt was piled halfway up the side and the metal was badly rusted. He saw the glass to the driver's door was slid down at an angle as he swam closer to shine his light inside. Silt had filled the truck almost to the top of the seats. He could see something white sticking above the silt line, but couldn't get close enough to determine what it was. He pulled on the door to try to open it. The frame around the window broke off and something shiny floated down onto the silt. It took a minute for the water to clear, but he located the object and lifted it into his light.

Ty floated there, confused, studying the silver object which he quickly recognized as an old class ring. The ring was bent where it had been lodged in the truck door. He turned it as he read the inscription around the top where the stone had once been, then inspected the raised numbers on the side.

1954
Robert E. Lee
High School

He pitched the ring into his salvage pouch and stuck his head inside the truck to get a closer look at the white object protruding from the silt. As he drew closer and his light began to reveal more definition, he could now clearly see and recognize what he was looking at. It was a skull. Sterman Moore was still in his truck.

~ 28 ~

Tyler set the light where it would shine on the skull and took pictures with his underwater camera. He wanted to dig out the skeleton, take more pictures and look for more evidence, but he knew better. He clinched his jaw, thinking about the ring and the damaged door and got mad at himself. He'd done it again.

As he took more pictures, a distant memory started playing in his mind; a late afternoon in the fall of his youth when he played catch in the front yard with Terry and his dad. He lowered his camera and floated, remembering the first time he'd seen the grossly deformed ring finger on Lester's right hand.

Bam! He had him. The only problem now was, if the ring was Lester's, he could never prove it was found on the scene because he'd destroyed where it was located. He backed away from the truck a couple of feet and took more pictures. At least there was a body to be investigated, and maybe, just maybe, somewhere beneath all this silt was a weapon.

He went back in for his light and circled around the truck to see what else he could find. The silt had piled unusually high in the bed for some reason. Why would it be so much higher in the bed than anywhere else? As he panned around the truck bed with his light, he saw where an old rope had rotted apart coming off the back of the bed and disappearing into the silt below the bumper. He'd seen that enough times on his father's truck to know there must have been a tarp tied down over the bed.

When he got back around to the driver's side, he noticed a hole in the corner where the tarp had rotted through. He stuck his light into the hole and waved his hand to blow away the silt. There was what appeared to be rusted ammo boxes stacked tightly together. The box nearest the corner seemed to stand a little taller than the rest. He blew away more of the silt and saw the lid was unlatched and slightly ajar. Carefully, he lifted the lid.

Tyler rushed back to the surface and dug through the rod box where he found some trotline and several floats. He took a moment to scan the horizon, then dove back in.

He was bushed when he finally headed to the surface and jumped into the boat. He checked his watch again; it was almost five-thirty. Feeling edgy and guilty, he stowed his gear and beat it back to the marina.

His nerves settled a little by the time he reached the cut and powered up. His inner voice kept repeating over and over. No one is going to know, no one is going to know. He knew what he had to do next.

Ty sat in front of his dad's old computer and sipped coffee waiting for it to finish a gruelingly slow startup. He was completely calm now, even tired, but he had to see his hunch through to the end. The website for the high school came up with no trouble after a few minutes. He looked up the class of '54, put in the name Lester Radcliffe, and up popped a greasy-haired punk with a smart-assed grin. "That son-of-a-bitch!" Lester Radcliffe literally had a skeleton in his closet. Now all he had to figure out was how to draw an investigation without anyone knowing he'd made an illegal dive. There was no way they were going to throw out such damning evidence if he had anything to do with it. Tyler felt a hand on his shoulder and jumped.

"What's the matter, son? You getting so old you can't hear an old man walking up behind you?"

He took a couple of deep breaths and chuckled. "Dad gum, I was so deep in thought that you caught me off guard."

"Why are you looking at a high school picture of Lester?"

"Dad, I went out early this morning and dove the truck."

His father frowned and snorted. "What in the world possessed you to do that, son? Do you just like being in jail?"

"Dad, listen. I know it was a huge risk, but I woke up in the middle of the night, and I knew I had to do it. I had to find something on Lester that would give us the edge."

"By God, I hope nobody finds out. What in the hell did you expect to find?"

"They won't. Dad, just look at this." Tyler reached into his salvage pouch that he had sitting next to him on the table and produced the ring. He gave it to his dad and sat back. "You know what that is, Dad?"

"Well, sure. Where did you get it?"

"I found it wedged in the door of old man Moore's truck. I believe that to be Lester's class ring. That explains his busted finger. Guess what else I found in that truck?" His father stared at him coldly. "That's right; Sterman Moore's remains."

"Well, I'll be damned. He did do it."

Charlie gave the ring back, shuffled over to his recliner, and sat there half shocked, reliving the drama and the headlines from forty years earlier. He cleared his throat and spoke with a crackle in his voice. "I guess he killed my daddy too."

Tyler rose and gave his father a hug. "We're going to get him this time, Dad."

Charlie grabbed a tissue from the table and blew his nose, then with a deep breath he said, "We got proof that's for sure."

Tyler dropped his head and folded his arms. "Listen, Dad, we've got one big problem. I can't tell anyone I found it or it'll cause me trouble and the evidence will be illegally obtained."

Charlie frowned and stared straight ahead. "Can't you say you saw it when you were diving nearby?"

"No, it's too late. Besides, it was still out of the authorized area."

Charlie thought for a minute as he took a sip of coffee. "Well, what if it wasn't?"

"How do you mean?"

"You didn't tell them about the second splash?"

"What are you talking about? Dad there was no . . ." Tyler smiled. "Nope, I sure didn't. The fact is, I didn't realize there was one since I was taking a pee at the time. Now, the question is, how do we bring that up?"

Charlie took another drink of his coffee and exhaled loudly as he set the cup down in front of him. "You just leave that up to your old Dad."

ON MONDAY MORNING, TYLER WAS sitting in the briefing room finishing some fried eggs when he saw his dad walk into the marina café. Charlie nodded at his son briefly, then went straight over and started jawing with Len. Tyler went back to eating, and before too long he heard Len hollering his name.

"Tyler Morgan. Get over here a minute."

Ty did as he was instructed, and when he walked up to Len, he reminded his father that he'd asked him not to come down there nosing around and getting in the way.

"Never mind that. Tyler, your daddy here was asking what we found at the second splash down at the place you guys call the Moore farm. You didn't tell me about that."

"Well, honestly, Len, I didn't actually hear it since I was relieving myself at the time. Dad didn't seem too sure about it, so I guess I just let it go. We became so preoccupied with the major splash that it never came up again. I had totally forgotten about it."

He turned to his dad. "Dad, are you sure it wasn't just the aftershock from the big splash?"

Charlie acted a little ornery. "Hell, I know damn well what I heard, and I'm sure I told you to bring it up to the boys here."

Tyler sighed and shrugged. "Well, we've already moved off the spot."

Len chimed in quickly. "Now, hang on, that doesn't matter. We have to investigate every possibility. We're finished at the current site, and before we move to the next location I want you, Frank, and Johnny to beat it back over there and at least give it one dive to clear the area. Are we clear on that?"

"Yes, sir. We'll head there straight away this morning."

As they reached the Moore farm, Frank shut off the motor and stood with his hands on his hips looking at the government warning sign and all the floats that were now in the general vicinity. He looked back at Tyler as he was suiting up.

"What's with all these jugs floating out here? I don't remember them from last time."

Tyler spoke casually without looking up. "Those are trot-line floats. This is the deepest water around here, so it's good for snagging catfish."

"Huh." Frank nodded and gazed around some more. "I figured it was something like that."

Tyler dove in and made his way back down to the truck. When he reached the scene, he unzipped his boot and pulled out the ring, placing it in the silt inside the truck next to a piece of the rusted door that had broken off. He then took a picture using the new roll of film he'd placed in the camera that morning. He swam around the truck and took a couple more pictures of the skull from the other side, then backed away and took some shots of the entire scene. When he returned to the surface, he raised a big commotion and jerked off his regulator and mask.

"There's a body."

Frank scampered to the side and Johnny began writing furiously.

"Wait." Ty swam closer to the side and grabbed onto the rail. "It's not an astronaut. It's a skeleton, and it's inside an old truck." The two men looked at each other, then just stared at Tyler for a moment. "Well, what do you want me to do? I took lots of pictures, but I was careful not to disturb anything."

Johnny stuck his pen over his ear and looked out across the lake for a minute. "I think we've done all we can. We have to turn this over to the local authorities."

Tyler nodded. "Shall I make one last sweep before we pull away?"

"Sure, go ahead."

Johnny was calling it in as Tyler descended for the final time on the old truck at the Moore farm. All those years he sat in the boat above it, dangling a plastic worm at old man Moore. He smiled to himself. Everything was going according to plan, and with any luck, Lester Radcliffe would soon be under suspicion again.

TYLER SAT, SLOUCHING A BIT, in an old wooden straight chair in front of Karl's desk at the sheriff's office. He'd spent the entire afternoon reporting his findings from the scene. The sheriff had plopped himself on the edge of the desk next to him and was recounting the story in disbelief.

The phone rang and Karl answered. He put the caller on hold, looked up at the sheriff, and said, "It's Lester."

The sheriff pulled off his hat and popped it against his knee as he rose from the desk with a long sigh. Karl sat back with his hands posted on the arms of his chair and grinned at Tyler as the sheriff slammed his hat back on his head with a disgusted frown and drummed his boot heels into the wooden floor.

"I'll take it in my office."

Tyler watched as the sheriff pulled up on his gun belt and headed directly into his office. Without slowing, he swung at the door as he walked by. Ty noticed that the door closed and almost latched, but it slowly creaked back open a couple of inches. He quickly switched chairs to the one closest to the door and cocked an ear.

"Hello, Lester. Boy, news travels fast in this little town. . . . Yeah, it's true. . . . What's that? . . . Hell, I don't know. It's too early to say. We haven't even gotten the pictures back yet, but if it's what he says it is, I expect we'll probably open a formal investigation. . . . What do you mean we can't do that right now? . . . Well, of course I remember I'm up for reelection; believe me, I've already thought about that, but with the Feds breathing down my neck, I can't exactly blow it off, Lester. Too many people already know, and Henry is probably already printing the front page headlines." All went quiet for a moment. Ty leaned over and peeked through the crack in the door. The sheriff had his jaw set, and his chest was puffing up like a bulldog. He stood, looking like he was about to explode, and turned toward his window. "Dammit, man, quit yelling at me. There ain't a shittin-assed thing I can do about it. What are you so damn worried about anyway?"

Ty watched as the sheriff's shoulders slumped and his head dropped. He lowered his voice. "Well, if they cleared you all those years ago, it shouldn't be more than a formality this time unless there's some kind of new evidence you're worried about. Is there something you want to tell me? . . . No, there's no reason why you would automatically be the prime suspect again. It's a whole new case, if there's a case to be made at all. . . . No, Lester, I wouldn't think you would do something like that. I'm sure folks won't jump to any conclusions. . . . Yes, sir, I know the money went in today. . . . Yep, twenty grand. . . . No, I can't afford to lose you as a contributor. Look, just relax for now, will you?"

The sheriff sat against the desk and started rubbing his head. "I can't formally open an investigation until the Feds leave because I don't have the manpower, and it'll probably take a couple of weeks after that before I can finish all of my paperwork with this damn shuttle. By then, your banking business will be complete and you'll already have your funds, so I wouldn't worry about them tying up your loan. Now I can't be talking to you about this anymore. . . . Yep, I will."

Ty heard the sound of the big man's boots on the wooden floor and jumped back over to the chair in front of Karl's desk. The sheriff pulled open the door, stopped and looked down at the latch for a second, then walked out. "Peggy, I need a list of the Class of '54 for Robert E. Lee High School just as quick as you can make it happen."

"Yes, sir."

He turned back to face Karl and Tyler. "Have you finished with his statement?"

Karl nodded. "Yes, sir, we are all done."

The sheriff looked at Tyler. "Mr. Morgan, the sheriff's department would like to thank you for your cooperation. You're free to go now."

"No problem, Sheriff." Ty stood and shook Karl's hand and started out the door. He stopped and looked back at the sheriff. "Just one thing, Sheriff; how do you plan to keep anyone from tampering with the crime scene?"

"Why don't you let me worry about that, Tyler?"

"With all due respect, sir, all I'm saying is the whole town probably knows about it by now. All someone would have to do is pull up there, dive down, remove that skeleton, and that would be the end of it."

"Just what would you have me do about that, Mr. Morgan? I've got three deputies and they're all out escorting federal marshals around looking for burnt pieces of spacecraft. Are you volunteering to sit out there all night for several weeks with a pea shooter and a spotlight?"

Tyler put his hands on his hips and thought before he spoke. He noticed Karl poking his head around the sheriff with his hat pushed back on his head and sporting his big, country-boy grin.

"Who are we kidding here, Sheriff?"

Karl's grin turned to a grimace as the sheriff bowed up again. "What's that supposed to mean?"

"I think you know. What you don't know is if that sonofabitch Lester thinks he's going to get away with this and then con my daddy out of his land, I'll take him down all by myself, one way or another."

Tyler stared him in the eye for a moment and then turned to walk out the door.

"Hey, Tyler." He stopped and looked back at the sheriff.

"You watch your back, boy, and stay the hell out of my way."

"That sounds like a threat, Sheriff."

"Dammit, Tyler Morgan, if I wanted to, I'd stick your gimlet ass underneath this jail and take my sweet-assed time coming up with a reason to keep you there."

Tyler walked out and hollered back at Karl as he was leaving.

"Later, Karl."

"Ty."

The sheriff slumped into the chair in front of Karl's desk.

"What a mess! Is it just me or do we have a good, old-fashioned family feud going on here?"

"No, it's alive and well. The Radcliffes started it a long time ago, and Tyler is going to finish it. You've seen that look in his eye before, Coach. Old Ty is back!

"Yeah, well, that's what has me worried."

~ 29 ~

Lester Radcliffe pulled off the highway at Cooter Faulk's place and drove up under the large oak by the house. As he stepped from his car, he heard Cooter cussing over his lawn mower that he had in several parts on his front porch.

Seeing he had a visitor, Cooter crawled over and sat on the steps, pushed his cap back on his head, and was cutting a chew from his plug of tobacco when Lester walked up to say hello.

"I'll be damned, Cooter, you ain't changed a bit."

"Afternoon, Mr. Radcliffe. What brings you out this way?"

"Your daddy would be proud of what you've done with this place, Cooter. It's prettier than a speckled pup under a red wagon."

Cooter looked around and spit. "Well, you know how it is. A little hard work, a few prayers, this that the other, and all. Too bad it ain't really mine no more. What can I do for you?"

Lester chuckled and picked up an acorn that he tossed out into the grass. "I might have a little job for you. You still do any diving?"

"Oh, I work out at the dam every once in while when they need me to check on things. What you got?"

"Well, it's a little embarrassing, but I was out fishing the other day and forgot I was wearing an expensive watch. I bent over the side to pull up an old bass that I caught and the damn thing slid right off my wrist. I've been meaning to get the band fixed, but I just never got around to it."

Cooter squinted and stared out at the highway for a minute.

"You know, times are kinda hard for me right now, Mr. Radcliffe. A good paying job, even if it was short-term, would sure plug the hole for me."

"I'll pay you well for your troubles."

Cooter nodded and played with his cap, then crossed his arms and squinted up at Lester. "I heard they found old man Moore's body."

"So they did. Hard to believe, huh?"

Cooter spit and studied some grease on his jeans. "Yeah, well, the way I figure it, if somebody needed it to go away, that would be a damn good paying job. You say you want me to find a watch?" He looked up at the highway again, avoiding eye contact with Lester.

Lester smiled, got back into his car, and started it. He looked over at Cooter, who was still sitting on the steps with his arms crossed and his head down. He rolled down the window and hollered at him. "I'll be in touch."

WITH ITEM ONE ON HIS list checked off, Lester jumped on the loop and headed for Terry's house. Tyler Morgan had become a thorn in his side, and he knew his son had similar feelings. It was cleanup time, and Lester knew better than to get his own hands dirty.

Deep in thought, Lester turned up Terry's long drive that wound through a strip of woods before heading up the long hill where the house stood. Suddenly, he remembered that his son had been ordered to stay away for three days while Jeanie gathered some of her personal belongings to take with her to Margie's. At least she hadn't tried to kick him out of his own house.

He decided to drive on past the wood line where he could turn around, hoping that he wouldn't be seen. He slowed as he made the last turn, peeking up the long drive to the house, and was flabbergasted at what he saw. Tyler Morgan was walking to his truck with a large box. Lester froze, watching carefully to make sure Tyler never looked his way.

He watched as Tyler strolled back into the house, then quickly turned around. Heading out the gate, he called Stacy on his car phone which came over his radio speakers.

"Good afternoon, Mr. Radcliffe."

"Stacy, where's Terry?"

"He just left. Him and Bobby was going to pick up Doyle and they was all headed to Houston on business. They won't be back till Friday. Do you want me to get ahold of him and tell him to call you?"

"No, thanks, I'll call him on his cell." He hung up and redialed quickly. "What's up, Dad?"

"Where are you going?"

"Houston. Why?"

"What the hell for?"

"Business."

"Business, my ass. Son, you need to get your shit together."

"What do you think I'm trying to do?"

"Did you know that Tyler Morgan is at your house right now loading boxes into his truck?"

"What?"

He could hear Terry pulling off the road and skidding to a stop.

"Listen, Son, you can't go there or you'll end up in jail."

"No, but I know who can."

"Good. Get 'em lined out and get your ass back on the road right away."

Lester smiled when he hung up. In just one short afternoon, he'd managed to get to a place where he was in control again.

~ 30 ~

Jeanie grabbed two bottles of water and sat at the kitchen table with Tyler. "I sure appreciate all of your help, Ty."

He winked at her and unscrewed the cap on her water for her. After handing it to her, he stood and looked out the window at the big pasture sprinkled with grand oaks. "This sure is a beautiful place. Are you gonna try to keep the house?"

"Probably. My lawyer says if I let him keep the business and split our retirement, then I should get the house. It's more than I need, but it's easier that way."

Tyler nodded and took a long drink of cold water. As he sat back down, a sharp pain shot through his hip. He winced, then reached into his pocket and pulled out the shard of taillight he'd found by Joshua Creek.

"What's that?"

He held it above the table and turned it in his hand.

"It a piece of taillight. I found it at the crossing. It must have flown out onto the bank when a tree or whatever it was hit our car. It's all I've got left from that day."

She put her hand on his and gave him a sympathetic smile. "I wish I had magical words that would make all the hurt go away forever."

He squeezed her hand and took a deep breath. "Thanks. Well, I guess we better get back to work, huh?"

She rose and gave him a quick hug. Tyler finished his water and watched as Jeanie walked past the pictures on the mantle and gave them one last look. Even though she had her back to him, he could tell she was wiping her eyes. He walked up behind her and held her as she broke down.

"I was so stupid."

He put his head next to hers. "We both were. I guess there's a reason and a season for everything."

"I'm glad you're here to help me through this."

"I'm glad I can be here for you, Jeanie."

Tyler heard the sound of a truck pulling up and two doors shutting. He gave her a peck on the cheek. "I'll go see who's here."

A hissing whistle caught his attention as he opened the door. Ty stepped out to see Bobby and Doyle slashing his tires. He ran toward them and Doyle started at him with his knife extended. He took a few swipes in the air and grinned at Ty.

"Hey, lover boy. Soon as we get through redecorating your piece of shit truck here, we're gonna rearrange your pretty face." Jeanie stepped out onto the front porch and Ty hollered at her to get back inside and call Karl. "That won't do no good. Get her, Bobby."

Bobby headed for the porch, and Ty tackled him into the bushes. Quickly he jumped out and looked for Doyle who was almost on top of him. He heard Bobby moaning as he inched away from the bushes. Doyle flipped the knife in his hand and begged Tyler to come after him.

Ty knew he could get the knife away from him, but he also knew he probably couldn't avoid getting cut somewhere in the process. He decided to let Doyle make the first move. He heard movement behind him and saw Doyle's eyes widen as fear gripped his face.

"Oh my God, Doyle, help me, man."

Doyle lowered his knife in shock. Ty looked quickly and saw Bobby heading out of the bushes with his knife sticking out of his side. When he saw Tyler wasn't looking, Doyle raised his knife again and started after him. Tyler came around with a tornado kick and knocked the knife from his hand.

Bobby cried out, "Screw him, Doyle. Get me to the hospital."

Blood was pouring down his side and onto his leg. Doyle quickly retrieved his knife and kept it extended as he worked his way over to help Bobby.

"You got lucky, Morgan, but your time is coming if you don't get your ass out of this town."

Tyler watched as they drove away down the hill, then ran into the house where he found Jeanie balled up in the kitchen floor, in tears and trembling, with the phone by her side and a large kitchen knife in her hand.

"It's okay. They've gone."

He reached down and picked her up, and she wrapped her arms around him. "Thank God you're okay. They cut the phone line and I couldn't call."

"It's okay. I'll talk to Karl. Let's get out of here."

WITH JEANIE SAFE AT MARGIE'S, Ty headed to his dad's house. He called Karl on his cell, but got no answer, so he dialed the sheriff's office. A few hours later, the sheriff showed up at Charlie's.

"Hey there, Mac. Come on in. You just missed dinner, but I can fix you a plate if you're hungry."

"Thanks, Charlie, but I stopped by Best of Texas Bar-B-Que and Doni loaded me up one of them monster baked potatoes with brisket. I'm so dang full I can hardly walk. You know that damn Bar-B-Que sauce of his is so good you can drink it straight. I think if Preacher Bill used it for communion, he'd have more takers, and even the good Lord himself wouldn't find fault with it."

"You're sure right about that. He says he's gonna bottle it and sell it down at the grocery store. I'm afraid if he does, I'll be putting the damn stuff on my eggs in the morning."

The sheriff laughed. "That don't sound half bad. Well, Charlie, is Ty around?"

After Tyler had given the sheriff his statement, they all walked out onto the porch. Charlie slapped his hand on Mac's shoulder. "So are you going to pick them up, Sheriff?"

"Soon as I find them. The hospital said they patched Bobby up a couple of hours ago and they lit out."

He looked over at Ty and put his hands on his hips.

"You ought to think about finding someplace else to hang out until you head back home. You could be putting your father in danger if they come here looking for you."

Tyler cocked his head, then glanced at his dad.

"Sheriff, why don't you go pick up the man who sent them and tell him to go someplace before I find him. I told you before, if you ain't gonna stop him, I will."

"Easy there, big boy. We all know they hang with Terry, but Terry left town this morning so he's not even under suspicion."

"I ain't talking about Terry. This ain't his style. He likes to get his hands dirty. This has Lester Radcliffe written all over it."

"Now, Tyler. Just what the hell makes you think Lester had anything to do with this? Terry's the one you've been having the pissin' contest with, and those boys are his friends, not Lester's."

"So why would they come after me and tell me to leave town? Why wouldn't they just beat me up or try to kill me? Who's paying them? Terry doesn't have any money right now, and like I said, if it was up to him, he'd come for me himself with his two goons as backups."

The sheriff removed his hat and scratched his head in frustration. "I just don't see the connection, Tyler."

"Well, you might at least investigate it unless you're worried about losing your main contributor. Have you questioned him about old man Moore's death yet?"

"Why, you little smart-ass. You think I drove all the way out here after dinner for my health? Let me tell you loud and clear right here in front of your daddy, if you get in the way of my investigation or cause any more trouble around here, I'll run you out of town myself." The sheriff nodded at Charlie and stormed off to his car.

Back inside the house, Ty stood around thinking as his father casually sat back in his recliner and crossed his hands in his lap. "Don't you worry, If they come around here, I got something for their ass." He pointed to his rifle in the corner. Tyler sighed and looked at his father. His mind was made up.

"That ain't gonna happen, Daddy. I'm going to stay with Vince until this blows over. If they don't see my truck here, they won't bother you."

ALL THE NEXT DAY, TYLER walked the woods around Vince's place. He helped Vince run some trout lines in the river for a bit, then helped him with dinner. Even though Vince didn't say much, Tyler bent his ear all day about how he'd screwed up everything since he'd come back. He told him that he thought the sheriff was corrupt, that Lester was a murderer, and that some bad guys might be paying them a visit. After dinner, his big brother wrapped his huge arm around his shoulders and gave him a good squeeze.

"The lady said it's time."

Ty's heart sank. All this time he thought things were pretty normal with him and Vince, considering. "What lady, Vince? Is this the same lady you told me about before?"

"Uh-huh."

"Where is this lady? When did you see her?"

"Today. She came to the river."

Tyler knew that he was never supposed to make a big issue out of his brother's occasional mental folly, but there was something about this story that made him feel like his brother sincerely believed it. He instinctively began to address it before he realized what he was doing. "I didn't see no lady today Vince."

"You were out in the woods."

"Really? So, what does this lady look like?"

"Rachel."

"Rachel? She looks like Rachel?"

"Uh-huh."

Ty was shocked. His brother barely knew Rachel. He'd only seen her a handful of times. How had he retained images of her in his mixed-up mind? Had the trauma of her death somehow affected him; why would it? "What exactly did she tell you, Vince?"

"She said it's time. You should look at the pictures now."

Vince smiled and plopped his paw on top of Tyler's head as he turned and headed out the door.

"What pictures? Where are you going Vince?"

"Gotta reset my lines."

"Vince, wait." Tyler gently tried to stop him from leaving, but he just shrugged him off and kept going.

"You gotta look at pictures. I gotta reset my lines."

"Vince, wait. There's a thousand pictures in here. All of them?"

He watched his brother's flashlight bouncing around in the woods until he completely disappeared into the darkness. He sighed, feeling stupid for getting caught up in the labyrinth of his brother's confused mind. He walked back inside and sat on the couch, staring at the walls and feeling more lost than ever.

Oh my God, look at me. What the hell am I doing here? A feeling of hopelessness soon came over him, and he started feeling sorry for himself. *Screw it*, he thought. *Dad's got his deal with Lester, everybody wants me out of town, Vince is Vince, and Jeanie has too much on her plate to worry with me. The sheriff is crooked and Karl is just trying to survive, broken long ago and wading through life with all the contentment of a fox squirrel. So this is what the great comeback was all about, huh Lord?*

Maybe it wasn't his purpose to fix everything. He'd prayed, thrown away the bottle, and tried hard to make a difference, but he didn't feel God's help. All he felt was lost.

He took a deep breath, pounded his fist on the table, then jumped up from the couch and headed into the kitchen. He'd seen the bottle of Dickel that he bought for Vince on his first visit still unopened in the cupboard when he was helping clean fish earlier that afternoon. *Might as well get drunk.* He located the bottle, grabbed a glass, and went back to the couch. He sat there feeling sorry for himself, and thinking about Celina and the guys back in Port Aransas. At least they would take him back. So much for his big transformation. He picked up his phone and dialed Celina.

"Hello?"

"Hey."

"Tyler? How are you? How's your mom?"

"She didn't make it, Celina. I, uh, I got here too late. I didn't even get to tell her goodbye."

"Oh, Ty, I'm so sorry."

"Yeah, me too. Well, I guess it's time to come home."

She stayed silent for a few moments. "Ty, maybe you should take some time to be with your father. Don't worry about things here. Ray is taking your clients out, and everything is running smooth."

"Yeah? Well, I appreciate that, but there's not much else I can do here. I've messed up everything I can. I tried to help, but Jeanie and Dad . . . well, anyway I need to get back, focus on building my business, and try to move on with my life. Maybe I can even try to raise some money for Dad."

"Raise money? What happened to him?"

"It's a long story."

"Well, we can send money for you. Take a little time to heal and help your father heal. He needs you right now."

Her words fell softly on his heart and he began to break down a little. "I tried to do what you said. My mom left me a note and asked me to help fight for my father. I even went to church and decided to stop drinking, but God didn't help me."

"Tyler, listen to me, you can't quit now. Just because you've decided to try to make a difference doesn't mean it's going to happen overnight. Before now, you weren't even recognizing your faith. Now that you are, your faith needs to be exercised. He'll help you, but in His way, and when He knows the time is right."

"You sound like my brother now."

"Tyler listen. Just believing, just praying is not enough to turn your life around. You have to show your faith, not just for God's sake, but for you to actually become an acting Christian."

Frustration shot through his body and he moaned. "Come on, how do I show my faith to a God whose supposed to know what's in my heart already? Why would I have to?"

The phone went silent for a moment. He heard a quiet sniffle. "I think it's finally happening."

"What?"

"Never mind that, Ty. Listen, if you knew everything about being the best running back to ever play the game, why would you ever have to play?"

"What do you mean? That's crazy. What's the point in knowing something if you don't use it?"

"That's my point. I'll keep praying for you, Tyler, but if you really want to fight, you have to keep getting back up. You have to show you believe. Read Galatians, chapter 5, it will teach you the difference between knowing and playing. We have to do our part, not just know it. True faith is when you physically put your neck on the line not knowing how it will turn out."

He sighed again in frustration. "Okay, well, thanks. Thanks for everything, Celina. I guess I'll see ya'."

"Tyler, you're on your way now. I feel your life is about to change. Try to find that glimmer of hope."

"Yeah, well, I don't think His timing is going work out for us here, but thanks."

"I'll always love you Tyler."

He hung up the phone without quite comprehending the last thing she had said. He sat motionless, staring at the bottle in front of him. He tried to deny the immense feelings of self-pity, and push away the anger building deep within, but he found himself reaching for the bottle.

AFTER A FEW DRINKS, THE whiskey was beginning to flood his mind. He started looking around at all the pictures on the walls. He thought of what Rachel had told him that day in his bedroom before the accident. "Vince says that photographs can show us secrets, things the world has hidden from our eyes to keep our hearts from knowing the truth."

"Okay, Vince," he said loudly, "I'm gonna look at the pictures." He strolled around the room, sipping his whiskey and exploring the world through the eyes of his brother. There were pictures of woods, creeks, the river, animals, and birds. Some of them were quite impressive. If he had a good camera, he could probably make a living with his photography.

As he walked around, he began to notice the pictures were placed in chronological order. The pictures from his mother's funeral were in the kitchen. He began to wonder what his first pictures were taken of. He followed the dates and ended up in the bedroom. Next to Vince's bed were pictures from the hospital, pictures of the doctor and his staff, and some photos of their parents at their house. He saw the pictures that were taken of him and Jeanie in the kitchen. Just on the left side of the closet, he saw a picture of Vince's four-wheeler. Ty knew that he'd gotten it a couple of months after he moved out here, but the pictures on the right side of the closet were still from when he lived at home.

He sat on the edge of the bed and took a few drinks while he pondered the progression of the photographs. There was some time missing. He wondered if Vince had stopped taking pictures for some reason. On a whim, he got up and opened the closet door. The light string was tied to the door knob and it came on as he opened the door. To Ty's amazement, the closet was covered in more pictures. He gazed for a moment, then realized his glass was empty.

Ty instinctively put his hand on the wall to turn off the light when he suddenly remembered it was controlled by the string. As he lifted his hand from the wall, he uncovered a picture that made his heart stop. There, in front of him on the wall, was a picture of two men in the swamp. As he looked closely at other photos nearby, there were several more from the same day, all appearing to be laid out in progression according to the content of the photos.

~ 31 ~

Karl Dupree lay in bed with his hands behind his head, staring up at the ceiling. He thought about how long he'd known the sheriff, his old high school football coach and player at the Pine Island Country Club. Ty had been hinting at it, and now his mind was crunching the data. *Would Coach really cover for Lester?* He knew the sheriff to be a man of principle, and he'd never seen him do anything questionable, but money did weird things to people. *Sometimes friendships can run deeper than values, and most of the time money runs deeper than both.*

The phone rang, and Karl jumped three feet above the bed. He reached over and pulled the receiver to his ear.

"I screwed up again, man."

"Ty?"

"What was I thinking? The sheriff ain't gonna do nothing to Lester. He's his bread and butter, man; probably owes him money, too."

"Are you drunk? What the hell is going on, Ty? It's almost midnight."

"I should have just hid the evidence or given it to you instead. We could've nailed him, but his buddy the sheriff has all the goods now and they'll find a way to make it all go away."

Karl rubbed his face and looked up at the ceiling. "I would have had to turn it over to him anyway. I gotta think Coach will do the right thing."

"You heard him talking to Lester in your office; 'yes sir, no sir, yeah, I got the money.' Shit! I screwed it all up again, Karl. I'm gonna fix it, though. Just as soon as I get done taking care of what I got to do tonight, I'm gonna fix everything for Daddy."

"What do you mean, Ty? What do you have to do tonight?"

"I'm a fighter, Karl. That's all I know how to do. I should've done it a long time ago. I know right from wrong, and I know who the enemy is. It's time for me to kick some ass and make things right. I don't care what happens to me."

"Ty, that's the whiskey talking. You know better than that."

"Oh yeah? You'll never guess what I'm looking at."

"The bottom of a whiskey bottle?"

"Nope, not even close. It appears my older brother here has been holding a secret in his closet."

Karl sat up on the side of the bed and rubbed his neck in frustration. "What the hell are you talking about, Ty?"

"If a picture paints a thousand words, how many words does ten pictures paint?"

Karl sighed and shook his head. "My God, Ty, go to bed, man. You've had enough. I thought you quit."

"Karl, listen to me. I just found a whole slew of pictures here in Vince's closet. It's his truck, Karl; out in the swamp, in the freaking bog hole."

"Whose truck? Dammit, you're not making any sense, Ty."

"Terry's. These pictures show Terry and Joe-Glenn Hill sinking Terry's truck in the bog hole, then leaving on a four-wheeler. Why did he do that, Karl?"

"I don't know; maybe for the insurance. Ty, I'm tired and you're drunk. Can't this wait until tomorrow?"

Tyler spoke in a monotone voice, pausing for a couple of breaths between each sentence. "The truck is damaged . . . It's all tore up on the back right corner panel . . . The pictures have time stamps . . . It's the day I lost Jake and Rachel."

Karl froze and tried to push the fog from his brain. He remembered the story Terry had told about his truck being stolen when he and Joe-Glenn were out hunting. Ice clinking against glass chimed through the phone. "Karl, Rachel talked to Vince. She appeared to him in the swamp and told him it was time. She wants me to make it right."

"Come on, Ty, listen to yourself. I'll swing out there in the morning, pick up the photographs, and I'll go talk to Joe-Glenn. Now you get some sleep. We'll go take a look in the morning."

Ty growled through the phone. "That evil coward Terry; I'll kill that sonofabitch. They killed my family, Karl. I'll tear him apart with my bare hands."

"Take it easy, Ty. You don't know that for sure. You gotta let me do my job here, Buddy."

Karl heard a mixture of crying and growling as Ty had let the phone fall into his lap. "Ty? Ty?"

After a few moments, he heard breathing again. "I'm going to get him, Karl. I'm gonna jerk a knot in his ass and beat him within an inch of his life. When I get through with him, you'll know the truth."

"You'll do no such thing, Ty. You let me handle this. Besides, Terry is out of town. He won't be back for two days."

Ty went silent for a moment; then his voice grew low and soft. "I know. I called him and told him if he valued his life, not to ever come back. Now I'm going over to see Joe-Glenn."

"Dammit, Ty, don't be stupid. Stay home, man. No good can come of that. We'll handle it in the morning. Ty?" The phone went silent. "Ty? There's a storm coming through tonight. He ain't going anywhere, and you don't need to be out in it. Now dammit, stay home Ty. Do you hear me?"

"Um-hum."

"Ty? Talk to me."

"I heard you, brother."

The phone went dead. Karl set down the receiver and rested his elbows on his knees. "Un-freakin believable."

Dim flashes lit the wooden floor in his room, followed by a distant, slow rolling thunder that echoed softly through the piney woods.

~ 32 ~

Tyler Morgan stared at the pictures on the table in front of him. He set his glass down and grabbed the bottle and his keys from the table.

He drove out through the main gate and went down the road six miles to Old Union Road. The road had been carved out of the virgin forest in the last century as a main artery to access a water station and a checkpoint for the railroad. Later years had seen it used for logging. Now it was nothing more than an old hunting road that led to the shack of the gatekeeper for the Pine Island Country Club, Joe-Glenn Hill.

The woods flashed with light that caused the huge trees to creep about in titanic shadows as he slipped down the road dodging potholes and straddling ruts. He thought about how he would address Joe-Glenn, and wondered if he'd be able to keep his temper in check. His head was foggy, and on second thought, he really didn't much give a crap what happened.

The house was dark except for the dim glow of a TV as he pulled up between an old Ford 500 on blocks and a red pickup with a camper. He grabbed the bottle from the seat and walked to the front door. The wind was just starting to pick up, lifting the dirt from the worn-out ground around the house. As he stood in front of the door, he felt outside of himself, like a predator stalking his prey. He pounded on the door and hollered.

"Hey, Joe-Glenn; open up, man, let's have a drink."

Joe-Glenn Hill was once a darned good mechanic. He was a

goodhearted, simple man who lived for working on cars, hunting and fishing. He worked for Lester until about a year after Ty lost his family in the accident. His wife and daughter left him after the rumors about him molesting his daughter's best friend, and he started drinking heavily. For some reason, the Radcliffes took pity on him and stuck him out here in the woods as a gatekeeper and errand-boy for the hunters.

"Hey, Joe-Glenn, it's me, Tyler Morgan. Open up, bud, and let's polish off this bottle." Lightning flashed and he saw the curtains move in the window next to the door. "Come on, Joe-Glenn. It's me; old Tyler."

The door crept open and a thin, hollow-eyed man with greasy, tossed salt and pepper hair peered out through the crack. "I got a gun. What do you want with me?"

"Don't you shoot me, Joe-Glenn. Dad-gum, you old hard-ass, I just came by to have a drink with you."

Ty held the bottle up and Joe-Glenn's eyes froze on it. After a second, he forced a crooked smile exposing his rotten teeth and opened the door. He set the gun in the corner and pointed Ty to a filthy, dilapidated sofa, then went to the kitchen for glasses. Ty pushed aside a pile of fast food bags and set the bottle on the coffee table. He heard the water running for a second, then Joe-Glenn appeared with two plastic party cups. He sat gingerly on the edge of a worn recliner that appeared to be a Lester hand-me-down, and wrung his hands as he stared at the pour.

"You wasn't gonna shoot me now, was you, Joe-Glenn?"

"Nah, it ain't got no bullets."

Tyler handed him his cup and watched as his shaking hands enclosed it with long, bony clamps and took it straight to his mouth. He finished the half-cup without taking a breath and set it down quickly. He stared at the bottle as he wiped his mouth and rubbed his hands against his pants.

"Boy, you must have been thirsty. Here, bud, go for it."

Tyler shoved the bottle toward him and tried to act relaxed even though the smell of the place was about to choke him. Joe-Glenn's T-shirt was almost black at the neck, and he had the big red nose full of blackheads common among mechanics and drunks.

He waited a little while so that Joe-Glenn could get well oiled, then tried to start up some conversation. "I haven't seen you in a long time, Joe-Glenn. You're looking good still."

Joe-Glenn set his cup down and ran his hands through his hair with a grunt. "Hell, I get by, I guess. Got real sick not long ago, and I lost a lot of weight. Life ain't been too good to me, Ty."

"So what the hell happened to you, Joe-Glenn? You used to be the best mechanic in Texas, man?"

He watched as the drawn, frail creature reached out for more poison. "Things just didn't go my way. My life has been cursed 'cause of the things I've done. God punishes the wicked."

Tyler looked him up and down. His heart was mixed with anger and pity. He clenched his jaw and reached into his coat pocket, withdrawing the picture, and threw it onto the table in front of him.

"Things like this?"

Joe-Glenn recoiled from the photo with raging fear in his eyes.

"Pick it up. Look at it, Joe-Glenn."

He unwound slowly, timidly slithering a boney, gaunt digit to retrieve the photo. He appeared to be in mortal pain as he turned it where the light from the TV could shine on it. His eyes grew round and he threw the picture back onto the table and retreated into a ball in the chair.

"What's the matter, Joe-Glenn? Is the past coming back to haunt you?" The ragged, caustic creature was overcome with fear, shivering and mumbling under his breath. Tyler stood over him and glared down at him. "You want to tell me what happened, Joe-Glenn? Hey!" Ty slapped him on the head just hard enough to get his attention. "You better start talking, asshole. This ain't looking good for you. The only chance you got is if you cooperate and tell me the whole story."

He grabbed him by the hair and jerked him back up to the front edge of the chair as the man cried out. "Get yourself together, Joe-Glenn. I ain't gonna hurt you unless you don't talk. Now, take another drink to calm your nerves and start spilling your guts, you worthless piece of shit."

Joe-Glenn poured another shot and slammed it. He dropped his head and started shaking back and forth as Tyler waited and glared. "I knowed what you was here for when I seen it was you. I always knowed this day would come. You gotta believe me, man. I didn't have no choice. Terry said he was gonna kill me if I talked, and I know he would'a done it for sure."

Ty shoved the picture in his face and yelled, "Start from the beginning and tell me what happened."

Joe-Glenn shook his head and starting crying. "I'm so sorry, man. I wanted to come clean. Hell, I didn't do nothing wrong. I was just getting a ride home." He stopped and wiped his tears while he poured another drink. Ty stared a hole through him, waiting for him to begin again. "Okay. I'll tell you the whole story, man, but you gotta promise me you'll protect me. Terry will kill me, man."

"Karl will be here in the morning to pick you up. Terry is out of town, so you'll be fine. Now let's hear it."

Ty poured a drink for himself and waited. Joe-Glenn reached for another drink and Ty slapped his hand away. "Not until you tell me the whole story, then you can have the whole bottle."

Joe-Glenn slumped and sat there shaking his head back and forth. "We was at Lester's for the unveiling and we all got to drinking. Lester was getting mad. He said we was an embarrassment. Bobby, Doyle and Cooter lit out pretty quick, but I stayed behind because Terry was supposed to take me home. We was gonna leave out earlier, but the storm came through and we had to hunker down. Terry got real drunk and highly pissed 'cause he felt his dad was cutting him out of the project. He was smartin' off and Lester told him to get the hell out and to take me home. We jumped into the truck and he lit out of there like his tail was on fire. He was driving reckless, trying to scare me. I told him that the creek was coming up and it might be flooded. He just said, 'Hell, I'll just speed up and jump the damn thing.'" He started shaking badly, trying to catch his breath. "Ah, come on man. This is hard. I need another drink."

Ty poured him a drink and held it up in the air over the table. "You're doing good. Give me a little more."

Joe-Glenn wiped his mouth with the back of his hands and squeezed his jeans. "He punched it going up the hill by the creek and we caught air going over the top. By the time he seen your car, it was too late. He slammed on the brakes and we slid sideways into the back of your car. I saw you get knocked into the water, man. Then I seen your kid. Oh my God! He was flying in the air, then he just disappeared into the current. Your car slid forward and it caught the rushing water and tumbled away. I thought you was dead." Joe-Glenn stared at the cup, wild-eyed and shaking.

"I took a sigh of relief when I heard they found you, but seeing your kid like that, then I heard your wife was in the car; I couldn't live with it. It tore me apart inside. I went to drinking and doing stupid things."

Tyler's body caved in the middle like someone had hit him in the chest with a hammer. His arm dropped, and Joe-Glenn scurried for the drink. Ty went numb as he watched the man sucking down the whiskey. He suddenly found him intolerably revolting, an infestation of filth that deserved nothing short of total annihilation. Something foreign brewed from deep within, an eerily confident quiet; something he knew wouldn't stay that way for long. He watched his hand grip the neck of the bottle and pour himself a drink. His words spilled forth involuntarily, as if spoken by a spirit within him.

"So you and Terry killed my family."

He slammed the drink and stared at Joe-Glenn with complete indifference. Joe-Glenn grabbed the bottle and withdrew into the sofa, looking like a starving animal that knew a big croc was waiting at the watering hole but had to have that drink anyway. He started talking again, trying desperately to buy his freedom.

"I told Terry when they fired me that I was gonna talk. He carried me out to the old train bridge and said we was gonna talk about it. When we got there, he went to whooping on me, then he grabbed a rope and hung me from the bridge by my foot. He said to remember what it was like to stare death in the face, then he took out his knife and asked if he needed to worry about me talking anymore."

Tyler slammed the rest of his drink and threw the cup at him. "Just shut up, I've heard all I need to hear."

He started out the door, and Joe-Glenn jumped up and grabbed him. Ty turned and knocked him back into the chair.

"What the hell are you doing?"

"Please, Ty. You gotta give me something to protect me."

"You're lucky if I leave here without killing you myself. I told you Terry was out of town and Karl will be here in the morning. If you ain't here when he gets here, I'll track your ass down and bury you in that bog hole."

Joe-Glenn grabbed him again. "What if Karl don't come? You can't leave me out here defenseless."

Ty clenched him by the neck and spoke through his teeth, "Why should I care? You let me throw away five years of my life thinking it was my fault that my wife and son were killed. You let everyone in this town think I was a drunk and a killer. Your life don't mean shit to me."

He threw the scrawny drunk back into the chair, knocking the chair over and sending Joe-Glenn crashing into the lamp and side table. He cried a horrible moan as Ty stormed out of the house without looking back. His heart was beating in his temples as he stomped down the porch steps, kicking up dust as he headed back to his truck. He took rest against the side of the truck and hung his head over the bed. He tried to slow his breath as the light show continued in the woods around him. In the flashes, he could see his spear gun in the bed. He thought about his wife and son, and about the senseless way their lives had ended. A foreign and hungry force was now coursing through his veins; it was evil and delicious at the same time. In a surge of anger, he grabbed the spear gun, cocked it, and headed back into the house.

TY JUMPED OUT OF HIS truck and ran up onto Vince's porch where he turned to listen to the rain coming across the yard behind him. He took rest in a rocker, listening to the thunder and watching the light show as the rain poured hard and heavy on the tin roof above him. Physically and emotionally drained, he watched the raindrops connecting on the ground until tiny streams began to form. He knew this night would change his life forever. The storm was a timely cleansing of his tormented soul.

~ 33 ~

Karl Dupree pulled his car up to Joe-Glenn's house and stepped out, taking a deep breath of the cool, breezy morning. The woods were playful and sunny, and the smell of freshly cleansed pine filled his senses, taking him back as it always did to a childhood full of fond memories of hunting the backwoods with his father.

He took a long gander at the woods around the house, then casually went to examine the tire tracks he'd noticed as he was coming in. His heart suddenly leapt with fear as he noticed the tracks didn't match Joe-Glenn's little truck. His inner voice was reminding him what Ty had said on the phone last night. He looked up and saw footprints in the mud leading to the house. He ran up and knocked on the door.

"Hey, Joe-Glenn, it's Karl. Joe-Glenn?" Birds chirped, and the oaks danced in the wind, but no sound came from the house. He tried the knob and found it open, sticking his head inside. "Joe-Glenn, you in here?"

Karl's heart sank as he saw Joe-Glenn sitting on the couch with a spear through his chest. As he started in, his boot heel caught the strap of the spear gun that lay just inside the door. The recliner was knocked over and there was a bloody rag on the coffee table next to a bottle of Tyler's favorite whiskey. Joe-Glenn's eyes were drying up in their sockets. His mouth hung open, and his hands were gripping the spear.

Karl turned and stepped back out of the house slowly. He stopped and put his hands on his knees, looking down at the rotting timber on the porch. "Dammit!" He jerked off his hat and slapped it against his leg in anger. He stood for a moment with his hands on his hips, then went to use the radio in his car.

He pulled the transmitter out and leaned against the car, pushing his hat up on his head and taking a deep sigh. "Peggy, this is Karl. You need to get the coroner out here to Joe-Glenn's place, and tell the sheriff to meet me at Vince Morgan's right away."

"What's going on, Karl?"

"Just get 'em out here, please."

~ 34 ~

A siren howled through the woods, growing louder as it got closer. The sheriff's car slid a little sideways as he pulled up to Vince's house. Ty stood up from the rocker and stepped off the porch just in time to see the sheriff stoop low with his gun drawn.

"That's far enough, Morgan. Put your hands above your head and move on out here slowly."

"What the hell's going on, Sheriff?"

"Just do it. Where's your crazy-assed brother?"

"He's fishing, and he ain't crazy."

Tyler set his coffee on the ground and did as he was instructed.

"Let's go now, just spread your hands on the hood there and don't move."

The sheriff frisked him, then put a knee in his hips and pulled his hands behind his back to cuff him. His other deputy, Bradley Sinclair, came out of the house with photos in his hands. Bradley's daddy was a Nam vet, a heavily decorated sniper, and as a result, Bradley had always been an over-enthusiastic military wing-nut. It was good that he was so proud of his father, but the four-eyed bean pole wouldn't make a pimple on his daddy's backside. He made deputy purely out of the respect that the sheriff had for his father.

"Looks like we got motive."

"The sheriff kept a hand on Tyler's back as he looked at the photos. "What the hell is this?"

Tyler turned his cheek to the hood as he spoke. "It's proof that Terry and Joe-Glenn killed my family."

The sheriff exhaled with a frown. "This don't prove nothing."

"Them pictures was on the table next to an empty glass that smelled of whiskey, Sheriff," Bradley added proudly.

Sheriff McKinney sighed and pulled Tyler off the car by the back of his collar. "Tyler Morgan, you're under arrest for the murder of Joe-Glenn Hill."

Ty glanced over as Karl pulled up and jumped out of his cruiser. He stood with his car door open and put his hands on his hips.

"You got it all wrong, Coach. You don't understand." Tyler grunted as he was being pulled up.

"No, Tyler, as much as I don't want to believe it, I think I understand perfectly. Now judging by the fact that we found your spear gun at the crime scene, a spear in Joe-Glenn's chest, an empty bottle of your favorite whiskey on his table, and because you still smell like a distillery, I suggest you keep your mouth shut."

After he finished reading Ty his rights, the sheriff loaded him into the back of his cruiser. Ty couldn't believe what was happening. He racked his swirling mind to remember the details of the night before. Heading down the road back to the highway, he watched the sheriff in his rearview mirror. The silence fell upon him like a sack of bricks. Sheriff McKinney's cold demeanor was downright insulting considering the past they had with each other. He heard Karl come over the radio, sounding distraught.

"Hey, Sheriff, Tammy just got a call from Terry Radcliffe saying that Tyler called him and threatened his life last night. He'll come in to give a sworn statement when he gets back in town."

Ty's blood began to boil.

He looked around out the window and sighed, feeling sick as he thought of the uncontrollable rage that had consumed him the night before. They stopped at a red light after turning off the loop, and Tyler saw the sheriff's eyes cut to him in the mirror. He stared back, defeated and empty.

The light turned and they pulled away slowly. "I told you to let me do my job, Morgan."

"Yeah, well, somehow I didn't have the faith that you would."

The sheriff cut his eyes to Tyler again and frowned.

"It must have been hard finding that picture, given the date stamp on it. I'm sure in your state of mind it all made sense, but it don't prove nothing. There was no evidence of another vehicle at the scene. Besides how would they have crossed that raging creek?"

"He could have easily taken the back way out to the old Nacogdoches highway."

"That's pure speculation. It don't look good for you, Tyler, but if it's any consolation, I can't say for sure that I'd have acted any different myself if I believed what you believe."

"Yeah, well it ain't just a belief. I know the truth. Joe-Glenn spilled his guts to me last night. I needed his testimony to nail Terry. Why the hell would I kill him?"

"Rage and alcohol don't mix son."

Tyler sat on a cot in the corner with his knees up and his head on his arms as the sheriff turned the key in the door of cell number 4.

"It's your lucky day, Morgan. The D.A. says the evidence is circumstantial. Turns out the tire tracks and footprints weren't yours after all, and without something proving you were the one to pull the trigger, we've got nothing to hold you on but motive. You're free to go – for now."

Ty looked up and nodded with a long sigh as he stepped toward the door. As he started to walk by, the sheriff posted a brawny paw on his chest and looked him in the eye.

"Moose dropped your truck out front. Don't go far. I'm sure I don't need to remind you that you're still our number one suspect. I don't know how you pulled it off, but it's only a matter of time, Tyler. I just wish you would've let us do our job."

Tyler stared back at him defiantly. "If you were doing your job instead of running favors, the Radcliffes would be in that cell."

The sheriff let his hand fall and cast his eyes to the ground as Tyler walked out. After Tyler left the room, he heard the sheriff cuss and throw his keys as hard as he could against the wall; then he slammed the cell door, shaking the building.

Tyler headed to his father's house to pick up more clothes before heading back out to Vince's. As he approached the turnoff for the house, his cellphone rang.

"Hi, Ty, it's Jeanie."

She sounded concerned.

"I heard what happened. Are you okay?"

"I guess. I may have stepped in it for good this time."

She took a deep breath and tried to sound more cheerful. "I'm all settled in here at Margie's. She's going to a party at Karen's house and will probably stay there tonight. I planned a little surprise for you. I wanted to thank you for your help so I thought we might have a nice dinner and catch up some more."

A fresh, relieving sensation ran down his spine and through his chest, much like a cool shower after a hard day's work. "Wow that sounds awesome."

She paused for a moment, and he could hear her breathing. "I would love for you to come if you think you can."

"I think it would be wonderful. I wouldn't miss it for anything in the world."

"About eight then?"

"I'll be there. Thank you, Jeanie."

He hung up and took a deep breath. Why now? Right when things couldn't be getting any worse for him, he was finally embracing a stirring in his heart that whispered magical promises to his soul.

When he arrived at Margie's, the house seemed a little dark. He knocked and Jeanie came to the door wearing a beautiful black dress. She was every bit as lovely as he'd ever seen her. He stood there for a second gawking until she rolled her eyes and giggled.

"Well, silly, are you going to come in or just stand there all night?"

"I'm sorry." He looked down at his jeans, sports shirt and blazer. "I'm feeling a little underdressed."

As she walked ahead of him, he couldn't keep his eyes off her beautiful skin in the backless dress, and the tantalizing roll of her flowing hips. She led him to the dining room where two large candles burned above an inviting table with a gorgeous setting of food, a bottle of wine, and two glasses.

"Hope you're hungry."

"Man, this is some spread. You've outdone yourself."

"Please tell me you like pork loin and asparagus tips. I wasn't sure about the wine either. You do drink wine, don't you?"

"Of course. Are you kidding me? Everything looks awesome."

She fidgeted a second, then slid up next to him and reached over for the corkscrew, holding it up with a sheepish grin.

"Do you mind? Even if I manage to get the darn thing in without tearing up the cork, I never have the strength to pull it out."

He found himself staring again, unable to answer as his mind contemplated a snapshot of what life would have been like with her. She smiled ear to ear and gave him a gentle shove.

"Open it, goofball. The food is getting cold."

Tyler savored every bite of the delicious meal. He had a wonderful time not talking about anything in particular, just sharing her company.

Helping her with dishes was all pleasure and no work. He found himself floating above it all, listening to her sweet, chatty voice as she giggled and talked about old times by the lake. He watched her body moving to the rhythm of the dish work, her arms flexing, and her soft breasts teasing in the black silk with a bit of whiter skin showing here and there. He was mesmerized by her hair falling off her shoulders and waving about as she turned, sending waves of warm perfume over him, tantalizing and sedating him at the same time. Now and then her shoulder or hips would graze his, sending his heart into a flutter.

Afterward, they took the wine out to the back patio and sat on a wicker couch with thick, inviting cushions. Ty bragged again about how great the food tasted, just trying to maintain the flow of conversation. He looked up across the backyard, listening to the sounds of the night and trying to drown out the shouting in his heart.

"Wow, it's a bright night. I can see all the way across the yard just like it was day."

She tossed her hair and stretched. "Well, enjoy it while you can. There's supposed to be more rain later tonight."

"At least we're finally getting some. I guess you could say the drought has finally ended."

The conversation tailed off quickly, and suddenly Ty was nervous that he wouldn't think of anything else to say. Jeanie shivered a little and rubbed her arms. He looked at her with a sweet grin. "Are you cold?"

"Yes, a little. It just hit me."

"It is a little chilly tonight. You want me to light the fire pit?"

"Oh, that's a great idea. There's some wood over there under the shed."

WITH A WARM FIRE GOING, Jeanie snuggled a little closer to Ty and laid her head against his shoulder. "Thank you, Ty."

For the first time in many years he was beginning to feel whole again. He laid his troubles with Terry, Lester, and the law aside as much as he could and concentrated on the sound of her breathing and the smell of her hair. A thought crossed his mind that this might be one of his last free moments, definitely one that he would cherish for a long time. He put his arm around her and kissed the top of her head. After a few blissful moments, he felt her sob and heard a sniffle.

"Are you okay?"

She rose up and took a drink of her wine. "I'm just so disgusted with myself. Have you ever realized you made a major wrong turn in your life?"

"I think that's all I've been feeling lately."

"I just can't believe I let myself be taken in by Terry and his lies. I keep thinking that if I hadn't been so stupid, you and I might have had a great life all these years and maybe you wouldn't have had to suffer the horrible things you've suffered."

"Now, hang on, Jeanie. For God's sake, don't go blaming yourself for that. If I hadn't been so proud, I could've just driven up to school and talked to you face to face. We might've known then what we know now."

"I can't believe my entire adult life has been cheated away from me. As if the drugs and the abuse weren't enough, now there are these pictures of what he did. I married a murderer who killed the family of the only man I ever truly loved. It's all so sick. Is this God's way of punishing me for making bad choices?"

His heart stopped. He put his arm around her and held her as tightly as he could. "Jeanie, don't start getting crazy on me. You had no idea; no one did. Don't dwell on it; it does no good to try to dissect the past. We can't change it; God knows I've tried."

"Oh my God, Tyler, all those years that you took the blame for it. You really didn't know?"

"How could I have ever imagined? I tried hard to remember, but my mind always came up blank."

She sighed painfully and snuggled into him. "I'm so sorry, Tyler."

"Yeah."

He stared into the fire, traveling back from that horrible day, through the years, and back up to the current moment. He felt her arms tightening around him as her head lifted slightly and her lips found his neck.

"I meant what I said; you're the only one I ever truly loved."

He closed his eyes and let her words slowly wrap around his heart. She slid up into his lap and hugged him with all of her might. He held her for a long time, caressing her back, watching the fire dance, remembering their first kiss by the bonfire at the point.

"It feels incredible to hold you in my arms again, Jeanie. In a way, it's kind of surreal; like I've been lost on a desert island and just found my way home again."

"Ty, one of the reasons I asked you here tonight was to tell you that I filed for divorce today."

He looked deeply into her eyes, not really knowing what to say. She laid her head on his shoulder and sobbed.

After a long silence, she lifted her head, wiped the tears from her face, then reached over for her glass and took a long drink, finishing off her wine. She set the empty glass on the table and, without hesitation, ran her hands into his hair and pulled his face into hers.

His entire life rushed by in a heartbeat. All the years of his youth, all the wanting of her lips against his filled him with ecstasy. With her taut body in his lap, he allowed his hands to roam freely, rewardingly, down her back and across her entire body.

She bit his lip and pulled out gently on it as she sat up in his lap.

"We never know what tomorrow brings. Today I want to have what I've waited a lifetime for. I want to feel what we were cheated out of; what should have been - so many years ago."

Slowly, the black silk slipped from her shoulders and crumpled away, folding into her lap.

"Jeanie, are you sure?"

She put her finger across his lips, and as she slowly pulled it away, she replaced it with her lips. He ran his hands across her shoulders and around to her hips, pulling her into him as she pressed her lips ever more firmly against his, kissing him with all of her might. The firelight shimmered along her curves as he leaned her back and examined her perfection.

"I'm sure I'm deeply in love with you, Tyler."

He looked her in the eyes, taking in the precious moment when a lifetime of fantasy and unrequited love would finally be rewarded. With a gentle kiss he said, "I love you my sweet Jeanie. I always have, and I always will."

As the years of longing replayed in his mind, he became one with her. The pleasure was beyond his ability to imagine. Tears flowed from both their eyes as they expressed the fullness of their love in the ancient embrace.

BLISSFULLY EXHAUSTED, HE TOOK SLOW, deep breaths as she watched him lovingly. Her fingers danced upon his skin, admiring the muscles in his back as he turned and reached for his wine. She fondled his chest and kissed his shoulder as he took a drink. She turned toward the fire and he immersed himself in her gorgeous blonde curls as she leaned back against him. Gently, he caressed her soft skin as he kissed the top of her head. After a few quiet moments, she slid lower and laid her head against his chest. He noticed her breathing stop, then start again after a long, deep sigh. She trembled and shuddered as her words whispered above the crackling of the fire.

"I've never experienced anything so wonderful in my life. Tyler; that was the first time I've ever really made love."

He stroked her back and kissed her head. "That was amazing, my love. I only hope that we'll be blessed to enjoy our love for a long, long time."

TY WOKE, NOT REALIZING HE had dozed off. Jeanie was laying next to him, touching his face and watching him rest. She sighed and smiled as she rolled over on top of him and softly kissed his lips. He watched as her eyes moved around his face, until eventually they stopped, staring into his. She sat up and took a deep breath.

"Ty, there's something I need to ask you if you don't mind."

"Sure, anything." He pulled her back down and gave her a quick kiss on the lips.

She pushed up again and put her hands on his chest, fidgeting for a second, then cut her moist eyes up at him. "Ty, I hope you aren't offended by what I'm about to ask."

He reached out and put a finger under her chin to look into her eyes. "Ask me anything you want, darling."

"I just have to know the truth. I promise I won't judge you."

"What, baby?"

"Did you get mad and kill Joe-Glenn?" He closed his eyes and let out a short sigh as he shook his head. "It's just that, well, they said it was your spear gun, and that it had your prints on it and no one else's. I'm not going to judge you, Ty. I just need to know."

He gently rose and turned for his wine. After a quick drink, he set his wine down and turned toward her, grabbing her by the shoulders and looking directly into her eyes. "Absolutely not; I was extremely angry with him, but I didn't kill him. I was trying to leave after I got him to confess, but he kept hanging on me and saying that he feared for his life. He had a gun, but he didn't have any ammo. He was convinced that Terry would kill him when he found out we had talked. When I went outside to leave, I had to stop to settle myself. I saw the spear gun in the bed of the truck, and when I grabbed it, for a split second, I really did want to put him out of his misery, but when I went back in and saw him there, bleeding and whimpering, I just set it inside the door and left."

She sighed deeply and fell back against the couch. "Oh, thank God."

He poured more wine for both of them, finishing off the bottle, and put her glass in her hand. "Sweetheart, I know you're going through a lot right now, and given my circumstances, I don't blame you for wanting to know the truth. Before tonight, I'd been trying to decide if finding you again was a blessing or some sort of twisted punishment designed to show me what I missed out on. I've decided that you're a wonderful blessing, and I thank God for you. As God is my witness, I didn't kill anybody."

"Do you think Terry did it?"

He looked over at her and her face was wrinkled with shame. He knew what he thought, but he decided to spare her for the moment. "He could have, or he could have had one of his stooges do it, but there's no point trying to draw conclusions. Let's just let them do their investigation. I'm not sure about the sheriff, but I know Karl won't let them railroad me."

DRIVING HOME, TYLER WAS BATHED in joy and contentment. That certain tickle he'd so long been without had returned, and he almost wanted to start singing even though he couldn't carry a tune in a bucket.

He turned onto the highway and the bright, moonlit sky was fading on him. He bent forward and looked through the windshield up to the sky and could see fast-moving clouds. They were a lot like his life right now; moving quickly through the darkness.

As he passed the auction barn, he saw headlights come on and a truck pulled out onto the highway behind him. It followed at a distance until they were well out of town, then started closing in on him fast. He picked up his speed a little, but the truck kept getting closer. Suddenly, he heard a loud crack and a zing. It took a second for him to realize he was being fired upon. The bullet sounded like it had just missed the back window, striking the top of the cab.

He floored his old truck and ducked down as much as he could. The cracks and pops continued. He knew he needed to get off the double lane highway before the faster truck could overtake him. He tried hard to concentrate, but couldn't focus. Fear had the jump on him.

He took deep breaths and tried to steady his thoughts amid the rush of adrenaline. Finally it came to him. The lower Kingtown road was coming up, and it was an old single lane oil-top. If he could just make it there, he could probably lose them on the old winding road. He'd driven it as fast as he could many times as a teenager when he was cocky enough to think he had what it took to make a career out of it.

He saw the stop sign on the hill ahead and prepared himself for a quick turn. The old truck almost rolled when he slammed onto the brakes, turned hard, and gunned it again.

The pursuing truck was almost on top of him when he made the turn, and it slid past the road, but he knew it would only be seconds before he saw headlights again. He positioned himself squarely in the seat, put his hands at three and nine, and gave it all she had. His mind replayed the old road configuration and he soon found that familiar zone. The only thing he had to worry about was a deer jumping out in front of him.

He hit the straightaway just past the cemetery and pushed the pedal to the floor. Behind him he could see lights making the corner. A light rain had begun to fall, and as he flipped on his wipers, he hoped the pursuing driver would lose his nerve, but the headlights seemed to close on him again. A light came on in his head, and he remembered there was an old dirt road ahead that used to lead across an old wooden bridge barely wide enough for one car. The dirt road was the old way into Kingtown, before they built the new bridge at Marion's Ferry. Not far beyond the wooden bridge was the town, an old liquor run for when the county was dry. Maybe this guy couldn't drive so well on dirt.

The headlights behind him disappeared as he topped the hill and came to the dirt road. He shut off his lights and made the turn, sliding sideways on the dirt before he regained control. He strained to see the road ahead, but all went black as he dropped down into the woods. He hoped that perhaps he might have given the truck the slip, but as he turned on his lights, he could see the dust rising from behind him in the red glow of his taillights. The dust would be a dead giveaway.

Sure enough, before he could get far enough down into the woods to lose sight of the oil-top completely, he saw the headlights turning down the road behind him. His mind raced to think if there was anyone in Kingtown who could help, maybe a house he could duck into, but he knew it was hopeless. There was no way he could use his cellphone now. It had slid off the seat next to the passenger door.

Another shot rang out and he could hear it kissing off the rocks in the road. They were trying to shoot out his tires. He wound around a quick turn, sliding through it and staying on the juice like a dirt racer. He gunned it up the next hill; now he could see the bridge a quarter mile below. It was still there, but he couldn't tell what condition it was in. The truck that had been following caught air over the hill and was closing fast. As he surveyed the bridge in front of him, a crazy thought entered his mind.

Tyler let off the gas a little and timed the vehicle approaching quickly from behind. When he was almost on the bridge, the truck was right behind him. He slammed on the brakes and the pursuing truck swerved instinctively and took out the guard rail before plunging rear-over-front into the river below.

Ty threw his truck into park and caught his breath as his windshield wipers swished rhythmically. He took a deep breath and shook his head as he reached into the glove box and pulled out his flashlight.

Carefully, he inched up to the edge of the bridge and cast his light below. The truck lay upside-down halfway in the river with its wheels still spinning. The front of the truck was rapidly filling with water while the bed had come to rest below the current. Slowly, the vehicle moaned and slid into the water, floating a little toward the middle of the river before slipping out of sight. Ty looked for another few minutes to see if anyone had been thrown out, but the river bank was empty and quiet except for the pitter-patter of soft rain.

~ 35 ~

A cool breeze lifted the curtain and the bright sun smacked Tyler in the eyes. All at once, he began to recognize how loud the woods were. He pulled a pillow over his head. He knew it must be midmorning, but after the trauma he'd experienced the night before, he just wanted the world to go away.

He was almost fading back to sleep when a boot planted in his backside gave him a gentle shove. He slid the pillow off and rolled onto his back, looking straight up at Vince.

"Hey, mornin', Bro."

"You gonna sleep all day?"

"No, I'm up, I'm up."

"You want bacon or sausage?"

"Uh, to go with what?"

"Pancakes."

"Sausage." He said as he rubbed his eyes.

Suddenly, something hit him in the chest. He opened his eyes and saw it was a bible. "There's somethin' your s'posed to read."

He watched with an eerie, yet comforting feeling as his brother sauntered out. He rolled over and pulled back the curtain to look at the sky through the trees. It was a beautiful bluebird day; a good day to sit out on the porch after breakfast, take a big dip of Copenhagen, and read the paper, but his world was in chaos.

He knew he was still the number one suspect for killing Joe-Glenn. Today Terry would probably file a formal complaint for the threat he made against his life, and now there was another twist. He didn't even know who the dead were, or how many, upside-down in a pickup truck in the Angelina River where he'd put them. How long would it be before they found the truck? He opened the Bible and looked for Galatians, chapter five.

AS HE ATE HIS PANCAKES, Tyler searched his heart and soul, all the while listening for the sheriff to pull up outside. After reading Galatians 5:16-26, He finally understood why his prayers never seemed to be answered. Like Celina had said, It wasn't in the knowing, it was in the doing. Now he understood. The doing was all about living in the spirit and denying the flesh. If he wanted his prayers to be heard, he must be willing to sacrifice the flesh. Otherwise, he was just praying one thing and doing another.

"Did you make this sausage yourself, Vince?"

"Uh-huh."

"I've never had pan sausage that was smoked, or that had deer meat in it either. You might just have something here, Bubba."

"It's got pork and venison. I use hickory to smoke it and mix in a little oak."

"Well, it sure is good. Maybe we can get Massingil to let you sell it in their grocery store. We could call it *Vince's Backwoods Blend*."

Vince smiled and nodded. His smile dropped instantly as he perked up and looked past Ty out the kitchen window. A diesel truck was approaching. Ty was suddenly gripped by fear.

They went to the porch and watched as Karl's cruiser popped out of the wood line and came up the drive, followed closely by a wrecker and another sedan. Ty's heart sank. All he could think was they had found the truck in the river and now they were coming to get him. He poured into the rocker on the porch and went stone cold as he watched the vehicles line up in front of the shack.

Karl walked up first, pushing his hat back and posting a boot on the first step of the porch. He said hello to Vince and looked over at Ty. "I hate to do this to you, Ty, but I have some questions to ask you before we get started here today."

Ty remained almost lifeless, giving only a slight nod to indicate his awareness.

Karl pulled out an envelope as Moose jumped out of the wrecker and started for the porch, followed by a small, portly man with a bald head and round, black-rimmed glasses. Ty hadn't noticed that the wrecker belonged to Moose when it was pulling up. He began to feel a little better when Moose jumped up onto the porch; shook hands with Vince, then offered his hand to him.

Karl handed the envelope to Vince and introduced the stranger. "Vince, this here is Mr. Hollis Greer, special investigator from Woodland Indemnity Insurance Company. You'll see here they have a court order to exhume the truck from your swamp back there."

Hollis shuffled his clipboard and papers around and stumbled up the steps to shake hands with Vince. Judging by the slightly horrified look on Hollis' face, Ty figured Vince must have appeared to him as a character out of a backwoods massacre movie. "Hello, sir; Hollis Greer. It's a pleasure to meet you."

Vince mumbled back at him. "Hey."

Ty looked at Karl and his face was expressionless, but his eyes told him everything he needed to know. Karl asked him to step out into the yard for a second.

"Listen, Bud; Terry might be on his way out here. He was supposed to meet me at the station, but he didn't show up. If he does, I need you to stay as far away from him as you can. I should lock you up in the back of my car, but I need you. Now, am I gonna have to worry about you doing something stupid?"

Ty took a deep breath and ran his hand across the back of his neck. "I'll be cool."

"You better, if you want to prove that your threat was just drunken stupidity. Don't forget, you still have a court hearing coming up."

"No, Karl, I'll keep my distance. Tell me something; how did the insurance company jump on top of this so fast?"

Karl smiled. "Well, the sheriff said not to put too much effort into it until we got through babysitting the Feds, but I had to file the report anyway, so I made sure I called the insurance company and told them I had heard the Radcliffes were going to send their own wrecker out to recover their property. As it turns out, that wasn't even necessary. They had another customer to come see out this way this morning; a fatal accident."

Ty stiffened. "You don't say."

"Yeah, well, about the accident; you wouldn't happen to know what happened last night up near Kingtown, would you?"

Ty froze for a second. He couldn't decide whether to confess or act ignorant. His heart pounded in his chest. Even though he'd acted in self-defense, he knew he was guilty for leaving the scene of an accident. Karl frowned at his hesitation and continued to fill in the rest of the story.

"Some old river rat out of Kingtown was running his lines this morning and found Doyle Kitchens crunched up in his truck and hung up on Gator Island. They found where he'd run off the old wooden bridge. We know he was up to no good. He had a rifle with him, a half-empty bottle of Southern Comfort, and several spent cartridges were found in the cab."

He paused and stared at Ty, who was looking off into the woods. "By the way, I noticed there were some bullet holes in your tailgate."

Ty dropped his head and kicked at the dirt. "Doyle Kitchens, huh? What should I say, Karl?"

"Just tell me the truth, Ty."

"Okay. I was with Jeanie last night at Margie's until sometime after one. After that, I headed for here. I picked up a tail when I passed the auction barn and he started firing at me. I couldn't lose him, so I slammed on my brakes at the bridge and he swerved and went over the side."

Karl heaved a deep sigh and put his hands on his hips. "Just so happens you knew right where to find the only one-lane bridge within twenty miles. Dammit Ty. Why didn't you call it in?"

"I don't know. I was scared and my mind wasn't clear. So what do we do now?"

Karl moved his hat back and forth and looked around. After a long sigh, he put his hand on Ty's shoulder. "Look, it's not every day someone gets shot at. Let's just pretend I haven't said anything to you yet, and you can report it to me before I leave this morning. We'll just say that you panicked, not knowing who was shooting at you or if anyone else was following you, and you fled here for safety. You would have reported it, but seeing how you had left the scene, you figured you needed to do it in person, so you were going to head in this morning."

"That'll work?"

"It'll have to do. With the bullet holes in your truck that will match up to his gun, I'm pretty sure you won't be charged with anything."

They stood and looked at each other for a second. Tyler sighed and shoved his hands into his back pockets as he looked back at the others. "Thanks, man."

Karl looked straight up. "Yeah, well, watch your ass, Ty. Doyle wasn't the shooter, just the driver. Ho-ho, boy, the sheriff is gonna love this. Let's go pull up a truck."

They walked back up onto the porch where the others were. Hollis had finally warmed up to Vince a little and the three of them were talking about fishing. Karl stood in front of everybody and got their attention.

"Okay, guys. If you don't mind, Vince, we'd like you to take us back there and show us the best way to get to that truck. Ty, I need you, if you can, to dive down and try to hook us up. Moose volunteered to do it, but without any gear it could prove quite challenging since no one knows just how deep that hole is."

Ty nodded. "No problem, I'll grab my gear."

THE BOG HOLE WAS DEEP and dark as Ty descended with the cable in his hand. Thoughts of the lake and the Moore farm ran through his mind as his light picked up a reflection below. The truck sat on an incline with the grill buried in the muck. He swam back around to the rear of the truck and hooked the cable around the trailer hitch.

Moose manned the winch, and Ty, with his gear now off and his jeans back on, stood alongside Vince and watched as the back bumper of the Ford truck broke the surface and bounced slowly over the cypress knees on the bank.

Vince put his massive paw on the back of Ty's neck and squeezed lightly. He looked sadly into his brother's eyes, then walked directly into the thicket behind them.

"Vince, where are you going?"

The sound of throaty pipes and an engine revving through the woods caused everyone to jerk around. A new, bright red F350 pulled up. Terry Radcliffe jumped out, looking furious. He marched up toward his old truck, which was now on solid ground, and hollered over the sound of the winch to Karl, who had intercepted him next to the wrecker. "What the hell is going on here?"

Moose shut off the winch and stepped over next to Ty while Karl talked to Terry. Karl was pointing over to Hollis, who was now walking around the truck.

"That guy is an investigator for Woodland Indemnity. They have a court order to exhume the truck. I told you to come to the station this morning so that you could come with us. Where were you?"

Terry glanced at Karl impatiently. "I had to drive in from Houston. Why are they getting involved?"

"I think you know that, don't you, Terry? A thirty-six thousand dollar claim for a stolen truck and a picture of you and Joe-Glenn out here sinking it in the swamp is bound to raise some questions."

Karl looked back to check on Ty, who was bowed up and taut like a tiger ready to pounce. He pointed his finger at Ty and cocked his head as if to say *Down, boy*.

Ty flared his nostrils and turned his attention back to Hollis who was waiting for the last of the water to spill out of the driver's side door. He then tried to pry it open farther, but to no avail, so he commissioned Moose for some assistance.

Moose grabbed the door with both hands and, with a loud grunt, jerked the door past the rust-fused section of the hinges. Hollis stood back and chuckled.

"Well, well, well, what do we have here?"

He took a couple of pictures and then reached down and pulled the hickory stick from the floorboard that was still wedged against the gas pedal.

Terry was beginning to twitch and pace about nervously. He took off past Karl and started walking toward Hollis. Ty glared and began walking around the other side of the truck as Karl joined Terry, trying to stay between them.

A call came over the radio in Moose's wrecker. The sheriff was asking for him to meet them out off the lower Kingtown road to pull a truck out of the river. Moose looked over at Hollis, who waved at him without looking up.

"It's okay, you can go ahead. Just leave this one here and we can come back for it. I'll need a few more minutes, then I'll catch up with you over there."

Ty left Karl, Terry, and Hollis standing by the driver side door as he made his way around to the right rear corner panel. He froze, studying the damaged panel.

Terry was trying to act surprised as Ty overheard him talking to Hollis.

"What's that stick all about?"

Hollis pushed up on his glasses and grinned, but didn't say anything. Ty suddenly hollered in a loud, but monotone voice. "Karl, there's something you need to see here."

Karl headed for the back of the truck with Terry following closely. When they reached Ty, he pulled the shard of taillight out of his pocket.

"I told you I had proof." He stuck the shard into an opening in the taillight where it fit perfectly.

"That's the piece of taillight you found at Joshua Creek?" Karl asked.

Tyler couldn't speak. He grabbed the tailgate and squeezed as the anger began to boil up from deep within. Suddenly, he glared up at Terry.

As Karl put his hands toward Tyler to calm him down, Terry freaked out, grabbed Karl's gun, and struck him in the head. Karl's eyes rolled and his body went limp. Ty reached over Karl as he was falling and punched Terry in the face, sending him falling backward, but he rolled up as soon as he hit the ground and had the gun aimed right at Ty.

Hollis pulled a revolver from his hip holster and pointed it at Terry. "Drop it, mister!"

Terry whipped around and fired at him, sending him ducking behind the truck. Ty ran behind Terry's truck, using the cover to slip out into the woods. As he legged it through the underbrush, he heard Terry firing again. A bullet whizzed by and struck a tree near him. He ducked behind a large oak and peeked out to see if Terry was going to follow him. Terry was looking his way, scanning the woods.

Behind Terry, he watched as Hollis retreated toward the giant cypress to gain better cover. The poor guy was moving the best he could, but he was having trouble navigating the array of cypress knees and he tripped and fell. He must have struck his head against one of the cypress knees because he never moved. As he lay there unconscious, Terry started walking toward him.

Ty decided to slip back up to Terry's truck knowing that he stood a better chance if he could find a gun inside. He rifled through the glove box and checked under the seat, but found nothing. As he looked back toward Hollis, Terry had stopped walking and was just standing there. Ty made a break for the house. He took Terry's keys and threw them off into the woods as he ran.

Inside the house, he looked for Vince's rifle, but it was nowhere to be found. He caught a glimpse of Terry out the window, coming up the path toward the house. As he neared the house, he stopped inside the wood line and listened. Ty knew he had to find a way to get the jump on him, otherwise he didn't stand a chance without a weapon.

He ran out the front door, jumped off the porch and ran to Hollis' car to check for his keys. The car was locked. *Where the hell is Vince?* Hearing the footfalls on the dry leaves, he quickly took cover behind his own truck. He watched Terry come from behind the house cautiously, and run over to Hollis' car. Finding it locked, he started for Ty's truck. He was almost to the door when Ty ran out from behind the truck and tackled him.

The gun went flying off into the dirt. They wrestled and punched at each other, rolling over and over in the dirt in front of the porch. Terry pinned him for a second and raised up to get a solid lick on him, but Ty looped a leg around his neck and pulled him to the ground. They both scrambled to their feet and sized each other up, but Terry saw Vince's walking stick leaning on the porch and decided he wanted an advantage.

He went after it and Ty followed, but Terry reached the long stick in time to grab it baseball-style and whirl it around at Ty's head. Tyler ducked just in time to avoid getting his head bashed in, but he wasn't prepared for Terry to immediately swing back the other direction. The stick caught him square in the side of his bad knee, sending him toppling to the ground.

Seeing he had Ty temporarily immobilized, Terry ran out and found the gun that had been knocked into the dirt. He picked it up and walked slowly back toward Ty, stopping just a few feet from where he lay moaning and clutching his knee. Ty screamed at him, "You sorry sonofabitch. That's the second time you took out my knee."

"You should've stayed the hell away from here, Ty. This ain't your home no more, this is my town, and you ain't never been a match for me."

"So are you gonna shoot me now or what, Terry?"

"Shut up and let me think."

"What's there to think about? You've already killed at least three people that I know of. If you don't kill me now, I promise you're going to jail or Hell, depending on who catches up with you first."

"I'm sorry about your family, man. It was an accident, an unavoidable accident. Whether they nailed me for it or not, I knew it wasn't going to bring 'em back. I couldn't afford to get taken down by that. I would've lost everything if I would've gone to jail for manslaughter. What the hell were you doing there anyway? What kind of dumb-ass parks his car with his family in it next to a raging flooded creek?"

"What kind of dumb-ass floors it over that hill knowing that creek was there? If I wasn't there, you and Joe-Glenn would be dead."

"I guess all things happen for a reason, even accidents."

Tyler sat up, clutching his knee, and took a deep breath. "Really, Terry? And poor useless Joe-Glenn? Was that an accident, too? Come on, man, did you really have to kill him?"

"You made it too easy leaving me that spear-gun like that, and as far as everyone knows, I was in Houston. Joe-Glenn was a weak, pitiful excuse for a human being, not to mention a huge liability for me. It was only a matter of time before he squirreled out and squealed on me. He wasn't going to live much longer anyway. He was dying of liver rot. The way I see it, I just saved him from a slow, miserable death. I couldn't have him getting all religious on me and clearing his conscience on his death bed. I just put him out of his misery before he could do any more damage."

Ty rose to his feet, still favoring his right knee, which was swelling fast. "I just gotta know one thing before you shoot me, Terry. That day you killed my wife and son at Joshua Creek and left me for dead; is that when you first knew you were evil? Maybe it was before that, when you broke Jeanie's heart and stole our love from us, or even earlier, when you ruined my career."

Terry's hand was shaking. He knew Ty was stalling him and he was running out of time. Karl or Hollis would be coming around soon. He should've taken Hollis' gun. He knew he had to make a decision. He strengthened his resolve and cocked the pistol.

"What are you going to do, kill all three of us?"

"I don't see as I have much choice. I'm sure I can make it look like you screwed up again. That's the one thing I could always count on. I was always better than you at everything, Morgan, but you always got the girl and all the glory. Life is a battle, my old friend, and I'll always be a warrior, ready to meet the challenge. I'll make it clean and painless for you."

He lifted the gun and pointed it directly at Ty's head. As his finger began to close on the trigger, he heard footsteps behind him and turned, leading with his gun hand, which was quickly forced up into the air.

Vince held Terry's arm with his left hand while he clamped his huge right hand around his neck with the other. The gun went off, shooting up into the air, and Vince growled, lifting Terry from the ground and tossing him like a rag doll against the tree by the porch.

Terry never moved a muscle after hitting the tree. The large meat hook mounted on the tree for cleaning catfish pierced the back of his skull just above the neck. He hung there twitching with his eyes bulging out. Ty looked away and fell back onto the porch steps. Vince grunted and looked around as if not knowing what to do with himself.

Ty watched as his brother turned in circles a few times, looking up in the air, then walked inside the house and came out with his camera. He took two pictures of Terry and walked off into the woods.

~ 36 ~

Tyler and Vince followed their father into the funeral home, and they slipped quietly into the back row. From the moment he sat down, Ty saw Lester staring at them. His eyes bored a hole through them as he motioned for Bobby Buell to come over to him. After a moment, Bobby walked over to Charlie, who was sitting nearest the aisle and put a hand on his shoulder while he spoke.

"Mr. Radcliffe says there ain't no Morgans welcome here. Now get your asses out of here before we ask the sheriff to escort you out."

Ty and Vince heard what he said, and they both glared at Bobby. Charlie put his hand up in front of the boys and shook his head. He stood and motioned for them to follow him and they started walking out. As they reached the door, Jeanie was coming in. She gave Charlie and Vince a quick hug and then grabbed Ty's hand and pulled him close to her. She whispered into his ear, "Where are y'all going?"

"Lester said we weren't welcome here."

"That's ridiculous. I say you are."

"Don't fight it, Jeanie. On behalf of my family, I want to offer you our condolences. We can pay our respects later."

He gave her a peck on the cheek and followed his brother out the door.

Sheriff Warren McKinney was sharing a cup of coffee with Karl and Deputy Sinclair when Lester Radcliffe's Land Rover pulled up in front of his office.

"Looks like you got company Sheriff," Karl noted.

Lester walked in, stopped, gave them a quick, cold stare, then continued without invitation into the sheriff's private office. The sheriff frowned, dropped his head for a moment, then reluctantly followed him.

Lester was seated in a chair in front of the desk with his head down when he closed the door and walked past him. After an uncomfortable silence, the sheriff took a drink of his coffee and set it down with a long sigh as he propped his elbows on his desk and clasped his hands, frowning sympathetically. "I'm sorry about your boy, Lester."

Without looking up, Lester began speaking. "What are we going to do about his killers, Mac?"

The sheriff leaned back and sighed again. "Lester, he accosted my deputy, fired upon an insurance investigator, fired upon Tyler and was ready to put a bullet in his head when Vince stopped him."

Lester began to swell up. "It's all circumstantial, Mac. My son ain't here for us to hear his side of the story. They provoked him and put him in a compromising position where he had to defend himself, then they killed him."

The sheriff clasped his hands over his stomach and took a minute to search for the right words. "I can appreciate how you must feel right now, Lester, but I don't think that scenario is going to hold water against four eye witnesses, my friend. Now, granted, Karl and Hollis weren't there when Terry was killed, but we're checking out their stories and gathering the evidence. Evidence don't lie. You never know what we might find, but I got to tell you right now, unless we find something that refutes their story, I can't charge them with anything."

Lester gritted his teeth and glared. "Ty Morgan killed Joe-Glenn Hill, then he provoked my son and they killed him, too. What the hell do you need to do your job, Mac?"

The sheriff stiffened at the insult and pounded his index finger onto his desk. "Come on, Lester, I've got an insurance investigator lying over there in the hospital with a crease in his skull where he fell trying take cover from Terry shooting at him." He stood up, snarled, and pointed toward the door. "I've also got a deputy outside that door with a knot on his head where your boy stole his pistol and knocked him out." He rumbled under his breath like an old grizzly, then walked past Lester out the door.

After a minute, he came back in, slamming the door behind him. He threw a file onto the desk in front of Lester and sat down as he was speaking. "That's the coroner's report on Joe-Glenn Hill. Unless Tyler Morgan can fly, he didn't kill Mr. Hill. The coroner says he was killed around five A.M. Karl found him around eight-thirty. When we got to Vince's that morning just before nine, we felt the hood of Ty's truck and it was stone cold. Vince's four-wheeler has a flat and it looks to have been sitting in the same place for a couple of months."

"That was plenty of time for the hood to get cold again."

The sheriff frowned. "It rained that night around three-thirty, and Ty's tire tracks were mostly washed away behind his vehicle where it was parked at Vince's, proving he was home by then. There was a fresher set of tire prints found at the scene, but they were tires for a large sedan, not a truck, and definitely not any vehicle owned by the Morgans. There's no way to walk by road or swamp back to Vince's in that period of time, and there were no fresh footprints in the wet dirt around Vince's house, proving that neither he nor Tyler had been out of the house since the rain."

He paused to give Lester a chance to respond, but he just sat staring at the desk with his jaw fixed.

"Look Lester, I've asked Dr. Mize to look over all of his findings one more time to be sure, but at this point, there's absolutely no evidence pointing toward either of the Morgan boys. Besides, there's this." He pulled another file from the corner of his desk and handed it to Lester.

Lester opened the file and looked at the picture on top. The sheriff put his finger on the photo. "This picture was taken the day after Ty's accident. The date and time stamp in the bottom right corner shows January 29, 1998. Lester, that's Terry and Joe-Glenn sinking Terry's truck in the swamp. According to Ty, both Terry and Joe-Glenn had confessed to running into his car when he'd stopped to look at the flood waters. From the looks of things, Terry had a reason to cover his tracks."

Lester stood and slammed his fists onto the desk. "According to Ty, my ass! This is an outrage. Dammit, Mac, the sonofabitch had a hard-on for Terry since he ruined his knee and had to watch Terry go to UT on a football scholarship. Don't forget, Jeanie was his girl until she dumped him and started dating Terry at college.

"Now he comes swinging into town, stealing my daughter-in-law, provoking my son, trying to raise a lawsuit against me, and telling everybody I killed Sterman Moore. For Pete's sake, Mac, the sonofabitch is crazy! It's clear he's been off somewhere for the last five years sulking and scheming on how to wreak vengeance upon my family, and he's come back to execute his plan. Now, I don't know how he pulled it off, but dammit, as your primary campaign contributor, I want to know what you're going to do to see justice done and things made right for me."

"Keep your voice down, Lester, and settle down. Now listen. We're doing everything we can to ensure a thorough investigation into Terry's death. If they're guilty, I guarantee you we'll find out. I promise you we won't rest until we're convinced we know the truth."

Lester puckered his lips and lowered his head.

"I know you're hurting, Lester. I can't even imagine how it would feel, but I don't have a magic wand. Now, if you're done with me, I have a couple of questions for you."

Lester shrugged and folded his arms.

"It's about this business with Sterman Moore, I've got to know the truth or I can't help you."

Lester shook his head and frowned. "What the hell do you want from me?"

"I want to know everything you know."

"Well, I think you do. Hell, that was thirty-eight years ago. They already cleared me. You're bound to have an old file around here somewhere. It'll show that I left town the day before he disappeared. I had to go take care of a sick relative in Nevada. They can't harass me about this, Mac. It's called double jeopardy. I'm protected by law."

"I know what the file says, Lester, and no, it's not double jeopardy. You were never charged, much less tried for his murder. You don't seem to understand the gravity of the situation. In a few weeks, the Feds are going to authorize us to exhume the remains of Sterman Moore, truck and all. Once we make a positive I.D. on the body, the case will have to be reopened, and I'll have Federal eyes on me, not to mention reporters from all over hell and creation. If there's anything I need to know, by God you better tell me now."

Lester slid up in his chair and started straightening his tie. After a few moments, the sheriff heaved a sigh, and reached into his drawer, producing a brown envelope.

"I shouldn't do this, but we've been friends a long time." He reached in, grabbed the contents, and rolled it across the desk toward Lester. Lester stared at it for a minute, then slowly picked it up. "Is that your class ring?"

Lester examined the ring closely. "Where the hell did you find this?"

"I didn't find it. Ty Morgan did."

Lester paused for a moment, then laughed. "That don't raise any questions in your mind? Did you ever stop to think that maybe his grandfather killed Moore? Angus Morgan was an ornery old cuss. If you got cross with him, he'd sooner smack you down as look at you. Moore owed him money, too; a lot of money. Hell, for that matter, I could've lost that ring to old man Moore or to Angus either one in a poker game when I was stoned drunk. I drank a lot in those days. That's the way it was back then; we gambled everything. I bet Angus had a stash of all kinds of things that he won in poker games that got handed down after he died. Maybe Tyler and his dad concocted the whole damn thing to discredit me."

The sheriff winced at the thought. His expression seemed to light a fuse in Lester.

"You know, Mac, Temple is running against you next election, and without my support you don't stand a chance against his money. What are you going to do if that happens? You ain't never done anything else besides coaching. You gonna be a coach again? Hell, the YMCA wouldn't have you."

The sheriff clenched his teeth and breathed through his nostrils. "I'm sure I'll land on my feet."

"Well, I'd rather you didn't have to worry about that, wouldn't you? Now I'm going to tell you one more time, Ty is a sly little sonofabitch, and he set everything up thinking you're just a dumb country sheriff who's going to fall for it. It's a clear case of framing. Granted, I ruined his grandpa and his daddy, but business is business. If you let this stuff fester, everyone is going to be in our business. You've gotta do what you gotta do to put Tyler Morgan behind bars and throw away the key. That's the way it has to be. We own this country, Mac. We make the rules, it's your evidence, so make it work."

"I've got to find proof, Lester. That's all there is to it."

Lester jumped up, sending his chair falling backward. He leaned over the desk, pointing his finger at the sheriff. "Screw proof. My son is dead because of him, and now he's got me in his sights. I ain't standing around and waiting for him to frame me. I didn't come all this way and build this empire and all my connections to let some punk weasel it out from under me and send me up the freaking river."

The sheriff stood and put his hands on his hips. He looked square-jawed at Lester to let him know he didn't cater to his aggression one bit. Lester looked up at the taller man and his disposition changed. He put his hands out, palms up, and smiled.

"Come on, Mac, like you said, we go way back. Can't you see through this guy? Let me help you out. Hell, he had his brother kill Joe-Glenn after he forced him to confess. That freak knows his way through the swamp. Terry saw he was getting framed and he panicked. They provoked him when he went out to identify his truck so Vince could kill him, too. Even if Terry did have that accident, it ain't no cause to go above the law and seek personal vengeance. That's murder, premeditated murder. That crazy brother of his is a menace to society. Don't forget the Cooper boy he killed for trying to steal his four-wheeler."

"Oh, come on, that was an accident. He was trying to protect his property."

"By jumping out of the woods and tackling a guy going thirty miles an hour on a four-wheeler?"

"He was stealing it, and Vince didn't use a weapon."

"Vince *is* a freakin' weapon! He broke his damn neck! Look, the bottom line is, they've got no defense other than their own word. Now he's gunning for me and if he frames me, he'll take you down too. Like you said, who wants reporters and investigators looking into my campaign contributions and asking questions about our poker games? Now that you get the gist of how this all plays out, I'm sure you can find the evidence you need to put him away. You're one of the smartest men I've ever known, Mac. Now do what you do best and go get those bastards."

Lester straightened his shirt and nodded before turning to walk out.

"I'll be needing that ring back, Lester."

Lester turned and looked at him blankly. "There's no point in tampering with evidence if there's nothing to hide." The sheriff added.

He pulled the ring out of his pocket and pitched it to him with a wink.

"Only as a last resort, right?"

~ 37 ~

Karl pulled his cruiser into the service area at Radcliffe Ford and took a box from the back seat. He was met with an unexpected silence and grim faces as he stepped from the car and headed into the dealership. He stopped at the service desk and waited for Brenda Hicks, who ran the service department, to get off the phone. Employees filtered by offering silent nods and glancing at the box that read "Terry Radcliffe" on the side. Brenda hung up and tried to hold back a tear.

"Hi, Brenda. Would you mind asking Jose to change my oil while I see Mr. Radcliffe?"

She nodded and wiped her face. "Sure, Karl. I'll get him right on it."

"Thank you."

He lifted the box off the counter and walked through to the showroom and up the stairs to the executive offices.

"Hi, Stacy, can you tell Mr. Radcliffe I'm here?"

"Hi, Karl. He knows you're coming. He said to go on in when you got here."

He took a deep breath, shuffled the box under one arm, and opened the grand oak door to Lester's office. Lester was leaning back in his chair facing the window with one arm draped on his desk.

"Come on in, Karl. Set that over on the table."

"Yes, sir."

Karl set the box down and started to walk out when he heard Lester turning in his chair. "You got a minute, Karl?"

"Sure."

He stopped and stood behind the chairs in front of Lester's desk. Lester folded his hands over his desk, looking down and frowning.

Although he'd grown up with Terry, Karl had never had many conversations with his friend's father. Lester hadn't been the kind of father to hang out with his son much. He'd always worked late and stayed busy on weekends.

"Please, take a seat. Does your cruiser need any work done?"

"Oh, no. I asked Jose to change the oil, but it's fine otherwise."

"Good."

Karl took notice for the first time that Lester wasn't as big a man as he'd always seemed. He probably went somewhere around five ten, but he'd always seemed much bigger. His hair that he always wore combed straight back was mostly gray now. His pointed nose seemed longer and his cheeks much puffier. He still wore the French cuff shirts with cuff links and collar bar. Karl's eyes walked down his sleeves and across the busted finger to his desk to find the gold coin sitting in the glass case just as he'd heard.

"Listen, Mr. Radcliffe, I'm sorry about Terry."

"Not nearly as sorry as I am, Karl. Listen, Karl, I've never been a man who beats around the bush. I like to lay my cards on the table and get straight to the point. I think you know that about me."

"Yes, sir."

"Karl, I need to ask you an important question."

"What's that, sir?"

"Is Jeanie still in love with Tyler Morgan?"

Karl shook his head and looked down for a moment. When he raised his head, he looked Lester straight in the eye. "Honestly, I don't think I am in a position to be able to answer that, sir."

"Well, of course not. After all, he's always been your best friend, hasn't he?"

"That's not it. I'm just not that close to Jeanie." Karl was a little confused. "Just what are you getting at sir?"

"Well, it's the way women are. When things get tough, they start looking for a way out, and what better way than to go back to an old lover who happens to show up just at the right time."

"I don't think I understand."

Lester chuckled and touched his cuff links. "Oh, I bet you do. You see, I've got it all figured out, Karl. Tyler Morgan has made it his life's purpose to see me ruined and his family back in control of everything they lost. That includes Jeanie. He set Terry up and had his brain-dead brother do the killing for him. They knew he would go out there and stand up for himself. All the while, Tyler has been coaxing Jeanie back. Now, the final part of his plan is to discredit me; first by suing my company, then by trying to make everyone believe I killed Sterman Moore."

"No offense, sir, but I was there. Terry stole my gun and struck me in the head. I think the evidence points clearly to what actually happened."

Lester pounded his fist on the table. "Dammit, you country bumpkin cops just don't have the brain power to see the bigger picture. People have to resort to extreme measures when they're backed into a corner. He didn't shoot you, did he?"

"No sir, but . . ."

"Well, there's your real evidence. Now you listen to me. I'm a powerful businessman. I'm successful at what I do. I've been all over the world and seen every trick in the book. I'm used to people trying to weasel away my fortune, so I have a keen eye for clearly seeing their game plan. It's all smoke and mirrors. Let me teach you something, boy. Now that my son is dead, Tyler Morgan is halfway there. Don't you get it? Jeanie gets everything that Terry had. Now, granted, it ain't a lot because he was having troubles, but once he gets me out of the way, everything I got goes to Terry's estate, which means Jeanie gets it all. Just like that, he gets his girl back along with everything I own."

Karl sighed and stood. He checked his watch. "Sounds rather complicated to me, Mr. Radcliffe. You honestly think he's that methodical?"

"Think about it, Karl. You haven't seen this guy in five years and you know he ain't the same man you used to know. Hell, he's been through a mess of major trauma. That sort of stuff can whack you out. He probably really believes he's due it all, and he's lost all sense of reason."

Karl's phone rang and he excused himself as he stepped toward the back of the room. "Hey. Ty, slow down, what are you talking about?" He looked back at Lester, who perked up when he heard who was calling. "Sorry, sir. I need to take this. Do you mind?"

Lester frowned. "Go ahead. You can use the conference room."

Lester walked over to the conference room door and opened it for Karl, closing it behind him.

"Okay, go ahead. You did what? . . . Tyler, that's a crime scene. You broke the law and I don't want to hear anymore . . . Gold? What do you mean there's gold there?" Karl raised his voice. "You've gotta be kidding me. So, how much are we talking about? . . . Holy cow. Wait a second, what are you thinking about doing, Ty? . . . Oh no, I was afraid of that. Now just hang on, I need to think about this for a minute. Are you sure no one knows it's there, and no one else saw you?"

Karl rubbed his face and took a deep breath as he listened. "Shit, Ty, how in the world are you going to get that much gold out of there without anyone seeing you? . . . Well, I've got an old steel case that locks, but I don't know, man, it sounds kind of risky. What do you think it's worth? . . . Oh, my God, that's crazy. Listen, I can't be talking about this here. Besides, I think you just need to cool it for a couple of days and take time to think everything through. I don't know when the Feds are going to be finished, but not long after they leave, the sheriff will call for the truck to be brought up."

He listened for a minute, then sighed loudly. "Okay, okay, I think it's crazy, but tonight is as good a time as any. I'll double check where the sheriff and the Feds will be. We wait till after midnight. You bring it back to your dad's and I'll be waiting there. We'll hide it in our old treasure trove under the house until things cool down. Okay, I gotta go, bud. I'm in Radcliffe's board room for Pete's sake. Later."

He found Lester standing with his arms crossed, looking out his window as he exited the conference room. "Sorry about that, sir. I guess you know who that was."

Lester sat in slow and deliberate movements. He put his hands together, forming a pyramid in front of him. "Listen, Karl, I've already talked to the sheriff. We're going to turn this around, and you better know whose side you're on or you could get mixed up in it." Karl fidgeted. "I've always thought the world of you, Karl. Fact is, I've been talking to Mac lately about who his successor should be. Mac's getting old, Karl, he's almost seventy, and it's high time someone started stepping into his shoes. He's ready to spend time with his grandkids and enjoy some travel and fishing."

Karl nodded and folded his arms with a slight smirk. "So what are you saying, Mr. Radcliffe?"

"Oh hell, Karl, I heard what you and Ty were talking about. I'm afraid these doors are super thin. Let me make it easy for you. It sounds like there's a huge stash of Spanish gold down there in that lake, enough to set us all up for life. Now that I know what's going on, I can assure you that neither one of you will get away with it."

Karl plopped into the chair in front of Lester's desk with a hard sigh. He bent over with his elbows on his knees and cut his eyes up to Lester as he spoke.

"Sounds like a whole lot of gold." He grinned and shook his head.

"Let's cut to the chase, Karl. You only have one option at this point. You're going to help me get rid of my Morgan problem. Mac is going to retire this year and you're going to become sheriff because I need someone I can trust."

"Now hang on, Lester. Tyler's my friend."

Lester leaned over his desk and looked Karl in the eye. Maybe I didn't make myself clear. I'm in control now, and you're either with me, or you're in the way."

Karl dropped his head and thought for a minute. "Just what did you have in mind?"

Lester relaxed back into his chair. "That's more like it. Now listen, I've got a couple of guys who can help us. Cooter Faulk and Bobby Buell are already beholden to me. We'll let Tyler do the heavy lifting and bring up the gold, then the boys can take care of him and bring it back to us. Cooter can do the diving for us to get rid of Moore's body after we have the gold taken care of. By the way, they don't need to know there's gold involved. We'll tell them the cargo is some precious part of the shuttle that Tyler conspicuously disguised in an old steel box and they can't open it because it could be contaminated."

"I don't want to be part of no killing, Lester, especially my friend. If we're going to split the gold, then let me give part of my cut to him and send him on his way back to the coast. He can't talk after that. If he gives us a problem, you can take care of him. At least I'll know I tried."

Lester frowned and paused for a second, then slowly began nodding his head. "We'll try it your way, but if he gives us any trouble, he has to be taken out."

"So what do you want me to do?"

"Just pretend you don't know anything. Do whatever he asked you to do."

"Well, I'm supposed to stay up by the house and make sure no one tries to drive up and attack us when he brings back the gold."

"Then do just that. Cooter and Bobby will watch him from a distance until he has the gold loaded on his boat, then they'll slip up on him, take over his boat, and bring him and the gold back to my cabin. You'll join us there and I'll pay the boys and send them on their way. Then you and I will split the gold, and if you want to give some of yours to Tyler to keep his mouth shut, that's your business."

Karl looked at the gold coin on Lester's desk. "Say, did that belong to Moore?"

"Yep, It's a Spanish doubloon. He lost it to me in a poker game. He used to wear it around his neck. Never did find out where he got it."

"Wow, I guess there really is gold down there."

Lester grinned devilishly. "I never would've bet on it, but it looks to be true. This will make a dandy way to get a big pay off and get rid of all my problems at the same time."

~ 38 ~

Ty and Karl stood on the bank in front of Charlie's house, shaking hands. Karl grimaced. "Be careful out there, buddy."

"Yep. You watch yourself, too, Karl." Ty untied his boat and shoved it into the gentle lap of black water.

It was a dark night, as the moon had not yet made its way to their side of the world. Ty putted slowly down the river, scanning the horizon as best he could, checking for visitors. He noticed the boat start to rise a bit in the front and immediately backed off the throttle. He backed the boat off the huge stump that lay just inches below the surface. He should've known better, but he was a little preoccupied.

He continued toward the sunken truck and was almost upon it when a strange light caught his attention. He studied it for a minute until he realized it was the moon coming up from behind some clouds. It peeped out for a second, and it was massive.

Ty went through his gear check, washed out his goggles, and dropped into the water. He made his way down swiftly, toting the large chest Karl had given him. He swam over to the truck, dropped the chest nearby, and cast his light into the cab. Old man Moore was still resting in peace.

He hadn't heard a motor yet, but Tyler knew Bobby and Cooter would be along soon, they were probably watching from a distance, and would try to surprise him after he got the chest back into his boat. That was okay by him, he had his nine millimeter strapped beneath the console, and plenty of rope to tie them up with.

He grabbed the chest and started back to the surface with it. As he broke the surface, he found himself staring down the barrel of a twelve-gauge shotgun. They had already taken over his boat.

"That's a good boy, Ty, bring that chest right up here to old Cooter so he can help you get it aboard. You drop it, and I'll drop you straight to the bottom with it." Ty swam slowly forward. When he reached the boat, he pushed the chest in front of him where Cooter could grab it. Cooter reached over the side and hoisted the chest to the deck. "Okay, climb your butt back in here real slow and easy, Morgan."

Tyler pitched his mask up, took off his tanks, and hung them on the ladder at the back of the boat. As he stepped up into the boat, he came face to face with the shotgun again.

"I told you I was gonna get you, didn't I, pretty boy?" Bobby leaned in with the gun barrel as he spoke.

Ty noticed their boat was tied onto his and Cooter was suiting up to dive.

"What are you doing?"

"I got a little business to take care of here, then we're all gonna take a ride to the big water up by the dam."

"Lester hired you to destroy the evidence, didn't he?"

Cooter looked up at Bobby. "Boy's a genius, ain't he?" He put on his mask and fell overboard backward.

Bobby shook his head and snarled. "We're here to destroy everything, pretty boy, including you. I can't wait to sink your ass in two hundred foot a water. You gonna pay for what you did to Doyle and Terry. Then I'm gonna go skin your brother, pour honey all over him, and tie his Frankenstein ass to the biggest fire ant mound I can find." He stepped toward Ty and popped him in the chest with the gun barrel. "See, it was my little stepbrother he done killed over that fuggin' four-wheeler."

Ty's mind was going a mile a minute. He flexed and gnashed his teeth. "If you're gonna kill me, at least let me get a last good dip of snuff before I go."

Bobby snickered. "Hell, I think I'll have one myself."

"It's in my jeans there."

Bobby reached over and grabbed his jeans and threw them to him. "Open it and stick it over here."

Ty packed it, took the lid off, and held it out while Bobby took a pinch.

"At least you're going out on a fresh can."

Bobby loaded the snuff, keeping one eye on Tyler. Ty put the can just below his chin and reached in with three fingers, grabbing as much as he could.

"There you go, man, get a biggun'. It's the last one you'll ever have."

Ty looked him in the eye. "You didn't see which way the wind was blowing, did you, Bobby?"

Bobby widened his eyes and looked up. "What difference does it make?"

Ty threw his hand full of snuff into Bobby's open eyes and followed with the rest of the can. He grabbed the gun barrel and pointed it to the sky as he swung around and punched Bobby as hard as he could in the nose, jerking the gun away at the same time. He threw the shotgun overboard and jerked Bobby up off the deck, socking him in the gut with a strong uppercut, then he grabbed his hair and the back of his jeans and threw him overboard as well.

"That's what difference it makes."

Quickly, he untied their boat, then went to the back of the boat and pulled his gear off the ladder. Throwing it to the floorboard, he jumped behind the wheel, snapped on the emergency cutoff switch, and fired up the engine. Bobby was thrashing around in the water and screaming as he headed toward the other boat. Ty thought about ramming it and trying to disable the smaller craft, but he didn't want to take a chance on wrecking his boat. He turned the wheel and gunned it, but the boat whipped around just as he gave it the throttle. He had forgotten to untie his own boat. The unexpected jolt tossed him onto the floor and shut off the engine.

Bobby was climbing into the other boat when Ty finally got the bow line unhooked from the tree. As he got back to the driver's seat, he saw Bobby helping Cooter on board. Ty backed up and was giving it gas just as Bobby was raising a rifle toward him. The gun fired, but the bullet missed and sang across the dark lake as he pulled away.

Knowing the area was full of stumps, Ty was careful not to go too fast until he could make it back to the riverbed. Cooter didn't take the same precautions, and they were on top of Ty's boat in no time. Ty sped up as he got the boat straight in the river channel. The small boat behind him was running full throttle as he heard another shot ring out.

The moon was still playing hide and seek with the clouds, but Ty could tell that a thick cloud cover was moving in. He wound through the river, navigating the large bass boat as best he could in the growing darkness.

He managed to get a little more space between them when suddenly it came to him. The mother of all stumps was lying at the center of the river channel just around the next bend. The way the tree line looked on both sides, it appeared that the river was a little wider there, but in reality, the true river bank was in the center of the opening, and the huge stump that he ran up on earlier was now his greatest ally. Thank God he'd spent a summer afternoon trying to free his dad's boat from it. *There's a reason for everything.*

Ty hit the turn on a tight bank, then gunned it toward the outside bank before swerving quickly back to the center of the channel and speeding up for the long straight section ahead of him. Two-seconds behind him, Cooter slid around the corner, keeping it true to the center line. Bobby stood and leveled his rifle at Ty. Ty looked back just as they straightened out and saw the boat careening into the air. Bobby catapulted into the sunken wood line. The motor whined like a mad hornet as the boat went air-borne and started listing onto its side as it descended. When it touched down, the bow dipped into the water and the boat flipped end over end across the stump-laden graveyard of what was once a dense forest.

Ty stopped his boat and cut the engine. He listened for a few minutes for someone to cry for help, but all he could hear was the dying gurgle of the engine as it sank. He sat for a second, watching the clouds zooming by overhead, pushed by a vacillating breeze that promised rain. The lake was silent except for the sound of small waves lapping the side of his boat. He took it easy getting back to the house as a light rain took command of the night, causing the wind to rest and the water to lay out, still and quiet.

~ 39 ~

Ty reached the shore in front of the Morgan house and sat for a second, listening to the woods before he climbed out of his boat. He strained to see through the darkness up to the house, but it was hopeless. He stood, grabbed the chest by the two handles on each side, and grunted the heavy load out across the bow, setting it on the ground just in front of the boat.

"That's far enough, Morgan."

Ty froze. "I figured you wouldn't be too far off, Lester."

"Well, you figured right. Now just turn around and grab that chest and bring it over here to my boat."

He turned and saw Lester coming out from behind a group of willows that hugged the bank, pointing an automatic pistol at him.

"By the way, I ran into your flunkies out there. They had a little boat trouble."

"Yeah, well, I figured they failed their little mission when I saw you come around that point alone."

"Yep, that's why they call them flunkies."

"They dead?"

"I figure as much."

"No matter; it's easier this way. Now I don't have to worry about any loose ends. Now get that chest over here."

"What about that skeleton? Cooter never took care of it."

"Oh, I'll figure something out, and if I don't, I'll be catching blue marlin on a boat three times the size of yours somewhere out of Mexico or Costa Rica before they ever get around to pulling that truck up."

Ty needed time to think. He hoped Karl had heard the boat and would come down if he didn't see him coming up to the house right away.

"Here's an idea. How about I go pull up that skeleton for you? You can leave me a little of this gold to keep me quiet and I'll go on my merry way."

"I'm afraid I don't have time for that. Now quit stalling and pick up that chest and put it into my boat."

Ty picked it up, walked it halfway to Lester's boat, and set it back down.

"Come on, Morgan, I thought you were a first class athlete."

"Yeah, well, I've got a bad knee, thanks to your son. Just give me a minute. It's heavy."

"Gold usually is."

Ty bent over with his hands on his knees. *Where the hell is Karl?*

"Why should I carry it for you if you're just gonna kill me? Carry it yourself."

"If I have to carry it myself, I'll kill you right now, then I'm gonna walk up there and shoot your daddy between the eyes before I leave."

Ty stood up with his hands on his hips and glared at Lester. He figured something must have happened to Karl. He should have been here by now. "Yeah, you probably would. Okay, I'll carry it for you, but there's just one thing I gotta know before I die. Why did you kill my grandfather and Joe Gentry?"

"It wasn't supposed to turn out that way, but things just kinda got out of hand. Your grandfather was a proud man. He wasn't greedy; just a player and a fighter who loved to win. It's hard to beat a man like that. Even Joe was tired of losing to him. He was in on it; we all planned to even the tables on old Angus that night by getting him drunk and working his pride. It took all night, but Joe didn't know I was going to go that far. I figured what the hell, if he's going to act all proud and hardheaded and keep playing, I'm going to clean his ass out; and I did.

"Joe couldn't stomach it even though he made out like a bandit. He gave his winnings to Angus to help him get back on his feet, then he tried to blackmail me saying he would tell Angus what we'd done if we didn't get another game together and play straight up. So, we played that game. Angus got just as drunk as he always did, but he won, and he won big. I'll be damned if your grandpa didn't win it all back plus some. I couldn't have that; not after we'd already transferred all that property and had been warned not to be gaming at the club.

"The rest was easy. I stole Joe's Valium and slipped a couple into Angus' drinks. I figured Joe would get in line after Angus was gone, but he didn't. He kept making trouble, so I gave him a dose of his own medicine, so to speak. Cooter was kind enough to help him with his chores that day. In the end it just looked like two old fools who were playing with the same drug ended up the same way." He pointed the pistol at the old chest. "Now pick it up. Let's get moving."

Ty nodded and hunched over the load. "And what about the gold? How did you know?"

"Your buddy Karl took your phone call in my office. He went into the conference room, but like any good business man, I made sure I heard what you were talking about. I gotta admit I was amazed at what I heard.

"Hell, I knew old man Moore had the eminent domain money on him that night, and that he'd be loading up that new truck to leave because he was ordered to be out the next day, but I had no idea the old fart had a stash of gold. Of course, I didn't have much time to look around. Damn if that storm didn't take us all by surprise. That lake filled up quicker than a cat can lick his ass." He started laughing. "Can you believe the old man found it? All those people digging around in the twenties, spending their hard-earned money to find Fletcher's gold, and this old man walks down a creek bank on his own place one day and finds a fortune."

"Yeah, life's funny that way. I hate to break it to you Lester, but there is no gold. This is nothing but a chest full of trotline weights. You've been duped, Mister Big Business Man."

Lester laughed uneasily as he stepped over to get a closer look at the chest. He pointed his gun at Ty's head as he inspected it. Once he saw it was locked, he relaxed a little.

"Nice try, Morgan, but your buddy turned on you. I made him a deal he couldn't refuse. He's sitting up there by the road right now pretending to keep an eye out for you."

"I wouldn't bet on that. Drop the gun, Lester."

Karl walked out of the tree-line with his gun leveled on Lester. Lester quickly jumped over by Ty and put his gun barrel against the back of his head.

"It's no use. Tyler's right, there is no gold."

Lester laughed, "Do I really look that stupid? I figured you would switch sides on me. You think you can pop me before I put one through his skull? I can assure you that nothing would give me more pleasure, seeing as how he killed my son."

"I didn't kill him, Lester. He was about to shoot me. Vince was just acting in my defense. He didn't mean to kill him. It was an accident."

"Yeah, that half-wit brother of yours seems to have a lot of accidents. He'll have a good one before I'm done with him. You stupid kids thought you could take old Lester for a ride, huh? I was playing these games before either of you was even born."

"You mean like the game you played on my grandfather?"

Ty felt the gun barrel against his head. He thought about making a move to disarm him, but he needed to see what kind of footing he had. "Just take the gold and leave. There's been enough killing."

"It's not that simple. I can't leave any loose ends."

Karl took a couple more steps toward them. Ty knew he was trying to give him an opportunity. "It's a Mexican standoff, Lester. If you kill him, I kill you."

"You stupid backwoods cowboy. You had it all and now you're just going to end up dead and forgotten like your hero buddy here. I'm a marksman with this forty-five. I can put a round in him and stick one in your heart before you get your safety off. Now drop your gun, deputy, or I'll drop him."

Ty checked his distance and planned his move, but a twig snapped in the woods and they all instinctively looked toward the noise for a brief instant. Seizing the opportunity, Ty dove to the ground to give Karl a shot. "Take him!"

Lester swung around on Karl at the same time Karl was getting the drop on him. They both fired, but Karl's round barely nicked Lester's ear. Lester's shot found the body, and Karl fell backward into the brush.

Ty scrambled to his feet, but Lester already had him in his sights. "Now get that chest into my boat or die right here."

Ty grabbed the chest, crab-walked it around the willows to Lester's boat, and heaved it over onto the bow. "Get in. There's been too much commotion around here. I'll take care of you out in the lake. Put that chest in the floor."

Ty hoisted the chest from the bow deck and placed it onto the floor. In the brief glow of moonlight that peeked quickly from a gap in clouds, he saw a paddle lying next to the chest. He shifted slightly, pretending to be stowing the chest, and grabbed the paddle as he came up. Twirling, he swung the paddle around as the gunshot rang out and echoed across the lake.

Tyler's heart exploded in his chest as his mind raced through memories of his wife and son. He saw Jeanie's smile and her windswept hair on a carefree summer day. He imagined the soft caress of his mother's embrace and heard her whisper, "I love you, son."

He could feel the cool, soft rain kissing his face, and heard it delicately striking the water. The paddle fell from his hand and landed at his feet. He sat with a thump on the bow deck and looked out across the lake.

Tyler heard his name being called and slowly opened his eyes. He turned to see his father standing over Lester's body with his rifle in his hands. "Are you all right, son? Damn gun, I would've had his ass a long time ago, but I couldn't get the damn safety off."

In relief, Ty ran his hands down the front of his shirt and looked up at the sky. The rain continued sweet and gentle, and the lake smelled like home again. The moon slid out from behind the clouds and the darkness lifted. His soul had reached the mountaintop; he could see all the way across the world.

~ 40 ~

Tyler and Charlie worked side by side pulling sweet potatoes and thinning weeds. The sun had slipped behind the house, casting a long shadow over the garden. Charlie let out a painful sigh and rolled off his knees and onto his backside. Hearing his masters' voice, old Speck sat-up from his favorite spot at the side of the house and cocked his ears.

Tyler paused to take a dip of snuff. He dusted his hands on his britches and packed the can as he slowly took it all in. The world around him was beautiful. He loved the old home place, the smell of East Texas, the way the lake looked like a sheet of gold glowing through the trees making a silhouette of the dog with his ears cocked, and the pleasant smile of his father who sat in the garden he had created with his arms around his knees, admiring his son.

The sweet, crisp song of the cardinal echoed across the garden as his father inspected some of the potatoes he had picked.

"I'm glad you never sold out, Dad. I just can't picture you anywhere else."

Charlie looked up and grinned. "I guess the good Lord really does know what he's doing after all."

"Yes, he does, Daddy; yes he does. You know, I was thinking just today about where I was spiritually when I got here. My friend Celina, back in Port Aransas, said that God has a plan for each of us and that his sense of time is in a different dimension that we can't comprehend. I started thinking about what's happened to me these last few days and what it took for all of that to come together. Do you realize that if old Fletcher hadn't stolen that gold back in the eighteen hundreds, and if Lester hadn't killed old man Moore, and if the shuttle hadn't broken up when and where it did, and if I wouldn't have had the faith to keep fighting, none of this could have happened?"

"Funny how things work out, ain't it, Son?"

"It sure is. I just hope Jeanie ends up with everything that belonged to the Radcliffes, after all they put her through."

"I'm sure she'll do all right. It was awful smart of you to remember that story about the gold and use it to fool old Radcliffe."

Tyler smiled back at his dad. "Karl deserves an Academy Award. Remind me to tell you about that someday."

Charlie smiled and pitched his potato back in the pile. He moaned as he rolled back up to his knees and started working again. "I talked to Sheriff McKinney today."

"Oh yeah? What did he have to say?"

"He said they was gonna pull up old man Moore's truck on Monday."

Ty spit quickly, looking surprised. "Is that right?"

Charlie cocked a half-grin. "How does that make you feel, son?"

Ty stood and looked out at the lake. "It makes me want to go run some trotlines."

"Now? We only got about an hour of sunlight left."

"Perfect."

A GOLDEN-ORANGE RADIANCE PAINTED THE lake before them and filled the air with amber dust as Ty drove down the cut toward the Moore farm. He looked over at his father, who was staring ahead, but looking back, as the wind tossed his silver hair behind him like a kid on a late summer day.

As the dying sun made a silhouette of Charlie leaning over the side of his boat, he hollered down at Tyler.

"Well, I ain't never heard of a man diving to run his trotlines is all I'm saying."

"Believe me, Dad, it's easier this way."

After a few minutes, Ty resurfaced and held his catch up to his father. Charlie looked confused as he hauled it in.

Tyler treaded water as he awaited his father's reaction. He set the ammo box in the floor and opened it. After a few moments of gasping, his joyful shout echoed across the sleepy lake.

"Woo-hoo!"

"That was just the first one, Dad. There's eleven more."

Charlie lifted his hat and sat back in the boat chair with a look of pleasant astonishment.

Tyler walked out onto the front porch rolling his sleeves down.

"Next time I do the cooking and you do the cleaning, Vince. You're messier than a rabid coon in a flour sack when you cook."

Jeanie interjected. "No way, if it's that big a deal, I'll do the cleaning. Vince's cooking is unmatched anywhere." She rocked in Katherine's old chair sipping sweet tea.

Tyler curled his brow. "Is that your third cup of tea?"

She smiled and raised her glass. "It's awfully good. Thank you, Vince."

Vince nodded from the love seat and smiled back at her as Tyler sang out. "The first anniversary celebration of our new blessed life has been a success!"

Jeanie turned to look at him, he paused and watched her rock for a moment. She had one leg up in the seat and her hair flowed beautifully, catching amber kisses from the late sun.

"You look mighty good in that rocker, Baby."

Her eyes grew moist. "I'm finally home with my husband where I should have been many years ago."

With one hand, Vince reached out and grabbed Ty's belt loop and dragged him backwards into the seat beside him. Jeanie grinned as a tear rolled down her cheek.

"You look mighty good sitting next to your big brother."

Ty put his arm around Vince and gave him a squeeze. "We got more letters from the RRC investors today. It was very kind of you to return their money, Jeanie."

"We've got more than we need, Ty. It's time to start giving back. I think I want to start a home for children."

Karl walked out burping and rubbing his stomach.

"My goodness, that had to be the best darn catfish I ever ate."

Ty elbowed his big brother lightly. "Vince is the best. Wait until the world gets to taste his sausage. It's taken almost a year, but *Vince's Backwoods Blend* will be on the shelves next month!"

Karl sat on the other side of Vince, working his mostly healed shoulder a little as he leaned forward, resting his elbows on his knees. Tyler grinned at him.

"How's that shoulder, Bud?"

"It's still not a hundred percent, but it's getting there. Listen, Ty – something's been bothering me for almost year now and never remember to ask you."

"What's that, Buddy?"

"When did you have time to tie those ammo boxes full of gold to your trotlines?"

"I found them the first time I went down."

"Why didn't you tell me that the gold was really there? Did you initially plan to keep it all for yourself?"

"Would you have agreed to my plan if you'd known?"

"No, probably not."

"Well, there you go."

Karl smiled. "I just think it's amazing. All those years ago, when we were just kids and first heard the story of Fletcher's Gold, you were the only one who was compelled to go looking for it. It's like you were meant to have it all along."

"Yeah, Karl, it is amazing, but the thing to remember is that I wouldn't have this reward if I hadn't found my faith first. Knowing Cartwright helped a lot, too!"

They exchanged grins. "Yeah it did. I don't think he's gonna have any trouble finding investors from now on."

They all laughed.

Charlie walked out the front door holding a tray with a large Pyrex bowl and four smaller bowls around it.

Ty looked over into the bowl. "What do you got there, Dad?"

Charlie grinned and slapped his hands together. "Okay, are you guys ready to try the best banana pudding in the state of Texas?"

"You mean she finally gave you the recipe?"

"Well, I think so, but we won't know for sure until we taste it."

KARL OFFERED TO DRIVE VINCE home, and after they had all said their goodbyes, Tyler and Jeanie sat back out on the porch with Charlie as the sun threw a long sheet of gold across the lake. Charlie rubbed his hands together and took a long, deep breath. "Feels like its cooling off fast. It's easy to see how much difference that sun makes."

Jeanie stood, wrapping the throw from the rocker around her shoulders. She smiled at Tyler and he read her mind.

"We're gonna take a short walk, Dad. We'll be back in a little while."

"All-righty, I'm gonna sit right here and count my blessings."

THEY WALKED DOWN TO THE shoreline and headed toward the point. The sky was turning a brilliant, fiery red as the sun disappeared across the lake. They sat beneath the huge virgin pine on the point and took in the painted sky as a lone crane bellowed from somewhere across the quiet reservoir.

Tyler put his arm around her and she rested her head upon his shoulder. "You know, Jeanie, it's almost impossible to believe we're sitting here together again after all these years."

She sighed and put her hand on his chest. "It's amazing Ty. All of my prayers have been answered."

He gave her a gentle squeeze. "Mine too, but why now? When I think about all we've been through since we last held each other here, the life we've lived, the heartache and tragedy, all the darkness and despair, it's just unimaginable that I find myself right back here where I always wanted to be. Why do you suppose we had to go through all of that? What's the difference?"

She looked up into his eyes and then gave him a long, sweet kiss. "Just look at how much closer you are to the Lord. You have a daily relationship with him now. That's what it's all about. That's why we're here. There's nothing more important. I really do believe in free will, Tyler. All of those things probably would've happened anyway, but what matters is how you react to it. That's where history is changed. Perhaps some people, whether they be destined for it, or whether it's just something God sees in them, are chosen to take on a bigger role in His Master Plan. You've always been a good guy, and a believer, but believing wasn't enough. When you finally let go of who you thought you were, He showed you all you could be. I think that's the difference."

Tyler looked out across the lake and nodded. "I look back on my life and I see people who appeared as angels or saints, and I see people who appeared as demons. I guess old man Parker was right, there really is a war going on between good and evil. Each day brings choices between living in the flesh and living in the spirit, and we are just fragile souls doing battle amid the ashes and the dust.

"He was one of your saints wasn't he?"

"Yes, he was. You know, He told me God's plans are beyond our understanding, and if we just keep our faith in Him no matter how dark it gets, He'll bless us in ways that we could never foresee. I wish the old guy could see us now."

Jeanie hugged him and sat up in front of him. "Oh, I bet he can, and he was definitely right about that, Tyler Morgan. God has one more blessing for you that you couldn't foresee." She took his hand and placed it on her stomach.

"We love you!"

The End

Clay Mitchell was raised in Houston, Texas, and currently lives in San Antonio. He graduated from Stephen F. Austin State University with a BBA in finance and is the owner and operator of Over the Top Window Fashions. This is his first published book.

WITHDRAWN